The Most Amazing Thing

Robert Grudin

The Most Amazing Thing

A NOVEL

knOwhere Press   PALO ALTO

A project of White Wolf, LLC

Copyright © 2002 White Wolf, LLC
All rights reserved

Library of Congress Cataloging-in-Publication Data
  Grudin, Robert.
    The most amazing thing / Robert Grudin.
      p.   cm.
    ISBN 0-9658995-1-9
    I. Title
    LCCN 2001094321

Design and composition by Wilsted & Taylor Publishing Services

To Susanna Bixby Dakin

CONTENTS

Sig Bazoom told me to write this, so here goes. As he knows very well, I'm no writer, so he'll have to be satisfied with what he gets. It doesn't take Shakespeare to tell the bare truth.

The bare truth in this case is two bare facts:

1. The book that follows is exactly as I found it on a computer aboard the *Iwa*, Desmond Ruck's wrecked sailboat, excepting as Mr. Bazoom has cleaned up a number of odd spellings and mistakes.

2. This story is published under my copyright and belongs, lock stock and barrel, by Law of Salvage to me, Cuss Nelson, skipper of the seagoing tug *Vettie*, Panama City, Panama. I hocked my car to buy the oil, and hired on a crew, and steamed out and hunted around for the prize like everybody else. I hit a storm so bad it picked up my dinghy and smashed my stack with it. It came like a big white hand and grabbed the kid Jose, who loved his joke, and when I went for him there was nothing there but spray. I busted my right arm and my mate Honus braced it with a

Publisher's Introduction

socket wrench and baling wire, only it didn't heal right and had to be broke again when we got back. I risked all this to salvage a boat, and Salvage Law applies to everything that's on a boat. And besides this story and the shell-shocked hulk of a trimaran, I got precious little for my pains, except for a few saleable pieces of equipment and a one-eyed cat that sits like a statue and never goes to sleep. Mrs. Ruck, or whatever her new name is, can be satisfied with her divorce settlement, and her lawyers can be satisfied with, well, whatever satisfies lawyers.

Finally, regarding complaints about the types of sex described in this story, I have one reply: Sex happens. People who can't stand the words describing things had better not do the things the words describe.

—CUTHBERT ("CUSS") NELSON, *Publisher*

It was St. Paul, I think, who said "Vanity of vanities, all is vanity." No saying applies more aptly, or more poignantly, to the rise and fall of Desmond Ruck. Immeasurably the world's richest man and arguably its most exuberant, Ruck lived a lion's life, etched in acrylics and rounded with drum and timpani. He rocketed out of an obscurity so profound that details of his youth remain unknown. For a few brief years his shoulders touched the clouds and he spoke with the voice of legions, only to vanish into an immensity vaster even than his own titanic lusts. The media, which followed him doggedly if from a nervous distance, have been crammed for weeks with speculation about his motives and conjecture into his character. Now readers can have the truth, as it were, ex cathedra: from the unexpurgated intimate journal that he kept first, fleeing for his life, as a means of clinging to sanity, and later as the record of his rise to empire, his bizarre gratifications and his outrageous predicaments.

I use the word "unexpurgated" in part as a signal of caution. Mr. Ruck led a vivid life and did not stint in relating it. His fierce determination and bizarre luck led him into human situations so unusual that, until the publication of these journals, they were undocumented in the English language. Not all editors feel that such disclosure is in order. As Professor Snell has remarked,

> There are some human proceedings that literary language cannot manage fairly, and among these is just about everything that goes on between the navel and the knees.

It is quite clear that Ruck would not have accepted Snell's words of caution. Ruck wrote of what he saw and felt, and he saw and felt things that few of us even dream about. The reader is forewarned.

The Ruck narrative begins on the fateful day of April 2, 1998. It comprises the last 623 pages of a journal approximately five times as long. Cuthbert Nelson's decision not to print the earlier pages, which dealt mainly with Ruck's domestic life in Eugene, Oregon, was based on a surprising disproportion between this period and what followed. Incredibly, the Desmond Ruck of pre-April, 1998, was not, except to himself, a very interesting person. He had glimmered in several fields but shone in none. A tennis player, he had never won a tournament. An amateur singer, he had never performed. An inventor, he had failed to gain a single patent. Apparently his good looks, great height, pleasant demeanor and jack-of-all-trades jauntiness won him a measure of respect in his community, but he was so professionally feckless and unproductive that, had it not been for the events of 4/2/98, Jean Michaux's epigram, used of another, might well have applied to him: "His life was little more than an embarrassed silence between birth and death."

By 1998, when he was in his mid-40s, Ruck had yet to hold down a steady job, and earned a small and irregular income from giving tennis lessons, writing technical instruction manuals and teaching the odd course in shop at a nearby community college. On these slender means, and despite increasing indebtedness, he had clung to life in a disintegrating brown-shingle home on Malaview Avenue with his wife, Glynda.

But time was running out. On the morning of March 10, 1998, apparently while Ruck was in the shower, a team from a Portland collections agency arrived unannounced and totally emptied his house. His mortgager had set a date of foreclosure on the house itself. Ruck's wife indignantly berated him for his failure to support her; and his self-confidence, built for years on rationalizations and hopes, began to crumble. In desperation he used his last valid credit card for a trip to New York, where he pleaded for help from his uncle, Titus Farnacle (owner of FARNACLE's department store). It was following this pathetic interview that the events of our narrative began to unfold.

One final unpleasant necessity. By the current high stylistic standards of American publishing, *The Most Amazing Thing* is something of an anomaly. It is written without the slightest concern for conciseness, restraint, originality, pace, subtlety, irony or any of the other standards currently observed in good writing. Ruck greets every topic with an unconsidered torrent of words, and he enthusiastically visits every available cliché, like a dog among fire-hydrants, until each facet of our language has been sullied anew. Were *The Most Amazing Thing* a novel, it might well be dismissed as the worst-written novel in American history. But that is exactly the point. Desmond Ruck wrote of real experience in a real America. What might have failed as fiction succeeds beautifully as historical testimony. You might say that Ruck ate up experience and vomited it out undigested, but the results, so to speak, often have an impeccably photographic resonance. He seems to have had an almost-perfect ear for other people's speech and, even when his own writing falls painfully short, it only serves to emphasize the intensity of the events he describes.

Thus where Ruck loses, he wins; and though tarnished by every human excess and passion, he is redeemed by simple honesty. Wherever he is, we wish him well.

—SIGMUND BAZOOM, *Editorial Director, Wolper McNab, Inc.*

Book One Ruck's Run

● ● ● ● ● ● ● ● ● ● ● ● ● ● ● ● ● ●

Chapter One   Bullets Are Good for You

This isn't happening.

I'm not in Newark, in a dirtcheap motel room stunk up by Lysol and
cigarettes

I'm not in Newark, scratching on a notepad held against a Gideon
Bible

There's not a naked girl on the bed, unconscious, blood caking on her
skin

There's not a bullet-ridden van at the door, with billions of dollars
soaking in vomit and blood

I'm not Desmond Ruck, clown, thief and madman, with maybe three
hours to live.

But is it a dream to have this streak of pain through your back, pain you
earned dragging a sumo-sized corpse out of the van and slipping in his
gore? Or the pain and ringing in the ruins of your left ear, pain and ringing acquired by having some scumbag fire a pistol point blank at your
face? Or the rain drumming against the window, or the newscaster in

3

the motel TV quietly yakking about everything, it seems, except today's mass carnage on Stuyvesant Avenue? Or the fat fly checking out your ex-earlobe and then buzzing lazily over to Sleeping Beauty's torso?

No, it's real, it's a fact, it's an outrage. Nightmares are piss-poor by comparison.

Yet somehow for the first time in weeks I want to live.

Cut the losses then, put one foot in front of another.

I rise, stiffening with pain, take off my smelly shirt, go to the bathroom, piss for about three minutes, wash hands, pull a plastic cup out of a plastic sack, drink the sulfuric tapwater and start the bathwater at coolish, so as maybe to wake up the lady. I go back to the bed, bend my knees as I get my arms under her, lift her in lower-back agony, carry her to the bathroom, gently place her in the bathtub and turn on the shower. As the cool water cascades on her and begins to loosen the bloodclots, her nipples pucker but she doesn't move. I strip to the waist, grab a hanky-sized washcloth and begin to rub blood away as the bracing water soaks my back and head. I get to the face and the cheeks flush as I rub them and the eyelids flutter but go still. I straighten up and look down at her. With the water bouncing off her she's like a statue in a fountain. Sexy? No, I don't feel sexy, because you see I'm impotent, but looking down at her I get this strange feeling, as though I've never looked at a naked woman before. What can I say? The girl is perfect, as if she were made in heaven. I turn off the water, take a towel and pat her dry in front. I kneel down and lift her. Her thighs and upper arms, still moist in back, hang limp and buttery soft. Holding her so close, I notice that her body has a special perfume, not from soap because I didn't use any soap—a sweet outdoorsy freshness that I've never smelled on anyone before. I put her down on the bed, roll her over, dry her back and

4

buttocks and legs, roll her over again, turn down the covers on the other
side, put her in there, cover her up.

As I turn I hear a low sigh, then silence.

My back twinges again. I towel down and put on my shirt. I look at
the wretch in the mirror and straighten its hair. I swab dried blood off
my black raincoat and put it on and bring the collar up to hide my
wound. I'm going forth into the night.

9:59 PM. I'm back. Ibuprofen, food, beer, and three changes of outdoorsy clothing, complete with floppy fisherman's hats, for both of us. A
bargain basement notebook computer with five spare batteries. A road
atlas. All bought in a barn of a place called the Essex Depot, full of types
so grubby and odd that I, hulking big guy with stricken face, didn't look
strange at all. I returned bag-laden through the parking lot past the
white bulging shape of Fatal Van and keyed my way into the motel
room. The girl remained still as death, limbs in the same position under
the covers. I leaned down and put my good ear close to her lips and hear
the weak shallow breathing.

Would she ever wake up?

I've showered and now am stained by no blood but my own. I've
booted up the computer and typed up what I'd just scribbled. I've eaten
black bread and Swiss cheese and drunk Jersey City beer, and it felt like
the first meal of my life. I could eat seven times as much. I could swim
in beer, crawl in with my Lady Eve, pass out and sleep with her till kingdom come.

Except, my conscience bothers me. I've had no one to talk to for years
and haven't levelled with myself for as long. I've kept a journal, but it's
full of lies. But now at last the shit has hit the fan. I've got to write this
down, confess my guilt, give my reasons. I can't live locked up with
them. I'll write the truth, in every detail I can remember, and if I live to
remember more I'll come back and add it.

The Most Amazing Thing

If no one ever reads it, I'll have said it anyway. Which calls for another beer.

How do I begin? With my birth? No time. How about this simple fact:

At about three this afternoon I left the Brazen Head Bar and turned left down the east side of Stuyvesant

But that's not a simple fact. The truth isn't just what we do, it's also what's in us when we're doing it. I can't say what was in me on Stuyvesant Avenue that day without going back a couple of hours to Titus Farnacle's house.

I went to see Uncle Titus because I'd gotten to be kind of poor. The kind of poor where the brake-job you need is worth more than your car. The kind of poor where you begin to notice subtle aromas as you pass KFC. And I more or less deserved to get poor. By more or less I mean utterly. I deserved to get poor because for fifteen years I'd avoided real work, and strung myself along on part-time jobs, and written endless bullshitting journals, and spent my mornings watching the Science Channel, and blown my afternoons playing tennis with the old boys, and joked with the neighbors like some big shot, while the economy ran away from me.

By the end of last month I realized, this was it. I'd have to go to work full-time. I'd have to take any job that was available. All I needed was a grubstake to keep the wolves from the door. For this I'd fly to New York. I'd ask Uncle Titus.

Except that my uncle, Titus Farnacle, is an asshole. I'd call him a sonofabitch, but that would insult the canine profession. I'd invent a new word for Titus, something with a clackity in-your-face ring to it, but I can't think of one right now. A word describing a shit who's proud of being one.

And Titus is filthy rich. His "house," as he puts it, is the whole block of brownstones having its southwest corner at Stuyvesant and Mc-Canles. You enter thinking it's a single address, or half-address sharing space with the Brazen Head Bar, you labor up three flights of steep dark stairs with little valleys worn right through the linoleum, you give your name to a horsefaced man in black who looks at you as if you were something growing in a tidal pool and, don't bother to sit down, you wait. Horseface has mumbled a few words into a phone, and soon an ancient stooped form of unknown sex appears from behind him, clad in a blotchy pink shawl, croakingly introduces itself as Patrice and motions you to follow. A narrow corridor to the left leads right through the wall of the house, as you can tell by the drop in level and the bare brickwork, then through the next house and so on, passing nests in the lair of Pack-rat Farnacle, storehouses of boxed and labelled engine parts, museums of old machine tools, a great dark chamber housing ornaments from demolished buildings, a smoke-filled chamber where lots of shirtsleeved men are torturing grimy computers, and finally Titus' inner sanctum, a dimlit high-ceiling apparition of tile, marble and tapestry that has to have been, in earlier New York days when blood ran high, a prostitutional steam-bath.

Titus, dwarfed behind a marble table big enough for sixteen or so jolly old Knickerbockers to have sat bare-arse on it, was visible as a grease-stained primordial Boston Red Sox cap pointed down at the table-top, where fingers like tapeworms protruded from cut-off gloves examining some object under a high-intensity lamp. Approaching I saw that said object was a small gold crucifix, probably fresh-stolen from a bishop's grave, and Titus looked up to reveal a small turtle-face with bright gray eyes and a beak so pronounced that he couldn't focus both eyes on you without constant sideward adjustments of his head.

"Desmond!" he squeaked, and rose with a cackle. "You've put on weight. Not playing enough tennis?"

This insult to my wage-earning manhood hit me where I lived. My lower spine felt like it was jellifying, and blood rushed away from my head as I managed, "Uncle Titus."

With him turning to Patrice to order a deli special for two, I was reminded that Titus himself was nothing to crow about in terms of good looks. Dirty tufts of gray hair stuck out through the moth-holes of his Red Sox cap, and it was pretty clear he slept in the damn thing. His chinless face was gaunt and unshaven, and his deep eye-sockets, together with his habit of looking sideways at people, gave him all the charm of a fresh corpse. He was wearing this old blue smoking jacket that looked like it'd been used to mop up an ER floor, and under that a faded plaid flannel pajama top, and around his scrawny neck, serving as cravat, a ragged item that might have been cut from a length of used fire hose. Titus's nether parts were left to the imagination, being cut off from my view by the marble table top, lying on which, I now noticed, were six or seven wads of $50 bills. The sight gave me goosebumps.

As Patrice left, Uncle caught me eyeing the loot. "Wistful thinkin', fellah?" He suddenly looked almost wistful himself. "That money ain't neither yours nor mine. That's *bosses'* money, by jiminy."

"Bosses?" I asked. "I thought you were boss around here."

"Don't mean around here," said Titus with a sneer. He grimly brandished a big wad of U.S. Grants. "This is for my old friend the Bronx boss, Guccio Imbratta. Lives right down the street. Mr. Imbratta fixes things so that my house doesn't burn down, and he seems to have a way with the tax assessor." He picked up another wad. "*This* is for Ercole Stramba and his likewise blessed assistance with FARNACLE's department store on Fifth Avenue and *these* (pointing to smaller wads) are for local bosses near my production plants in Asia. Don't know what I'd do without 'em."

Titus motioned me to a chair and launched into a major speech in praise of Organized Crime, itemizing all that it's done for American civilization. His point, as I pretended intense interest with my gaping pig imitation, was that without organized crime you'd be stuck with *disorga-*

nized crime, a fate worse than death. Titus was getting almost weepy about this when Patrice limped in with the lunch and spread it out on the marble table: hot pastrami on rye, big pickles, pastries and coffee in white cardboard tubs. I ate ravenously and sloppily. Food brought courage and I popped the question. Can Titus, my mother's brother, my veritable flesh and blood, see his way clear to help me redeem my furniture and save my house?

The big room went silent. I tried to bolster my spirits with a pickle, but in the stillness my chewing sounded gross and hideous, like Swamp Thing sloshing along on his way to a rumble.

I gulped coffee and looked up at Titus, who'd gone all gray and rolled up his eyes so you could only see the whites. Titus was throbbing, sort of, and my fond hopes that the old fart was in cardiac arrest (I'm his only living relative) were dashed when I realized that he was actually laughing. He caught his breath, picked up the Stramba wad and shook it at me like some phallic baton. "Desmond," he croaked, "you disappoint me. Do you reckon I'm stupid enough to waste money on a no-account like you? Didn't you realize I wrote you off when you married that Irish lunatic? You're a mental butterfly, just like your dad. You're no Farnacle but a Ruck through and through."

The food was literally curdling in my gut, and I was thinking about throwing my chair at him but feeling the pain in my ruptured disc. I pleaded, "But to someone of your wealth . . ."

"Wealth!" he exploded, "Horsemanure! I'm a poorer man than you are, Desmond Ruck! How much are you busted for, ten, fifteen grand? I'm leveraged *seventeen million dollars* beyond my assets! How did I manage it, fellah? By smart borrowing. How do I sustain it? By cash flow. Where do I get the flow? By retail sales and floating debt. Those men in my computer room are manipulating my three thousand, give or take, personal credit card accounts and adding about eighty new accounts a day. The banks love it! When I go into debt, they lap up the interest. When I cash out a loan, they raise my credit! Don't you get it, bright boy? I'm priming the great economic pump. Everybody's happy! In my humble way I help the US economy. I massage the system, I power the Ship of State! Ho ho!"

Titus was on his feet now, geriatrically bouncing up and down and waving his wad of greenbacks like a flag and nasally humming Souza's *Stars and Stripes Forever*. That was it. I couldn't take this kind of heat another moment. Convulsively I wheeled about and rushed from Titus's office and through the Farnacle complex, hotfooting it through room after room like a whipped and pummelled cur. My lower-back pain had climbed up my spine and was now radiating into my throat, where like a little hand it grabbed at my adam's apple, producing the terminal snit that's been with me since childhood, hanging somewhere inside me like a framed motto:

> YOU'VE LOST IT ALL, KID, AND
> NOTHING'S GONNA MAKE IT BETTER,
> AND IT'S ALL YOUR FAULT

I slunk past sneering Horseface and headed for the stairs, but by the third flight my legs went out of sync and I lurched downward, desperately grabbing for and catching the handrail. I needed a drink, and the suggestion was no sooner raised than I was out the front door, entering the Brazen Head Tavern, sitting down at the bar and ordering a double gimlet on the rocks. The bartender was quick to oblige.

Discreetly two-handing my gimlet to make up for violent shudders, I drank deep, and the gin began worming its way into my sorrows with tidings of comfort. Like a friendly hand it caressed my innards, but it couldn't touch the core of my sorrow, my sense of being finally and hopelessly alone, my hopeless dilapidation. Looking up as I ordered a refill I caught myself in the mirror and silently cursed the swarthy good looks that opened so many doors for me when I was young, made things seem so goddamn easy. How come I looked so good, when I'd just been crushed under heel like a roach? Turning my eyes away from this, and from my deceptively capable-looking hands on the counter, I focused on the bottles lining the wall, and as I tuned out my mental theater did a screening of *Ruck's Year in Review*: the grim scenes with Glynda, the ever-weaker excuses and rationalizations, the putrid failures and finally, last week, the morning I sang a Rodgers and Hammerstein medley in the bath and came out to find the furniture gone, including several pieces I'd built myself. I ordered a third drink, kind of like dessert, but instead of improving things it got me a little confused. I checked my watch, found out it was after 4 and decided to head for my hotel. I set down a tip and wobbled out the door.

I wobbled straight into hell.

Looking south from the Brazen Head, Stuyvesant Avenue runs downhill towards Tamany Boulevard, where there's a subway stop. Leaving the bar I turned left and headed down Stuyvesant to catch the subway.

It was raining now. I wove downhill among the foot-traffic, noticing that a couple of houses ahead of me there was a white unmarked delivery van pulled up in a waiting zone, with its driver's door open and a group of men discussing something or other on the sidewalk nearby. What struck me was that these guys were all well-dressed in suits and that they were all big fellas, not nearly as tall as I am but all real hefty and broad in the beam. As I walked towards them I half spaced out, thinking, *Hey, maybe that's Guccio Imbratta's house, and I wish I had the tailor's fee for all those fancy clothes.*

But I woke up quickly because somebody'd screamed. I saw people running for cover all over the street, but what I didn't see until it was too late was one of the big guys in suits heading straight for me like a train. He caught me off balance and tipped me sideways, which definitely saved my life, because right then the shooting started, you can't believe how loud, and the first casualty was a woman who was walking directly behind me, who took a body shot. She dropped her shopping bag and just stood there. She was an older lady, with olive skin and deep lines beneath her widow's kerchief, and in that split second I saw centuries of Italian tragedy written on her face. Then she toppled backward onto the pavement.

Now bullets were flying all over the place. I was wedged between two parked cars, looking for an escape route, but going back uphill was no good. The guy who shoved me was cornered on a stoop and firing down at another colossus who'd taken cover in the street behind a car. Meanwhile a can of Casa Mia tomato sauce—funny how you remember these things—a can of Casa Mia tomato sauce from the Italian lady's shopping bag, was rolling down the sidewalk toward the van. Down thataway two men next to the van were firing their pieces up the front steps at two others who were wedged in the entrance way of the house and blasting back at them. I thought *How can they miss? These guys are three feet wide.* But it turned out they weren't missing. Both men in the entrance way were clutching bloody wounds as they fired, and when I looked at the van I saw that one of the others had fallen behind the truck and could be seen only as a pair of splayed and motionless feet.

I wiped rain out of my eyes and glanced back uphill to see the man behind the car take aim and suddenly crumple up as his head exploded into a rosy mist; and the guy who shot him from the stoop was now staggering from his perch and towards me, with blood oozing from his neck. He let go from the hip as he reeled forward and the slug dinged into the trunk of the car two inches from my left leg. I lunged streetways and was almost demolished by an eighteen-wheeler winding uphill in low.

I'd nowhere to run but downhill on the sidewalk towards the van, and I did so like an animal who's been so frigging terrified that it can't fear anymore. There was big carnage down there. One of the men in the entrance way had left his position and was rolling slowly down the steps like a spent beachball. His partner, a fountain of blood, had dropped his gun and sat down on the steps and was making Wa-Wa noises and pointing at me. The survivor by the van was now halfway *in* the van, and from six feet away he aimed at my head and fired. I thought it was the end but it was only an earlobe, and lurching against the side of the van I opened up a clear shot for the bloody-necked man who'd been staggering up behind me. He fired once, and the guy in the van screamed and toppled back into it.

With a neat sound like a rotary saw a bullet creased the side of the van next to me and *That's it, folks, I've had enough fun for today.* I jumped into the goddamn van. The guy inside must have fallen into the back, because the driver's compartment was empty. Instantly I released the handbrake and was coasting downhill. I heard two more shots, but Bloodyneck had no angle, and my panic wasn't about him but about finding the windshield wiper switch so I could see through the rain to steer. I switched them on and set the gearshift on Drive. I glanced over my right shoulder just long enough to see that my companion was on the floor and dead still. I put a quarter mile between me and the bloodbath, pulled up at a red and signalled left onto Tamany. My head rang with pain but I was alive, and the thought made me want to jump for joy.

Breathing again I caught a couple of green lights, and as I drove it suddenly occurred to me that I'm safe, I've escaped. I could park now and exit the van and go find somebody to sew up my ear and answer a few questions from the police. I could leave all this blood and danger behind me. Yet somehow I didn't stop. It's like something'd popped inside me, like the proper grownup had been kicked out and an angry kid appeared, a big angry kid with no respect, who was saying, "*OK, YOU TURKEYS, THE LAUGH IS ON YOU. YOU CAN DISS ME AND SHAME ME AND PUSH ME DOWN AND SHOOT ME, BUT SOMEHOW I SURVIVE. AND BY THE WAY, I'VE GOT YOUR TRUCK!*"

You see, it'd come into my head that there was something valuable in the van, that it was the van those guys were having their little spat about, and I wasn't going to make any rash moves til I found out what it was.

An intense knifelike voice, Glynda's voice, said inside me, *"YOU'RE STEALING A VAN! YOU'RE STEALING A VAN!"* But Angry Boy replied, *"OK, SO I'M STEALING A VAN. SO ARREST ME, WHY DON'T YOU?"* I pulled onto the Cross-Bronx Expressway and took it to West Side Drive, leaning on the gas. I wanted to be in Jersey before they sent out an All Points and I got snagged in the evening rush. Why Jersey? The Hudson River's a barrier, man. Unless you cross it you can only drive north and south. Jersey's the West, man. It's the whole USA.

I hit an onramp for the George Washington Bridge, and traffic slowed down, but I could see it moving along pretty well on the bridge itself. The rain was heavier now, and the windshield wipers, in their military rhythm, quacked and yakked to me of crime and punishment. At one point traffic stopped and I could check on my passenger. He was on his back, just far back enough in the van so that he wouldn't be noticed at the toll booth. His belly was so huge that it would have blocked out his face, but his head was propped up on something. He was looking sort of dead, with one eye covered in blood and the other wide open and pointing sidewards. What was propping up that death's-head? Suddenly I was nauseous.

I must have spaced out, because before I knew it there was a great blare of horns behind me. I goosed the gas and hot-footed it across the bridge. What was propping up Monsieur's head? I didn't have time to look back until the wait before the toll booth. It was a briefcase, a fat black briefcase, and there were lots more like it!

The toll-woman, probably strung out on cocaine, dropped a quarter as I paid her. She looked at me angrily, then motioned me on.

Now at turnpike speed I opted for US 80, which would take me, if need be, all the way to San Francisco. But nearing Hackensack I got qualms. The gas read half-full, but the oil pressure was low and the temp needle was in the red. I couldn't afford a breakdown, and I had to get rid of Monsieur before my next gas fill-up, so I took the Hackensack exit, turned north onto Wagner and started looking for a lonely place. It was getting dark already in the grim spring rain, so I switched on the head-lights. Three blocks down Wagner on the right was a shopping mall under construction, and what with the rain it was deserted. I drove com-pletely past it and turned right. There was a service road running be-tween the half-built mall and the privacy wall of a housing development on the other side. I ticked halfway down this service road and stopped the van and killed the lights. Still nauseous and dizzy, I got out into air smelling of damp concrete, walked around the van and checked up and down the road. 150 yards of clearance on each side, everything quiet but not a minute to lose—police cars patrol alleys like this.

It was time for the reckoning.

I got back into the van. Reaching back over the dead man I grabbed a heavy briefcase and put it down on the console next to the driver's seat. I switched on the map-light. The briefcase wasn't locked. It contained about forty large white envelopes made of soft clothlike paper. I took one of these envelopes and undid it by unwinding a little thread in back. A packet of stock certificates slid out. In the dim light I read that the firm was Consolidated Silicates, Ltd, and the quantity was 200,000 shares. I needn't ask what Consolidated Silicates, Ltd, had been trading for, be-cause a handwritten pink post-it told me that it was $103\frac{5}{8}$ as of March 15. I turned it over and noted that it had been duly signed over for redemp-tion by Leonard Jacobus, the registered owner.

The math made this certificate worth over twenty million bucks. Enough to bankroll Uncle Titus's entire debt, with spare change for a Roman palazzo. I checked the others in the envelope and there were about fifty of them and they were all a lot like the first. A teasing little voice started singing to me, "They're neGOSHable, they're neGOSH-able."

Uncertain of what else to do, I puked all over them.

I caught some more vomit in my handkerchief, got out of the van, doused handerkerchief in puddle, wrang it out, got back in van and

wiped as much barf as I could off the loot. I restowed certificates, envelope and briefcase. I turned off the map-light, leaned my head on
the steering wheel and thought, There's billions in this van. The police
search will be colossal. But Angry Boy, still inside me, answered: *No,
sonny, it won't be so colossal. Billion-dollar van deliveries aren't advertised
transactions, they're secret deals. The police won't know what's in the van.
If they think that the Stuyvesant Avenue action was an in-house mob ad-
justment, they may not even prioritize the search. Chill out, man.* That's
easy for *you* to say, I shot back, but suppose the police are grossed out
with mob adjustments and want to play for keeps this time. Or suppose
the mob has its own police. Where does that put me, wise guy?

If you can separate yourself and the money from the van soon enough,
said Angry Boy, *IT PUTS YOU ON MARVIN GARDENS IN FAT
CITY!*

But first I had to separate the van from the corpse.

I swallowed hard to settle my guts. I opened the door and stepped
down into the rain. I keyed open the rear door and climbed in. The van
was awash with big black briefcases, but by rearranging them I could
open up a path. Without looking at the face I grabbed the corpse under
the arms and lifted with all my strength. There was a spasm in my back
as my left foot slipped on the bloody floor, but I ignored my back, braced
myself and lifted and pulled harder. The dead weight moved and slowly
painfully I pulled it up and towards the rear. When he was close enough
I got down from the van and grabbed him by the armpits again, this time
with my head horridly close to his, and when I'd pulled far enough I
couldn't hold him up any more and the body slipped from my grasp and
flacked down on the pavement. As the barrel-shaped carcass hit, it made
this low gutteral grunt, and I jumped in fear that he was still alive, but
in a second I realized it was just air forced out past the vocal chords.
Trembling now, I felt for his wallet, which I needed in order to slow up
a police search that could mark Hackensack as part of my trail. I found
it in his inside jacket pocket, alligator skin, jumbo-size and bulging,

one side still warm. I tossed wallet onto driver's seat, returned to corpse, checked out other pockets and finally, with my last remaining oomph, dragged the stiff behind a big pile of re-bars.

I got back in the van and saw the girl.

She'd been under Monsieur, lying face up. She had no raincoat, just a woolen suit with a white blouse, and they were both soaked with blood. Suit, nyloned legs and high-heeled shoes suggested some pathetic plan for an evening on the town, perhaps with Monsieur himself. *He's crushed her*, I concluded, but as though answering me she groaned and stretched slightly. Those briefcases near her must have cushioned the body's impact. I kneeled next to her and examined her carefully enough to make sure she wasn't bleeding herself. I searched the van for her ID, but there was no handbag.

Before starting the motor I checked one more thing—Monsieur's wallet. As I expected, it was loaded with a wad of big bills thick enough to choke a moose.

Monsieur's name? Michelangelo Imbratta, probably a son of Uncle Titus's friendly godfather, a prince of the royal line.

I hit the starter and crept forward down the service road. It was almost 6 and quite dark. My intention now: to get the van off the road and out of circulation, preferably at some dumpy motel, as soon as possible. But the van had other ideas. I was no sooner onto Wagner but the engine got rough and clouds of steam started rising from the grill. Going all sweaty I shifted to neutral as the engine died and, running a red light, I took a right and coasted to a stop on the left side of a one-way street. I'd fetched up in front of the Pillar of Fire Church, fifty feet from the corner. Rush-hour traffic was lively, but there weren't many pedestrians. I leaned on the steering wheel again, physically exhausted. A little bird told me that all I had to do was grab one briefcase, abandon the van and the girl, taxi to Newark Airport and fly away rich as Croesus. But another little bird squawked back that if the police found the securities, they'd contact the SEC and be onto me when I sold mine. Besides, I now felt that I *owned* the van, and all the wealth in it, by law of conquest—that it was kill or be killed, and I somehow was not killed and had survivor's rights.

I got out, locked the van and opened up the engine compartment, which was soaked and stinking of coolant. There was no mystery what had happened. Steam was still hissing from a half-inch split in the heater hose. I left the engine open so the night air and the rain would cool it down.

I hoofed it back to Wagner, noting near the corner an abandoned and partly dismantled bike locked to a parking meter.

One block north on Wagner I hit an A & P and was out of there almost at once with a gallon of springwater, a pocket flashlight and a penknife. On the way back I stopped at the abandoned bike. The front wheel was missing, and the rear tire was flat. I checked for passers-by and then got to work. With one hand I pulled the rear tire off its rim, with the other grabbed the inner tube. I cut off about eighteen inches of same. Back at the van I used the flashlight to locate the slit, which was no longer hissing. I looped inner tube over it, made a knot on the other side and pulled tight. The inventor in me smiled—the glory of this jury-rig was that the expansion of the hose from heat would make the patch even tighter. With a little luck this hose would be good for miles.

I topped up the radiator with springwater and drove the van away.

Back on Wagner I headed for the freeway. In five minutes I was on the Garden State Parkway, heading south at 60 MPH in heavy traffic as the wipers beat back the rain. I exited at Newark and moseyed along looking for the right motel, but they were all too well lit and close to the street. I opted for the truck route and within a few blocks came upon the Dallas Motor Inn. With faded flickering neon name-sign, another red neon sign reading -ACANCY, and a parking lot extending clear around to the back, the Dallas Motor Inn filled my bill to a tee. In the lobby I liked it also that the front desk was back far enough from the window to make it hard for the clerk on duty to see what I was driving. I offered credit card, asked for a ground floor room away from the road and signed my name. The clerk was too busy with a phonecall in Spanish to notice anything about me. Funny how people's infernal apathy can sometimes work in your favor!

Only one tricky maneuver remained. Getting the girl into the room. I propped open the motel room door with a wooden chair. I wrapped her in my raincoat and was just out of the van when we were caught in the headlights of an approaching car. This car parked two doors down, and the passenger window came down, and somebody was watching us. What did I do? Of course, I sang. I started singing A Hard Day's Night, complete with Liverpool accent, but once I was in the door and out of sight I donned a ladylike falsetto, shouted "Put me down, you brute!" added a Goldie Hawn laugh and barked out a meaty guffaw in my own voice.

I put the girl down on the bed, and when I came back to close the door I heard a woman outside say, "Why don't you ever carry *me*, you clown?" and after laughter, "Hey, that big guy's got *some great voice*."

It's 4:30 AM. I'm going to lie down next to her soon, without much hope of sleeping, but first I'm going to take some Magic Tape to those bullet-holes. Give myself half a chance or, if you will, more rope to hang myself with.

O the power of art! My singing must have livened up conversation between the couple in the car, because I'm now being treated to a virtuoso performance of the Bedspring Concerto, complete with impassioned vocal duets, from the room next door. Could they please stop?

Chapter Two **Special Rates for the Dead**

There is no rest, not even a minute, for the wicked on this earth, especially when they've stolen a few hundred billion from ravening killers. Such thieving dunces enter a special zone where every little thing in life has blatant symbolism, where every word has echoes, where the click of a lightswitch takes time. It's like reality becoming an opera, or vice versa. Something like what Johann Sebastian Bach would have written if he'd been reborn in a concentration camp.

But rest I must, at least rest in the sense of stopping for a few days. You see, I've hurt myself in a tender part of the body, and I have trouble sitting down, so we're holed up at Buckeye Grove, a trailer park near Carpathia, Ohio.

That's right, we. Mara is still with me, and she's talking now. *Mára* that is—get it right, man, Mára Deláno, a name that sticks with me as though from some old dream.

Mara's talking buckets, but that's for later.

It's noon, and she's asleep, taking what she calls a traumatic nap, and of all things it's snowing, and through the windows of this strange contraption I see major cemeteries on all sides—to the left Shadow Acres, to the right Elysium Section, and stretching out before me Rest Domain—all white with snow. Can you believe these places are competing with each other for corpses? Elysium Section offers Larger Plots, Shadow Acres says it's a Family Cemetery, but I think I like Rest Domain best. They have Special Rates.

Sitting by this little table in my land-ship, drinking lukewarm instant coffee out of pitted styrofoam, I space out and imagine the snow lasting forever, hopelessly burying all the roads in and out, and Mara and I, safe and snug among the dead, cruising through years in this tiny room with our hook-ups and electric heater. All the things we could talk about, all the memories we might share.

But my sweet dream ends in a grimace of fear. The money in this van—it's burning a hole in time.

How we got here was amazing. I woke up at 7 AM yesterday in the Dallas Motor Inn. One moment I was dead asleep, the next moment I was sitting straight up, blinking and groaning as I slowly glommed onto where and what I was. I got out of bed and almost doubled over with aches and pains. I limped over to the window. It was still dark and raining, but when I opened the window for air, the air was mild and smelled sweetly fresh. I showered, dressed in my new duds and ate some bread and cheese and four shots of ibuprofen, washed down with tapwater. I pocketed Monsieur's wad and padded it with two neat packets of C-notes from one of the briefcases in the van. Back inside, I checked on the girl. She was still asleep, lying as I'd left her, on her back. The weak window-light of the rainy morning etched her face, neck and margin of bare shoulders like a close-up in a black-and-white forties movie, and I was stymied again, as I'd been the night before, by her beauty, wistful, earthy, beckoning. Had her eyelids fluttered? I reached down and shook her, very gently, but no response. She was somewhere else.

I laid out her clothes on the couch, wrote a note saying "Back by noon. Don't go anywhere or answer the phone," and left it by the bed. I undid the phoneline for good measure. Would she bolt? Given her condition and the gory details and the van being locked, it was unlikely. Still, this was the chanciest angle of my scheme. But I had to take the risk.

I donned my new raincoat and hat, hung up the PRIVACY PLEASE and walked out into the parking lot. Now I was ready to rumble.

I hiked up the truck route towards the nearest traffic light. My reasoning was as follows: I knew we couldn't stay with that white van in that motel. We had to be hauling ass somewhere else in some other set of wheels. Also the new vehicle shouldn't be bought anywhere near the Dallas Motor Inn, because then anybody who asked about me at either the motel or the car lot would have an easy time tracing me to the other place. So I got on a bus. I got on a bus that said STATION and shuddered and swayed down Jersey morning streets, past auto repair shops and fast foods and grimy closed pizzerias, past dingy shopping malls, past bombed-out town centers with charity shops and sad-looking old churches and used clothing stores and bail bondsmen. In the bus were a sparse collection of kids on their way to school, probably Catholic school because they were up early and decently dressed, and spaced-out night watchmen on their way home. I was beginning to feel together again. My ear still hurt, but the buzzing had gone away. I could have used a monster breakfast, but even the hunger, clean and raw, made me feel focused, directed. I had a mission.

I got off at the main station. It had stopped raining. I bought a *Star-Ledger* and hopped on the Number 7 for Passaic. This bus was crowded as hell. I squeezed into a seat, pulled my fisherman's hat down low, cowered a bit to conceal my size and got my nose into the *Star-Ledger*. You can bet I wanted to see the morning news. But there wasn't a thing in it about the Bronx shoot-out. Not on the front page, where it ought to have been, or 2–3, or News-in-brief, or anywhere else.

But there was no end of talk about El Niño. Two articles on p. 1: one a twister demolishing most of Ayre, KS; the other, with a headline like EL NIÑO ON WARPATH, WANTS REVENGE, quoting a Green group that El Niño is a kind of demon created by global warming, which was created by the Greenhouse Effect, which was created by us. A Green spokesman compared El Niño to Frankenstein's monster. Not exactly a reassuring read, as I sat in a fume-filled bus and looked out on the architectural dump-heap that was greater Newark. I'd seen disaster footage that looked better than this.

If El Niño wants more work, he can start here.

I pocketed the newspaper and got off at the Passaic city limits. I'd gone far enough, and I'd seen what I wanted.

I'd seen a sign saying MEHBUB ALI SHAH HAPPY MOTORS under a weird neon shaped like a sun with rainbow-colored rays, and the sign hung over the entrance to about an acre of aging cars, vans and trucks.

I crossed the street and sauntered onto the lot. I picked my way through a jumble of Mustangs, Rams, Chevelles, Charades and Caprices towards the office, a little frame structure well back off the street. Mr. Mehbub Ali Shah was quick to appear, and as he sallied forth from the office to greet me I noticed motion behind him, and an indistinct pasty face appeared furtively at the office window. Ali Shah was a tiny dark-skinned man in his forties, with the delicate features, luminous eyes and perfect teeth of ancient royalty. He wore a befeathered Swiss hiker's hat and a fleece so violet that it looked about to jump out of the spectrum. From his relatively low altitude he beamed up at me as one might admire a tree, and announced in a high, tuneful voice, "I am thinking Mistah requires something uncommonly big."

I'd been thinking minivan, but all of a sudden I realized, Ali Shah had a point there. Something bigger than a minivan would give us privacy. We could bypass motels, spend whole days and nights without being seen. But I didn't want a giant blunderbus that would be unparkable. "Big but not too big," I said.

The Most Amazing Thing

Ali Shah bent his head forward and put the knuckles of his right hand to his lips, as though lost in thought. As he did this the office door opened and a pudgy man in a Seton Hall sweatshirt, younger than Ali Shah and lighter-skinned, emerged onto the little deck and scuttled down the stairs and away from us into the maze of vehicles. He held a book-bag but wasn't carrying it like one. Ali Shah turned and sang out "Farrukh!" but almost swallowed the last syllable, as though he'd changed his mind. A pained look crossed his face but he quickly caught himself, regained eye-contact and touched me lightly on the arm. The starry brightness came into his eyes again.

"Mistah," he said, "I am considering I may have just the right numbah." Right away he was leading me far back into the lot, so far in fact that at last we reached a metal gate opening onto the bordering alley. Parked just to the right of this gate and facing toward the alley was a cream-colored vehicle the likes of which I'd never seen before. It was as tall and wide as a minivan, but about twice as long, and this extra length allowed for lots of living room. Under the driver's window was the name VIXEN 21. Ali Shah allowed as Vixen had been a small company that didn't make these things any more. He showed me through the incredibly neat and new-looking interior. "You use it for a house, you drive it like a cah," he said.

I did a little bargaining just for credibility, and we agreed on a price of $22 thousand. We went back to the office for the keys and the paperwork which, thanks to my obscene wad of cash, went like a breeze. Ali Shah made space for me on his desk by neatly piling his Kelly Blue Books on one side, and under his admiring eyes I dealt hundred-dollar bills in piles of ten. He didn't bother to recount the loot, but in short order signed off on the title and handed me the keys to the Vixen, as well as the key to his back gate, which he told me I could leave in the lock.

But all of a sudden I had to pee. It wasn't the polite little tickle that says I can wait thanks, or the sharper bladder-twinge that says Why not now? It was more like the surge of the Yukon River on the summer morning when the ice breaks up, saying, Man, I'm outta here, I'm headed for open sea.

I asked Ali Shah about the facilities and he motioned to a little door behind his desk, saying he hoped I'd fit. I wedged through the door, edged past the grimy sink and banged both elbows against the walls getting my fly open.

During these proceedings I heard Ali Shah exit through the front of his shack.

Out came Lefty in the nick of time, and I was well into a relieving cascade when All Hell broke loose outside. First there were sirens, door-slamming, lurid flashing lights through the bottle glass of the little window in front of me, several gutteral shouts, as in "NO!" and "DON'T!" and then, God help me, gunshots.

Desperately groping to zip up, I caught my penis in my fly. I tried to free it, but got nothing but pain because the zipper was firmly lodged in underwear and flesh. POW! a bullet rattled into the water closet and the tiny room started to flood. The pain was major, but I decided death is worse, and gripping his Nibs in one hand to reduce turbulence I turned and burst out into the office, seeing through the front window that the principal shit was happening off in the right front corner of the lot, where Farrukh had scuttled off. I minced down the steps, all hunched over, and started weaving my way towards the back rear corner and the Vixen. You'd have thought my tool was shrivelling up in the process, as though in fear, but in fact, maybe because of a blocked vein, the damn thing was getting bigger until it felt like some useless third leg that was almost dragging on the ground. I looked back towards the shit. The shooting had stopped, but there was a blue cap with a badge on it bobbing among the cars, coming towards me. I panicked. In the far corner of the lot was this monster green truck, with a kid working on the engine. He had a Walkman on and apparently hadn't heard any of the

25

commotion. I darted around to the back of the truck and crawled right onto the right-hand set of double wheels, so as to be invisible from anywhere except the very back corner.

But I'm no sooner in position than there's a door banging and a great big roar. The kid has started the fucking truck. The gears are grinding. I try to ease off but O God it can't be. *My dick is stuck between the wheels!*

Damn! Mara stirring in her sleep has let out a moan wrung from the deepest sorrow—a moan to wake the dead. I rise and survey the snowy graveyard, and there they all are out under their snowy stones, the sedate and respectable Dead, at rest at last after living responsible Carpathian lives, many of them enjoying Special Rates. Staring at them in the grayness I fade back to Ali Shah's used-car lot and cringe in shame. What special rightness that at last I should show the world a great limp dong, me who hasn't made a buck or had a boner in years, me whose worth and character are neatly symbolized by a sagging male member. Why should a big brute like me go impotent? You may well ask. I thought it was Glynda's fault at first, with her refusal to have sex with me and all that. But who can blame her for being sick and nauseous?

I finally decided to see a psychiatrist and maybe invest in some Viagra, but that's just when I ran out of money. I'm glad I'm writing this. Impotence is the secret sorrow, you clam up about it and it gets worse. Talk about it, and who knows? Not that, I mean, Glynda's any man's cup of tea. She's small and slim and since her illness a little bony. But I used to revel in her, make her disappear inside my big arms (she'd go all quiet then), cherish her dearly. Erections were no problem then, though I wished she'd let me do it more than once a week (she favored Sunday afternoons, when the opera was playing on the radio). But then that changed. She developed this eating disorder, which is supposed to be psychosomatic, and began seeing Dr. Jezra. Jezra, wiry little facial-hair type in a tweed jump suit, holing up with her in the bedroom for primal scream sessions.

But one day the noises coming out of the bedroom sounded a little *too* primal. Even money, he was jumping her. Odds on, Glynda and the good doctor were playing a round of tummy-rummy.

At least, that's what I feared, and Glynda's behavior did nothing to calm me. In short order she was pushing me away in bed, saying I stank, or I was too big, or that I treated her like a piece of food, or that I didn't support her right. At one point, she even vomited, and I got the general idea and started camping in the music room.

After that I wasn't attracted to Glynda or anybody. Women make me cower. I have sexual stagefright.

It's early afternoon, and sun is starting to dapple the snowy graveyard slopes. There's action in the trailer park now, old folks visiting each other, nursing on cigarettes and sipping steamy coffee from big campy mugs. A Saturday get-together? No way. It's Saturday all the time here—they're retired. Retired, isolated, forgotten—impotent like me.

Of course, impotence has its consolations. You don't have to carry condoms or worry about wet dreams, and you're a sure winner in paternity suit situations. You don't have to give a damn about whether or not women like you. You can even play God and laugh like hell at the dumb-ass messes that lovers are always getting into. Pretty good. Almost good enough to compensate for feeling like a worthless piece of crap.

But if Desmond Ruck repays the national Debt, he's not so impotent, is he?

Mara sleeping on the bed in back, lying on her right side, facing me, except all I can see of her is a shock of brown hair on the comforter, which covers a sweet hillscape of shoulder and hip, with the line of her thighs foreshortened in my direction. A pain in my crotch. How long, I wonder, do penis lacerations take to heal? Are there ever complications? Why the blazes did I

Forget it and tell the story.

So, what do you do when you're lying on the rear wheels of a big truck with your dingus pinned between them and somebody's just started up said truck and shifted into low, and you're suffocating on exhaust fumes and the engine's so loud you can't call for help? What do you do? You shit in your pants, that's what you do, and that's just what I was just about to do, when the gears disengaged again and the motor died. I pulled again and what do you know? My prong came free easily. No problem. I suppose with the almost-shitting and all, the blood supply had shifted, and the once-bloated organ was now shrinking into parity with a piece of elbow macaroni. But as I slid off the wheels and into daylight I saw that the space before me was no longer empty but occupied by a woman in uniform. A short square young woman in a bulletproof vest. She looked away while I zipped up, then fixed me with an intense and urgent stare.

"You OK sir? Not shot or anything?"

I said I was fine thanks.

"You know this man Farrukh?"

I said no, I was just a walk-on customer.

"That what Mr. Shah told us. He got all upset about you, after that round hit the office."

I asked why the bullet had been going in that direction.

"It wasn't us, Sir. That bullet was Farrukh's. He drew his weapon on us and we had to kill—I mean, defend ourselves. Sure you don't need a medic?"

I looked her in the eye for the first time. Her face was sort of white, and her right hand trembled as she tried and tried to close the snap on her belt-holster. "I'm fine, thanks," I said. "But are your sure *you're* OK?"

She had trouble answering. "Sure. It's only that I never—I mean, til today . . ." Her eyes went vague and she turned suddenly and walked back towards the street. What was the matter with the cop? It must have been her first fire-fight, her first kill.

I made for the Vixen. Using Shah's key I opened the back gate, left the key in the open lock, climbed into the van, turned on the ignition and, it being a diesel, waited for the glowlight. I started the motor and began coaxing the big boat into a position where I could exit the gate. As I prepared for the third run, somebody knocked hard on the driver's side window. It was Ali Shah. His hat was off and there was a big bloodstain on his violet fleece. His face was transformed by grief. I lowered the window.

"Don't worry, mistah," he said. "I'll lock the gate after you."

"Your son?" I asked.

"Nephew, my nephew, my dead sister's son, all I had in life. Fundamentally a sweet boy. Always I warned him not to deal."

I offered sympathy. Stretching up as far as he could, he stuck a small fist through the window and opened his hand. In it was a pair of tiny sealed leather pouches on a frayed black necklace string. "I want you to have this, mistah. It was Farrukh's, what we call, *taviz*. It contains Koranic verses to brighten the human path. It did no end of good for him."

I stammered, "But Farrukh . . ."

"Farrukh kept his promises to God, and God rewarded him for those. But promises to men, that is anothah mattah."

"But how can I see the verses if the pouches are sealed?"

"No problem, sah. Being sealed just makes them more powerful. I'm weeshing you a safe voyage, mistah, with many good lucks."

I nosed the Vixen out onto the main drag and followed signs to the Garden State Parkway. The motor home handled OK, but you needed patience getting the little Diesel up through the gears. I steered south on the Parkway and set the cruise at 55. There wasn't much traffic, and the road was drying out. But as soon as I pulled my foot off the accelerator, my crotch started hurting like hell, and I was going into a full-body shake when I noticed Farrukh's taviz on the passenger seat. I reached over and gave it a pat. Somehow that calmed me right away.

As I drove I started thinking about things. OK, I thought, suppose that in fact the Bronx episode has been hushed up. We then ask why. To avoid Imbratta family embarrassment? Don't make me laugh: for these gangsters, wasting rivals is a matter of professional pride, and getting wasted yourself makes you a fallen hero. Why then, it's plain as the nose on your face! Imbratta covered it up to keep the money secret! If the feds know that that kind of money exists, they'll have a pretty good idea *why* it exists, and that won't be very good for Imbratta. And if *that's* plain, then it's plain as the mouth in your head that he's going to come after me. But how? He doesn't have police search-and-pursuit resources, so unless one of his people fingers the van this AM, he's out of luck. But he's got two more hopes down the line.

The first is that money shouts. Unless I'm really cagey, I mean wise, I'll blow my cover through gross extravagance, like buying Key West or something.

The second is the girl. Why the hell didn't she have ID? *She may be an Imbratta herself.*

Yet somehow I doubted it.

I took the first Newark exit and made for the Dallas Motor Inn. I did a test drive-by—the place looked almost abandoned—then parked half a block down the road under the sign for Kosciusko Tire and Brake. I locked up the Vixen and eagle-eyed the motel and street again. No unusual goings-on, except that from this angle I could see that two adjoining Dallas rooms had their doors open, with a chambermaid's cart at one of them. I strode past all this and around to the back of the motel, and there was the white van, looking much the better for its Magic Tape body-job.

I remember just at that moment having this strange thought, that the world, which makes a horrendous fuss about minor fuckups like poor

Farrukh's drug-dealing, never seems to notice the major monstrosities that go on in plain daylight. I was thinking this while fitting the key in the motel-room door.

I twisted the key, leaned on the door and went inside. At first it was too dark to see, and in the darkness all I recognized at first was this strange smell, not perfume but like the air on a spring day, that had to be the girl, and then I saw a lightness in the far corner and saw that this lightness was the white bedside curtains shifting in the breeze, and saw that the girl was lying in the bed as I left her, face up. I walked in and sat down on the window side of the bed and looked at her. In the dim light, with her eyes closed and her face so serene, she had a magic look about her, like the faces children see in dreams. But now I had to wake her. I touched her shoulder, and she shifted slightly, and I got to thinking, suppose she wakes up and sees me and gets scared to death? So I thought, God damn it, I'd better sing something, and I picked out the sweetest, least abusive song I knew, "Oh What a Beautiful Morning."

I crooned it the way Bing Crosby might, but softer. I hadn't gotten further than the corn and elephants when the girl opened her eyes.

I hadn't counted on the eyes.

The shifting curtains must have parted as her eyes opened, sending a glimmer of light that bounced off of them, because my first impression unforgettably was that they were luminous, that they were casting light on me. Large, perfectly shaped, intensely focused but somehow calm and spacy, like a jungle cat. And the color! Long ago, as a child sitting by the window of an airliner that was coming in over the ocean to land in Los Angeles, I watched as a ray of sunlight broke through the clouds and fell right on the fringe of water where the deep blue of the ocean ended and the sandbank began, beaming up a blue-green that was brighter than either blue or green and seemed almost like the color of happiness—her eyes were exactly that color. They were the most beautiful eyes I'd ever seen, except there was something a little scary about them,

31

as though they not only had lucid sight but the weird power to reshape what they were aimed at.

I realized I was singing out of tune.

She shook her head as if to clear it and pulled the covers up around her shoulders.

I said, "You're safe."

She blinked at me and said in a husky whisper, *"You should have let me die."*

"But you weren't dying. You were just—"

"They told me I would die." This sentence, spoken like an accusation, now carried the full power of her voice, which was rich but soft, like the lower range of a flute. It cut through the air like a ray of suffering. What with the eyes and the voice, I was getting dizzy.

"*Who* told you?" I asked.

She just stared at me and zapped me with the voice again. "What place is this?"

I jumped up, feeling major pain in the crotch (which was feeling worse and not better) and started futzing around, turning on lights, getting her new bathrobe and clothes, heating some coffee water, all the time trying to explain things, and finally turning to the wall as she donned her bathrobe, grabbed the clothes and made for the bathroom. By the time she got back, I had sandwiches and coffee ready. We tore in greedily, and I finished first and realized it was time to sock it to her. As best I could, as she munched and sipped and held me in her eyes, I made the following points:

1. I had the money from the van.
2. I meant to keep the money and run.
3. She was free to go right now, with any amount of money she needed, if she'd be good enough not to finger me to the fuzz or to old man Imbratta.

4. She was also free to come with me, share the wealth and the danger and finally escape into some other part of the world with a laundered identity.

After I finished, she was quiet for the longest time, as the window-light darkened and little bullets of rain smacked on the window. Then she said, as I'd somehow expected, that she'd hang on with me, at least for a while. "I'm dead here, you see," she said. I asked what would happen if she contacted the Imbrattas and offered to return the money. "*I'm dead then too*," was the whispered reply.

I asked her to pack up, pronto. I walked around front to check out. What with the busride and drive and all, I'd had time to make some plans. At the front desk I paid my bill in cash and pocketed the original credit card paperwork. That left no trail, except word of mouth. We stowed our gear in the white van, but it reeked so badly of old blood that she couldn't get in. No need, I said, and I pointed by line of sight to the left and just up the street, where we were headed. In the van I inched through the parking lot, keeping her in the mirror as long as I could, and took the left onto Kosciusko in heavy lunchtime traffic. I didn't stop at the Vixen but went a block beyond it, to a big Sears Roebuck parking lot that I'd seen from the bus. I parked in an empty corner of the lot and walked back down Kosciusko to the Vixen. Mara was standing on the sidewalk next to it, in her new raincoat, facing me, her feet wide apart as though for better balance, looking like a lost soul beside the wide eye-like windshields of the supervan.

I somehow thought, *I'll never forget this sight.*

The next step was insanely simple, compared with what I'd been through before. We drove the Vixen to Sears and parked next to the van. I walked into Sears and bought four gray duffle bags. In the van, while Mara sat in the Vixen, I packed the loot into the duffles. Some of the briefcases had blood on them, but that would have to wait. The sacks were heavy and sagged like dead bodies. I manhandled them into the Vixen and packed them in the privy.

I jumped into the white van, parked it in a crowded section near the Sears storefront, where it wouldn't stand out, and locked it.

Then I climbed into the Vixen and belted up. I revved the diesel and looked out on the full sweep of the parking lot, using the mirrors to boot. A normal lot, a normal day. No lurking patrol cars or goggle-eyed spectators. I felt almost good. Sure, my crotch hurt, but you take that in perspective. The parkway was just a few blocks up the street, and we took it north and made for I-80 West. As we cleared the on-ramp onto the big road and I pulled into the middle lane and wound out in fourth to get by a big slow Ballantine Beer truck, I saw brightness far ahead and a patch of blue sky right over the vanishing river of road, and it was like the whole West and freedom were opening up in front of me.

Near Stroudsburg, PA, we pulled in for gas and Mara bought chips and Coke. No time for anything fancy—I wanted to be out of Pennsylvania and well off I-80 before we slept. Back on the road we started eating and drinking, and after a few minutes Mara asked me to tell her about myself—what I did, that sort of thing. I felt a pang of shame.

I said, I'm a Nobody from Nowhere who does Nothing. Up ahead the overcast had relaxed into broken clouds, and the low sun was making sly remarks from the southwest.

Mara laughed mockingly and said, "That can't be. It takes more than a nobody to pull a solo job like this."

I told her I hadn't planned the job. I asked, How could I have? That made her think a minute. I looked up, and she looked different, like somebody who'd just read a letter.

I told her I taught wood shop and sometimes built furniture. All of a sudden it welled up in me to tell her more, to share the joys of working wood, to tell her how there's no fresher smell on earth than a fresh-milled Doug fir two-by-four, and what a turn-on it is to look at a stack of new-bought lumber and see the table in it, or the bed or what-have-you, that I'm about to make, or to strip the cloudy varnish off an old piece that looks like junk and bleach out the stains and patch the veneer and sand it down and finish it til it looks like new. It welled up in me to tell her I was good at this and at a baker's dozen of other odd jobs, and how I had an instinct for the way things worked and sometimes could even see into the hearts of things from their outsides, and how I loved listening and talking to people, and how the whole seeable and touchable world, the lakes, plants, rocks, machines and people, made me mad keen to know everything about it, and how I would never, could never, forget a fact I'd learned. I burned to tell her how strange it was, wasn't it, that a guy with my looks and arm-strength and know-how and pure amusability could never, would never, learn a profession or keep a steady job or support a family. *Sort of a mystery, right? Something a doctor might study.*

It welled up in me, but I couldn't speak. Not that I couldn't find words, but more like I found too many and felt drowned in them. I'm full of words, but I'm as useless with them as I am useless with women.

So instead of opening up with Mara, I asked her about the shootout. Turns out, it *was* the Imbrattas who were involved, except they were financially much bigger even than Uncle Titus thought. Not even the Mob, I mean most of them, knew how big the Imbrattas were. (You can bet it was strange, hearing these things in a space-age van from a woman who spoke pure flute.) For starters the Imbrattas ran the East Coast and the Caribbean, and not just drugs, but they were into gambling, prostitution, weapons, terrorism, slavetrade, spare human body parts, etc. Etc.? For example, they netted about six billion a year fencing stolen US technology to mainland China. They bought and sold drugs and weapons, on a GNP scale, in Asia, Eastern Europe and the former USSR. They also owned a "legitimate" bank and a "legitimate" mutual fund, just to make their financial dealings less of a bother. This family business turned more of a profit than Microsoft and GM combined. On top of this, except for their front activities, they paid no taxes. And they were expanding, just like any other successful operation. The money in the van, that I had now stolen, was for a buyout of the whole drug syndicate in South and Central America, owned by the granddaddies of all Colombian druglords, an infamous family named Sturm.

But it was a brokered buyout.

The brokers were the Calandrinos. These Calandrinos were a Chicago family who were cousins of the Imbrattas but who had their own operation.

I interrupted to ask Mara where she fitted in. "I'm the Imbrattas' comptroller," she said. "Or was."

The Calandrinos couldn't afford to corner this Colombian market themselves, but they had "superb" South American connections (meaning they owned four or five provincial governments), and they could sure use a few billion in commission. So that explained the transfer of loot. Mara had driven uptown with Mickey (Michelangelo) Imbratta and had been joined by two other Imbratta brothers (Luca and Oliviere) in the van. The Calandrino brothers (Zach, Lenny and Xavier) arrived in their own van to make the pickup.

In broad daylight? *Right there?*

Mara took a sip of Coke and made a funny wad'ya-wad'ya face, like somebody in an Italian movie. "The Imbrattas *own* that block, shops cops and all. They do what they please there, things that wouldn't be as safe somewhere else."

Why didn't she have ID? She'd left it in Mickey's car.

I said thanks for sharing all that but why pray tell did everybody start shooting each other?

She looked at me like I was E.T., and the flute lowered to that hoarse whisper. "*I thought* you *did that.*"

What did she think now?

"I don't know *what* to think. I'd gone with Mickey to the van to get the briefcases. We heard shots and he pulled his gun. I must've fainted." She slowly shook her head, as though confused. "Something must've gone awfully wrong out on the street, who knows? There was this *thing* between Luca and Xavier Calandrino. Xavy's a mean SOB, and he and Luca tangled over a franchise in Pittsburgh, a few months back. I'm thinking maybe Luca didn't feel so easy trusting Xavy with all that money."

"Betcha he's feeling easy enough now," I answered and then remembered I hadn't told her they were pretty likely all dead. Telling her this and hearing her respond (she whispered a sizeable obit for every Imbratta and every Calandrino), and musing with her on why the slaughter had been hushed up, took about half an hour.

I had lots more questions for Mara, but by then I was getting drowsy and we both needed a bathroom (there'd been no time to service the john in the Vixen). So we pulled into the next oasis, and what do you know? The place had an espresso machine! A double latte was very much in order—the double shot for uppers, the milk for energy. She wanted one too, and by the time I'd been served she was out of the bathroom and we were heading back to the Vixen. We set our javas, fat and hot, in the drink cradles on the console, and once we were cruising she pulled out a cigarette and lit up. In this coziness, as the afternoon passed and twilight settled on the road, I heard, in flute and whisper, the story of Mara's life. It literally took hours. Telling it all would take a book, and one you wouldn't soon put down.

She told stories within stories within stories.

I'm still feeling weak, but I've got to write down some of this. I'll put Mara's intense whispers in italics.

Mara comes from Chile, where 27 years ago, she was baptised (pardon my spelling) Albamara Serena Baquedeno Balmaçeda Santa Maria.

Her family in Chile goes way back to a day in the 18th century when Jorje Manuel Balmaçeda, a daring Spanish sea captain who'd been abandoned in a dinghy by his mutinous crew, saw what he thought was a beached sea lion as he drifted near Punta Angomos. Dying of *mortal famishment* he leapt from the boat and swam ashore and discovered that this wasn't a sea lion at all but a *naked sunbathing native maiden* who'd *fallen into a trance.* This *native maiden* turned out to be *the Princess Galapaga,* who was on the verge of a deadly sunburn and who (when he saved her life by waking her with handfuls of sea water) mistook him for *Kanaloa, the God of the Ocean.* News of this so-called miracle quickly spread among the native folks, and Captain Balmaçeda, now honored as *something divine,* was married to *the Princess Galapaga, as soon as she had healed,* in a ceremony full of golden gongs, conch horns, grass harps, solemn ritual and drunken binge.

Here Mara paused and sighed and I wondered, was she maybe homesick? But before I could ask, she went on.

Captain Balmaçeda became the force to reckon with in those parts. After a couple of years he introduced *the Mother Faith,* which became known to those simple souls as (??) *Gextabaga: the religion worshipped by God.* First thing they all did was build a tiny thatched chapel at Point Angomos *to the Madonna of the Tides.* It stands to this day.

Then Jorje went into mining and made it big on nitrate of soda.

I asked, was the family still in the mining business? She paused for a moment, then almost hissed, *"Sure, but the imbeciles have ruined it!"*

When *interrupted by death* the good Captain was building a huge villa by the sea. He called it *El Rosario.* Galapaga and the children later completed most of the villa but (*as a sign of their piety*) left *a noble vaulted chamber open to the elements. It's become a sanctuary for migrating butterflies. In March the walls are great vertical meadows of living saffron, vermillion and indigo. On hot days we'd take tea in this room, soothed by the breeze of a million wings.* (The beauty of that image floored me!)

As centuries went by, and Balmaçeda cousins kept meeting and marrying and breeding with each other, or meeting and breeding with and marrying each other, or just meeting and breeding, family affairs got a wee bit eccentric. An inbred streak of lunacy, fire in the villa library, a killer plague of influenza, and continual misreadings of church records, led to the family belief that Captain Jorje Balmaçeda *was not only Kanaloa the sea-god, but that he had pearls for teeth, that his skin was green and luminous and extended in flaps between his arms and abdomen to form wings, and that he had an insatiable sexual appetite and a mean streak.* One Esmarelda Remedio, etc., etc., Balmaçeda, a 19th-century spinster *admittedly not famous for her veracity,* claimed that *Kanaloa appeared before her as she lay in bed, magically elevated her body and ravished her in mid-air.* Two weeks later her naked corpse was found at the base of a cliff. Since then, other Kanaloa sightings have been recorded, and always with deadly results. In 1853, 1878, 1883 and 1901, Balmaçedas of both sexes insisted that the god had appeared before them while they were looking out the window, and that he in a thunderous voice had asked *"HÉ PASSA?"* and that they were tongue-tied and could not answer. *Each of them was found, stark naked and stone dead, soon after the sighting.*

("Hé passa?" is the local way of saying, What's up?)

This explains the notorious Balmaçeda phobia for windows.

Here I felt a chill and asked Mara if she believed in any of this stuff.

"NO!" she exploded. "That is, not since I was a child. When I grew up I stopped believing in that *silly goblin story.* That's why my family called me *The Freak.*"

Mara went on to talk about her favorite aunt, Big Cuerva. Aunt Cuerva was hot stuff. Sitting in her ancient eagle-clawed chair in the immense sundrenched kitchen, her casements open to the roar of surf on the rocks beneath, drinking brimful tumblers of Mexican tequila, rolling her own maduro cigars against her naked thigh, flanked on one side by her huge purple parrot and on the other by her indoor housepet stallion, Big Cuerva told her niece a bookshelf full of stories, so full of local lingo, unbelievable fantasy and far-out wit that *it would take a poet* to put them down in writing. Mara remembers these like yesterday and told me enough of them to keep me enchanted, in spite of nagging crotch agony, all the way to Carpathia.

God I'm hungry, and it's getting dark. I'm going to open a few cans of hash and hope that the smell wakes her. She's still asleep, turned towards me, and it's strange that her face, so pleasantly round in its features when awake, takes on the straight lines of a Japanese sketch, mouth, eyelids, eyebrows, when asleep. Like a child she looks, the innocent child whose wide eyes opened to the horse's whinny and the woosh of parrot's wings.

Must say a prayer for Farrukh tonight. Strange, I never told Mara a word about him or what happened at the car lot. I guess that's for the best.

People can only take so much.

Almost forgot. What became of Mara's parents? Died mysteriously— she won't say how. How did Mara get to the States? Simple. Big Cuerva dies. Cousin Osvaldo inherits—Osvaldo a sadistic bastard from Santiago who banishes animals, dismantles Kanaloa shrine, takes down all the paintings in the villa and replaces them with ornamental whips. (*He'd better not look out any windows!*) Mara, who's learned English at school, escapes to Vassar, where she meets Claribel Imbratta, Guccio's niece, and so on, so all that stuff is clear.

But when I ask her how come her last name's not Balmaçeda, she almost clams up tight. "*A marriage . . . to Osvaldo's son Raul,*" she whispers. "*It went bad . . . very bad.*"

I wonder if he used the ornamental whips on her.

I called home from a gas station in Carpathia. Glynda answered, and I swear you could hear the enthusiasm deflating like a punctured tire when I said it was me. She probably expected a call from fuzzy Jezra. I said I was still in the city, and I had a new opportunity and things were going OK, and I'd be sending money. I think she must have zoned out at the mention of money, because she didn't ask any questions when I said I might not call for a week or so.

Let sleeping dogs lie.

MIDNIGHT. We've gorged ourselves on hash and bottle beer and now Mara's in the sack again. Sleep welling up in me too. Signs of healing in the groin area—I should be truckin' by Monday, maybe even tomorrow. Trailer park hookups make the Vixen john usable, so after dinner we pulled all the fat black briefcases out and carefully cleaned them and stored them in a compartment under the bed. One of them, as I discovered earlier, has about a million in unmarked C-notes (that would have been for the Calandrinos to pay off their pilots and guards with, and maybe a few local officials). The other briefcases have the real money. The clean briefcases had a nice leathery smell, somehow taking me forty years back to a time as a kid when my parents bought new luggage and we all went on a trip to Hawaii. Hey, *that's when, from the plane, I saw that sandbank, blue-green like Mara's eyes!*

Those blue-green eyes this morning came near turning me back into a whole man. I may not be able to screw, but at least I can steal.

Hey, I feel almost good. *Can sin be purifying?*

No way, man. Guilt is eternal.

But it sure helps to know what you're feeling guilty about!

Chapter Three The Misfortunes of Bod

PART ONE: THE WOMUBA APOCALYPSE

MONDAY, APRIL 6, 1998

I have seen the glory and felt the horror, I have snatched a glimpse of the promised land and slid back into the pit of Hades, I have tasted joy's grape and dashed it into smithereens against the teeth of folly. In short, I've fucked up.[1]

I've had it all and lost it all, Mara, the money, the van.

I'm in a cell in the county jail, Pilotsburg, KY. It's grim and fluorescent and overheated in here, and the overheat is vaporizing the disinfectant in my uniform and making me smell like a latrine, and in fact I'm sitting on the toilet because there are no chairs and the bed's too soft, writing on a gray confession pad given me by Schultzie, the sheriff's deputy.

Not that I'm minded to make a confession. These notes will become

---

1. This chapter was later retrieved and keyed into the computer. —Ed.

a confidential letter that I mail out of here, which is part of my rights in this jurisdiction.

My stomach's sort of bloated and acidy, from having drunk two or three gallons of the Sacannah River when the water wasn't so clean.

Schultzie's a red-faced sausage of a man who seems to be OK. He's taken a liking to me, maybe because, as he puts it, it's not every day you see a big man cry, and I'm crying now, even as I write, forgive me World, for what I've lost.

It's still raining hard outside, the same apocalyptic demon storm that screwed me up yesterday, and everybody here in the slammer is talking flood. The Pilotsburg levy is 27′, and they expect the Sacannah to crest at 33′ around 3 this PM. What happens to us prisoners? Only the Sheriff knows, in his wisdom, but right now he's up in Louisville, defending himself against a construction fraud indictment, and he's cellularizing Schultzie at short intervals.

It's OK boys, leave me here to drown. I'm grossed out on life.

Blame the entire mess on the Vixen. Here we are, yesterday morning, driving south because I decided (shit!) that getting on I-40 would buy us some better weather. As I drive I'm drinking lukewarm instant coffee, while Mara regales me about how her aunt and guardian, Big Cuerva, owned three pets that she kept right in the house—a horse, a goat and a parrot. I'm starting to giggle about the parrot, who liked to quote bawdy tidbits from the Song of Solomon, when all of a sudden the rig loses power, and there's no way to pull over to the right because I'm in the passing lane in traffic. I pull left onto a little grassy median that gives me about a yard of clearance from the fast-lane traffic, and as luck would have it the engine's to the rear on that side. Wait for help? Fuck that, I don't want to schmooze with any state troopers. Letting the engine idle in neutral, I grab tool kit and slide out the driver's door and, feeling doomed in the strange warm air, am crouching and opening the engine compartment as God knows whatall races and roars just behind me. In spite of all this excitement, there's still room for a nasty shock when I see the engine. A BMW diesel!! Beemers are great but quirky, and for motorhome use I'd have preferred something much plainer, like a GMC. As traffic fans up warm air around my buttocks I lean deeper and squint.

Sure enough, this engine has quirked out real good. The throttle works fine, but the throttle-line's corroded and parted right at the valve, and there's no way of fixing it out here. But what's that rattling? A double whammy: *the clutch in the fan is shot!*

So what's the problem? In my current mood, these things don't bother me at all, for somewhere along the road to insanity I have developed Self-Esteem. I inch around the back and sit down in the driver's seat, thinking hard.

"Tell me the matter!" whispers Mara, wide-eyed.

I let her know.

"Can you fix it?"

"I think so." She gives me a long look, like I'm some kind of magician. I tell her to go back to the duffle-bags and pull the tie-cords off them and tie these cords together at the ends to make one big line. When she reappears I test the connections: I've now got a thin strong line about 25 feet long. I turn off the ignition and tell her to start it and rev it up again when I bang on the side of the Vixen. I bend over Mara and throw most of the line out her window, leaving her with one end, and in short order I'm around the front taking up the line. Back at the engine I disconnect and remove the fanbelt and tie the line to the throttle. Then I bang on the side of the truck. Engine starts, and I yell at Mara to pull on the line.

Vroom, Vroom.

I get back into the cab. Mara looks stricken when she sees the fanbelt. "You mean it'll run without that?"

"I aim to find out."

We're truckin' again, sort of. Through trial and error I learn how to pull or ease up on the throttle line as I go up through the gears. This works OK, it turns out, but the situation forces a change in plans. We've

44

got to make Louisville, which I'd hoped to bypass, so as to do repairs, and we've got to make it by the levelest possible road, because I'm gonna have to remount the fanbelt before we climb every hill. On an easy stretch, where I don't have to shift, I take the throttle line and tell Mara to open the road atlas to Kentucky and find a red line to Louisville that looks straight.

It turned out the next exit was as direct a way to Louisville as any. Or so we thought.

Fate takes strange turns. Immediately off the highway we were simultaneously hit by the smell of what seemed like (and was) 10,000 barbecuing chickens and consumed by the desire to eat a couple of them apiece. I guess that's what emergencies are always like — you go through them in a kind of trance, and when they're over you all of a sudden need food. The irresistible smell led us a quarter mile upwind to a pair of huge gates opening on a humongous grassy lot where every vehicle in Kentucky seemed to be parked. Between the gates was a billboard with permanent brass letters announcing that this was the Womuba Recreation Area and big movable letters proclaiming that today was the

5TH ANNUAL
UNITED CHARITIES CHICKEN ORGY

and that the entertainment would be

PLATINUM JAYNE AND THE GROAN

Mara and I looked at each other in surprise. Charity chicken orgies aside, what really boxed us was how they'd gotten Platinum Jayne and her Groanykins to come to Kentucky, which was more or less like getting the mountain to come to Mohammed. Last time I'd seen Jayne on network news, she was doing a benefit wingding with Madonna and Pavarotti (talk about mutual starfuck!), who'd both come (with about 65,000 other folks) to her entertainment-palace in Aspen. Word was that the White House wanted to give her the Medal of Freedom but was afraid she would come to the ceremony in costume (or lack of same) and make Daughtergate[2] look like so much spilled pablum. *Platinum Jayne!* Even the demure Mara whispered the name in amazement.

At this point we were slowly weaving our way through the unpaved parking lot between cars and vans and tailgate parties that involved every social class, age group and lifestyle, all clumped together in a Sunday mood of group frenzy. Even from the cab of the Vixen, you could smell a summery medley of booze, perfume and pot. I was then about —oh God!—to take a turn into a vacant parking place when Mara grabbed the wheel and shouted "STOP! DON'T MOVE!" and was out of the van like a shot. In seconds she was at the driver's window holding up an open, empty-looking Budweiser case that I'd just been about to run over.

It had a live baby in it. The baby in the beercase was smiling up at me.

I parked the van and found Mara nearby, kneeling in the grass next to a motionless supine woman whose pregnancy looked as though it'd run beyond term. Passed out on beer, indicated empty cans. Behind her, a redheaded man in a terrycloth robe emerged from a beat-up microbus and took delivery of beercase baby with no word of thanks and a holier-than-thou look.

Feeling faint, I remembered having left the keys in the Vixen. Mara went back to get them and lock up. And then, together, we walked out through the lot, towards chicken aroma and distant music, onto a graded road that led us up a little rise. The air was uncannily warm, like around 75 degrees. Blossoming cherry trees lined the road and black-birds were singing in them, and I remember feeling for a second as though we were Adam and Eve (not that I was in shape to have carnal knowledge!) leaving Eden and going forth into an unknown world.

"How'd you know the baby was in that case?" I asked.

---

2. Daughtergate: apparently Ruck's idea of a witty term for the scandal involving President Bill Clinton and Monica Lewinsky. —Ed.

"*I had a feeling*," she whispered.

"Thank God!" I burst out. Was there something extrasensory about this girl? Of course not, I thought, looking down at her as we walked. But the look of recognition that those aqua eyes shot back at me made me think she'd known what I was thinking at that very moment!

Just then we topped the rise, and a scene unfolded that I'll never forget.

We looked down on a vast panorama.

Imagine a plain about ⅜ of a mile square, stretching from the rise and dropping off in cliffs over the Sacannah River. Imagine the whole left-hand side of this plain being full of people, all of them facing a big stage that was right at the edge of the cliff. Imagine on the right smoke rising as thousands of chickens are barbecued in huge pits. Imagine all this lit by a sun that's slowly being smothered by mammoth black clouds, throwing off a light of supercharged lurid whiteness, like concentrated moonlight, without a touch of gold.

Now imagine a wall of noise, heavy metal to the tune of 200,000 watts, almost drowning out the even deeper noise of approaching thunder.

The air must have been very heavy because the noise was drubbing us almost like a wind, louder and louder, and the crowd was so big and scattered, with people straggling in and out all the time, that we could get almost to the front row and see everything. What a sight to behold! We were maybe 35 feet away from the opera-sized stage, and standing on this stage to the right was a very colorful but mysterious group of ten or twelve people. Each of them was holding onto a lifeline attached to a big orange balloon that floated in the air above him or her. On the left-hand side of the stage, the Groan were making big-league noise in their famous rendition of *Sixteen Tons*, with Fallic Devine sitting (as usual) at the drums in front of everybody, and Ditto Kelly and Nether Cleavage and Jerusalem Scratch (just back from rehab) pumping guitars right behind him, and tall Orville Negombo bouncing up and down in back as he punished his bass boomer, so that from the front they looked like one superhuman creature with lots of never-stopping arms and legs.

But nobody was looking at the Groan. How could they, with Platinum Jayne standing center-stage? Not that she was singing or dancing — she was just sort of undulating to the music, but what undulating! It was as if she was the conduit the music was flowing through. As always she was topless, and as her arms and torso moved, her boobs followed in private epicycles, as if they had minds of their own. And the metal! Believe me, Jayne was fitted out like a steamship! Three rings in each nipple for starters, a ring through the navel and, as she turned and you could see the swell of her rump under her Daisy Mae skirt, a large ring through each buttock. Down her left inner thigh ran a chain with a locket attached to it, also wigglewaggling to the music and leaving its point of origin to the imagination. Bracelet-sized earrings, elbow-rings, knee-rings and smaller but shinier equipage on the eyelids, nose, lips, fingers and toes.

I was still counting rings when the music stopped, punctuated by a heavy crack of thunder from behind us. I looked down at Mara, who looked up at me with a frown, suggesting maybe that she hadn't liked the music, or maybe that it was going to storm.

That was the last time I saw her.

Platinum Jayne's voice was suddenly drowning out everything. Standing tall at the mike in the deepening gloom, lit intermittently by lightning from the approaching storm, Jayne launched into a major speech. First off, she explained as how this whole performance was aimed at the welfare of disabled Americans everywhere. Next, she introduced the folks with the orange balloons — Flo, Fuzzy, Herschel, Baxter, Pedro, Wendell and I forget the rest — as disabled Americans from twelve different states. They're standing up, she said, for the first time in years, thanks to them being fitted with body-braces attached to helium balloons, and even those folks whose legs were totally paralyzed could still get around, in a vague sort of way, with the help of special canes (as an example of which Fuzzy, the oldest of them, navigated his way up to the mike amid applause). Jayne allowed as the technology of this balloon stuff wasn't very well developed yet (*she was right about that, poor devils!*), but that she'd bankrolled these getups so the Womuba Twelve, as she put it, could be symbols of the quote-unquote Empowered Body. Then she introduced Fuzzy, a smallish bearded coot who looked as though he'd rather be somewhere else, like maybe at the dentist, as Ira "Fuzzy" Blomsky, her own father.

The rest of the Womuba Twelve didn't seem so happy either. They were all looking helplessly westward at the approaching storm, and for an instant I saw lightning reflected in their eyes.

But none of this fazed Platinum Jayne. With breasts heaving and rings clinking she was now into the main course of her performance, a singing sermon that she called *The Gospel of Bod*. Her sermon really rattled me. What did she think, that she was going to convince this huge audience, a lot of whom were probably Baptists, to turn away from Jesus and start worshipping the human body? Many in the audience were getting fairly riled up. I looked back to see a number of pretty tough-looking customers standing up and shaking their fists. But lots of others were cheering. Accompanied by the Groan, Jayne started belting out this medley of hymns, with Bod always substituted for God, as in "Nearer, my Bod, to thee," and "A mighty fortress is our Bod."

Then came this colossal roar. I looked back at the multitude, thinking for sure that this was a riot, but it was worse. It was some kind of devil wind—El Niño I'm sure—come up out of the river gorge, and it blasted down on the people behind, so awesome and loud you'd have thought it was some monster helicopter attack right out of *Apocalypse Now*. A tornado for sure! Like a big angry dog, it tore into the roasting pits behind the seats, and in a moment all of us were being barraged by a hail of flying barbecued chickens, whizzing sizzling featherless birds, and I'm afraid some people may have been badly singed.

But even while fending off chickens with both hands, I couldn't keep my eyes off Platinum Jayne. In the melee she stood firm, grasping the mike and shrieking something about Bod with all her might, and in the middle of that shriek,

I shit you not,

the sky opened and a bolt of lightning as thick as a tree transfixed her where she stood. There was a thunderclap such as almost knocked me down, while the lightning, which seemed to hold itself still in time, played horribly over all her rings and ornaments and her voice stopped and Platinum Jayne burnt to a crisp before my very eyes, an ashen crust that was quickly swept up by the wind.

Then in a flash, as luck would have it, things went from bad to worse. The wind had died down for a minute, and I'd barely realized that the smell in the air was Platinum Jayne's roasted flesh—which was especially gross because it had all the chemicals from her melted rings mixed in with it—when I noticed that something was very wrong onstage. The Womuba Twelve were taking off into midair! It must have been a sudden drop in air pressure—or was it a sudden rise?—but there they all were hanging from their orange balloons, floating five, seven feet in the air, arms wagging helplessly about as mischief-gusts whirled them in little circles around each other, some shouting "GOD! GOD!" and others "BOD! BOD!"

I had to help them. I bounded forward and jumped up onto the stage. Old Fuzzy was in the greatest danger, as some kind of felon wind had caught him alone and was pushing him out over the Gorge. I hate heights, but there was something about Fuzzy's utter helplessness that drove me on. As I made for him, he'd floated just past the back end of the stage which, as I immediately found out, was the edge of the cliff itself. He had nothing under him but 300 feet of space to the rocks below, and the cliffs on the other side loomed gray behind him, and he had this sad, confused, wistful look on his face, and as I reached out to him he asked, "Are *you* Bod?"

That's when I fell off the cliff.

In mid-air I grabbed Fuzzy and held on for dear life as wind rushed up by us faster and faster. My face was all fouled up in his beard, but I knew that, balloon or no balloon, we were headed towards the rocks at increasing speed. I reached out an arm to change our trajectory, but it was no use, and we both would have been gull feed if it hadn't been for a terrific river updraft—a blast of air related maybe to the tornado—that cushioned us and sent us careening off toward midstream. The Sacannah is about half a mile wide at that point, and we made splashdown smack in the middle.

The first thing I remember was that the water had a disgusting warmth to it, like falling into blood, but worse than that it was cloudy and foul. I could taste all kinds of floodcrud in it, like car and animal and house. For a few seconds I couldn't find Fuzzy among the brown whitecaps. But then I heard his cry above the din of rampaging water. I paddled over and grabbed him. I'm a good swimmer, but I was being dragged down by my shoes and clothes, and the balloon was now partly deflated, and it was all I could do to keep the old guy afloat. I could see him swallowing water, and I couldn't do Jack shit about it. It was raining buckets now, making things even harder to see, but I made out a large form floating next to us, and whatever it was had a leg, so I grabbed the hock. Turned out to be a big dead bloated pig. Holding Fuzzy with one hand I held onto the hock with the other, for flotation and balance and the stability of its mass. Now as a summer rafter I know a little bit about rapids, and I guess that's what saved us. I knew that the water would be faster in the gorge, because gorges are steeper, so the gorge was no place for trying to get out of the river. Beyond the gorge things would slow down, and with luck I could let go of the carcass and paddle towards the inside of a bend, where water tends to eddy. Even then I would need strength and luck pulling Fuzzy onto dry land, not to mention what it would take to revive him and get him to a medic.

The Most Amazing Thing

Maybe from the tension or who knows what I was getting groggy, and I must've zigged when I should've zagged, because I was dragged across something sharp, maybe a snag, that opened up a few inches of my right arm. I was bleeding into the river now and slightly zoning out about the evil results accruing to all those who celebrate the Gospel of Bod, when an image flashed into my mind's eye, complete in detail and clear as day. It was of a walkway back at the University of Oregon, where the path passes between the School of Ed and the backyard of Theta Rho, and a sycamore limb from the backyard stretches out over the path. Spring of junior year, just after I had to quit basketball when I hurt my back in that collision with Shakeem, I would meet Glynda there, days when she got out of her Ed Psych class and nights for secret kisses. She'd rub my back where it hurt and try to comfort me. That spot behind the frat-house meant happiness to me, memory as sweet as dreams. I was trying to open my eyes—you've really got to keep on your toes at times like this—when another image zapped me. I was a little boy, maybe six years old, walking with Uncle Titus (who looked old even then) in Golden Gate Park in San Francisco. After much pleading and whining I'd just persuaded him to buy me an ice cream cone—the kind of vanilla they don't make anymore, that had little pieces of real ice in it, and the ice cream man mustn't have put the scoop on very tight, because as soon as we left the stand, the cone tilted a little and the ice cream fell right off and plopped onto the sidewalk. I looked down at my lost joy, and I looked up at Titus's accusing eyes, and I wanted to disappear from the face of the earth.

Well *that* woke me up all right. I opened my eyes at the moment we were rounding a right-hand bend and I saw what I'd been waiting for, a village on the inside bank. It had everything a drowning man could might want—docks, ladders and ramps—but it was almost too damn close, and I let go of the pig and paddled like hell with my right arm. It was a nightmare watching that village go by. Even in the rain I was close enough to see the faces of those who reached out to help me, a red-faced clergyman (I got close enough to smell the booze on his breath!) and, next to him, a strikingly beautiful black woman in a red mackinaw who almost fell in trying to reach us, and finally, at the last put-in, a kid wearing an Atlanta Braves cap and holding out an oar. As my fingers slipped from the oar, he shouted something about a mill. I went under, swallowed about a gallon of river and came up passing a bank of willows. Sure enough, there was the mill close ahead, an ugly old monster with a white stack and, just for Fuzzy and me, a monster intake port that must have led down to a nest of hydraulics. And damned if I didn't see a big paddle-drive down there, waving to us, waiting to turn us into gruel. *Not on your fucking life*! I reached up and grabbed a willow branch and begged it not to break. The branch bent round until Fuzzy and I had completely reversed positions and I was hopelessly strung out between him and the limb but, thank God, it dumped us in an eddy.

I let go of the branch, found my footing and—strange that my back didn't hurt me—pulled Fuzzy onto the bank. He was unconscious. I undid his body brace, pulled him away from the brace and balloon and did what resuscitation I could. I was still at it, with no positive results, when a pickup pulled up nearby. Without really meaning to, I lay down on my back. Before I passed out I recognized the Reverend and the boy in the Braves cap, and above them, finally free of its tether, the half-inflated orange balloon wandering up through the willows on its way to heaven.

The Most Amazing Thing

I must have been unconscious, or semiconscious, for 18 hours. You know how sometimes you'll be lying in bed, late at night, thinking of something grim, it seems like forever, and then look at your watch and see that only a few minutes have passed? In those 18 hours I dreamed my way through several lifetimes of loss and loneliness.

A hundred times I was with Mara, carrying her, helping her, chatting with her, feeling the warmth of her presence, or I was back years ago in her childhood with her, eavesdropping on her as she sat on Aunt Cuerva's knee.

A hundred times I fell off the cliff and into the foul river, swept past all hope of return.

The next morning—this morning—I woke up in this cell. I'd been washed down and dressed in jail clothes. My right arm was bandaged and my other arm ached, probably from a tetanus shot. When I could stand up I went to the john and pissed out a tributary of the Sacannah River and went to the door and shouted. This bought me a visit from the Sheriff himself, big hawk-nosed honcho, chewing a foul dead cigar, introducing himself as Luke Thrumble, reading me my rights in a sadistic drawl and telling me that I was going to be charged with the murder or attempted murder and/or kidnapping of Platinum Jayne's father, Ira "Fuzzy" Blomsky, but that my case wouldn't be "processed" until a) the flood danger was over and b) Blomsky had died or pulled through—they weren't sure which—and they could then decide what was the most damnable charge they could pin on me.

Murder! Ira Blomsky! My selfless act of mercy mistaken for a crime! I was so eaten up with shock and rage that I almost keeled over on the spot, which gave the Sheriff his chance to get out of my cell and hightail it to Louisville. I lay down on my cot and thought unpleasant thoughts.

About how hard it would be to prove my innocence. About how, even if I proved it, investigators would connect me with the Vixen and the money. About the freedom I'd had before the Vixen broke down and we got hungry for chicken. I started crying, but left off when Schultzie appeared with a tray of biscuits-and-gravy and some black coffee. I was wolfing and slurping down same when Schultzie came back with the Reverend, who was shaking rainwater off his umbrella. The Rev, a fine figure of a man with a handsome red nose and a blue-eyed look at once suspicious and comic, as though he was trying to sniff out a joke, introduces self as Howard Keane, sits himself down and, apparently aware of my depressed state, offers me a slug of bourbon from the biggest hip flask I've ever seen. Over this profoundly refreshing drink, which he said was made by a family named Wharton, I told him my plight, skipping of course what brought me to Womuba Park. He'd already seen on TV about Jayne's tragic end and how a stranger named Bod had made off with her dad, but he was especially interested in my side of it, and after each new little episode of the story he'd nip on his flask and shout "Capital!"

"What d'you mean, capital?" I finally asked.

"Mr. Bod," he said, "you are a historian of the times." I couldn't get him to explain this, but he was off on a tangent, some of which made me laugh in spite of myself, about people who'd been wrongfully accused or otherwise had gotten ear-deep in shit. He ended up by saying, yes, that he knew of eight or nine people who were even more unfortunate than I, but that they were all dead. All, that is, except one.

"Who's that?"

"Mordecai MacCrae," said the Rev.

"What happened to him?"

Priming himself with sour mash, Rev described MacCrae as an old Gulf War buddy, a war hero and "the most capable man I've ever met," later an LA cop whose exploits had been (though he never boasted of this) the source of three hard-hitting Hollywood movies. But MacCrae had apparently run out of luck. He'd been brought to Louisville on special assignment, because the Feds needed somebody who wasn't known in the area. Peter Carrarra, who was a big deal in the FBI (I'd heard of him myself), and Taylor Munson, the local DA, wanted an informant on Death Row at the Kentucky Pen. They were mad keen to get the goods on Eddie Moon, the underworld kingpin, and figured they could do this by planting a mole next to Eddie's old pal Fats Vukovich, a Death Row inmate. But the plant had to look legit. Carrarra and Munson met with MacCrae in total secrecy and asked him if he would take a bum rap (under an alias) for murder. He agreed as that was probably the only way to get Moon. So the next time they had a suspectless execution-style crime, they pinned it on MacCrae, and he was prosecuted as a virtuous-cop-corrupted-by-money and cycled through the system to Death Row. And there he is, getting the goods on Eddie Moon, when he sees in the paper that Carrarra and Munson have both been gunned down, in two different cities, *on the same day*, and that they were both deader than King Tut. Seems that Moon had a contract out on 'em. And Carrarra and Munson *were the only two in on the secret.*

"How come you know it?"

The Rev said he'd visited MacCrae in prison.

"Why can't you help him?"

Because he'd only MacCrae's word to go on.

"What happened to MacCrae?"

He's still on Death Row. The stays and appeals have almost run out, and he's got about two months to live.

Suddenly feeling ornery, I told the Rev that if he knew my full story, he'd see that I was even unluckier than MacCrae, because I had more to lose.

The Rev looked up in mock surprise. "MacCrae's a good man. You don't have more to lose than that."

That stung. A good man? I hadn't heard that phrase in years. And whatever it meant, it pretty well didn't mean *me*. For a moment I wanted to stop the Rev and ask him what exactly made his friend MacCrae such a good man, and what makes a good man in general. For a moment I forgot my money and my danger and own miserable selfish lot.

But the preacher was still talking. Hardly pausing, he made a broad sermonizing sweep with his right hand. "Now your Sheriff Luke Thrumble here, he's got an awful lot to lose, but he's not such a good man. He and his brother Art (who's a *real* asshole) own most of this old town. But if they don't watch out, the State's Attorneys are gonna take it all away—that is, if there's anything left of Pilotsburg to take away."

I asked why.

" 'Pears a while back the Sheriff and brother Art put in the low bid for building the Sacannah Dam, and now it transpires that instead of building it with rebar or concrete or whatever expensive stuff you're supposed to build dams with, they dumped in 100,000 tons of landfill, and nobody found out about it till the County went to repair a hole in it, and out pops an old washing machine."

I asked if the dam in question was upstream of us. "You bet your balls it is!" exclaimed the Rev.

"Then how come the river was flooding when I fell in it?"

"If you call *that* a flood, you ain't seen nothin' yet. If that dam breaks, you're talkin' *WALL OF WATER*," said the Rev, refreshing himself with more bourbon. His face was beet red now. Before my eyes, in the middle of the day, this preacher was getting pie-eyed drunk. I wondered how this could be. Was something gnawing at his guts?

I wouldn't have found out if I hadn't asked him about that beautiful black lady by the river. The poor guy starts sobbing! Turns out he's head over heels in love with her! But there's more. The Rev is gay, or at least thought he was. All this goes way back. Until the Gulf War, he was celibate, though he didn't have to be, being Protestant. But as a chaplain under fire he began to feel love for his comrades. It was a kind of love he couldn't understand, seeing as in the church and the Army homosexuality was swept under the rug, so to speak, I mean, not discussed. He thought there was something wrong with him and tried to cover it up. But it got to be too much for him, and one day he more or less propositioned the company captain, Mordecai MacCrae.

MacCrae turned him down politely, but told him he didn't think there was anything wrong about being gay. All that was wrong, he said, was to have emotions and keep them a secret or lie about them.

But the Rev didn't see things that way. "God's work comes first," he'd told MacCrae, and he knew that he wouldn't be allowed to do God's work as a self-confessed gay. Back in the States after the war, he set up shop in the church at Pilotsburg, and for years he cooped up a secret he couldn't tell and passions he couldn't express. Imagine that!

The Rev got resigned to this fate, and even began thinking that it was God's way of punishing him for his lust, until a couple of years ago, when he met Heidi Frederick. She's a social worker assigned to his church. Right off he was amazed at how she worked with the poor and the suffering. "She was getting paid for it, but you wouldn't know it," he said. She worked as though helping people came naturally, even as though it was some high-class kind of self-expression. It was the first time he'd ever respected a woman professionally, and what made it worse was that in her case professionally meant spiritually. Add to this that she was obviously some kind of genius in understanding people's problems, and you've got a powerfully attractive mix.

And her manner with him! Direct, warm, and without a hint of female/male or black/white uneasiness. Everything she said or did was full of heart.

One morning last summer Heidi and the Rev ran into each other under an apple tree in the parish garden, and he realized he was in love with her (I know exactly how this is, because it happened like that to me with Glynda). It was very warm, and she'd left an extra buttonhole of her blouse unbuttoned, and when he'd seen the top curve of her breast and smelled her morning soap on her, he was suddenly a raving hetero and hopelessly in love. *How do you explain these things?*

The Rev said nothing about this to anybody, especially Heidi, because he had this habit of stewing over things secretly rather than blurting them out. He says those were the most precious weeks of his whole life, the weeks when he worked with her, chatted with her, all the while silently adoring her every move and word.

I asked if it mattered that they were of different races.

Yes, he said, the race thing made his love and desire that much more intense. He saw God in her, but it was like no God he'd ever known before — it was a God who coursed through his veins like fire. In the end he couldn't hold out. After all, why should he? One October evening he found a way of getting her under that same apple tree again, the apples being ripe this time, and he told her that he'd loved her for many weeks.

"What happened then?" I asked.

"Then God struck me down," said the Rev. Heidi replied that she had lots of liking and respect and even love for the Rev, *but that some years before she'd discovered she was a lesbian!*

What irony! How do you sort out a mess like that?

"You don't," said the Rev. "Except maybe you pray." Saying this he staggered across the cell and took a long loud piss in the john and then went and banged on the bars to be let out.

I asked him if getting drunk was his way of praying, and he half turned toward me and said it was his way of staying alive so he could pray.

As the cell door slammed shut I fell back on the cot. I must have been asleep before my head hit the pillow. I slept about an hour and had a single dream. There was Heidi Frederick by the river again, reaching out to help a drowning man, her face so beautiful that you didn't know whether to kiss it or pray to it, but the drowning man wasn't me or the Rev. *It was my father!* I yelled "Hey Dad, watcha doing there?" (how's that for a silly question?), and instead of answering he gave me, from the waves no less, one of those long sad looks of his, those sort of Oliver Hardy looks that suggested he knew some fault or limitation of mine that was such a bad one that I'd never understand it myself no matter how hard I tried, and at that instant I remembered he'd been dead these twenty years, and I woke up. I woke up and rubbed my eyes and tried to blink away the sadness of never having made the grade in Dad's opinion, and how he'd never had the heart to tell me so, except with those sad looks.

And I'd never redeem myself to him, or be a man with a woman, or see Mara again.

Never, never, never—the word sounded like the lapping of muddy waves.

Chapter Four   Señor Lodoso

You won't believe where I am. I don't believe *what* I am. Looking out at the green trees of Langhorne Park in Louisville, I'd think myself gone, transposed, in heaven. Except for a few details. I'm short on sleep and have hiccoughs that smell of mud. My left eye is half closed and feels as if some of its goo is leaking back into my brainpan.

The rest of me feels like God.

You want to feel like God too? No problem! I'll tell you exactly how to do it.

For starters, try getting carried unconscious into a Blue Ridge Mountain jail, accused of mayhem and locked up while floodwaters mount and the fraud-filled county dam is burping out old washing machines and looking to bust wide open. If this doesn't work, add a throbbing wound in the arm, a belly-up preacher and the loss of all your hopes, and then try finding out that the damn dam *was* busting wide open and you were sure to drown.

That should almost do the trick.

It did the trick for me, though it's weird how one thing led to another.

The Most Amazing Thing

To begin with, there was the panic. Schultzie the Deputy came on the PA sounding very weak, like he was in shock, and talking almost too fast to understand, but the general idea was that the Shawnee Dam had just *exploded* and that a wall of water about 100 feet high was moving down the canyon towards us at 30 mph, which would bring it to us in about three-quarters of an hour, minus the time of reporting. There was no way of getting us to high ground because we were low priority. Even Schultzie's own pickup had been grabbed up by a day-care center, and he and the Rev were getting bussed downriver to help evacuate the mental patients at the State Hospital. We prisoners were going to be released and left to fend for ourselves. Schultzie and the Rev, one on each side, came down the alley of cells, opening doors and saying "God bless you" to every prisoner. We grabbed our effects from the front desk and straggled out onto the street, dazed and forlorn.

Main Street was empty. It was exactly three in the afternoon of a black day. It had stopped raining but looked ready to start again. Standing in the gloom, wondering which way to run, I got the idea of how Schultzie could let me, a possible murderer, go free.

I had my death sentence one way or the other.

Main Street runs parallel to the river, so most of the guys took off at a gallop towards the downriver side of town. But three or four of us were standing there, as if we were made of wood. Nobody talked. I was struggling to get my jacket on, and my eyes were fixed on the empty drycleaning shop across the street, that had a sign, HELP WANTED.

God, how I wanted help.

I didn't hear the noise of the truck until it was right in front of us—a big old optic-yellow six-wheeler with a red rotary warning light on the cab roof. Out of the passenger's side jumps Sheriff Luke Thrumble himself, holding a 12-gauge repeater shotgun that accidentally goes off BANG when his feet hit the pavement. The other prisoners scatter down the street, but Thrumble's got me by the lapel with the smoking gun-muzzle at my chin, and before I know it I'm handcuffed to a short chain in the truckbed right behind the cab's cracked rear window and we've taken off like Gangbusters on the road downriver.

In a minute we were past the mill and hightailing it down the road at 60, maybe 65 mph. A burly grizzled man, who turned out to be brother Art, was driving, and he didn't spare the horses. My hunch was that they were just looking for the first road up out of the river valley, but that didn't explain why they were saving me. Through the blown-out rear window, listening to their barbarous slang in a blast of cigarette smoke, I learned that Luke and Art would be under indictment for murder if anyone died in the dam debacle and were aiming to make a run for it out-of-state. But first they wanted to pick up the family treasures. That's why they needed me. They were headed for Art's house, to gather some of their loot, and they needed a big mule like me as their baggage-man.

I was just getting used to their lingo when the following item came up:

"Wha bout thaym lil luv-cuddlies o yourn, Art?"

"Yo mean mah fookin dodders?"

"Dodders, luvvers, same difference, big guy. We tayken thaym?"

"We fookin well not fookin taken mah fookin dodders! Hayl, thaym fookin dawgs is half fookin wodder rayt anyways. Let the cridders swim!"

At this pronouncement Art turned to glare at his brother, and I looked at his face for the first time. This had to be the ugliest dude I'd ever seen. One bulbous eye was about an inch lower than the other, and the free areas of skin were a nest of flaming filbert-sized boils. The upper front teeth were so off-kilter that they stuck out between his closed lips. It was a face that looked angry at being a face. He looked like somebody'd slipped a cherry bomb into his Big Mac and it went off while he was chewing.

Art turned his head back to the road, and immediately we swung sharply to the left. Only the great weight of the truck kept us from flipping, and I was smashed hard against the side of the truckbed. We were on a muddy dirt road now, tearing great ruts into it and hurling waves of mud to either side. A hundred yards in we pulled up at a gate made out of railroad ties, and after unlocking it Luke let it hang open, and we drove on.

It started raining hard again.

As I ducked oak and maple limbs I could see a big old Victorian house looming ahead and almost covered in dark vines. One wing on the right had been crushed by a falling maple tree, and the old snag was still lying where it fell. The garage was a burnt-out hulk next to which was sitting a 20-ton bulldozer that was aimed right at the house, as though about to demolish it once and for all, but the bulldozer was all overgrown with honeysuckle.

We'd come to the back of the house (the front most likely faced the river), and just out of the rain in the kitchen doorway were standing two half-dressed mulatto girls in their late teens. The *luv-cuddlies*! They looked like sisters, and Thrumbles at that, but handsome in their way, although like wild things. The girl on the left was in nothing but a negligee that she held closed with one arm, and the other one's total outfit consisted of jeans and an unbuttoned cowboy vest. At first they watched us arrive with slack-jawed amazement, but then they started babbling at each other and nervously trying to cinch together their clothes. You could tell they weren't all that used to company.

The Thrumble brothers didn't dawdle around for any amenities. Art heaved his gut out of the truck and headed for the house at full speed, while Luke locked his shotgun in the cab and climbed up onto the bed to get me. He showed me a serious-looking police .38, in case I got any ideas, and led me into the house.

As I passed the girls (who smelled of bubble gum and river water and kept leering at me and giggling) I caught an earful of what they were saying. It wasn't English and didn't sound like anything I'd ever heard. It sounded like the kind of sister-speak they'd have made up if they hadn't been taught anything. That's when I caught the idea. *These were ART'S OWN DAUGHTERS, and he'd raised them to be his whores, and he had no mind to teach them anything else.* The bastard probably didn't even have a TV.

And now he was going to feed them to the river. When I thought these things, and of the person that Art was, and the sort of town that would let him be that way, I felt a pain right through me, as though somebody had latched onto my spinal cord and was trying to pull it out all at once. As I picked up the Thrumble worldly goods in various dark corners of the house and lugged them downstairs, I thought of things I'd want to do to Art and Luke if I could, like for starters running them over with the truck. But I have to tell you that every time I thought these things, I'd almost die of fright. No kidding: abject fear, blatant terror that made my thighbones feel like refrigerator pudding. And don't get me wrong, this wasn't because the Thrumbles were big mean honchos with guns. No way, man. I've *always* gone to pieces when confronted angrily by adult, child or animal. Just thinking of somebody else's anger makes me paralytic. As Luke and I grappled a stuffed bear down the back steps and I looked into the bear's glassy eyes and silently snarling snout and even the goddamn stuffed bear scared me, it was brought home once and for all. I was a worm. I'd always been a worm, and I'd no choice but to keep behaving like one.

But this time, I decided, the worm would talk. The worm would warn. Art and Luke were out by the truck, squabbling over whether to load something or other, when I approached the girls in the kitchen. I started speaking to them, but instead of hearing me out they both turned and scampered into the front hall and upstairs, squeaking with delight and motioning for me to follow them, which I did, three stairs at a time. We ended up in a room I hadn't seen yet, a front bedroom with two big windows looking down on the river. It was *their* room, I could see, because they'd made two beds out of heaped-up old clothes, and stretched them side by side in front of the windows, with big old Raggedy Ann type stuffed dolls where the pillows should be. Rain was dripping in from a few brown cracks in the ceiling, and under each crack the girls had set an old coffee can with dirt and honeysuckle that was send-ing flowery tendrils out in all directions. But that wasn't all. Instead of regular furniture they'd brought in all kinds of river flotsam—a boat's steering wheel, a cow's skull with the horns on, a surveyor's tripod and a few strangely knotted pieces of wood—and placed them here and there as nicknacks, the way a stockbroker would bring home Tiffany or Chip-pendale.

I got it then! Deprived of human care, the sisters had turned into water nymphs! It was like a story from a fairy book! Did they sing to fishermen too?

One of the knots of wood was still wet and smelly, and a dank-coated black and white cat was crouched on it, gnawing on a barnacle. The poor cat was skin and bones and had only one eye, but somehow, perched on its own snag with its own tiny meal, the critter looked com-pletely at home, as though the ragtag room was its castle. For a moment I marvelled at this bizarre boudoir, the home that the two waifs had made out of the nothing that Art gave them, and the sudden impulse welled up in me, If only I could save these girls, protect them, educate them treat them right . . . .

Just then the girls grabbed me, each by one arm. The flotsam wasn't what they'd brought me to see. Madly giggling they turned me to the right-hand wall, where they'd tacked up one of those posters you've seen everywhere of Clark Gable carrying Vivien Leigh in his arms in *Gone with the Wind*. They were pointing to Gable and back to me, as though I was something like Gable or even was Gable himself, and it was pretty clear that I must have been the only guy besides the Thrumbles they'd seen for years, if they were somehow comparing me to Gable. I didn't know whether to laugh or to cry.

But I had no time for nonsense like this, because I had to warn them about the wall of water.

So I said real loud, "Listen! There's this wall of water coming! There's gonna be a big flood! You've got to get away!" But they just looked at me and giggled and blushed and looked at each other and squealed with glee. *Damn Art for never teaching them English!* I ran to the window and pointed to the river and made upward moves with my arms meaning flood, but they both just grinned at me and made as though they were swimming.

"Packapinga," remarked the girl in the cowboy vest.

"Wunnagunna!" shouted the other, and they both burst out laughing. Talking to them was hopeless, but I was going to give sign language one more try when Art himself walked in, toting a pistol the size of a chainsaw and looking a mite out of sorts.

"What are their names?" I asked him.

"Thayre fookin' both naymed Yo," he muttered, and with a devilishly quick move he whacked me on the side of my face with the gun. I lurched back and fell over one of the knotted branches, and the water nymphs were on me in an instant, making soft cooing sounds, stroking me, kissing me, trying to pull me up. (*Could they still feel sympathy for a man after what Art'd put them through?*) Art barked out some strange incomprehensible syllables clearly meant to warn them off. He pulled me up and forced me downstairs. I looked back once over my shoulder to see two forms in the dark hallway by their bedroom door, silently watching.

(*WHERE ARE THEY NOW?*)

Out back Luke was bashing at the truck's driver's window with a splitting maul and cursing up a storm. He'd locked himself out. After breaking into the cab he handcuffed me up on the truckbed again, but this time I wasn't alone. As we careened out through the open gates and down the drive, I was bouncing around with all the Thrumble heirlooms—Snarling Bear, a life-sized wooden cigar-store statue of Tecumseh, a few silver ingots, an electric wall-mounted Moxie sign, boxes of pawnshop trinkets and watches, numerous Persian rugs, a couple of massive trunks, a Buck Rogers pinball machine and, of course, the family Bible. Probably enough stuff there to hang them each three times, if the truth was known. We turned left at the county road and made tracks downriver. With all the noise of shifting baggage, it was hard for me to hear what was going on in the cab, but I was able to make out that the final alarms had rung at Breedsville and the wall of water was only five minutes away up the canyon. Luke, who was driving now, said something about crossing the hills at Ambush Pass, making a "dropoff" and heading towards north up the Ocalona Valley, and in short order we veered right, onto a very narrow road, and started to climb.

That's when I got to see the wall of water. The road switched back and forth as we climbed, and looking to one side or the other I could see up-valley clear to Pilotsburg. The rain had let up again. The sky was overcast but the seeing was clear, unforgettably clear. I could see the town and the bright tongue of river just beyond it that was the first reach of the canyon—the same reach I'd floated down. But I'd hardly looked for 30 seconds when things started to change. The tongue of river was shortening, as though the darker hills behind it were gradually eating it up. And when I squinted I saw it wasn't the hills at all, but a dark mass, sometimes flickering with white surf, that was closing up the canyon, irresistibly, like a moving dam. I mean, it looked almost like a machine—it was that steady and regular. How tall? Taller than the Rev's steeple, that's certain, because being farthest upriver it was the first landmark to be hit. The flood ate it up in seconds. So much for the church.

But would the apple tree resist being torn out by the flood? And would there be a Rev and a Heidi to meet there one more time?

By the time the wall of water reached the center of town, its face was changing. It broadened, lowered and seemed to get more turbulent. Why? *That* was it. Water was behaving like water. In my terror of the wall of water I'd forgotten that it would flatten out and slow down after leaving the canyon. But not enough to save the houses near the river. From the hilltop, the best view of all, I could see the river opening up like a fan and licking at the valley floor.

At that moment, just when we cleared the hill and the view was gone,

I felt something licking on *me*. Damned if it wasn't the girls' cat! The critter had somehow made it onto the truck! I wanted to pet it but the handcuffs wouldn't let me. It was shivering to beat the band, and its one eye looked terrified.

It sure had reason to be. The road down to the Ocalona was as narrow as it had been uphill, and Luke was driving it like Indy. Why the rush? Maybe they thought that the flood would back up the Ocalona, or maybe they'd suddenly been hit by the fear of God.

I'll never know which because of the crash.

It was really a two-part crash, and I saw only the first half of it, but the first half went this way. We were racing downhill towards the road that ran along the Ocalona and were about ⅛ mile from the stop sign, but instead of slowing down, Luke was speeding up. The reason? There was an ungated railroad crossing between the stop sign and us, and a freight train with endless boxcars was closing in on it from the right. Luke wanted to beat the train across, and he probably would have made it, if it hadn't been for a flatbed tow truck that'd been barrelling up the river road from the left and that suddenly turned into our path. Its driver, I bet, had the same idea as Luke—to beat the train across the tracks— and hadn't seen us at all. That last instant before the crash I saw him, a middle-aged black guy, with a smile (from some earlier happy thought?) still on his face and his eyes frozen in surprise and fixed on mine. He looked like a person I would kind of like.

I must have been the last thing he ever saw.

At that same instant I heard from the cab an enormous, explosive

"FOOK!"

which must have been Art's final comment on his own tragic doom, and we collided head-on right at the tracks.

My world exploded. One second I was on the bed of the truck, handcuffed to my own death so to speak, the next split-second I was flying through the air, having been thrown by my own inertial force over both crashed trucks and towards the river. The last thing I heard before hitting was the horrible smashing and grinding and scraping of the freight train as it demolished both trucks. I remember looking at the river speeding towards me and seeing something strange, something my mind couldn't process, and the reason I couldn't think straight was the realization that I'd finally run out of miracles.

I hadn't been thrown far enough to land in the river. I was hurtling towards the mud on the near bank.

I lost consciousness.

I woke with no memory and every symptom of death but two—I was feeling pain and tasting mud. Vision, hearing and breath were all cut off, and I was completely upside down, and my arms were pinned to my sides, and an awful tightness in my chest told me I hadn't been breathing for some time. The pressure on my closed eyes was most awful, as though somebody was trying to push my eyeballs back through their sockets. I felt the inexpressible terror of live burial. But strangely it was the terror and pain and taste of mud that reminded me who I was, where I was. They gave me a river and the river gave me a name again, and a story, and the name and story and something mysterious I couldn't quite remember about the river made me fight for life.

My legs were free, and I worked them until I could feel friction and freeing around my arms, and when my arms were usable I worked them with a kind of upside-down lifting motion until I'd budged my body an inch or two upward. Then, almost unconscious again from stiflement I did a fair amount more kicking, and finally some upside-down jumping motions, till I'd kicked and bucked my head out of the mud. But I still couldn't breathe, because my mouth and nose were still full of it.

I staggered towards the river and fell headlong in. It was shallow there, and for a long time I half-sat half-floated, up to my shoulders in water, coughing and spitting and sucking in air and ducking my head in water to clear my eyes and ears.

When I could see, I looked down at my hands. On impact the hand-cuff chain had parted right in the middle, and half the chain hung from each wrist. I looked out at the river. Tecumseh and Snarling Bear had also taken little flights, Tecumseh having come to rest, like me, head first up to his waist in the mud, while Bear (I suppose having better aero-dynamics) had made it clear into the water and was eddying around with his feet in the air.

When I could stand—surprisingly my back felt great—I turned to look at the accident. The first diesel engine (it had four others behind it) had carried the tow truck about two hundred yards down the track, crushing it as it went along. Flames from the truck were playing against the locomotive's side. Higher flames from the other side suggested that much the same thing had happened to the Thrumble truck. Two men, I guess the engineer and his crew, were standing back from the flames, surveying the wreck.

I turned again and looked upriver. It was an astonishingly peaceful scene of water and willowed banks and pasture hills, and in the middle of everything was what I'd glimpsed from mid-air and hidden from my-self as unbelievable.

There, about 100 yards upstream, halfway around a bend in the river, was the Vixen, parked under a big sycamore tree.

For a moment I stood there like a stone. Just as the mud had locked me in pain, I now stood stunned by joy.

Then I took off along the bank at a trot.

Fifty feet away I slowed down, to make less of a racket. The Vixen seemed to be undamaged, in fact shinier for all the rain. Twilight was coming, and it looked like we were going to have another thunderstorm, so when I peeked in at the big window behind the passenger seat, I could barely see into the darkened van. All I could make out was Mara's profile. She was sitting at the table across from me, facing the front. She was perfectly still. I've never seen such sadness, or rather wistfulness, in the simple tilt of a woman's head. Was she grieving for me?

71

"Mara!" I called softly through the window. She jumped a mile but in that instant must have recognized my voice, because her face relaxed into gladness, and she said, "I *knew* it, I *knew* it."

She was up and at the door, reaching out to me, but I said, "Mara, I'm a mess."

Gently, thoughtfully, she took some river mud off my shirt, rubbed it between her thumb and forefinger, smelled it. What was on her mind? Then her face brightened. "Go to the river," she said. "I'll bring a towel and clothes."

By the willowy bank I removed my wallet, which was soaked, pulled off my clothes and in the cold water washed most of the mud off my head and upper body. The place was completely deserted, and the train-truck accident, which had now attracted a lone siren, was out of sight downstream. Mara arrived in my nakedness but I thought nothing of it. After what I'd been through I was flushed away, spiritually wrung out. I'd clean run out of fear and embarrassment.

Back in the Vixen we turned on the lights, and Mara gave me hot tea. I wanted to wolf down some hash right out of the can, but she insisted on chopping some onion, frying it and then adding the hash for a hot meal. Finishing my tea, I pulled out a bottle of Gallo Cab I'd bought in Carpathia, and as I gulped and she cooked, above the rumble of the approaching storm, she told me how she'd fetched up under the sycamore tree.

"*Paralysed with fear and grief,*" she'd watched as I fell off the cliff and grabbed hold of Fuzzy. A home video freak, who'd followed me to the edge of the cliff and photographed us all the way down to the water, told her he thought we'd survived the fall, so she raced for the Vixen and ("*almost crashing seventeen times*") got back on the freeway to the first downstream exit, Breedsville, trying to get some word of me.

Of course all this was happening while Fuzzy and I were floating downriver and getting found, so Mara heard nothing about me in town and decided I'm probably dead, but maybe not. She drove on downriver on the county road in hopes of some sign of me, but there was no bridge at the Ocalona, so she had to drive upstream a ways. She stopped at the Ocalona Wayside to take a rest, but coming into the Wayside she hit a big bump, and maybe because of that the motor wouldn't start anymore when she tried to leave. She'd been stuck there a night and a day, *"trying to dope out what to do."*

I asked how she'd managed to drive the Vixen. She said, not easily.

It was dark out now, and the rain was drumming on the roof, with thunder and lightning much the same as it'd been on Sunday. She served me hash and I served her wine. To conceal our presence we turned the lights down and ate and drank in a soft orange glow. As I told Mara my story, she sat spellbound, as if I were some kind of enchanter. Especially, she couldn't let go of the Thrumble girls. *"What was their language like? Do you think they were twins? Were they really beautiful? Could they really have had no names? What happened to their mother? Do you think they are still alive?"* I suspect she actually wanted to go searching for them then and there.

In the middle of all this, we heard scratching on the door, and a weak wailing sound, and all at once I remembered the one-eyed Thrumble cat. Could it too have miraculously survived the wreck? I opened the door and, sure enough, in it walked, wet as can be but otherwise in one piece. Mara took a shine to it right off and gave it some cream on a plastic dish. The cat lapped up the cream, gave another faint wail (as in "You've *no idea* what I've been through") and fell asleep on the floor in its own little pool of water.

I used my towel to mop up and dry the cat, which opened its eye and gave a feeble purr, and when I got back to the table and sat down I must have gotten distracted by something, because when I looked up, Mara was gazing at me. She had that wistful look again, or rather a look of inexpressible loss, yet the look expressing that loss sought compassion and oddly, as though sensing that I felt some echoing loss, gave compassion too. In the golden lamplight that darkened her bluegreen eyes, she was the most beautiful thing I'd ever seen. So beautiful, so unspeakably beautiful, that she eclipsed my sense of past and future, I don't know for how long, my sense of who I was, why I was there, eclipsed what I hoped and feared. It was as though we'd walked into a painting, and I remember actually asking myself, *Why can't this last forever?*

But the moment brought its own end, because all of a sudden I wanted to kiss her. I wanted not just with my mind or lips or other male equipment, but as if my whole self, from sole to scalp, from birth to death, purposed the kiss that was the inevitable answer to the compassion of her eyes. And all of a sudden I was kissing Mara. How'd I gotten around the table? Had I lost consciousness and sleepwalked? Had the painting changed from one scene to another like two frames of film? I'd come around the table and was leaning down and kissing her, at first a soft feather-kiss and then becoming, as she rose and pressed fragrant against me, a kiss so long and deep as to drink up my soul and drown it with fulfillment, a kiss that became a universe with its unique god and creation and cosmology and climate and growth and seasons and fruition, a kiss with its own countryside of oak groves and poppy meadows, a kiss with its own city of ancient marble monuments, bright shops and green parks bursting with happy children, a kiss with its own myths, legends and history, its own poetry and song and dance, a kiss with its own wildness and tameness, its own sin and forgiving, its own sleeping and waking, a biblical kiss of the mouth. This kiss had windows in it, opening through blue mists to distant towns on brush-stroke hills beside the sea. This kiss was a sea into which I sailed until there was no substance but itself, and my whole past was dumped and jettisoned into the depths of this embrace, this enveloping caress, this communion. It was some kind of kiss.

Yet the kiss-universe also came to an end, or rather brought about its own mind-blowingly surprising outcome, for in the process of this encompassing kiss I realized that I was having the surprise of my life, and that this surprise wasn't coming from outside, but from inside me, being the return of my manhood, returning not hesitantly or tentatively but blatantly, like some wild third presence between us, interrupting one sweetness to suggest another, and suddenly Mara and I were rolling over each other on the bed together, with clothes flying off in all directions.

We rolled here and there on the Vixen bed, and each new position was like meeting her in a new way, as though she'd just breezed around a corner and come into sight and smiled with recognition for the first time. Mara made love as if there was no tomorrow, and for me it was more like there being no yesterday, because she made me a new person, and together we burned those moments into time, as though somewhere in time we will always and always be doing it just like that. If you've not made love like this, you haven't made love at all. It wasn't like anything I'd ever done or felt, leastways the laced-up lovemaking with Glynda, not actually *done* I mean, though it was like daydreams I'd had as a kid, of being with a girl who answered my passion with her own, but in those daydreams there was always some sort of interruption, like police sirens pulling up at the front door or the girl's father showing up to clobber me with a baseball bat, I guess because in my heart of hearts I felt I didn't deserve the joys of love. I just couldn't imagine myself being that happy. Yet what I didn't and couldn't know as a child was that when I finally got such happiness, it wouldn't be *me* who was happy—not, I mean, in the sense that I would be the person I'd been before. Deep inside Mara, in the heat of the moment, in the very moment of orgasm, I changed. My senses opened. My past self curled up like a burning October leaf, and I was born full grown into a new time, with the certainty that sink or swim, win or lose, I would gain some kind of dignity.

We didn't talk, except once, when in the midst of some inexpressible delight she felt behind my ear and whispered, "*Señor Lodoso.*"

"What does that mean?"

"Mister Muddy," she said, and for the first time since I met her I caught the trace of an accent.

I was going to sleep, all entwined with her, when I remembered the flood. I threw on some clothes, and so did she, and in the dim light we had a laugh about whose clothes were whose. I had a vague idea about what was wrong with the Vixen and asked Mara if the engine had died right when she hit the bump or not. She said no, and I told her I thought it was a battery cable. She asked how we'd had juice for lights and dinner then, and I showed her the Vixen's auxiliary batteries for running the accessories. Outside there was about an inch of water on the ground already. (Things must have been a *mess* back on the Sacannah.) It took maybe two minutes to fit and tighten the cable. It took longer to get the Vixen out of the rest area, because there wasn't any way of knowing where under the water the potholes were.

Out on the road it was better. We turned left and were soon winding our way into the hills. In twenty minutes we hit the freeway. The rain let up, the traffic was light, and on long easy stretches I tied the throttle line to the window crank, our version of Cruise Control. It was along one of these easy stretches that we heard about Fuzzy and me on the radio. Fuzzy had survived. He would be well again. And he'd exonerated me, "the fugitive known only as Bod" (Schultzie'd never gotten around to booking me!), "now presumed drowned in the Sacannah River flood."

I raised a big cheer and grabbed Mara's hand. She tried to share my joy but I noticed, she'd gone pensive again.

Some other radio news followed that wasn't so good. Mordecai Mac-Crae, the Rev's friend on Death Row, had started a hunger strike. Doctors expected that if he held onto it, he wouldn't be alive to attend his own execution.

Seeing as nobody was looking for me anymore, I thought it would be OK to bed down in Louisville. We pulled into town about 11. It was amazing, after all those emergencies, to see a town going about its business as if nothing had happened. Here, on the second floor of the Aberdeen Inn, I'm sitting and looking down at the park on a sunny morning after the best night of sleep of my life, typing with one hand and petting the cat, whom Mara's calling Paws, with the other. I've got a new beginning. My slate is almost clean.

I say almost because last night, just before sleep, I asked why she seemed so sad, and she said something I still can't fathom.

"*I saw HIM,*" she whispered.

"Saw who?"

"*Kanaloa!*" She was close to me in bed, and the whispered word almost burned my ear. Kanaloa, the demon-god of ancient Chile, the so-called harbinger of death!

I asked where and when.

"*Last night, he came to the same window you did. But before you.*"

"And said?"

"*What else could he have said? He said, 'Hé passa?'*"

I don't believe in spooks, but anyway this made my blood run cold. There's something so damn *real* about Mara. She speaks, gazes, kisses from the roots of her being. I'm certain that at least she *thought* she saw this thing.

I asked her what she answered.

"*Answer!! I threw the whole book at him! I called him every bad word I ever heard of! I told him he was an evil wicked god, and he had no business with good people! I cursed him by his own ancestors.*"

"What did he do then?"

"*He made a little wave, like good-bye for now. Then he was swallowed by the night.*"

In the darkness I heard a sound like her deep whisper but deeper and rhythmic. She was crying. How can you tell her that something simply didn't happen? Then I remembered what was around my neck, what neither law nor flood nor mud nor Thrumble had torn off.

I gave her Farrukh's taviz.

Chapter Five **The Glass Needle**

APRIL ?, 1998 *(later established as Saturday, April 11. —Ed.)*

We all live—breathe and pump blood, I mean, pretty much the same way, but there's infinite ways to die. In the past week I've seen two or three of the God-all strangest, and almost saw my own, watching from a cockeyed position somewhere outside of my own head. I've seen a grown man reduced to a mad thing with hair and horns, and another man who took to being an insect, and a third man who exploited both of these two for his own unspeakable evil, and I've seen them all die, neat as a hat trick. I've seen a strong woman felled like a tree. I've lost my loot and found it again. I've seen

Must have dozed off. Can't even stay awake describing my own (almost) death! You see, I've been on drugs, I mean mainlining (though I didn't shoot up on purpose!). Takes a while to get back.

Distracted, I pick up yesterday's *Rocky Mountain News* and read a front-page article. PIT BULL MIX MAULS IOWANS. It's about this creep named Winthrop C. Boylston who crossed pit bulls with greyhounds till he produced a freak-dog that was both fast and mean. He went out to the desert, it looks like, and all in secret, to train the beast to chase cars. Why? You guessed it! Last Monday there's this family from Iowa passing Boylston's place, and the dog takes off after it, jumps in (it's a convertible) and disembowels all the people. Boylston is nabbed by State Troopers as he tries to rip off the deceased Iowans, and he and the dog are in custody. *Is nobody safe anymore?*

Am I spacing out again? *Drinking coffee, I try an exercise to clear my head:*

> Estes Park, CO, that pleasant valley in the boonies that I'm now looking down on, was first settled in the early or middle old days by a Mr. Estes, who then brought his wife, and for the next few years they hunted and trapped, alternately crowing about the scenery and freezing their buns off, until they just bagged it and went downcountry.
>
> NB: Mrs. Estes made brooms of eagle-feathers.
>
> But in the 1880s along comes this kid of 14 named Enos Mills who's trekked over from Kansas because he's "too frail" to live back there. Frail Enos camps at 9000 ft and builds a cabin single-handed, then proceeds to jog up and down 14,000-foot Longs Peak until he can do it blindfolded (which, by the way, he did). Somewhere along the line he pauses to found Rocky Mountain National Park.

I can think again.

Mara and I were two days and three nights in Louisville. Tuesday AM Mara filed the Thrumble handcuffs off my wrists, and I dropped the Vixen at BMW (who did a real good job on the fan and throttle line). For the next two days and nights Mara and I ran up a tab with Room Service and managed to see all the sights of the city without leaving bed. Nobody bothered us except Paws, who perfected a way of following a ledge that was just under one of our windows out to a neighboring balcony, where he hunted birds, and sometimes would meow (he has a low voice for a cat) or scratch the glass to get back in.

As far as the room service menu allowed, we had the best of everything. Mornings Mara would have fruit salad and I'd order the three-egg omelette with cheese, mushrooms and a couple of bangers. For lunch Mara would favor a Gruyère fondue with a small bowl of gazpacho, while I'd opt for a mixed grill with scalloped potatoes. Dinners, we both inclined towards a strange blend of cob chowder and shellfish called Contrescarpe Marseillaise.

It's almost as though, by ordering the same meals each day, we were trying to write those moments into memory.

We quaffed Moselle by the magnum, and I laid in a case of Wharton's Rare Olde Bourbon, the Rev's favorite. Paws, whom we hid when the busboy knocked, lapped up so much triple-cream and ate so many leftovers that he must have put on a pound and a half in two days.

Between meals, and long rounds of lovemaking that somehow got better and better, we'd ask each other questions and swap stories. Mara had an armful of memories about her ancestors and her relatives and the antics of the childhood pets. Remember that, inside her palace, El Rosario, Aunt Cuerva kept a horse, a goat and a parrot? Each of these critters got a master bedroom (Balmaçeda cousins being kicked upstairs), and *"each of them had the run of the house. These animals could do no wrong."*

Mara remembers being woken at night by a loud whinny at her bedroom door, followed by the outrageous racket of the stallion thundering down the marble steps (together with the goat and raucous parrot) into the front hall as the three headed out for a moonlit romp in the garden. She remembers sitting at dinner and feeling the goat eating the laces of her tennis shoes from under the table, and then looking up to see *"a blinding flash of green and crimson"* as the parrot swooped in and snatched a breadstick from the hand of the local Bishop.

She remembers the goat falling ill and being serenaded by four musicians who played again and again, *"with a repetition both lunatic and divine,"* the same movement of a Haydn nocturne. And she broke me up with a story about the stallion, who one day was being ridden by the Bishop in a formal parade, but in the middle of same sniffed the air, bolted away, found a mare that was in heat and *"answered the summons of Venus"* while the Bishop, *"splendid in his feast-day habit,"* clung terrified to the saddle on his back.

There was just no way I could match her yarn for yarn. My boyhood in Portland was pleasant, but so mudpuddle dull that the quaintest thing I could remember was the Trailblazers' mascot. But Mara, who seemed to understand this, kept after me to tell and retell my experiences of the past week: Uncle Titus, Ali Shah, my trip downriver with old Fuzzy, the wicked no-account Thrumble boys and (her favorite) the unbelievable Thrumble girls and their made-up language. At times she'd get caught up in one of my stories, or hers, but ever that look, the sad Kanaloa-look, would return, and then we'd usually make love again, until I wondered whether, just as with our meals, she wanted to engrave a memory (for herself? for me?) in limited time.

She's taken to calling me Desi. One morning, I'm coming out of the bathroom wiping shaving cream off my mug, and she's lying on the bed without a stitch on, on her back with her head propped up on the bedstead and her hands behind her head, a position that deliciously raises the elbows and the breasts, and she says real solemnly, *"Desi, look at me. Remember me this way."*

On Thursday we went forth.

There was a rash of twisters in the south, so we opted for I-64 to I-70, a straight shot that (I thought) would take us through Indiana, Illinois, Missouri and Kansas and bring us into Vegas by Sunday at latest. We left Louisville on a perfect spring morning, blue sky with puffs of cloud, 60, green lights clear to the on-ramp, the radio playing Billie Holiday and fields at roadside breaking into bloom. I had a pretty good espresso buzz going, thanks to iced cappuccinos Mara'd gotten for us just before we left. An hour down the road, as the highway curved left and uphill, a ray of morning sun glanced through my window onto the instrument panel, and at that very moment I remember thinking, "Fancy this!" and it was a long, long thought about all that I'd gone through and what I'd come out with and all the wonderful things that might be possible, if only . . .

I dreamily checked the side mirror, and that's when I saw the VW for the first time. It was a gray-green ancient bug, maybe late 50's, and its windows were dark, like heavily tinted glass, only they didn't have tinted glass back then, so somebody'd retrofitted it or glued on that chintzy tinted cellophane you can get at stores. It was hanging back behind me maybe 30 yards, seeming to mind its own business at 55 mph while faster traffic wove in and out between us, and there's nothing the matter with that, because your old Bug is not about to wind out through the gears on a long uphill grade, but there was something about it that troubled me, like a chilly wind on a late summer day at the beach. Maybe I just didn't like the cut of the VW's jib. Maybe the darkened split windscreen and its round headlights gave it the look of a nasty little spider-face.

We topped the grade and I slowed down to 45, to see if it would pass me. It didn't. I took it up to 60 and alerted Mara, who, with Paws asleep on her lap, had been checking the map. She looked up at me with concern. *"Who can it possibly be?"*

We brainstormed a while, ruling out possibilities. Any police force in its right mind would move in on us without any namby pamby VW jazz, and the Imbratta folks would follow us covertly and strike when we were alone and unprotected. If the VW was really tailing us, it was most likely just some dude who'd gotten fascinated by the lines of the Vixen (this happens pretty often on the road) or somebody who'd seen Mara back in Louisville and couldn't get her out of his head.

Given all this, we could have just driven on and waited for him to lose interest. But there was something else. Mara'd gotten a stomachache, probably from the espresso, and needed an Alka-Seltzer and a restroom.

We decided to take the next exit (St. Lorenzo, in about 5 miles), head for a busy roadhouse, use the facilities and find out what this flake in the VW would do. Mara opined that seeing my *titanic shape* as I got out of the Vixen might cause him to wither away. On top of that, we might be able to shake him (that is, if he wasn't concentrating at that moment) by swerving onto the off-ramp suddenly enough. And finally, there was the chance that he, or even she, was just following along in a fit of distraction—maybe from doing pot or frying on acid or popping uppers—and had no interest in us at all.

What it really was, we'll probably never know. I veered onto the St. Lorenzo off-ramp and braked hard on the sharp right turn. The Bug put-putted on along the freeway, as though we'd never mattered at all.

The off-ramp curved down through an underpass, and in the deep shadow, with my sunspecks on, I felt almost blind. But in a second everything was bright and green again, with signs announcing that this was Indiana 238 South and Abe Lincoln Country. Sure enough, a mile down the road we found the Honest Abe Inn, a massive log house with a neon face.

Mara managed to dislodge Paws from her lap without waking him.

The Inn was swarming with coffee-break business. I went to the men's room and afterwards found my way into the high-ceilinged dining salon where I saw Mara approaching a table by the far windows. She seemed to pause for a moment by the next-to-last table, where a well-dressed woman was standing in the aisle, leaning over and serving something to a person sitting there. When I reached Mara and sat down, I could see that these people at the next table were both quite striking: a tweed-suited middle-aged woman, with a strong build and a handsome squarish face, and a younger woman in white, a big-eyed girl really, who'd remind you of the young Audrey Hepburn, except that this gal was blond and seemed rather frail.

They were a pretty interesting pair, but they were none of my business, and there was something I'd never got around to asking Mara. I forgot the ladies and ordered Alka-Seltzer for two, and my big hands were fumbling with the tablet wrapper when Mara reached over, took it from me and opened it easily. As I looked at her and she back at me, her great turquoise eyes narrowed slightly, as though I were her whole world, but sort of a clod.

"Mara," I asked her, "how'd you get to be the Imbrattas' comptroller?"

Her eyes froze for a split second, but then softened almost to tears. "*I was deceived*," she whispered. "You should have seen Mickey five years ago, when we first met. He was *beautiful*, not heavy like later. He behaved like a prince, and at first I thought he'd come from a good Italian-American family that'd gotten rich quick on restaurants. He went *crazy for me*, and when he couldn't get me to bed he tried to marry me, and when I said no to that *he lay low for a while* and then offered me this job. At first it looked like a decent job, and the money was so much better than I could get elsewhere that *I took it, even though my ex-husband Raul in Chile was writing letter after letter, desperate to have me back*. I'd been on the job for a few months, working on the restaurant accounts, before I realized that the family had other interests, that the restaurants *were just a front*. I *faced Mickey down* and told him I was quitting, but he said, people don't just quit the Imbratta Business and that even though he liked me himself, his dad the padrone might *do something bad to me*."

I asked how long she'd been working under this threat. A few months. Mickey said he might be able to "let her go" after the Calandrino deal, but when she found out how big a deal it really was, and how much was at stake, she began rethinking what the words "let go" might mean in the Imbratta lingo. She was planning to take a chance and bolt during the family bash that was planned to celebrate the transaction. That would have been the very night of the Imbratta-Calandrino shootout.

I could see Mara watching my responses as she spoke. How would Big Desi take her admissions of weakness? She needn't have worried.

I'm an utter freeloader and sissy myself and am not about to add hypocrisy to my stable. And I liked it that she was levelling with me.

She was explaining her game plan for escaping the Imbrattas when something caught my eye. The two women at the next table had been rising to leave when all of a sudden the young one lurched towards the other and began to slide down to the floor. The older woman gave a low cry and with surprising strength grabbed her friend under the armpits and put her back in her chair, where the poor girl lolled as though nearly unconscious.

Mara, who followed my eyes, turned and jumped up and almost instantly was beside them, offering help. I dropped money on the table and was over there in time to hear the older woman identify herself as Bessie van Ardsdale of some clinic at the Skythorpe Institute and ask if we could possibly help her bring Isobel, her patient, to the parking lot where they were going to get picked up by the Institute's limo. Isobel momentarily perked up a bit and gave me a pleading look that would have melted a Buick.

"Try to walk," I said. "I'll support you." This plan worked out OK, and in a minute we were all standing in the sunny lot. But no limo, and as the clock ticked on, Isobel leaned more heavily against me, and it was obvious she needed a doctor right away. Before I knew it—and despite a stern warning glance from Mara—I asked how far away the Institute was, and Bessie said only a mile, and we packed ourselves into the Vixen and were off.

But it was well over a mile. It was long enough to learn from Bessie, who sounded polite but sort of official, that the Skythorpe Institute had been built on the campus of San Lorenzo College because Myrdal Hwang, a billionaire donor, had wanted to establish a research facility there, and that at Skythorpe a number of research teams "pursued a variety of studies for the good of man," and that the Hauck Clinic was run by one of these teams. She added that the philosophy at Skythorpe and

Hauck was "psychosomosophy" and that what this amounted to was that "healing" concerned the whole mind and spirit rather than just the disease. Isobel, for example, was a cancer patient whose treatment included homeopathy, physical therapy, music, chapel and an occasional treat at the Honest Abe. Jesus had a role in the equation, too.

Bessie added that this year the Clinic had gotten an $800,000 grant from the US Defense Dept., of all places, because Mr. Hwang had friends on the right House Committee.

As Bessie spoke she was directing us along 238S down to College Road, and then up through woods and meadows to the stone gates of San Lorenzo College ("The School of Jesus"). We drove on up through a college campus only a little bit better landscaped than the Augusta National Golf Course, past widely spaced white college buildings that Bessie said were all made of Mexican alabaster, and spaced between these were pillars engraved with "THINK JESUS," "DRINK JESUS," "BREATHE JESUS." I wondered what the folks around here did for laughs. And not a student in sight. You'd think the place was deserted, if you didn't know that everybody was in class.

At the very top of the hill, we stopped at a modern building that had no windows in front and was eight, maybe ten stories high. Above the wide entrance was engraved SKYTHORPE INSTITUTE, with a smaller title, Hauck Clinic, underneath. Bessie trotted in the front door and was back soon with a big hulking albino in a white nursing frock. The big guy picked Isobel up, I thought a little carelessly, and strode off with her into the building. I wanted out of there, but Bessie insisted on running into the "galley," as she put it, to fetch a tub of iced tea for the road, and she was off before we could say no thanks.

She reappeared amazingly soon with two plastic glasses and a plastic beverage container full of tea. Mara and I, who were both parched, drank a glass apiece and stowed the rest, before thanking Bessie and setting off.

We hadn't gotten past the first curve when the Vixen felt strange to me. It seemed to be oversteering, and the brakes felt squooshy, and I looked up to see that we'd screeched to a stop against the curb. I glanced at Mara in dazed confusion, but she wasn't looking at me or the road— her face was turned away and her head was slanted down and to one side, as if she was trying to get a new angle on the landscape. For a moment I realized it wasn't the Vixen that was squooshy, it was me, but then I was slumping forward, without any strength to catch myself.

The last thing I remember was the sound of the horn, coming it seemed from miles away, as my inert sack of a body hit the steering wheel.

● ● ●

I woke up looking at something gross and hairy. It was large and horned and close to me and evil-smelling and making unthinkable noises. I wanted to be far away from it, but I couldn't move a muscle.

Then I woke up more and realized that this thing in front of me was speaking a language, and I felt like a baby, who hasn't learned language yet.

Then I woke up enough to understand that I had one language, and the hairy thing had another, and I also realized something completely different: that though I could see, hear and smell, I could not feel, speak or move a muscle.

My eyes wouldn't even roll in their sockets.

I can say *now* that I was in some sort of madhouse, some section of the Clinic reserved for folks who'd gone wacko. I can say *now* that I'd been given something like what they call the date-rape pill, because I've read interviews where women said they'd been quite conscious of being raped without being able to move a muscle in defense or even make a peep. Somebody'd even rigged up an IV to my arm, probably so I could be date-raped in regular scientific doses. And they must have originally given me something else in the iced tea, some pharmacopoeial hors d'oeuvre, to knock me out completely.

But I couldn't think those things *then* because my inboard computer was down. Yet maybe even *because* of my utter helplessness, I truly saw and heard, and my memory of everything is clear as crystal.

The unholy furry mass began to droop, and there were two short raps as the horns attached to the fur hit the floor, and a man emerged, a man as rank and smelly as the fur, a man so gaunt and thin you'd say he'd been buried in that fur and then dug up again. You couldn't give this man an age, because most of him looked outright dead. He propped himself up on his knees in front of me, the way a marmot or squirrel might, but mind you much more slowly, and he looked at me with silent helpless surprise, the way a mountain ewe once looked at me when she found me hiding in the brush beside her trail.

Then he back-pedalled, very deliberately, still on his knees, dragging his fur and stink away from me and opening up my field of vision.

There were other people sitting in the room. I could see seven of them, but I could *feel* several others around me. One of them was speaking to me, trying to get my attention. He was a gray-haired man, with a broad kindly blue-eyed Irish face, and his voice was sweet and mellow like a healer's.

"That's Red Wind of the Lakota people you just met, my friend. He's registered in this establishment as Arnold Wain of Laramie, but that's just a paleface name and place, and now he's got nothing but his native name and his buffalo skin to call his own. Red Wind has AIDS and Alzheimer's, and he's a junky to boot, which is perhaps just as well, considering. But in his day he was a man to see. Or listen to, rather. He was an orator like as we don't see in the reservations today. He could speak such words as gave people visions. Maybe he could do this right now, if any of us could understand him. On the other hand, we've got plenty of visions to go around without Red Wind's help. Let me introduce myself, sir. I'm Doctor, you heard me, *Doctor* Bevan Slattery, and but for one minor *detail* I'd still be in practice in Minneapolis and on the faculty of the University of Minnesota Med School. And your name sir—ah, but I see you are inconvenienced."

When Slattery said "one minor detail" there were wild shouts of "DETAIL! DETAIL!" from all around the room, as though his mates wanted him to go into it. The room was about 15 feet across and, I later learned, about twice that in length, lit by fluorescent from above, with walls and floor of bathroom white tile. All the inmates I could see were tied down in wheelchairs (I wasn't because I didn't need to be) and sat side by side, except that I could also see, just to Slattery's left, a table of instruments and drugs.

Red Wind was curled up on the floor like a dog in front of Slattery and was hiding under his buffalo skin, except when he stuck his head out and moaned "*hinske uye-kiyin*," which I took to be Lakotan for something awful.[3] Slattery kept talking, as though he meant to introduce me to everybody in the room, while a gravelly voice still shouted "DETAIL!" and I began to hear murmurs on all sides, as though the audience was getting worked up.

The whole bunch seemed to be male, and all ages, except for no kids. Slattery introduced Jock the burnt-out hipster, Travis the bombed-out Nam vet, Norman the traded-out stockbroker, Phil the grossed-out ER physician, J. T. the spaced-out trial lawyer who'd escaped from reality and into the world of *Honeymooners* reruns, and Sid the flipped-out rabbi who'd suffered from laughing fits during holy service, until one day he blew his marbles altogether.

Slattery finally got around to somebody I could see, a man to his right who had his mouth taped shut and was being fed by a tube up one nostril. This guy had *enormous blue eyes*—I mean, the size of golf balls.

---

3. Actually, it is Lakotan for "He has grown horns," which is short for "He has become a buffalo," which means, metaphorically, "He has gone mad." Here, as elsewhere, Ruck's ear is perfect. —Ed.

Slattery explained as how this was Ray, and how he was under restraint for being abusive. Ray looked like I felt.

Ray's eyeballs suddenly got even bigger and he made a guttural two-syllable noise that everybody but me seemed to understand, because again they all started shouting "DETAIL!"

Slattery pulled a long face and shrugged his shoulders, as though the wretches around him were kids asking for an extra bedtime story. As he spoke, the gang threw in comments of their own, which I'll quote in brackets.

"All right. Enough. OK. I'll tell you guys this story one last time. Why it's the last time, you'll soon find out. As I said before, except for one minor detail I'd still be in practice in Minneapolis and on the faculty of the University of Minnesota Med School. ['SHAME ON YOU!'] Pipe down, Sid. I was an anesthesiologist, and like others in my trade, I had lots of money and expensive hobbies. My own favorite pastime was jungle exploration. ['RIGHT ON, MAN!'] Years before I'd gotten bored stiff with the guided tour sort of thing, you know, the Congo/Amazon rat race ['ONE OF THESE DAYS, ALICE!'] and opted for solo treks up out-of-the-way canyons and into areas that even anthropologists and linguists had left alone. I'd gone beyond amateur exploration and become a back-hills fetishist. ['KNOCK WOOD!']

"This explains my presence, in October of 1995, in a remote corner of the foothills of the Moake Mountains on New Guinea. It was a brilliant Sunday morning. Tuman, my guide, had heard that a native coronation was to be held upcountry, and all morning long, through dense forests dinning with the calls of blue-eyed cockatoos and tiger parrots, we'd hiked upriver in order to get to the village on time. At about noon, sweating profusely, we reached a small plateau with an oak grove and a number of round houses. About 100 villagers, all in festive dress, had thronged together in a meadow just beyond the houses. In a loud voice Tuman called for attention and explained my presence, and the crowd of natives buzzed with excitement, for it's likely they'd never seen a white man before. [*'FAR OUT!'*]

"The coronation ceremony began almost at once. It was long, complicated and painfully slow. I was standing, or rather leaning, soaked in sweat and half-asleep, with my left arm propped against the trunk of an oak. I woke up suddenly. Tuman had gasped in horror. The ceremony had stopped, and the entire crowd was gathered around me, wide-eyed in amazement. They were all looking just to the left of my head. My left arm felt heavy, and as I turned to look at it Tuman cautioned me to stay calm. [*'OY VAY!' 'PROZAC!' 'AIR SUPPORT!'*]"

Slattery paused a moment to prolong the tension and then extended his left arm and turned his head towards it, as if he was reliving the moment. "There, sitting on my outstretched arm, was the biggest insect I'd ever seen. [*'INCOMING!' 'FLAT-LINING!' 'SELL SHORT!'*] It was drinking my sweat. It was like the sweat bees that I'd run into near the coast, but many times as long and proportionally more massive. My arm must have fallen asleep, or I would have noticed it. I was frozen with shock. [*'HINSKE UYE-KIYIN!'*] The natives were looking at this insect with more than just curiosity. Some of them fell to their knees. Led by their priest, all of them began moaning some sort of incantation.

"Their voices swelled to a fever pitch, and at the crescendo I felt a sharp pain in my arm. The beast was stinging me. [*'SHAME ON IT!' 'MORE SUTURES! SHE'S STILL BLEEDING!'*] I banged at it with my other hand, and with a terrific BUZZBUZZ it took off and zigzagged into the woods, leaving its one-inch sting in my arm.

"At that moment I saw something very strange indeed. As the bee disappeared into the woods, I saw a naked young woman, who'd presumably been watching the event from cover, disappear into the woods after the insect. A native next to me, who'd also seen this, whispered the word *'ranguma.'*

"As I pulled out the sting, the crowd went wild. I'd definitely become a star around there, but was worried about exactly what sort of star I'd gotten to be. Tuman was having a little powwow with the priest and the prospective chief. Then the other two fell back, and Tuman spoke to me in English. 'Sir,' he said, 'I have momentous news! You have been touched by a god! The elders have made you king! You'll be crowned tonight at a pig feast! The priest is preparing a delectable punch in your honor! Tonight you will be obliged to make love to every grown woman in the village! That is the good part, sir.'

" 'If that's the good part,' I answered, rubbing my sore arm, 'I don't need any bad part! But maybe you'd better tell me the bad part anyway.'

" 'The bad part, sir, is that you'll die of the sting tomorrow, no remedy. And after that the villagers will fry you in lard and eat your divine flesh.' ['BUMMER!' 'MEDIC!' 'HEART MASSAGE!' 'SHAME ON ME!' 'ONE OF THESE DAYS!']"

With both hands Slattery motioned for silence. His audience had gotten pretty worked up, but you could tell from the twinkle in his eye that he thought it was probably good for them. How many times had he told this story before? Was it a sort of local ritual? Whatever it was, it was having a weird effect on me. It was bringing my spirit back to life. It was reminding me that I, like Slattery, was a kind of cursed king.

When the room got quiet, he continued in a tone of hushed excitement:

"I recoiled in shock. The full range of possibilities, or rather lack of them, quickly ran before my mind. 1) I could stay in the village and die. 2) I could trek out of the village and die. I was just about to choose number 2 when a thought struck me. It was the word that had been muttered when the girl disappeared into the forest.

" 'Tuman,' I asked, 'what's a *ranguma*?'

" '*Ranguma*, sir, that's a sorcerer.'

"I'd felt it in my bones. And now I was certain that somehow this sorcerer held my only chance of life. After all, many European women healers in the Middle Ages were denounced as sorcerers — the more so when their cures worked. After all, the sorcerer had been watching the bee-scene. I burst from the clearing into the woods, with Tuman straining to keep up with me. Life has never been so vivid to me as those first few moments in the forest. I'd been harmed by man (those stinkers should have warned me!) and now sought salvation in the heart of nature, as the vicious poison raged in my arm.

"In the dark greenness of that jungle, lush and mysterious, I knew that I was racing for my life.

"About a hundred yards in I saw her, a deer-like young woman, graceful, tan, naked, like some creature of Henri Rousseau.[4] She looked at me for only a moment, then turned and, without seeming to hurry, moved rapidly deeper and deeper into the forest. Out of the darkness she broke into a sunny clearing—I remember it was like a temple of sunbeams—and stopped and turned back towards us. We approached her. Her beautiful face showed not a hint of fear or guile. She explained to Tuman that she knew my plight and that, though she couldn't completely save me, there was one way of prolonging my life. ['*KIN EINA HORA!*'] Through Tuman she told me that she was part bee herself, and that I would have to take on some of the bee's character.

"Telling Tuman to wait in the clearing, the girl led me to a thatched hut just beyond. The air was alive with buzzing. The girl lived with those big bees! ['*OY!*'] She used the front door, and the giant creatures the back. On the floor of her room lay a dying bee, I guess the one that stung me. Gently she removed its honey sacs and made me chew on them. She fed me propolis and royal jelly that she'd stored in large hollowed-out coconuts. She brought in two other bees, this time much smaller ones, and, motioning for me to drop my pants, had one of them sting me in each buttock. Immediately the pain in my arm began to lessen.

"Then she pulled me down onto her grass bed and we made the

---

4. Henri Rousseau, French naturalist painter, 1844–1910. —Ed.

most passionate, sensual love I've ever experienced. [*KNOCK WOOD!' 'NURSE!' 'GERONIMO!' 'BUY CALLS!' 'OUTTA SIGHT!' 'ENJOY IN GOOD HEALTH!' 'HINSKE UYE-KIYIN!' 'VAVA-VAVOOM!'*]"

Everybody in the room was pumping up and down in his wheelchair and shouting with brutal glee, but Slattery's cheeks now were wet with tears. He waited for the uproar to die down, then went on:

"Over the next week, Tuman half-dragged, half-carried me out of that land. I was feverish, raving about sunlight, sex and stings. From Port Moresby they flew me to Sydney and thence to San Francisco. I was a year in the Veterans' Hospital there. They did what they could, but the *ranguma* was right; I've never been myself again. I've lost my muscle tone and 45 pounds. I have visions. And occasionally . . . every so often . . . *I become a bee.*"

I'll be damned if a low buzzing noise didn't start coming from Slattery's throat. As everybody else shouted and clapped, he freed his hands from the wrist straps with surprising ease, rose and walked across the room towards me. He grabbed my date-rape IV with one hand, held my arm with the other and skillfully removed the thing. "I'll pull out *your* sting buddy," he buzzily whispered, and then, "We're not patients here, we're prisoners and guinea pigs. Doc Hauck's growing Ray's eyes on purpose so he can remove and study them. He's got me on insect hormones, and everybody else in the room is a living microbe farm. I wouldn't like to think about what he's got planned for you. You'd better vacate these premises."

Slattery stood up and grabbed for something in his pants pocket. Before I knew it he'd rammed a handful of blue and white capsules into my mouth. My gullet reacted automatically by trying to swallow, and Slattery helped by dumping his glass of water down me. "These uppers will counteract your downers," he said. "Relax while I attend to some medical business." He turned and walked off towards the left. As I was realizing that I could move my eyes again, Slattery disappeared through a door on the other side of the room.

Only a few seconds passed before another door opened behind me and to the right. Two people strode in, a doctor and nurse. The nurse was Bessie van Ardsdale, now clad in white, looking God's-wrath neat and official. The dude had to be Doc Hauck. Straight off they noticed Slattery's empty wheelchair, and Bessie reached into her breast pocket and pulled out a phone the size of a pack of cards, keyed in an extension and gave a muffled command, I reckon, to call out the dogs. Meanwhile, Hauck was going about his business. He was the size of an NFL linebacker and looked just as fit. He was about 45, ruddy, balding, handsome until you spotted the stony gray eyes behind his MacArthur-shaped eyeglasses, and he moved with the grace of a cat. I could see the patients cringing in their wheelchairs as he passed them. The whole gang of them had gone silent.

With Bessie still on the phone, Hauck strode to the table next to Slattery's empty chair and busied himself with what was on it. When he turned to face me I saw something on the table I hadn't noticed before: an adjustable frame combined with some sort of gas torch. Hauck spoke with the voice of a radio newsman, precise and numb. "Mr. Ruck, you're a very sick man, and I'm afraid you're soon going to become much sicker. But not to worry, it's all for the good of humanity. See this instrument? Guess what I'm doing."

From a box on the table, he carefully pulled out a very narrow glass tube and fixed it in the frame. Then he threw a switch. The gas blower hissed into action up and the frame moved upward till the heated glass stretched and snapped apart. He detached one piece and held it in front of me. "See this, Ruck? It's the world's sharpest needle. Properly managed, this needle can puncture a single cell. But we've got a different use for it in your case. We're going to find a special part of your throat that channels right up to the brain." He leaned over me more closely so only

I could hear. "We're going to send your brain to Never-Never Land to help the little fairies make honeydew, and then we're going to drop in on your pretty friend and do the same for her."

I could smell the cinnamon mouthwash on this bastard's breath as he said he was going to wipe us out.

This is making me sick even as I write it. I'd better knock off.

TUESDAY, APRIL 21, 1998

I've been down for a while with the flu. Should have listened to Glynda last fall and gotten a shot.

Mara's taken care of me like an angel, with fresh oranges and special barley soups and her warm quiet presence in bed. It's really been rather nice, in this campgrounds above the pretty town, lazing around in the absence of madmen and sadists and little green gods. May rest a while longer before making the run to Vegas.

Dreamt about the Thrumble girls last night. In my dream they were both happy as larks, dressed in luscious finery, and they were waited on hand and foot by a lot of strange bright-colored animal creatures that had scales instead of fur. Then I realized that we were all of us under water.

Where was I? Oh, the mouthwash.

As I said, *I could smell the cinnamon mouthwash on this SOB's breath as he said he was going to wipe us out,* and I remember thinking, *he buys this mouthwash with US Defense money.*

After showing me the glass needle, Hauck went back to the equipment table. Bessie gave me a fishlike look and turned to help him as he attached the pieces of glass tubing to two wicked-looking syringes. I've always admired doctors' hands: so steady, so precise, so gentle yet so strong. Now as I watched, a helpless halfwit, I saw nightmare written in his elegant moves.

Hauck tested both syringes and set one of them down on the table, point outwards. Then he came towards me, holding the other. I noticed that the door behind him had opened a crack: spectators? His left hand reached at my face and pried open my jaw, while with his right he inserted the syringe into my mouth.

That's when true Bedlam broke loose. The door behind Hauck burst open and Bevan Slattery bolted in, livid, wild-eyed, possessed, and with him the unbearable, unforgettable BUZZ you hear from high-voltage power lines when you get near them, or (as was probably the case) from Slattery's fellow prisoners buzzing in unison, or, if you insist, from giant bees. Slattery caught Hauck as Hauck was rising and spun him around as the syringe dropped and splintered. Hauck had 6 inches and 100 pounds on Slattery, but this was no ordinary Slattery. This was a man driven by a power. And it's almost as though Hauck realized as much. Finally you could see an emotion in those gray eyes: rampant terror. Slattery had grabbed Hauck two-fistedly on the front of his white jacket and was moving him backwards, faster and faster, to my left. Bessie went after them but I tripped her up—my God, I could move my legs! She caught herself on hands and knees and gave a cry of anguish that was almost lost in the buzzing. Meanwhile Hauck had stopped his backward motion and was aiming a Sunday punch at Slattery's head, but before he could connect he was thrown off balance by a second attacker. Red Wind had risen in his full buffalo suit, and as Red Wind rushed forward Hauck took one of the buffalo horns in the neck and was forced backward again. At the far end of the room, as I could now turn my head to see, was a yellow bottle-glass partition. Slattery and Red Wind and Hauck hurtled towards it with Slattery's rubber-soled shoes squeaking with stress and Red Wind shouting *"HINSKE UYE-KIYIN!"* They crashed WHAMMO into the partition, which shattered with a sharp report, revealing that it was no ordinary partition but rather a second- or third-story window opening onto some large inner space—down into which the trio disappeared. There was an instant of grim silence and then POW! a terrific crash, together with a blinding flash like blue lightning and the hissing of ruptured electrical circuits.

Instantly all the lights went out, and we were left in the dull amber of the emergency power supply. Except that the room beyond the broken partition was lit by something besides this, something bright orange, flickering, alive.

The place was on fire.

Bessie pulled herself up, hurried to the broken window and looked down into the room beyond. Apparently she didn't like what she saw, because she turned roaring and came at me like a tiger. The image of her coming, outlined against that horrid fire like some avenging demon, gives me fits even as I lie here days later. I can imagine she had some interesting things in mind for me, but what they were I'll never know, because just at that moment I had a huge rush of sensation in every limb. Slattery's uppers had kicked in with a vengeance.

By the time Bessie got to me I was on my feet, and I was feeling like Goliath on a good day.

I suppose she meant to knock me over with the force of her rush, because she hit me at full speed, but I just shifted my weight and, with almost no effort really, deflected her towards the instrument table. She smashed backwards into it with a shriek which meant that she'd taken the second hypodermic needle in the rump. And that's exactly what must have happened, because right away her arms dropped and her face went dark and her body stiffened into a board and stood there, propped against the table, for just a moment, until some minor imbalance caused her to roll leftward and smash to the floor like a log.

Without knowing exactly why, I reached down, grabbed her cellular phone and dropped it into one of my jacket pockets.

Quickly I released Phil and Travis from their wrist straps and, as they turned to their cheering comrades, I shouted a word of encouragement and hotfooted it out the same door that poor Slattery'd come in by. I could smell the smoke now but didn't have much trouble breathing. Alarms were going off everywhere, and orderlies running in every direction, and I was temporarily ignored in the confusion. My mind wasn't firing with all its eight cylinders yet, but still I was clear about what I had to do. I had to find Mara and the Vixen—and then vamoose.

I pulled this off by remembering a couple of obvious things about public architecture. Since the men's ward was at one end of the hall, and I was now passing the men's and women's bathrooms, the women's ward had to be at the other end. Sure enough, when I blundered in, there were a lot of women strapped down in wheelchairs just like the men had been. Some were shouting for help, others were doped up. Something caught my eye to the far right. It was the big albino attendant, and he was standing with his back to me. He was holding a lifeless woman in his arms. As he turned towards me, the lifeless woman turned out to be Mara. She was unconscious and white as a sheet. The big lug must have been abusing her, because her patient's robe was down around her waist. When he put her down onto a bed and came towards me, I saw under his gown an erection the size of a handsaw.

This was the last straw. I let out a cry of rage, which he answered with a lionish roar. He tried to come at me in a rush, but he must have tripped over his own dong, because all he could manage was a kind of John Wayne swagger. He telegraphed a haymaker, but in my pumped-up state it seemed that the punch took several seconds to throw, so that I had time to brace myself, grab his wrist with my left hand and his upper arm with my right and, and, turning leftward, toss the man over my shoulder to the floor. I heard a snap as the shoulder separated en route, but he couldn't have felt the pain for long because he immediately landed on his head.

He lay dead still where he fell.

I went over to Mara, pulled her robe up over her shoulders and picked her up in my arms. This seemed to take no effort at all. I was just leaving the ward when I noticed Isobel, whose wheelchair was right by the door. She was tied down like the others, and her mouth was gagged, but her blue eyes looked up as though they wanted to tell me a long story. I reached down to ungag her, but as I did, she passed out. I had no time to help Isobel. To be frank with you, I wasn't feeling very humanitarian at the moment. As I whisked Mara out of the ward, through an EXIT door and down the stairs, I started giggling and realized I was looped to the gills.

At the next floor down I had to leave the stairwell in order to escape a great flock of footsteps and voices coming upstairs, so I exited the stairs at 2 and hid out for a minute in the Ladies' Room. When the voices and steps had passed, I reemerged and found myself alone in the hall. That's how I managed to get a gander at the room into which Slattery, Red Wind and Hauck had fallen. With my free hand I half-opened one of the double doors and furtively peeked in. It was a big room full of separate workstations, with some sort of major power source in the middle. The fire, doused in extinguisher goo, was still smoldering and smoking there, and the place smelled positively lethal. But instead of escaping into the fresh air, a bunch of workers, about 25 of them, were frantically trying to hide their work materials in boxes next to their tables. I'd seen materials like that before in films. Chances were this was some major cocaine operation. The workers all seemed to be from the same East Asian country, Korea maybe, or somewhere in China.

All, that is, except for the dude who, with his back to me, moved from table to table and who looked like he was giving instructions. He was just under medium height, and his wavy brown hair gave him away as caucasian, and there was something about his manner that reminded me of something I still can't place.

I backed through the door without being seen, and from there I took Mara clear down to B. You see, most public buildings will, if possible, have their loading docks downstairs from their front offices and in back, and I didn't see why this shouldn't be the case with the Skythorpe Institute. And why did I want a loading dock? It was the logical place for them to hide the Vixen and process its cargo. Logic is the shortest distance between two points, so bad people, just like good people, behave logically whenever they can.

As luck would have it, I was right. The Vixen was parked by the loading dock. I checked my watch. It was 2 AM, dark as pitch. I strapped Mara into the passenger's seat, found the key in the ignition and went aft to look for the briefcases. They were all gone. Where would they be? Of course, in the shipping room, which is what you have whenever you have a loading dock.

I went back in and got them. I lugged them back to the van in four brief trips.

Along the way I met with a few nuisances. A number of Hauck's assistants offered me medical care that I didn't really need. A speedy little fellow in white administered orthopedic therapy from behind me as I was coming back into the building the first time, but he developed a sudden case of cloutnosia and rolled into a corner for a bit of R & R. A minute later a pair of burly honchos tried to perform an examination on me at the loading dock, but in a flash one of them was complaining of acute groinal footitis, while the other was stricken suddenly by kickguttarrhea, with complications for both patients that included falloffdockonassia. And there was also that big guy in the shipping room who was about to give me slamdunk cranial typewriter shock treatment when he was taken from us by multiple sockosis. The others aren't really worth mentioning.

I fired up the Vixen and tromped on the gas, checking the rearviews all the way down to campus entrance, where I started passing the fire trucks coming in. No one behind me. Once on I-64 I pulled out Bessie's cellular phone and hit 911 and told the dispatcher I was San Lorenzo campus security and I'd found a big-league drug factory on the second floor of Skythorpe, as well as a couple dozen human guinea pigs on the third. Then I set the cruise just below the speed limit and drove through the night, still high as a kite, loudly singing golden oldies like Turkey in the Straw and My Darling Clementine. In about an hour Paws crawled out of wherever he'd been hiding and jumped up on Mara's lap, and just about that time pale moonlight glimmered on the countryside.

As I drove, my mind mumbled and rumbled to itself about my own behavior over the past few days. Does beating up on a dozen or so white-coated grunts and racking up multiples with a beautiful gal turn me into a new man? True, it doesn't hurt the self-confidence. I had to admit that at last I'd become what I wanted to be, what I'd dreamed of being: a vested member of that Ancient Brotherhood, the Fistful-of-dollars For-nicating and Ass-kicking Community. But was that all there was? What did it mean, for example, to be a good man?

Suddenly I remembered—so vividly that I nearly swerved off the road—the face of the black man in the flatbed truck just before the head-on collision at the tracks. Such a pleasant, gentle face. A man you'd like to know. Why did I now feel guilty about his death, just as though I'd been to blame for it?

I'd slowed down to navigate the morning mists when Mara woke up. At first she was disoriented and asked questions about the flood, the Thrumble sisters and the Louisville hotel, and when was dinner? But soon she got back in shape, with no hangover at all. That confirmed in my mind that we'd been given date-rape potion, because I've read that people who are given the potion wake up feeling pretty good, that is, ex-cept that they've been raped.

My own medical condition was more complicated, because I'd been given a medley of drugs, first by Hauck and then by Slattery. I was riding high but riding for a fall. I could drive OK, but kept hallucinating that nasty little VW Bug into my side-view mirror.

I drove clear to Kansas City, where at a truckstop I ate a chicken steak, drank a light beer and blacked out on the bed in the Vixen. Mara drove the rest of the way here. She figured I needed some rest, so she took a scenic route out of Denver, and that's how we fetched up near Estes Park in the Rockies.

She's lying beside me on the bed right now and making one side of me much warmer than the other. She says she wants to write something in my book, and I say, No you can't.

DESI ¡ LOVE YOU   REMEMBRE ME

Chapter Six **May Day**

PART ONE: THE SILENCE OF THE WOLVES

"It cannot be."

That dim and misty morning Mara's eyes, as she sat across the table from me in the Vixen near Estes Park, were wet with tears and seemed aglow with light. We were talking about the Skythorpe Institute. We'd gone over every step from our departure out of Louisville to our arrival at the Honest Abe, and the whole thing seemed no more to me than a bizarre coincidence, but Mara thought otherwise. She thought she'd been slipped some kind of stomach mickey in her cappuccino at the Louisville hotel and that the VW bug was a plant to get us to leave the freeway at the San Lorenzo exit.

I said, "No, Mara, that plan's got too many loopholes."

"Loopholes?"

I explained as how a plan like that left too much to chance.

She looked at me reproachfully. "*What do loopholes matter if the plan succeeds?"* I didn't quite follow this and told her so, but that didn't phase Mara in the slightest. In her mind the whole deal at Skythorpe was part of an Imbratta plot to nail us. It was a subtle, far-reaching diabolical plot, she insisted. *"There were wheels within wheels."*

I could see that Mara was in a snit, so instead of jawboning with her I just let her ramble on. It was as though she'd gone back in time, from modern America to the folklore of her native Chile. She said she was doomed, that her *"death warrant was signed and sealed."* She said that wicked people like Guccio Imbratta *"have wicked gods they pray to,"* and that these wicked gods have special ways of getting things done, *"loopholes or no loopholes."*

I asked why, with all these dark powers at work, she and I were still among the living, but obviously she'd given this some thought.

"They don't just want us dead. They want us to die in agony. They want to prolong the torture. They want us to love each other and know what we are losing."

This rattled my china. It was just like it'd been before. I didn't agree with Mara, but there was this way she said things—her deep whisper, her eyes full of urgent dismay—that made you half-believe the strangest things. It also made Mara damn sexy, in a film noir sort of way. I wanted to gather her in my arms right then, and God knows I should have. But Desmond Ruck was in a hurry. It was May Day, and my strength was back. Las Vegas was 15 hours of map-time away. With luck we could make it by midnight.

As we stowed our gear for departure, we talked about the Hauck business, and there was less disagreement. We'd both read about deals like this in the papers. San Lorenzo College might be a genuine article—a right-wing Christian-mill—but it was also a protective front for Myrdal Hwang's institute and clinic, which were themselves fronts for Doctor Hauck's biological experiments and the drug operation. Peel back one more layer and I bet you find the oriental warlord himself, using drug money to buy weapons, and paying Hauck to get him eternal life.

The Most Amazing Thing

It's just that Mara took it far beyond this. According to Mara, Hwang's drug connection was a sign of his link with the Imbrattas!

Turns out she was probably right.

I'm going to have trouble writing this. But maybe I can write some of the horror out of me.

We pulled out of the Deer Mountain Campgrounds at about 8:30 AM. We were headed for Rte 36 back to Denver, which was the best way of hitting I-70 again, given the snow in the mountain passes. This would take us through downtown Estes Park, which was convenient, because Mara wanted a decent breakfast before the long haul to Vegas. It was a gorgeous morning, with the sun shouting in our faces and melting the roadside snow.

We parked near the Brewery, set up the litter box for Paws and then pieced our way among tourists, mountain bikers and skateboarders, down the sunny street to the creekside mall, where she picked out an eatery called Freda's Fresh Feeds. Mara was in an upbeat mood, but none of this was my idea of a good time. I didn't like being so far away from the Vixen, and this eatery looked like one of those incense-reeking vegetarian money-mills where fat yuppies congratulate each other on their high morals while they dope up on peasant-exploiting espresso.

That's exactly what it was, with a few added attractions. The little dining room was sauna-hot and smelling of burnt sandalwood, and the walls were matted with limp ivy, and the stereo was playing a CD of humpback whale love songs.

Only two tables were busy, but they were really rocking. At one of them, which was piled high with steaming tofu, a clutch of dark-bearded men in pink turbans were having a prayer meeting. At the other table, nearby, were five florid real-estate-type women who, every thirty seconds or so, would all start snorting and barking and gagging with laughter.

In the midst of all this, Mara and I sat across a tiny table from each

106

other, eating potato pancakes and feeling in love. Above the din of turbans praying and female cackling and humpbacks humping, Mara asked me what we should do for starters when we got to Vegas.

I thought for a second, then answered, "We check into a big hotel, maybe the one that's shaped like a pyramid, and start behaving like the other rich nobodies that Vegas is full of. Tomorrow AM I'm off to the bank with our cash and to the stockbrokers with our securities. Once the account or accounts are in place, we get rid of the Vixen and disappear. We can't disappear out of the country without passports, but we can disappear almost as much inside the States, by finding a few acres in the wilderness or hiding somewhere in the California suburban sprawl. Holed up there, we check newspapers for developments and hope for none. After a year or two of that, we can go where we want and do what we want."

"*But what do we want?*" she whispered earnestly, as though that question had to be answered before anything else.

I was fumbling for an answer, trying to think of a plain manly way to tell Mara that I wanted to live with her forever, when she ran out of patience and rose and excused herself for the Ladies' Room. She stood and paused for a second, looking at me, and I read the same look in her eyes I'd seen once or twice, the sweet-and-sour look, the *Why Do I Love Such A Dunce?* look.

Then she was gone.

It hadn't been ten seconds when I heard a Godawful burst of laughter, together with a strange hissing noise. I looked up to see that things had turned ugly between the turbaned men and the laughing ladies. The men, who all had their hands clasped in prayer, were vehemently hissing the women, who it turned out had been laughing all the while at *them*, and the ladies had their own hands cupped in mock prayer and were red-faced and convulsed in laughter. This was too much for the mullah who sat directly facing them. He rose to his feet, picked up something from his plate — it was some kind of tofuburger — and hurled it right at the women's table. The tofuburger landed smack in the middle of a jumbo bowl of café au lait, splattering all the women.

That's when the restaurant exploded. It was the strangest and most terrible coincidence I've ever seen, but just at that moment, when the rowdy women were rising from their table to take revenge on their turbaned foes—it was almost as though some god wanted to punish these kooks just for being kooks—but right at that moment there's a terrific BOOM from the kitchen, and an explosive wave of hot air smashes all of us, and the whole back wall of the dining room buckles outward like a cardboard cereal box.

A screaming cook with her hair on fire runs in from the kitchen right at me and, suddenly on my feet, I soak the cook's head with our pitcher of ice water and rush past her into the kitchen.

The right-hand kitchen wall has blown away and I can see clear through the restrooms, which have lost their outer wall. Both rooms are empty. The air is still and the stench of chemicals is suffocating.

Too scared to breathe, I race through the restrooms into the alley. No Mara! But there's her scarf on the pavement half a block away, and beyond it, just taking off into traffic, is the unmistakable shape and color of

The same ancient wicked VW bug that had tailed us in Indiana!

Mara was right! And now they had her.

Next thing I was running after the car. The street was clogged with traffic and I could hear sirens coming, but the sidewalk was pretty clear and people shrank back as I thundered by. About the middle of the second block, a kid passed me from behind on a mountain bike that was grossly too big for him. I grabbed the bottom of the bike's seat and held on. It stopped real fast.

I said, "Sonny, I need that bike."

He looked up at me in a funk. "Sure, sir," he stammered. "I didn't know—" Before I could offer money he jumped off the bike and took off at a gallop down the street.

He'd stolen the damn bicycle himself!

I jumped on the bike and left rubber. I used sidewalks to get around the motor traffic, just as the kid had. The bike, a dual suspension jobbie, was nearly big enough for me and perfect for curb-hopping and the like. As I cleared the center of town I glimpsed the VW turning out of traffic onto an uphill road to the right and disappearing around a curve. In about three minutes I'd made it up to the intersection and a sign that read MACPHERSON ROAD/TO DEMON'S GULCH.

Puffing like crazy I swept through the curve on the shoulder and engaged mid-range with the front derailleur. The next grade was tough. The little road was taking me right up to the base of those mammoth piles of boulders they call the Lumpy Mountains. I recognized it from the map—MacPherson Road led along the range to the north, then after a few miles fell off through Demon's Gulch and met 34 to the east. My chest was busting and the rest of me was a web of pain, but I was still thinking, *this VW's got to be heading for somewhere on MacPherson Road—otherwise they could've taken 34 right out of Estes Park!*

This meant I hadn't all that far to go.

Just as I cleared the crest, the road turned eastward toward the morning sun, and every square inch of me burst into a sweat. The mix of glare and dripping sweat blurred my vision, but I shifted into the high range and the rush of air began to dry my face. I had my second wind now, and a few miles of level riding ahead. The Death Bug had disappeared, and MacPherson Road was empty. To the right, hay fields sloped down to a line of aspen that probably hedged a creek. To the left was the base of the Lumpies, which towered and glowered like an avalanche waiting to happen. No driveways, no side roads, no traffic. I could hear thrushes sing, and the buzz of my cleated tires on the pavement.

It was like that for about five miles. I'd clear run out of valley, and was beginning to freewheel down into the Gulch, when I saw the hotel.

I'd just rounded a turn when I saw it. It came on me like a nasty surprise. I don't believe I've ever seen anything as desolate. It was a mammoth old Victorian pile, dingy white with a great black mansard roof that had a lantern-like tower at the top, and the building clung so close to the steep slope that some of its walls seemed to press against the rock itself. Its countless windows were boarded up, except for a few that were like open black wounds, like the eyes in a Death's Head.

There was a big chainlink fence all around this wreck of a hotel, except where it backed up to the mountain. But somewhere there had to be a hole in the fence, because there was a little huddle of cars, pickups and ATVs near the garages over to the left.

And sure enough the VW was among them. I'd arrived.

At this point a few ideas might have come to me. I might have noticed that the people who took Mara were there in force, while I was only one unarmed man. I might have considered biking back to Estes Park for the law. It might have struck me that I'd been through a number of hairy scrapes in the last ten days, and that maybe I'd better quit while I was ahead.

But not a single one of those ideas occurred to me that fine morning. Instead of reasoning logically, I was just remembering the cockeyed look Mara'd given me before leaving the table. I was just thinking, if you can call it thinking, that she was part of my life and I wasn't about to let go of her.

I biked downhill and around the property. About a hundred yards down, just in front of the old formal entrance to the grounds ("PEN-UMBRA HOTEL, HISTORIC SITE"), was a metal gate chained shut with chainlinks the size of your fist. But I could see mud tracks on the road coming from further downhill, and sure enough, just past a little stand of Jeffrey pine, somebody'd cut the fence so that enough of it could be pulled out to get a pickup through.

I slipped in and hid the bike among the pines.

My plan was to sneak into the hotel and find Mara without a big commotion, so I began working my way to the right behind an overgrown hedge, hoping to enter the hotel through a window at the far side. But a strange place lay right in my path. It was a little round clearing ringed by cypress trees. What it'd been I don't know—maybe a place to dance— the slate paving was worn in places. But at this moment, with its ghostly trees and the old hotel looming above them and the cruel mountain above that, it seemed especially grim, and I shivered, even in the bright spring sun.

I'd gotten to the middle of the courtyard when the sky darkened. I looked up to see that a great big cumulus cloud, like the ones you see late in summer, had inched across the sun. Rain coming?

When I looked down again I wasn't alone any more.

All around me, in the courtyard just inside the cypress trees, stood a circle of big gray wolves. How they'd gotten there so fast I haven't a clue. It was unreal. They stood there motionless and silent, with all eyes on me, and the eyes were distant and intelligent and commanding, without a glint of friendship or recognition. I was paralyzed. I marvelled at them. They weren't like your normal seedy zoo wolf, hangdoggedly prowling his cell. These were magnificent animals with lustrous bushy fur, as brawny as if each of them had just eaten the lion's share of a moose. Their calm stillness and steely gray eyes suggested utter control. They had more presence than as many people.

And just as suddenly there was a woman standing among the wolves. At first I thought that one of the animals had somehow *become* a woman, but she must've been standing behind a tree and come out when I wasn't looking. She was tall and thin, clad in a sewn-together rabbit skin cloak, and she had straight gray shoulder-length hair and a young and angry face. She was stock-still, leaning on a hefty wooden staff and glaring at me like a picture of Fate. In the seconds she stood there her burning dark eyes must've killed me in seven different ways.

Then, without saying a word, she motioned me to follow her. The wolves fell into line in front of and behind me. I was so near them that I could smell the woodsy freshness of their coats, thinking all the while that at any moment one of these splendid creatures might develop an irresistible yen for one of my extremities and lop it off with a single chomp. But they didn't so much as growl, as we entered the hotel through a side door, marched through the empty ground floor and up the wide main staircase.

I shambled up the stairs, feeling like a fool. *How was I going to rescue Mara, now that I was wolf-chow?*

Near the second floor the wolves began some nasty muttering, but soon I saw that it wasn't at me. There were two armed men on the landing up there, guarding a line of shut doors. The men were burly and hairy and dressed the way a ranch hand might dress, except that these honchos were encrusted with pistol holsters and hunting knives, and each of them held a wicked-looking M-16 rifle. No question, there was bad blood between these lads and Wolf-Lady, because the beasts kept growling, and the men had them in their gun sights all the time we were passing, except when one of the men took aim at me and snarled to his partner, "Howsabout we bag the big one, Varrick? There's an empty spot by the farplace."

"Dincha know I jess do laydies?" roared the other, and both of them laughed Ha Ha as our little band headed up to the third floor. "See ya tonight, beeyatch!" he shouted at my guide.

As we climbed, Wolf-Lady without looking back spoke to me for the first time in a high voice that seemed hung up between loathing and fear, "He's not kidding, slimeball. Those monsters *stuff* people."

I asked, "Then why do you hang out with them?"

"Because Our Beloved is here," she hissed. "He is their lord and ours."

Who was Our Beloved? I didn't dare ask.

Hearing us talk to each other must've made an effect on the wolves, because when we got to the third floor landing, and met two more of the animals who were standing guard, all the beasties crowded around me and started busily sniffing my trousers with their great vacuum-cleaner noses. I wouldn't call them exactly friendly, but they must've finally decided I wasn't something Wolf-Lady had brought home as a family snack. Now everybody wanted to know more about me, and maybe in particular about Paws, whose smell must have been all over my trousers.

But they didn't get much chance, because there was a noise of heavy locks opening behind a pair of double doors, and the doors sprang open and the wolves brushed roughly past me and swarmed into the dark room beyond. I went in too, followed by Wolf-Lady, who was prodding me with her wooden staff.

She closed the doors behind me, and I stood blinking in the darkness. At first I couldn't see, but I was sure it was a large space, with wolves' and women's voices coming hollowly from many directions, and it smelled of lamp oil, old bedding, incense and wolf. There were excited squeals from one direction, as a mother wolf, probably, returned to its whelps. Then all at once I could see a monster room, maybe 100′ by 50′, with its windows all boarded up, and lit by a scattering of frontier-style oil lamps. At the far end was a big fireplace, bordered on each side by what looked like old-fashioned naval cannon. Wolf-Lady and I were standing on a kind of low stage that looked down the length of the room, and I could see that there'd been a number of thatched huts built right inside it, in three rows. Several of the women stood outside of their respective huts, watching me, and each of the wolves sat by a separate hut. All in all it looked like a Girl Scout campout held in the school gym because of rain, excepting as there'd been no rain, and these dames would have gagged on the Scout Oath.

There were two big bathtubs near the stage, both occupied. One lady, who stood outside of the tub, was shampooing another lady's hair, while to the right a gal was shampooing a wolf (so much for the animals' fresh woodsy smell!). The washers at first seemed naked, but then I could make out something black strapped around each of their groins—those artificial erect penises you see at sex-novelty stores. That touch made the scene just perfect!

But as the sisters became aware of me everything—shampooing included—stopped dead, and those seated rose to their feet, and they all stood silently gawking at me, as if I were some kind of sideshow freak. Me, the only normal person in the room! Yet to them I was strange, and they burned it into me, until Wolf-Lady, who seemed to be some sort of leader, shrieked out in her high voice, "Sisters! I am bidden to speak!"

The wolf-shampooer, who had a rich contralto that rang through the room, demanded, "You're going to speak, Ould Chattox, in front of Mr. Wonderful here?"

There was much noise of disagreement, together with the baying of three or four wolves. Finally it was agreed that Wolf-Shampooer, who was called Nurse Gowdie, should "fix" me before anything else went on. Nurse Gowdie approached me, saucy as you like, a fine figure of a woman with big breasts, lightly freckled shoulders and rich flowing red hair. She menaced me with her eyes as she approached, and her strapped-on penis waggled impudently with each stride. Her wolf followed, trailing bathwater and shampoo.

Nurse Gowdie stopped about three feet away from me and, facing me, started making cat's-cradle motions with both hands and chanting something in Latin. It all dawned on Bright Boy then. This was a genuine witches' coven—I hadn't known they really existed!

It also dawned on me that Nurse Gowdie was supposed to be putting me into a trance. This struck me as a good idea, so I waited for her to reach a crescendo and then did one of those backward ass-flops we used in college basketball to draw a charge and convince the ref we'd been fouled. There was a big THUMP as my rump hit the stage, and I managed to end up on my back with my head propped up against the far wall.

I hadn't closed my eyes.

The other witches applauded Gowdie and started wildly laughing as Gowdie's wolf took that opportunity to shake water and foam over everybody nearby. Even though a wad of foam hit me smack on the nose, I stayed coffin-still, listening in on what turned out to be a satanic town meeting.

I'll tell you I got such an earful that I'm almost not sure what to mention first. From Old Chattox's and her sisters' rantings and ravings, I gathered that group called itself the Lupus Coven and the wolves, who were named Gibbe, Hattock, Jannicot, Hern, Pyewackit, Pharaoh and the like, were each supposed to be the familiar spirit or demon attached to each witch for life. The witches' Grand Master was known to the women as Our Beloved and lived in the lantern-like tower on the roof. Our Beloved was supposed to be some kind of god, and it's pretty clear that each of the ladies was on X-rated terms with him.

Also, it so happened that Our Beloved was the big enchilada of the survivalist clan who lived below; they called him Saint Crivellius and themselves the Crivellian Risen.

How Beloved/Crivellius could have appealed so much to both groups beat me, because the two groups disagreed on everything else. The Lupus Coven were into astrology, vegetarianism, free love and everything else New Age, and I'll bet they were season-ticket holders at Freda's Fresh Feeds. The Crivellians were hard-line neo-fascists who'd probably bombed the place. But the spark that lit the tinder was reproductive rights. The Coven's Pro-Choice position went along with the their fierce independence and their penchant for sex. The Crivellians were Pro-Life, so Pro-Life that they would kill for it. Their idea of Hog Heaven was to abduct an abortion doctor and his whole staff, and kill them and stuff them, but they hadn't been able to manage this as yet, thanks to problems in logistics.

What was Our Beloved/Saint Crivellius's take on this hot-button issue? The great leader had maintained a demonic silence, saying only, "All things in their time."

But this uneasy standoff was crumbling. The Coven held their May Eve Sabbat last night, and the Risen disrupted it with beery insults. Our Beloved himself couldn't quell the riot, even though he threatened to "rain thunder down" on anybody who bucked him. Especially uppity was an unholier-than-thou Crivellian named Reuben Sauers, who shouted that the Risen would be back on May Day, in full metal jackets.

Any fool could see that Our Beloved was losing his control over the Risen and that they were fixing to settle the witches' hash real soon. In her powerful contralto, Nurse Gowdie sounded the call to arms. "Lupine sisters! Beware of the Crivellians! They've talked the talk and they'll walk the walk! They're a bigoted malodorous uncivilized horde, and they don't respect our difference, and they'd curb our liberties and enslave our precious bodies to their foul practices, and they will stuff us for their unthinkable iconographies! Alarm! Alarm! Beware of them, for they will come on us in numbers! They raise the obscene symbol and pray to the hated name! Woe to the Crivellians! Drink to Liberty! Arouse thy beasts! Prepare thy weapons!"

Then somebody banged a gong, and the witches broke for lunch. At one big table there began a general devastation of watercress sandwiches, while at another the women started swilling a mix of Southern Comfort and canned cappuccino out of pint schooners. In preparation for battle, the Coven was tying one on!

I was famished and stiff and wanted to pee, but I kept on faking the trance.

PART TWO: DIES IRAE

The witches ate and drank and sang and shouted and raved for what seemed like hours. When they reconvened, they were a raucus caucus, drunken and disagreeable. The bone of contention and group debate was what they were going to do with Mr. Wonderful, that is, with me. A few different plans were submitted, roughly as follows:

PLAN A. Ould Demdike, who'd mixed the drinks, asserted that I'd make a terrific stud stallion—what with Our Beloved recently begging off his sexy duties and complaining of stress and fatigue (did His Godship have a case of Erectile Dysfunction?)—and that I should be treated like one of the wolves and kept around indefinitely.

PLAN B. A loud faction in back wanted me hanged by the neck until I got a gallows erection, then communally raped, then butchered and thrown to, I mean really thrown to, the wolves, except for my penis, which was to be frozen and used now and then as a ritual pestle.

PLAN B, Alternate Motion. Ould Redfearn applauded this suggestion with a loud toast to her sisters' "thumping buttocks" but submitted the alternate motion that, instead of being frozen, my member should be freeze-dried and then ground into a powder, to be used as a fertility drug, together with various herbal mixtures.

PLAN C. An unruly type named Jonnet, who was stripping to the buff as she spoke and revealing some bodacious tattoos, said that was all nonsense, and that I'd do the most communal good if I was buried alive, and pointing straight down, by the front door of the hotel, as a preventive against botched abortions. At this the group broke into three or four local squabbles, and the wolves started up baying.

It looked like the women and animals were going to give each other some major grief, when the door behind me creaked open. Everybody suddenly went silent. There was a shadow cast over me, and I felt chilled. A massive dark presence strode into my line of sight.

I tell you I haven't seen a man this big in years, except for me. He was up to here in black leather, which stretched where his muscles bulged, and this blackness was topped off—his back was still towards me—by a bushel of black hair, dank and curly, that hung down to his shoulders. He stood silently, his brawny arms stretched sideways as if to make him a human cross, until somebody must have drawn his attention to me lying behind him, and then he turned to look down at me.

I didn't bat an eyelash, but his face branded my eyes. It was the most evil face I've ever seen. Evil not from having anything deformed, like

The Most Amazing Thing

Art Thrumble's face, nor by looking blankly malignant, like Dr. Hauck. Evil by expressing, in every feature, heinous blatant self-indulgence. Our Beloved was obviously some sort of racial mix. His pockmarked skin was halfway between black and white, and he had a big eagle-hook nose that could have been Arab or Jewish or Italian or Welsh and sensually half-closed eyes that would have looked oriental if it hadn't been for their WASP-like cold blueness. His ears were hidden in thick hair, as if they didn't exist at all, and hanging lazily open under a pirate's mustache was an atrociously large mouth, a mouth lined with thumbnail-sized yellow tobacco-washed teeth, a mouth framed by taut dark brutally emphatic thin lips themselves lavishly festooned with demagogic spittle, a mouth that seemed like a blind sea-monster with a life of its own, waiting to gorge itself or spew out curse words or bite your ass.

And on top of that, or rather just below, this dude was a walking jewelry shop. His motorcycle jacket was blazing and jangling with brass pins in different shapes. As he stood there, leering down at me, I spotted the Nazi swastika, the Peace Symbol, the Native American calumet, the Star of David, the Islamic crescent and scimitar, the Irish clover, the Soviet hammer and sickle, the crucifix, the French and Italian tri-colors, and, biggest of all, the Great Seal of the United States of America, together with trinkets from other countries and states, the gay community, the anti-gays, Pro-life, Pro-choice, environmentalists and lumbermen, as well as military units, colleges, trade unions and pro athletic teams. If his jacket was any sign, Our Beloved believed in, or pandered to, every cause in Creation.

But even wilder than what was on this jacket was what was under it. No question about it: this giant of a man had woman's boobs—by far the biggest pair I've ever seen—pushing out against the jacket like blunderbusses, as though they were competing for attention with what was pinned onto it. Whether they were real or not I hadn't a clue, but I can tell you, I didn't mean to find out.

Our Beloved must have been cocksure that I wasn't a threat, because he turned around again and harangued the Coven. You won't imagine his voice or way of speaking unless you've been near a major logging operation and heard a heavy-duty chainsaw snarling its way through big tree-trunks. Just like that big chainsaw, he alternately rumbled and whined. His voice had a wide range from low to high, and when he was in low, the words rolled out slowly, like cannonballs on a marble floor, but when he was in high they sputtered out fast as a tommy gun. He spoke in anger, and after each exclamation the body of witches swayed and hissed like palms in a typhoon. It was all in Latin, but this time I recognized a couple of phrases that put me in mind of his general drift. "Dies irae, Babylon magna mater fornicationum": the words could have come from a Christian sermon! In his lowest voice he kept using the phrase "turbo lapidum" like a weapon against the witches, and every time it caused them to wail and their wolves to howl.

I didn't understand much Latin but I hadn't the slightest doubt what was happening. Our Beloved was turning against the Coven. He'd left off leading their orgies and was now roasting them for their sins. What could be in the works? Had he made a pledge to the Risen? Had his own sexual impotence produced an onrush of PC?

I'll probably never know, given what happened then. Just as Our Beloved was ripping his way through an especially nasty stretch of fire and brimstone, there was a terrific din from the stairwell. I raised and turned my head to see the doors burst open and one, then another, ATV roar into the room, bestridden by Risen members in crash helmets. All hell broke loose as other Risen militia followed on foot, firing assault weapons in the air.

I looked around for Our Beloved but he'd vanished, as though in a puff of smoke. I was fixing to copy that act, but two of the Risen were too quick for me, and before I knew it I was roped around the legs and drawn clean across the stage to the ATVs, hitched to the back of one of them and, as the other Risen held off the coven, dragged on my back into the hallway and down the stairs. That trip by itself came near killing me, except that the ATV couldn't handle the stairs very fast, so I was able, by straining and craning upward, to keep from bashing my head on each stair, but the stink and noise of the ugly little motor were almost too much to take.

Passing the stairwell window, I could see that it was getting dark.

Downstairs they dragged me into their headquarters, and I was no sooner inside the Risen's lair than the other ATV barrelled in, hot on our heels. The doors were shut and heavy bolts rammed home. The light was almost blinding. From where I was on the floor I couldn't see much besides the bright fluorescent ceiling lights, but I could hear helmets being unbuckled and the unmistakable noise of beer cans opening.

I heard somebody give a command, and a man who looked all hair and smelled of puke leaned down, frisked me and loosened the ropes on my legs. Then they let me stand up. I towered over them, but that didn't keep me from being scared shitless.

I was ringed by a scruffy lot of ten or twelve men, some in jeans and cowboy shirts, some in motorcycle outfits and some in what looked like makeshift uniforms. What they all shared was at least two guns apiece, an awful lot of hair, an aroma of armpit and stale cigarette smoke, and eyes that looked haunted and obsessed. The one who was giving commands was little more than a kid, a blond kid who resembled those romantic paintings they used to do of Jesus Christ. This must be the famous Reuben Sauers.

"Herman," he ordered, "get Dumbo here a brew." Pukesmell obliged.

I asked if I could go and piss. "Sure thing," said Reuben. "Condemned men always get their wishes." I parked my beer on a counter. We were in a large kitchen area, and as Herman marched me to the john I passed piled cases of beer and canned hash and spaghetti. The john opened right off the kitchen, and Herman let me go in by myself.

120

I blinked. Unlike the galley, the bathroom was hardly lit up at all, with nothing but a single flickering fluorescent light.

As I headed for the toilets I saw that I wasn't alone. A man dressed as a cowboy was standing at the group urinal, his back to me. I walked right up next to him and started pissing, but all at once it struck me as weird that somebody'd be pissing here when I hadn't seen anybody leave the galley.

I turned and looked at him and froze. He wasn't alive. He wasn't dead. He wasn't even a man anymore. He was stuffed. On his flannel shirt was a badge that said Tanabe County Sheriff's Deputy. His cock protruded through his fly. His head was bent intently, the way a guy does when he's being careful not to miss his target. Except that for eyes he had white marbles.

Trying to finish up, I suddenly thought of Our Beloved's speech. *This place is damned. Fury will rain upon it.*

Outside the door was Herman, making through his mass of facial hair a faint whimpering noise that was probably his idea of a laugh. He pushed me to the left with his pistol and marched me back through the galley, which was now empty, into a room that was just as bright but much bigger. It must have been a combination living space, because the far wall was lined with bunk beds, while right in the middle was a big wooden table, and this table was piled high with guns and six-packs, and the Risen were standing around it, hollering at each other and popping more cans of beer.

I glanced at the other end of the room. To the right was a long row of boarded-up windows. To the left was a hearth and what looked like another group of partying people. But this time I knew what to expect. Herman, gun in hand, proudly walked me over to them. The females were eerily real. They were all prostitutes, with a couple of madams, and they were all done up to the gills, as though ready for business. One of the girls was about to light a cigarette, with her head cocked and her thumb on the serrated wheel of her Zippo. Another, in a pink see-through gown, was leaning against the hearth, pensively toying with a lock of her own platinum hair. Yet another, with riveting dark eyes, was frozen in the act of seductively brushing the left strap of her yellow chiffon nightgown off her shoulder. One of the madams, dressed in bright red, had her right arm raised towards you with the index finger curled, and she was grinning and winking, as if to say Howdy, come on in. The other madam, a heavy woman, was sitting on a bidet, with one hand holding a washcloth between her fat veinous thighs, and her outsized panties lying on her patent leather shoes.

The women all smelled of institutional soap and cheap perfume. I stood there gaping at them. Even the desperate danger I was in couldn't keep me from being yanked by uncontrollable feelings. The Risen had *killed* those women, *murdered* them. Imagine the colossal gall!! And just to set them up again, real as life, with hatefully excellent art. *Why?*

Well, why do hunters stuff animals, like the Thrumbles' Snarling Bear?

I guess, to steal their power.

Herman goaded me with his pistol, trying to push me away from the prostitutes and on to the next group of stuffed people, but instead of budging I asked him what the Risen were fighting for.

He went purple under his beard and got flustered and waved his piece in the air. "The flounders!" he squealed.

"Flounders?"

"I sayd *founders*, yasshole. Jefferson an' Davis. The flounders sayd evurbodees got the rot to life, an' we can tayk liburtees with our god-given waypuns. It's guaranteed by the bill of rots! How'd I know? Saint Crivellius himself says so, Gudfuckya, an' so does Yankee Doodle Dandy, an' so do the Father an' the Wooly Ghost. They all say we got four rootin' tootin' crackerjack rots, the rot to free speech, the rot to bear arms, the rot to remain silent an' the rot to a shyster jewboy. Now suck on that, buggerbuns. Lookee here!"

Before I could say a word he prodded me on. To the right of the prostitutes and madams was a bunch of stuffed men. There was an Air Force private, always saluting, a couple of snotty-looking businessmen in suits, a balding professor in turtleneck shirt, tweed jacket and khaki pants and a balder Franciscan monk, smiling blissfully, with his eyes shut and his hands together in prayer. These were much shoddier efforts done up than the females—stiff, wooden, more like student jobs—and from the way Herman was behaving, they were his own work.

But at the far right was something way beyond Herman's artistic powers. It was a County Sheriff. He was tall, though a little stooped over, and he wore mudcaked black boots, jeans with a silver-buckled belt, a faded denim shirt and a tired-looking suede vest with mother-of-pearl buttons. Under the dusty broad-brimmed Stetson his face was tan and deeply lined, but you could tell at a glance that the lines weren't just from stress but also from loving and laughing. The guy had been around and taken his knocks, but he liked his work. The set of the mouth, the firm gray eyes, gave him a look of quiet resolution. He reminded me of what the Rev had said about his friend MacCrae—he looked like a good man.

This sheriff was frozen in the act of drawing his gun. His left arm was bent slightly out in front of him as though to protect his midsection; his right hand was drawing a hefty six-shooter out of a big black holster on his belt.

I bet he looked just that way when the Risen wasted him with their Uzis.

Above the uproar I heard Sauers's squeaky voice shouting to Herman, who then pushed me back toward his gang. While I'd been getting my guided tour, the Risen were arming themselves to the teeth and now, topped up with beer and bristling with semi-automatics, they were on their way upstairs to kick ass at the Coven. The Risen seemed to have no plan or organization for the attack at all—they were just going to ram the doors with their ATVs and blow away every woman and wolf in sight.

The only question was what to do with Dumbo. A bunch of them wanted to gun me down right then, but Sauers nixed that, saying he had "other ideas" about how to whack me and when.

Sauers decided to leave me with Herman and the Peacemaker, as Herman called his .45 magnum pistol. After the gang left he kept it pointing at me and told me to open a can of beer for him as we stood facing each other on the hearth-side of the big table. As he swilled beer and I pondered ways of getting the drop on him, we listened to the battle going on above. It sounded like the Coven had a little surprise in store for the Risen, because the noise of the ATVs as they splintered through the doors was cut short by a pair of large-bore explosions, followed by the rattle of small-arms fire and more big explosions.

The witches must have loaded those old naval cannon they kept by the fireplace and set up a barricade back there. No matter who, if anybody, won it, this battle was going to take time.

But Herman kept his little black burning eyes on me like a snake. You can imagine he was a bit worked up, not being invited to the battle. Turns out he was pissed off at more than that. In half-human half-sentences he explained to me that it was he, Herman, who'd stuffed all the male figures by the hearth (except the Sheriff which, along with the Deputy, Herman's now-dead father had done), while Herman's brother Varrick had done the females ("all the wumfolk studmuffins"). Now Varrick was going to get to do all the witches they bagged ("'bout a hunred") and Sauers had said that Varrick would stuff me too ("cause of him been' gyuder at it").

As Herman sputtered and whined about this unbearable insult to his pride, I saw I had a homicidal maniac on my hands. This point was driven home in full force when he shifted the revolver to his left hand, reached towards the table and grabbed a Japanese military sword. He raised said sword over his head unsteadily, hissed, "Varrick ain't gwine to do nothing nohow with you, pretty boy, 'cause I'm gwine to *rune* you. There won't be *anythin'* of you left for Varrick to patch together!" and staggered towards me, flailing away with the saber.

It was then or never. With my left hand I grabbed his hand and the sword-handle, and at the same time my right hand went for his left wrist. Both weapons clattered on the floor. I gave Herman a shove to send him towards the stuffed figures and away from the weapons on the table, but on the way he fell backwards over a case of spaghetti and lay still.

I took a small pearl-handled revolver from the table and put it in my jacket pocket and ran over to the bank of windows. I had a straight shot at escape now, but that's not why I'd come to the hotel in the first place. I'd earned the name Dumbo by walking unarmed into a rat's nest, and now I had to go upstairs and drop in on the Chief Rat.

Why? *Because Mara had to be up there.*

But how? What with the Risen/Coven battle raging, the central stairwell wasn't an option. There might be staircases at the end of each wing, but I didn't have time to go exploring. I hadn't any choice but to try to exit out a window and scramble up to the roof.

I strode to the nearest window and kicked and battered away its boards. As the cold mountain air rushed in, I leaned through it and looked out and around. No ledges, ladders or railings. I climbed up to where my feet were on the sill, and held on hard to the lintel with my left hand and reached outward and upward with my right for the lip of the raingutter. At full extension I found it. All stretched out like that I couldn't test it, and in fact it felt shaky, but I really had no choice, so I held onto it for dear life, swung myself into space and grabbed the metal gutter with my left hand.

With an awful groaning noise the raingutter parted from the siding, and I began going down. I thought I was in for a quick trip to the ground, but this gutter stuff was old-fashioned heavy-duty copper, and instead of breaking clean off, the point of attachment above was just slowly bending. It stopped groaning and bending about a quarter of the way down, and now my way up to the roof was actually easier than before, because I could work my way up a diagonal that was a good deal shallower than a sliding pond.

In less than two minutes I was standing on a firm section of gutter next to the roof, which was a mansard number with a sharply-angled border about eight feet high supporting a level main section. I latched onto the ridge at the top of the border and hoisted myself up. There was the lantern-tower, only a hundred feet away. The lights were on.

The shooting continued downstairs.

I made my way towards the tower. Anger and fear flirted with each other in my gut. My legs trembled, but continued to carry me forward.

At least this time I was armed.

The tower had large multi-paned banks of windows on each of its four sides. The windows were above my head, so I walked around the place looking for the service door that had to be there. I found it on the mountain side of the tower. Before trying it I looked up at the mountain. In the moonlight it loomed like a monster ready to leap on me.

The door was unlocked.

I opened it and felt my way up a dark narrow staircase. At the top was another door like the first. I pulled the revolver and blundered in.

I was in a big room, Persian-carpeted and lit from the walls by candles on tall stands. Between the candles all around the walls were potted palms in Mexican ceramic urns. The many-paned windows that I'd seen from outside stretched on three sides of me, but the far end of the room was blocked off by two curtains hanging from the vaulted roof. There was no furniture to speak of, except for a tatami mat and low table crammed with liquor bottles. The second-floor stairwell opened to the middle of the floor.

Too much! I thought. Our Beloved, master of all causes lives in an empty room!

126

The air was strangely warm, as though the full heat of the spring day had floated up through the stairwell. The din of battle continued from downstairs.

Something at my feet caught my eye. It was Mara's taviz, lying next to the tatami mat. I grabbed it with my free hand and pocketed it. But in that moment my world changed. *The fallen taviz shouted to me that Mara was dead.*

I first felt, then looked up and saw him. Across the room, in a dark triangle formed by the parting curtains, stood Our Beloved. His body seemed still but got bigger and bigger, until I realized that he was walking towards me with a pace so steady that he seemed to be floating. As he passed the stairwell, I held up the gun for him to see I was armed, but he kept coming. Our Beloved was smiling. I pointed the rod at him and pulled the trigger, but just like in one of those dreams there was no explosion, only click, click.

As he covered the final yards, and I kept going click, click, I felt fear like you'll never believe. By the time he knocked the gun from my hand my legs were Jell-o and a mere slap on the face sent me tumbling to the floor. I nearly fainted of fright, but by reflex action I struggled to my hands and knees, and at that point he pulled me up by my hair and caught me in a headlock so powerful I thought he'd put me out of my misery then and there, and almost wished he would.

He roared, "Trying to shoot me with my own gun, Wunderkind? You should be so lucky." I couldn't speak. He pulled me out by the stairwell and tried to throw me down it, but I managed to veer off and catch myself on the railing. In a flash he had me in the headlock again. His voice was hideously loud. "Have a care, laddy, you might fall down and get hurt!" He started walking me towards the curtains. "We don't want you getting hurt before you see your girlie, do we, sweetums? It's time for Show and Tell!" He dragged me between the tapestries. We were now in a continuation of the big room, its far end really, but this part was set up as an operating room, or rather, for taxidermy. It was well lit from above.

He let go of my neck and let me stand up. He'd been blocking my view of the room's middle but now he stepped aside and stood at my right, still facing me.

Mara was lying on her back, stark naked, on a taxidermy table in the middle of the room. Her eyes were closed and she was stone still. Blood had flowed from a slit around the front of her neck, a slit so deep that, like in the Simpson case, you could see an artery, a severed tube, protruding a little. Like somebody in a trance I went up and touched her cheek. Even in the warm air it was clammy and cold.

"I screwed her before I did her," shouted Our Beloved. "Wanna know why, sonny? *'Cause she begged for it!*"

Something went out of me then. It was like Our Beloved had raped and slaughtered *me*, and gotten Herman to *stuff* me for an encore, and suddenly I was standing there without a soul. But as I lost feeling, I lost fear, and when I looked up from the table at Our Beloved, as he stood leering at me in mock sympathy, he wasn't a terrible devil anymore, or even a terrifying man, but just an overgrown perv who'd floated a couple of con-jobs. Our Beloved had lost his vicious charm. Even the outrageous tits didn't fluster me any more.

I measured the distance between us, faked a gesture towards the table and came at him with a long right hand. It was a little like Floyd Patterson's famous leaping left hook, because I felt myself leaving the floor in order to make up for the gap between us. I missed his face but lucked out by catching him in the neck, and I felt the blow with much of my weight behind it smash into soft tissue. My trajectory carried me up against him and we both slipped on something wet and hit the floor with me on top, and it was clear I'd messed up his vocal cords because a great whoosh of voiceless air came out of him when we hit and I was suddenly in a cloud of tobacco, pot, whiskey, beer, garlic and everything else Our Beloved had enjoyed that day. On top of him I struggled to one knee and clumsily tried to pepper him with everything I had, missing mostly but connecting a few times and at last feeling his nose-bone shatter under my fist. Just for good measure I hit him in the same place again.

This beating would have drained the spunk out of your average tough, but Our Beloved was a mega-stud fighting for his life, and as his arms hadn't much purchase he gave his legs a powerful flip and sent me sprawling against the taxidermy table. He was on me before I could get up, and for a few seconds I could feel the blood from his nose dribbling onto my cheek and the breasts pushing that horrific bevy of badges into my chest, but with robotic strength I bench-pressed him up and off to the left, and I heard another whoosh of air as he landed on his side.

Right away we were both up again and squaring off. I landed a couple of good shots and could see that his mammoth boobs were keeping him from crossing a left or a right, and from the way he shook his head to clear it I could tell I was wearing him down. I doubled him over with a body blow and had cocked my right to finish him when BOOM! BOOM!! Two massive explosions shook the hotel. I took it for thunder, but Our Beloved sure didn't, because a look of utter shock crossed his face, followed by one of panic, and he hissed something like, "The fucker's screwed up again."

Then, before I could stop him, he spun around and hot-footed it out through the tapestries.

I was after him in no time and might have caught up with him as he made for the service staircase, except that I was knocked off my feet by a gigantic crash that made the floor throb under us, and he managed to scramble away. That's when I finally got the idea. This had been going to be Our Beloved's revenge against the Coven and the Risen! He'd plotted with somebody to bring the whole mountain down on the hotel, only it was happening too early for him!

I suddenly wanted to save my own life. The soul had gone out of me, but not the animal fire. In fact, I was off like a shot. Our Beloved must've known some fast way across the roof and down by ladder, but rather than follow him I took the main staircase. On the second floor landing I had to hurdle over the bodies of fallen Risen, and also leap across a big hole where a cannon-shell had blown part of the staircase away. I took the rest of the stairs two at a time and stumbled into the big front hall and out through the main doors.

I was just beyond the doors and under the entrance portico when there was a giant CRASH and a hurricane of air pushed me away from the hotel. A great boulder that must have freefallen a thousand feet had hit the building almost dead center, smashing through the roof just beside the tower and destroying some of the hotel's central supports. The back end of the portico smacked down onto the drive like a great hammer-blow just behind me, and I could hear beams groaning like giants in pain as the big old building began to collapse.

But even louder was the hideous explosive rumbling of giant boulders down the mountain. I was almost to the stand of Jeffrey pine near the fence when I heard something like a freight train behind me, and I dodged to the left as a fifteen-foot wide ball of rock, that must have missed the hotel, rampaged past me and walloped into the grove, turning most of it into a mass of fallen trunks and splinters. Luckily my bike was on the other side of the grove and even more luckily the boulder, which came to rest in the middle of the trees, protected me from two other big mothers that'd been playing tag with it.

Amidst this pandemonium I dragged the bike out through the wire fence, staggered onto it and scratched out without sitting down or engaging the toe-clips. The road was clear, mainly because it didn't offer any obstruction to the house-sized boulders that happened to be roaring through. In about a minute I was up the hill and out of danger.

Or so I was thinking, when I saw them. Sitting in a row across the road and blocking my way were seven or eight of the Coven's wolves, their eyes reflecting a terrible orange light from the now-burning hotel. Just off to the left was Ould Chattox the Wolf-Lady. Her right arm was in a makeshift sling, and she was glaring at me much the same way as the wolves. This little welcoming committee wasn't ten feet away, and I'd stopped my bike and was standing astraddle the bar, helpless as a snared hare. Mentally I ran the numbers and didn't like them. It would take me three seconds at least to turn the bike around and start to peddle. It would take them one second to be on me.

Wolf-Lady hissed a ferocious command, and the wolves sprang as one. I braced for their impact but was stunned by a bright streak that I couldn't at first understand. Something big and white had flashed in front of me and stopped the wolves in their tracks, and now it was wreaking havoc among the pack. It was moving so fast on the attack that it was a moment before I could make out that it was itself a wolf, huge, brawny, eerily graceful and white as snow. Its tactics were a sight to behold. It wheeled and bit so fast that it was able to keep the pack together like a bunch of sheep and deal handily with only the two or three in front. Within seconds it was clear that these tactics were paying off. Through fear or, who knows, maybe some sort of wolfish respect for authority, the wolves in back were turning to escape, while the ones in front began to backpedal.

Ould Chattox was standing where she'd been before, but now her face was a mask of terror. She let out a wail to wake the dead and turned tail into the woods. And then it was over in an instant. The white giant, who'd been driving the front wolves back, suddenly pulled up short, and at once its enemies spun around and disappeared after their leader.

I remembered to start breathing again. The white wolf turned and solemnly approached me. It touched my left hand with its great black nose and then looked up at me. We shared a moment of silent communion. In the brightening glow of the fire its eyes—could it be?—were blue-green, like Mara's. They held a million years of wisdom, but more as well. They held compassion.

It was like a religious experience.

I tell you I no more than blinked, and this wolf was gone. I stood there for a few seconds, with chills chasing each other up and down my spine, and then I set out for Estes Park. I stopped only once, to piss, and made it into town about 1 AM. They'd rolled up the sidewalks.

On this day of stark surprises, the Vixen was where I'd left it. I made sure Paws was OK and revved up the diesel. I headed for Route 36 east and took the mountain road at a safe pace, stopping only once, to cry. And I'm crying now, four days later, parked on the north side of Flatirons Park in Boulder.

I miss her.

Chapter Seven **Death in Vegas**

PART ONE: THE BOOK OF LOUIE

FRIDAY, MAY 29, 1998

I'll be indisposed a few more days while Dr. Auchinleck follows up on the reattachment of my right hand.

Writing left-handed is a slow deliberate task that makes you think about what you're writing, which isn't exactly my cup of tea right now, because I'm not sure I want to think about writing, or about anything else.

Because when I think, I think of *her.*

For about a week after surgery, as I lolled around in bed at night half-delirious from painkillers, she was with me a hundred times, either striding in right *through* the closed door, or standing by the bed and holding out a glass of cool water I couldn't quite reach, or hovering in the darkness like a pale golden cloud, or coming in the shape of the white wolf to keep me from reliving a certain majorly horrible event that I'd just gone through, and yesterday I woke with my face cooled by the touch of her tearful cheek.

I swear, she was with me. Then, when the delirium was over, the dreams began, or rather the dream, because there was only one dream, and it played like a hit movie six nights in a row. I was the heavy in this particular movie, and I was brutalizing and killing Mara with my own hands in that foul taxidermy studio on top of the Penumbra hotel. You can bet on it, this dream woke me up every time. I'd wake up cold and shivering and in a sweat, and my arm pumping with pain.

Except yesterday I figured it out and the dreams went away. I figured out that I was making myself the dream-heavy because I was guilty over having involved her in my escape across country in the first place. But no! (I thought) It was I who'd saved her life! The Imbrattas would have killed her if I hadn't taken the van. She knew too much. *Rewrite these paragraphs in short, clear sentences.*

But in another way, I *am* responsible. If only I'd believed Mara when she told me her suspicions. She had a kind of sixth sense. If I hadn't been such a damned fool—*Unfinished sentence. Organize your thoughts better, don't just belch them out.*

Hell, at least I've avenged her.

Dr. Auchinleck described the replantation roughly like this: first they refrigerated my severed hand, so it wouldn't rot out while I was getting prepared for surgery. Then in the operating room Auchinleck cleansed both the hand and the stump and trimmed away damaged tissue. He then transfixed the hand to the stump with temporary metal rods, just to stabilize it. Then he reattached the two main arteries, radial and ulnar, and the two main nerves, median and ulnar, and followed that up with the muscles and veins and skin. There were no bones to reattach, because Our Beloved had struck right at the wrist, "disarticulating" the hand.

All this took the surgeon 9 hours 25 minutes. What a thing! It's so goddamn elegant you'd almost want to have your right hand lopped off by a machete wielded by a maniac in order to have Auchinleck put it back on for you. Almost, but not quite. *Do we really need this paragraph?*

Even more amazing is how I got here, I mean, to Victor Bellows's clinic in the Music Mountains. By rights I should be in the Las Vegas city morgue after being hacked to death in my room at the Tour d'Or, or shrivelled up from parching in the desert. It's almost as though something's protecting me. *Capitalize "something"?*

I should add that Bellows's clinic doesn't specialize in reconstructive surgery. I'm driven into Vegas for that. Bellows' clinic is a kind of sanitarium for non-threatening disorders, cum health spa. There are fifteen or so other patients, who are all pretty well off and treat each other like buddies, the way people do who meet on ocean liners. One of these is Mega Klein, a U of Texas professor who's recovering from something she won't discuss. I told her I was writing, without saying exactly *what* I was writing, and she said she'd like to see it. Why not? Maybe she can help me write better. *What's this, metafiction? How exciting! Let's discuss it over coffee.*

I'll take up my story where I left off, in Boulder, Colorado:

Curse Boulder, Colorado! It's a beautiful town, but rotten at the core. I drove downtown on the night of the 5th to get some toothpaste and some beer. I parked the Vixen on a residential block and walked down 13th towards the mall. I was half a block onto the mall when two mall-rats, or mallrats emeritus—they were both tall men in their thirties— loped past me from the opposite direction. I noticed that they smelled foul, that they were giggling manically and that one of them had a satchel that swang wildly as he ran, but I was too spaced-out on my own woes to give that or anything else much thought. *What woes? Write 'emeritī.'*

I was on the mall about half an hour, finding the toothpaste and the beer. When I got back to the Vixen, I saw that it'd been looted and trashed. It had to be the two mallrats I'd seen, but there was no sign of them anywhere: they'd shimmed the driver's window and glommed up everything they wanted. All the valuables were gone—that is, except the securities, which we'd locked in a hidden compartment near the rear—but they got the briefcase with all the cash, which had been stowed in the loo.

That was the rub, that was the grief. I'd lost a million bucks, but that didn't matter a hang. What mattered was that I lost my gas and food money to get to Vegas. *Don't exaggerate.*

I walked back to the mall, stuck my credit card in an ATM, keyed in my PIN and asked for $50 cash. The screen read ACCESS DENIED, but at least it gave me back my card.

I thought of selling the Vixen, but no way. I'd put the title in the briefcase with the cash.

I thought of bagging the Vegas idea and setting up shop in Denver, but I couldn't stomach it. Anywhere in Colorado was too close for comfort to Our Beloved, if he'd escaped from the hotel and was hankering to renew the acquaintance. Besides, I was still dead set on Vegas as the safest bet for laundering money. *Seven clichés in three sentences! Isn't that laying it on a bit thick?*

I counted my assets: a bottle of mineral water, a can of hash, half a loaf of day-old French bread, a few camping supplies, ten bottles of Wharton's Sour Mash, three fivers in my wallet and enough securities to run the British Empire for a year. I drank the water and ate most of the hash cold and gave the rest to Paws. I revved up the Vixen and said Ciao to Boulder. The tank read almost full. *Now that's a much better paragraph, hard and clear. But you can't 'rev up' a vixen.*

Twenty-five minutes later I was hauling ass on I-70. As I drove I did the math, which was simple and unforgiving. Vegas was over 750 miles away, and the Vixen could truck at 25 mpg, and the tank was near full. With $15 and change, and no money for food or anything else, I could buy 10 gallons of diesel fuel. With luck I'd make it to Vegas.

Eleven, midnight, 1 AM went by, but I had no trouble staying fresh. The theft of all my cash was a wake-up call, and the freeway served up enough curves and grades to keep my attention. For the first time in three days, the curtains of my grief parted and I started to think. *? LOVE "curtains of my grief".*

I thought, first of all, of the mallrats. They'd pulled the oldest trick in the book on me, and I'd fallen for it. What would they do with all that loot? Buy condos in Aspen and gross out on dope? Open a shop and become yuppies? Keep running, just like me? I'd have levelled them if I caught them, but now that they were out of my life I almost wished them well. *This lacks credibility. Try pure abject hatred.*

As I drove on through the darkness, I thought of Mara. I conjured her up and put her on the bucket seat next to mine where Paws was curled up asleep. From there, without speaking, she gazed at me, with her passionate reproachful eyes, for mile after mile after mile. Finally she spoke, in that husky whisper that seemed to travel straight from soul to soul. *"Why didn't you come sooner?"* My fingers clenched the steering wheel until they ached. Sooner? How much sooner would I have had to come? She was already stone cold, even in that tepid room. I checked the fuel gauge, and Mara faded. *Who's this Mara? A femme fatale?*

Other faces came to me in the dark, some to ask questions, some to be asked. The sleeping cat became Uncle Titus, his Red Sox cap cocked back on his hairless noggin, his Adam's apple bobbing above the greasy scarf. "You're sure as hell no Farnacle!" he kept snarling, and then began to list the dire events that would befall me for stealing so much money without a front. Titus's face dimmed, to be replaced by a kinder one, the used car dealer Ali Shah, whose eyes glowed in the dashlight with vicarious excitement. "You *like* this rig, mistah? You *like* it? You are thinking it's the right numbah?" I was about to ask Ali Shah if he'd ever been to Vegas, but just then we hit a speed zone, and when I looked his way again it was into the sad old eyes of Platinum Jayne's bereaved dad, Fuzzy Blomsky. Fuzzy wasn't in a very talkative mood. Neither was I. Tears glistened in the creases of his old face, and his eyes showed that he understood my grief. This got me feeling sorry for myself, and I was starting to cry too, when Fuzzy's face suddenly broadened and brightened into the beaming mug of the Reverend Howard Keane.

"Rev!" I shouted, "Talk to me, man! Did you make it through the flood? Did you find Heidi?" *What an imagination! Have you been taking drugs or something? Got any extra?*

"My lad, I can speak wonders," he whispered, and faded into the gloom. I reached back for a bottle of Wharton's, uncorked it with my teeth and took a slug. If these were hallucinations, I wanted more! I wanted a few inspirational tales about the Rev's hero, Mordecai Mac-Crae. I wanted the wild lingo and fragrant honeysuckle smell of the Thrumble water nymphs, and the bee-buzzing of Doctor Slattery. I wanted to ask poor Isobel what she so burned to tell me before passing out in the Skythorpe clinic. I even hankered to hear Art Thrumble's uncensored opinion of the Underworld, and to find out how the Risen got the idea of stuffing people, and to chew the fat with a witch or two. *You should have introduced these characters.*

But the dawn had crept up and surprised me. There was sunlight on the mountains ahead of me to the west, and I was catching whiffs of sweet morning air. Paws stretched his legs and opened his good eye. I gave him a pat and he settled back to sleep.

I drove and drove. *So what else is new? Good fiction is a matter of details!*

By nine I was in desert country in the middle of Utah and nearly out of fuel. Just as bad, I was finally starting to fall asleep, and the sleepiness wasn't just your normal nagging sort: it was oozing through my body and limbs without stint down to the fingers and toes, making me feel like a glob of warm caramel. The road in front of me took on a killing sameness. I bit my lip and knew I had to stay awake and find a gas station, but a wave of sweet numbness washed through me, and when my eyes blinked open the Vixen was kicking up pebbles on the right-hand shoulder. *That* woke me up all right. *You should take better care of yourself! The human body needs sleep!*

I pulled up and checked both mirrors. Sure enough, I'd dozed off for a second and missed my off-ramp, about 200 yards back. I threw her into reverse and started backing up slowly. Vixens aren't hard to back up, I mean, compared to semis, but anyway the shopping-cart effect is much worse than in cars, and the sun was glaring at me from the rear, and each little wobble made me feel more uptight. By this time of morning the traffic was pretty lively, and I was getting a lot of action from truck horns as the big rigs swept by.

I'd reached the off-ramp and was half across it when a flash of crimson came out of nowhere, and a sports car shaved by me down the ramp with a throaty roar and a blare of horn. I was totally flummoxed but managed to finish backing up and follow the red car down the ramp. *I'm getting really excited!*

The gas station was a dismal hutch that looked as if it had been tacked together from dried-out cactus trunks. Looking for the diesel pump, I ticked past the sports car. It was a Dodge Viper—you could tell from the side-mounted exhausts—and its crew, so to speak, were two willowy numbers in pastel sweats, one blonde, one brunette, with brimmed white pitstop caps over straight cropped hair and dark glasses over porcelain skin. The blonde was pumping gas while the brunette did the windshield. When I slid out of the van they both checked me out, and I could feel their eyes on me as I went up to the pump.

I pumped $10.53 in fuel, which was every penny I had, and replaced the hose and paid the kid in the office. It felt real good to be up and moving, but I knew I still had to worry about sleepiness, hunger and thirst for the many miles to come. I madly craved the dried-up French bread but decided that it was too early to risk eating it. Back in the Vixen's galley I found an almost empty jar of instant coffee, filled it with cold water, closed it, shook it fiercely and drank up the resulting mess. It tasted like mud puddle, but it woke me up.

On the way out I glanced over at the gas pumps. Team Viper seemed in no hurry to split. *Why should anybody want to split?*

The Most Amazing Thing

Before leaving I rifled the Vixen's glove compartment and discovered an old cigar. It was a Dutch Masters Corona, still in its wrapper. I slid it out and lit up. Cigars are the last word in fighting hunger and drowsiness, especially if you're a bad smoker and cough on every other puff.

Blowing clouds of smoke I swung out of the gas station and onto I-70. The gas gauge read half-full and I had about 225 miles to go. If I free-wheeled all the down-grades, I could cruise into Vegas in style.

Two minutes later I glanced at the mirror. The Viper was following me, even though I was doing only 60. What if the girls were—No, they *couldn't* be—

I decided to take them at face value, as frisky young gals with a little time on their hands who'd taken a passing interest in a big stranger and a big van. *Don't repeat adjectives. Besides, weren't they sort of young for you?*

Three hours later they were still dogging me. We were on I-15 in Nevada now, in desert country about an hour out of Vegas, and I was counting my money. It was roaring hot, and I'd had the A/C turned off so as to save fuel, and my mouth was sand-dry, but I was feeling no pain. The girls had been brandishing cans of Sprite at me, and when I looked in the mirror to see if I could signal them, it seemed at first glance as if the red Viper had grown a fat white tail, until my blood curdled and I focused on the awful truth.

IT WAS THE VW, THE GODDAMNED DEATH BUG! *You don't prepare readers for this shock.*

I looked ahead again. I'd been veering slightly over into the passing lane, so I corrected. Then I checked the side mirror again. It was no mirage, and behind those black windows had to be Our Beloved, because he's the guy that escaped from the hotel, and Our Beloved had to be packing heat, because that's what I'd be doing in his position. I looked in front again. We were going up a long grade at 60, and 60 was the most that the Vixen could manage. *Why call him Our Beloved? Shades of Evelyn Waugh?*

I had a feeling I've never felt before, or rather a kind of mixed cocktail of feelings: fear, determination and poison spite. *Not very likely.*

My left hand's exhausted. I can't type any more.

SATURDAY, MAY 30, 1998, THE BELLOWS CLINIC

Mega, I've read your comments and I've got news for you. This isn't fiction. This really happened. How'd you think I lost my hand? This is a sort of journal, a place where I can make sense of what's happened to me and record facts that I may need some day and come out with things that would like as kill me if I corked them up. I'm grateful for your suggestions, but mainly I can't use them. If I wrote better, I'm not sure I could get these monsters out of me. *You're hallucinating. Coffee together might help.*

As I was saying, as Our Beloved followed me down that highway, I had a mixed cocktail of feelings: fear, determination and pure spite. I had a scheme of sorts, but first I had to save the girls in the Viper. Our Beloved would think nothing of blowing them away just to get at me with no witnesses. I parked my cigar and with my left arm reached out and motioned for the girls to pass. It was a very rapid motion, like saying, "Something's the matter, get out of here!"

Thank God they understood. The Viper pulled left, thundered past me and burned a hole into space down the freeway.

They weren't gone a second when my sideview mirror exploded, sending slivers of glass through the cockpit. One sliver hit the left lens of my sunglasses, which shattered without hurting me. I tore them off. Seven thoughts went through my mind at once, but the upshot of all seven was a single brutal action: I hit the brakes with all my weight and tugged on the emergency brake for good measure. Vixens have good brakes, front-disk rear-drum, and the result was a really impressive deceleration from 60 to 0, excepting I didn't have to get down to zero, because well above that I felt and heard the VW smash into the Vixen's stern. It wasn't the all-out pulverizing total-wrecking call-the-coroner memorial-plot-digging crash, followed by a few tinkles of broken glass and maybe the sound of a gas tank exploding, that I might have hoped for, but nevertheless it was a good solid walloping thump, with a cry of twisting metal, and my hopes were answered when I checked the right-hand sideview mirror and saw the Death Bug spinning out and coming to rest, backwards, on the right shoulder. Our Beloved, if he could still drive, would have to find new wheels. *Have you flown this by the VW Company?*

Which seven thoughts went through my mind before I hit the brakes? 1) Our Beloved had shot out my mirror just to intimidate me, soften me up. 2) He did this because he thought I scare easy, which I do. 3) He was about to shoot out my rear tires, because 4) his VW didn't pack the mass or the power to force the Vixen off the road. 5) Having no weapon myself, I couldn't let him do this. 6) My only hope was using the Vixen's mass and good brakes, and 7) surprise. All these thoughts ran through my head all at the same time. *That's impossible. Rewrite.*

I freewheeled the long downgrade, watching for the next exit. My hands were on the wheel, my eyes were on the road, but my thoughts were with Our Beloved. Why did I want to exit the freeway? I was giving my enemy his due. He was one sick dude, I'll allow you that, but he was a man like me, and his strength lay in his resourcefulness and his desperate stubbornness. I put myself into his sick brain. I figured that, if he wasn't badly hurt, he could turn his wreck into an opportunity. The wrecked end of the bug was facing traffic, and all he needed to do was kneel down (concealing his huge size) next to the wreck and woefully beckon to traffic. Everybody loves a wreck, and soon enough, maybe even now, some cocky cowboy in a pickup, on his way into town to lose some money and get laid, would pull over to help, and Our Beloved would have no trouble getting the drop on him and commandeering his rig. If this happened soon enough, he could overtake me, and *there'd be hell to pay*, because that type of magnum weirdo will risk anything, and I'd become his jihad. *Watch those run-on sentences.*

All this reasoning made sense of course, but at the same time it was the acme of silliness. You see, it was the reasoning of fear, and fear never reasons straight, I guess because fear is afraid of the truth as well as afraid of the enemy. I was forgetting that just as I, the hunted, was trying to put myself in Our Beloved's place, Our Beloved, the hunter, would put himself in mine. Worse, I was forgetting that I was low on fuel. These mistakes almost cost me my life.

Shit, my hand's cramping up. *I take dictation!*

SUNDAY, MAY 31, 1998, THE BELLOWS CLINIC

Mega and I have talked about her possibly taking dictation, but I've asked if we can put that decision off. Pacing is enormously important when I write, as in sometimes writing fast and sometimes slow, and I wouldn't feel at ease if somebody was waiting for me during the slow spells. Besides, ever since I started putting myself in Our Beloved's skull, I've felt my mind expanding in bizarre ways, as though in mid-life I'm finally growing up, and growth is a clumsy and embarrassing condition, like nudity.

Now that I'm not being rushed, I should get up to date on a few fronts. I've been reading the *New York Times* and tuning in NPR every day, trying to get news about fifty-odd things that matter to me, such as the Imbrattas, the Calandrinos, Fuzzy Blomsky, the Rev, Heidi, the Thrumble girls, the Skythorpe Clinic and the Penumbra Hotel, but at best the news hounds have come up with even less than I already know. But a few items should be noted:

1. The first is very sad. Mordecai MacCrae, the soldier-cop whom the Rev called "the most capable man he ever met," has died of

hunger on Death Row, proclaiming his innocence to the very
end.

2. The second is pure American wacko. Winthrop Boylston, the
psycho who trained his dog to run down convertibles on the
freeway and maul everybody inside, will be electrocuted today
with his dog, Nipper, eight miles above San Diego in a specially-
fitted Boeing 747, complete with doctors, coroner, priests, press
corps, TV crews, and, as audience, 100 or so of America's
leading talk-show hosts. The DA in charge, Marvin "Smartass"
Smalley, calls this $12.7 million venture "an example to all
Californians," but to some it looks more like hype for his race
for governor.

Just for the record: Boylston's the son of Sumner Lowell Boylston, ex-
senator from Massachusetts. Kid had the best of everything, including
prestigious Stockbridge Academy and Harvard U. How'd he turn out
so nasty? When Smalley asked him at the trial why he did these things
to animals and people, all Boylston would say was that he'd decided to
"push the envelope."

Finally,

SUPREME COURT RULES REBEL SERMONS LEGAL

The Supreme Court of California has ruled that the sermons of Herbert
"Dominee" Lockforth, pastor of the First Gombeenian Evangelical Anarchist Church of Escondido, CA, are a legal expression of faith. Lockforth preaches the overthrow of order "by all available means."

But my story makes Boylston and Lockforth look like Quaker Oats.

I exited I-15 about ten minutes after smashing Our Beloved's VW.
As I'd hoped, one option after the exit was a graded road signed LAS
VEGAS 32. I took it without a thought.

The road was white gravel that seemed to throb with midday heat. No
kidding, it was hot. I was gasping for air, and my front teeth heated up

when I breathed in. The road crossed the valley floor in a straightaway for several miles, then lifted into some low hills. I wasn't five minutes onto this grade when it got steeper and broke into switchbacks. I was checking the coolant temp when I remembered the fuel gauge. It read empty. I didn't know *how* empty because I'd never run out of fuel before. The switchbacks never seemed to end.

I began having that LOSER feeling again, same as I had back in the Brazen Head Bar after seeing Uncle Titus. But I fought it back. "Hang in there," I whispered. "Hit the summit and six'l get you a half-dozen you can coast down to Vegas."

I almost made it. The diesel gasped and died just after I'd cleared the last switchback. Coast to Vegas? No way. There was still a mild upgrade ahead of me, reaching a quarter-mile towards a left turn that might mean more upgrade still.

I set the shift in park and got out of the van. The country was ugly but also awesome. Up here the sandy soil, spotted by sage, cactus and parched grass, broke into mighty escarpments of rock, while the other way looked down over all the switchbacks, into the vast dry valley, and back to where I-15 ran like a barely definite line, maybe 20 miles away.

I'd see him if he was coming.

It occurred to me that I'd passed nobody on this road. I walked around front of the Vixen. No tracks there at all, only the hardened pockmarks of some rain that could've fallen weeks before. I began to realize what a fool I'd been to exit the freeway. What a loser! And I'd left fresh tracks.

I tried to think about what I was going to do, but I was all out of thoughts at the moment. In any case, I desperately needed something to eat and drink. I grabbed the old bread off the front seat, got out of the Vixen and started climbing up what looked like a goat-trail to the right of the road. About 150 yards uphill was a lone pine tree—if a spring was anywhere, it'd be there, feeding that tree. I climbed hard, knowing there'd be tough decisions to make, and soon, and knowing also that

The Most Amazing Thing

Our Beloved or no Our Beloved I'd be a goner if I didn't find water. I was so dehydrated, I couldn't even break out a sweat.

I was almost there when I tripped on a stone and stumbled into the little clearing in front of the tree.

Then I saw the man. *Wow!*

I don't think I've ever been so surprised in my life. I swear, he wasn't ten feet away. He was stone still, looking diagonally away from me and towards the valley. He was leaning back against the tree, and his skin was reddish-brown like the pine bark, and his eyes were the same color, like some desert animal's. He was about average height but thin as a rake, and with his dented cowboy hat and broken nose and lined face and dusty deerskin jacket and threadbare jeans, he looked like the hills had chewed him up and spat him out a dozen times. *Very compelling! Ever hear of Louis L'Amour?*

Without batting an eyelash, he spoke in a deep low rusty voice. "I could use some'v that bread."

The bread meant my life to me, but I couldn't say no. There's no refusing a beggar in the desert. I cracked the bread on my knee and handed him the bigger piece. Without thanking me he went at it like a squirrel, with a satisfied grunt or two and flashing of fine white teeth. The bread disappeared in seconds.

I started munching mine and choked on it. "Any water around?" I coughed out.

He turned and pointed. A few feet behind the tree, the face of the sandstone was sodden, and just below this was a horizontal rock holding a tiny pool of water, maybe a gallon. I went down on my knees, stuck my face in it and sucked up about half. It was like dying and going to heaven.

I sat down on a rock in front of this lizardlike man and asked him what he was doing there. "I live here," was the low, melodic reply.

"What do you eat?"

"Cactus."

"How can you eat cactus?"

"Very slowly. You find the right sorta cactus and bite off a chaw and chew your chaw slow and easy, like for fifteen minutes or more. I've been here seven months, chewin' cactus. Folks call me Pecos Louie, considerin' I once almost drowned in the Pecos, but if I stay out here a couple more months, I'll be 90% succulent, and they'll have to call me Cactus Louie."

While Louie checked his deerskin jacket for spare crumbs, I asked him if he did anything else, that is, anything besides chew his chaw.

"Write poems in my head." The light brown eyes moved slightly. "Your man is comin'," he said.

I looked back down into the valley. A car was nearing the end of the desert straightaway. From this distance it wasn't much more than a glint, but you could tell it was coming fast.

Gulping down my fear, I asked Louie how he knew I was being followed.

"Your eyes told me," said a voice like the desert wind.

I wondered out loud if he'd like to know why. "No need," he said. "I've seen pilgrims before."

Pilgrims? I let that one go and asked Pecos Louie for his help. I told him about being out of fuel. I told him I was no angel, but compared with the creep who was chasing me, I was something like Mother Theresa. Louie understood without a word.

By the time he and I got down to the Vixen, I could see the approaching car clearly. It had left the straightaway and was into the switchbacks. I could hear it too, even at that distance. It was a police car, and it had its siren on.

"The bastard's killed a cop," I said.

"How'd you know that's not a cop drivin'?"

"Why would a real cop use his siren on this road?" It was Our Beloved's usual way. He wanted to scare the shit out of me before he nailed me.

The Most Amazing Thing

I asked Louie how much time he thought we had. "About ten minutes."

As we climbed into the Vixen, Paws hopped down from the passenger seat, raced for the rear, jumped up on the bed and hid under the comforter.

Louie stood behind me, checking things out, while I opened the secret compartment and started stuffing briefcases into a duffle bag. "Why'r you doin' that?" he asked.

I looked at him in annoyance and kept packing.

"Why 'r you doin' that when you can ride this rig out of here?"

"I told you I've got no fuel!" I shouted angrily, but Pecos Louie smiled, and I suddenly knew that there *was* fuel, though I'd been too lame-brained with fear to realize it.

There was half a gallon of heating oil for camping. And there was bourbon!

As I dumped a second bottle of Wharton's into the gas tank, I asked Louie how much farther up the road it was to the Vegas downgrade.

About a mile.

There wasn't any time for thanks. The engine started with a roar, and the whole van started to vibrate in the oddest way, like one of those paint-mixing machines you see in paint-shops, but I threw it into gear and it lurched forward. I waved at Louie and tromped on the gas pedal and the Vixen, which had just now been a fairly respectable cruiser, became a shivering sputtering popping mental case of a van, staggering like the wino that it was up the road at 30 mph. Our Beloved wouldn't be gaining on me right now, because he was still piecing his way through the switchbacks, but he *would* gain on me plenty when he hit this stretch. Luckily it was only a mile, but before that mile was driven I'd taken back every bad thought I'd ever had about the BMW diesel and vowed, if I survived, to send presents to all the Bavarian engineers who'd had a hand in it. And you can bet I will. *Take it easy!*

The far edge of the summit came so quick that I thought I was being thrown into empty space. I veered to the left, and suddenly the whole Las Vegas area was stretched out beneath me as I started down a zigzag of switchbacks much steeper than the other side. This was bad news. I'd been hoping that gravity would help me keep ahead of the much more powerful cop-car on the way down, but now I had 3–4 miles of hairy driving ahead of me, where the cop-car's greater mobility would gain on me at every turn. I'd no choice but to punish the gas and the brakes with two feet, sometimes even holding them down together to come out of turns the quicker. Everything loose in the Vixen, pots, pans, silverware, equipment, briefcases, even Paws and the cat litter, was swashing around the van like jetsam in a storm.

Two turns down I looked up and saw him hit the switchbacks. He saw me too and waved something out of his window and slugs zinged through the Vixen's roof to the floor three feet from where I sat. I took my eyes off the road for an instant and looked ahead again to see that I was coming into a right-hand curve too fast. I braked and spun the wheel. The Vixen went into a major skid, during which I thought I'd finally bought the farm, but the turns had been banked for a margin of error, and amazingly the skid had aligned me just right for the next straightaway.

All at once I remembered. This was called a four-wheel drift. Race-car drivers did it *on purpose*! I gunned her into the next turn and skidded my skid again.

This maneuver brought me up to speed with Our Beloved, who it seemed hadn't learned this novel way of taking turns. And parity was all I needed. Looking down and ahead I saw that the switchbacks ended in a straight section about a quarter-mile long, that T'd at a main road amidst a huddle of gas stations. Even Our Beloved wasn't crazy enough to chase me in there. Right now he'd be thinking about ditching the stolen patrol car and cutting his losses. I looked back from the straightaway and saw him pull up short on the last switchback and aim at me one more time. POP!

The Most Amazing Thing

I crept toward the gas stations. Now I needed one more than ever. Our Beloved had finally shot out one of my tires.

Desmond, this is a promising first try, with gripping emotional power. But isn't the story just a trifle over the top? Do Vixens really run on bourbon? Can the human gastro-intestinal system subsist on a diet of cactus? Is there such a thing as a 4-wheel drift? Also, this seems very short on social consciousness and moral meaning. You've nothing to say about the rampant economic inequalities that turned Pecos Louie into a hermit, or the cruel social conditions responsible for Our Beloved's life of crime. Finally, ever hear of such a thing as style? Style is hard to describe to beginners. But let's call it the variety of techniques by which an author controls a reader's mind. Instead of style, this narrative is just a headlong rush of your hero's responses to experience.
We must discuss these points in detail over coffee as soon as possible. Tonight?

PART TWO: A WORD FROM OUR BELOVED

MONDAY, JUNE 1, 1998, THE BELLOWS CLINIC

Mega, I can't omit minor details—they're the keys by which I can open up my memory. Re: your questions about bourbon, cactus and car-racing, the answers are yes, yes and yes. But the other things you have to say strike at my very heart. Yes, I'd *love* to be a good writer, chock full of commanding style and deep moral meaning. I try again and again. The trouble is, life keeps getting in the way. Sometimes it sneaks up and surprises me, sometimes it hammers and tortures me, sometimes it turns and runs faster than I can follow it. Maybe, once I've caught up with it, once this journal is done—I can take a Lit course taught by an expert like you.

Also, Mega, I'm afraid I won't be able to have coffee with you any time very soon. You see, I'm in mourning. *Desmond, I'm told I have a special talent for soothing the bereaved.*

First off I have to bring a dismal story to its end. It *happened* yesterday. I mean, *the worst:*

WORST-EVER AIR CATASTROPHE
CLAIMS ONE THOUSAND LIVES

I knew they shouldn't have tried to electrocute somebody in an airplane! And the whole thing was captured on tape! 40,000 feet above San Diego County, Smartass Smalley was just about to order the switch pulled on Boylston and Nipper, when Nipper somehow yanked himself free and started mauling people right and left. A deputy, who mustn't have been the sharpest knife in the drawer, drew his rod and fired, but instead of hitting the dog, he hit the transformer, electrocuting himself and everybody else on the plane, which then plummeted like a rock, down, down, down, finally slamming into, as fate would have it, the First Gombeenian Evangelical Anarchist Church of Escondido, where Dominee Lockforth was preaching revolution to a house packed with faithful! Everybody perished except for 213 children who'd been left to watch inspirational videos in a nearby Sunday school.

Save me from California!

Who's going to do all those talk shows?

Who's going to take care of those kids? Connect these sentences!

But back to Vegas. I knew that Our Beloved would find me again but figured it would take him a few days. During this grace period I had to protect my wad and gear up for his visit. Given that I hadn't a cent in my pocket, this wasn't going to be a breeze, but since Boulder some thoughts had been fitting together in my mind, and I had the germ of an idea. It wasn't a very fancy plan, but when you have a few hundred billion in negotiable securities, all you need is a little push to start the ball rolling. *"Billion"? Why exaggerate, when readers don't even believe the simple truth anymore?*

As the bullet-riddled Vixen limped towards the gas station corner I did a quick check of the facilities. All the stations had tow trucks, but I picked the station with the biggest and shiniest truck, on the hunch that pride of ownership would breed good humor. I didn't have to toot: the wobbling, wheezing, sputtering Vixen brought all the staff and customers to attention. I slid out of the Vixen into a crowd of eight or nine curious faces. The boss was an athletic-looking black man sporting a green paratrooper's beret over immaculate white cover-alls. "You been upcountry, sir?" he asked.

I said yes.

He fingered two bullet-holes in the window just behind the driver's seat. "Get these there?"

"Drive-by," I lied, and everybody nodded with compassion.

"Been there myself, sir," said the black man. "Want us to call the law?"

I said no thanks, and everybody grinned in understanding. I told him I needed a tow to the local BMW franchise, and he said no problem. I said I'd also appreciate the name of a decent hotel that had its own restaurant, and one of the customers, a well-heeled older guy, said to try the Tour d'Or, if I didn't mind the price. Just to keep a low profile I asked how much it was, and when he said $600 I said I could manage that for a couple of nights.

They all wanted to know more but I begged off, saying I was zonked, which I was, but that in a few years they could read my memoirs, which got a laugh because nobody believed me. The raucous laughter, combined with the ready grins and smiles, gave me the impression that even though it was only about 4, the sun had already gone over the yardarm for most of these Las Vegans.

I shook hands with the boss. He introduced himself as Augustus Randolph, and I told him I was Desmond Ruck.

For the first time literally in years, it was fun to tell somebody who I was.

While Randolph was lining up his tow truck and unpacking his towing gear, I called the Tour d'Or from his office. I told the lady I'd been bumped out of my reservations at another hotel because their computer crashed (nowadays a likely excuse for almost any atrocity) and that I needed, if possible, a suite. She said that Henri Quatre was available for a couple of thousand bucks a night. I said that I'd need it for at least a week (which got me a lower rate) and that in a few days I'd let her know if I wanted to stay longer. The lady asked for my gold card number. I gave it to her but told her I meant to pay my bill in cash (which it turns out Las Vegans sort of prefer), and that I'd leave a surplus of cash on account with their cashier tomorrow.

So far, so good. The phone call was a freebie, and the tow would be courtesy of my Oregon car insurance. The tow truck would taxi me to the hotel. How would I get this surplus of cash tomorrow? I had a plan. *I'm all ears!*

Only a few details were left. Before Randolph winched up the Vixen I popped in, put on clean clothes and made sure that all but two of my precious briefcases were in the duffles. I put the last two briefcases in my overnight bag, to make it look full of clothes, propped the bags in the driver's compartment, stumbled out of the van and gave Randolph the high sign. *You gave him the finger?*

In the truck I asked Randolph if he'd board Paws for a few nights. From the way he said Sure I knew that I liked him and that he had some respect for me, or at least polite interest. *You can tell these things? I can't.*

In ten minutes I was striding into the cavernous green-marble lobby of the Tour d'Or. I managed the check-in without flubbing, pocketed my plastic key and hit the Special Suites elevator with a compulsory bell-boy at my side. I can remember opening the door to my room and telling Wilbur the bellhop I'd have to tip him the next day. I can remember finding my way to the bathroom. But I don't remember flopping onto the bed. I was dead to the world. *I'm feeling sort of sleepy too.*

WEDNESDAY, JUNE 3, 1998, THE BELLOWS CLINIC

What a beautiful day!!

Recovering is like being reborn. As a kid I used to get real sick: high fevers and sometimes something they called the croup, which is like getting strangled from inside. Slowly but surely, after boring sleepy days in bed, I'd get better, and the first orange juice and milk and Triscuits and even tapwater I drank would have strange strong flavors, as though I'd never tasted them before, and when I finally went outdoors the air itself was like a bracing soup of ozone and pollen and the distant ocean. You could get drunk on it.

It was like that today. I had Vic Bellows's OK and was raring to go at 6:30 AM. Catherine, my favorite nurse, gave me a thermos of iced tea, and I walked out into the fresh air for the first time in a month, out through the Zen garden and up the arroyo to the east. Somebody'd built a bench at the top of the trail. I sat there and bird-watched and day-dreamed and tasted the spring mountain air. Then I came back here to my room, feeling like a million. *Just a million?*

Where was I? Waking up on that fateful day last month in the Tour d'Or Hotel!

I was fully-clothed, lying on my back, half on, half off a gigantic canopied bed. It was a corner room (King Henri Quatre would have demanded no less), and one French window framed a brilliant view of the mountains, while the other featured the pyramidal Luxor Hotel. The din of jet engines from the nearby airport shook everything every two minutes or so, and I was smelling their exhausts as well as auto fumes, new leather furniture and everybody else's breakfast.

154

Pulling my feet up onto the bed, I kicked off my shoes and stretched and slowly remembered who I was. Then suddenly, with a big adrenal rush, I remembered what I was supposed to be doing that day. Wow!

It was going to be the most important day in my life.

Such days not being for the weak of stomach, I called Room Service and ordered ham and eggs *à la mode d'Albuquerque*, with a side order of hash browns. I also asked for the local paper, but he said it was lying on the mat in front of my door already. *You can't write "he" without first identifying a person.*

I let it lie there. For the next twenty minutes, until breakfast came, I did my homework, which that day consisted of figuring out exactly how fast Our Beloved could get at me. Of course he was wanted for taking a cop car and doing something unsightly to the cop in it. Right now he could be in jail or even dead. But for my own life's sake, I had to give him the benefit of the doubt. Thinking *that* way meant assuming that he'd killed the highway patrolman so there'd be no visual fix on him in the Vegas area, that he was free and that he'd decided to look for me in Vegas and not farther down the road. Sure, the odds were against all these chances coming true; but Our Beloved was powerful, smart and motivated, and he seemed to have a special line into my psyche.

The way I figured it, Our Beloved's best-case scenario gave me about 24 hours of safety. First, he'd need to ditch the cop car, probably by driving it back up the switchbacks and stowing it up some jeep trail. Then he'd want to walk overland to central Vegas (to evade the All Points that the law will post in his honor) and establish a pied-à-terre. That meant a motel room, but you can't easily register for one of those without a car and luggage, so he'd have to get ahold of those first. When all of this was done, and after a trying 36-hour day of murdering, lying, cheating, stealing and high-speed chase, he'd be dead tired just like any of us, and being a slob he'd probably sleep late this morning, and today he'd buy some clothes and start his search. I'd asked at registration for them not to release my name, but Our Beloved could almost assume that, so he'd start his search some other way. Auto repair shops? Scuttlebut? Pure instinct?

Still I gave myself a day and night. I was wrong again. *Don't telegraph your punches!*

I showered, shaved and made myself as decent as I could. While I was in the bathroom Wilbur (who must have been working a double shift) had keyed himself in and was laying out breakfast and the local paper on a silver-inlaid antique table by the mountain-facing window. As I sat down he straightened up and, being about 6' 4" himself, gave me one of those recognition looks that tall folks give each other. *I didn't know tall people gave each other looks. Short people don't.*

I asked Wilbur if he was a student. Yes, he was working his way through a biology degree at UNLV. Earning a living *and* going to college? That would explain his pasty face and the bags under his eyes.

I asked him if he could help me with some luggage in half an hour. Sure thing. *Not a sentence.*

Breakfast with its crispy hash browns was delicious, but I barely noticed it. I was busy with the Las Vegas *Review-Journal* and a city map. Also I made two phone calls. *Why get so mysterious?*

Before Wilbur got back I visited one of my briefcases, and stowed it again in its duffle bag. Then we schlepped the duffles downstairs and saw them into the hotel safe. I left my Oregon driver's license as photo ID (in case Our Beloved got any ideas about impersonating me), and the desk clerk and I agreed on my father's date of birth as my PIN. I thanked Wilbur and told him to get a little rest some day.

Outside, in blinding sunlight, waited a metallic-gray Mercedes 600 with "DUKE'S" in black on its front door. Holding the back door open and smiling at me hopefully was a sleek and husky young Latino in what looked like an old admiral's suit. *We have special ways of speaking about ethnic groups these days, and this isn't one of them!*

I'd barely stretched my legs and relaxed into the dark leather interior when we arrived at Duke's. I got out of the limo, put my hands on my hips and looked at the building the way some conquistador must have looked at the Pacific. It was a spanking new block of glass and metal about 125 feet on each side and the same in height. The whole ground floor was neonized casino, and the nine upper floors were office space, about 100,000 square feet of it, almost all of it advertised For Rent.

A man could hide there in broad daylight.

My driver Paco led me through the joint towards the elevators. The casino was a big, high-ceilinged, columned room taking up the whole ground floor, done up at major expense, but I thought pretty chintzily, to look like an ocean liner. The help, barmaids, waiters, dealers, were dressed to suit, and to my mind they looked damn silly, but then it *was* my first visit to Vegas. All the same, they could have done something about the smell. The place stank to high heaven of detergent and bleach! If I was some Texan tourist fixing to sip Irish coffee and blow a week's pay on the bandits, I'd sure give *that* place a wide berth. *You'd 'steer clear' of it?*

In the elevator Paco took a key from around his neck and stuck it in next to PENTHOUSE, and we whooshed nonstop up to the top. We stepped out into a big skylit foyer with windows on each side opening onto a roof-garden of palms, cactus and flowering vines. Facing us were three doors: one on the right made of glass and looking into a secretary's office, a nameless metal door in the middle and on the left a wooden door with brass fittings, that ought to open into the penthouse apartment. A maid was just coming out through this last door and, sure enough, I caught a glimpse of lavish living room.

I followed Paco to the right, past a smiling secretary and on through a massive mahogany door.

The office was so big and bright that at first I didn't see the man in it. Then something materialized from behind a haze of cigarette smoke near the desk, and I saw him walking towards me. This would be the boss, Curtis "Duke" Crouse, and frankly there wasn't much left of him. He must have been in his sixties, but he looked almost mummified. His face was airline-pilot gray and hung on his skull so sadly that you could see the insides of his lower eyelids. Heart and lung trouble, as a nurse might put it, but behind that I saw decades of whipsaw smoking and drinking: smoking so that he could have another drink, drinking so that he'd need another weed. Habits like that, along the way to killing you, destroy the sense of smell, which probably explains why Duke didn't mind the stench downstairs. *'Airline-pilot gray' won't work.*

Duke and I shook hands, and Paco disappeared. I followed Duke to his desk, avoiding the cloud of smoke, which smelt of rotting lungs.

You've probably guessed why I went there. Duke's had been advertised for sale in the *Review-Journal.* It had everything I needed to start setting up shop: a legit address, a business front, acres of office space, computers, security, ready cash, you name it. The roof-top lodging made it just perfect. I could move in and disappear.

Duke showed me the mortgage and accounts, which told a sad story. He'd put up his whole wad to build the place two years ago and gone $9 million into debt. He was clearing about $100,000 per month, which was just about enough to service his mortgage and taxes, but nothing to live on. He was asking $15 million, exactly what he'd put into the place, but $15 million was a tad spendy for earnings of $1.2 million a year.

I asked him what was cash on hand. He phoned down. "$209,632.52."

I told him he could have his $15 million if he'd let me have the cash on hand. I saw ten years drop off his face. I saw his lips forming the word "why," but then he thought better of it.

From my jacket pocket I pulled full payment for the ducal palace, a signed and negotiable certificate from Omnium Limited worth $19,377,000 at yesterday's closing. By phone to Omnium (with me holding my breath) Duke verified that it was authentic and hadn't been reported stolen. Duke would express it to them right away and have a new certificate, issued in his own name, in his hands by the end of the week, at which time he could sell the stock and give me the deed and the change. Until then I could start moving into the office space and use the limo and the cash on hand as needed and even move into the penthouse apartment, which Duke had been keeping for guests and high rollers.

Duke led me back into the foyer and around the private apartment. It was mogul-class, decorated in the mauves and ochres of Arizona desert style and hung with Navajo rugs. It had a big sunny kitchen sinfully packed with commercial-grade equipment and butcher blocks and Mexican tiles, opening into a walk-in wine closet. And said closet was about as stuffed of Bollingers and Rothschilds and Chateau d'Yquems as the architecture allowed. Much material for celebration, if celebration would ever be in order.

Then we went out and strolled in the roof garden. Security was OK. There were a few other high-rises in the area, including the Tour d'Or itself, from which somebody could draw a bead on me, but the nearest was about a thousand yards away, and that was no cheap shot.

Besides, I thought, I can buy all the high-rises and tear them down. *Buy them all and tear them down,* I thought and started to laugh, but swallowed it, and the swallowed laugh turned into a thrilled feeling just at the base of my skull in back, a feeling of pure animal delight. I'd bought a building! A building of my own! I could barely hold back a shout of pure adolescent glee.

But there was still Our Beloved. I glanced at my watch: 11:30. My whole world had been transformed in the last hour, but there was still a lot to do. Once I had liquidity and the deed to Duke's I could burglar-proof the place, beef up security and even hire my own posse to hunt down Our Beloved, but for the next few days I'd be at risk.

I asked Crouse if I could borrow his secretary for the afternoon and use the limo again. Back in the office I instructed the secretary, Milly Beth, to phone Augustus Randolph and get him over there pronto, and then to contact Federal Express and tell them to bring over lots of envelopes and forms and make sure that Duke's fedex account was still current.

The Most Amazing Thing

I also had her get three desks and chairs together on one of Duke's vacant floors and to have coffee and sandwiches brought up. Finally I told her to find me a security agency that had operatives to spare today, so that Crouse's penthouse would be as safe as possible when I moved in that afternoon.

It was time to kick ass. I turned down Crouse's offer of champagne and said I'd be back soon. Downstairs I found Paco chatting with the bouncer, who introduced himself as Doc Sheehy. He was a rangy redhead, tough-looking enough but with some empty space in the back of his blue eyes. I asked him if he'd mind riding shotgun with us back to the hotel, and he phoned up for permission from Duke.

In lunchtime traffic and blare, we motored over to the Tour d'Or. Wilbur was just emerging in his street clothes, looking like something the cat dragged in, when I pounced on him and told him that great things were in store if he could keep awake three hours longer and help me out. I got him into the limo and trotted in to the front desk. In the hotel safe I took one briefcase out of its duffle. I didn't take more because I hadn't seen Duke's safe yet and was being super cautious. If I hadn't been so cautious I wouldn't have lost my right hand. On the other hand, if I hadn't lost my hand the way I lost it, who knows where I'd be today? *Good writers don't speculate!*

SUNDAY, JUNE 7, 1998, THE BELLOWS CLINIC

Augustus has gone to Oregon to ask Glynda, on my behalf, for a divorce. He'll offer money. I somehow can't stand the thought of seeing her right now.

They say that money talks, but I wonder how many people listen to what it's saying. My money's been talking a lot recently. Its voice sounds a bit like Mara's voice, urgent and whispered. *"You'll lose me, Desi, you'll lose me unless you protect me."*

Protect you how?

160

"You can't just leave me hanging out here. I have to look like other people's money."

But how does other people's money look?

"It looks, Stupid, as if it isn't theirs. Like, man, it's hidden, same way we hide our genitals. Hide it like that, keep your books straight and pay your taxes, and you'll attract less attention." [5]

Notes for the use of floor-space, at *Duke's*, 800 Kingman Rd., Las Vegas:

Floor 9—White Wolf Foundation (for organized giving)

Floor 8—Weather Company, employee benefits, public relations (the Weather Company owns White Wolf Associates, called Weather Company because the title won't interest anybody)

Floor 7—White Wolf Associates, which owns Duke's (called White Wolf just to sound wacko and too risky to be interesting to would-be investors)

Floor 6—Refreshment floor, master of the revels (every two months we take 10 days off, go somewhere en masse and celebrate being alive)

Floor 5—The Gardener Bank, security (wealth has to be gardened, like a living thing)

Floor 4—White Wolf architects, engineers, planners, information seekers

Floor 3—Duke's front office, White Wolf accountants, tax advisors, legal division

Floor 2—Library and communications

Floor 1—Duke's Casino, soon to be a worldclass brewpub

But all this has to wait till I get back to town.

---

5. Ruck here interrupts his narrative for some informal notes, which we reprint because of our commitment to publication of his journal in toto. —Ed.

The Most Amazing Thing

Hire the information-seekers first, from a pool of reporters, PI's, cops. Their first work: missions and probes.

Missions to discover the identity of the poor old lady killed in the Bronx shootout and to check up on how Ali Shah's doing.

Missions to find out what happened to Fuzzy Blomsky, to the Rev and Heidi, and Schultzie the jail-guard, and the Thrumble girls.

Missions to trace the poor cancer-ridden Isobel and the residents of Hauck's loony wards and to test the slim possibility that Bevan Slattery and Red Wind survived their fall onto the generator.

Missions to contact Pecos Louie and discover the trail of the White Wolf and reward the BMW engineers. Finally a sad mission back to Chile, to reach Mara's people.

A polite probe into the incredible finances of Uncle Titus.

A very quiet probe into the Imbrattas and Calandrinos. A relentless probe into the dealings of Colombian druglords and the connections of the bumptious billionaire Myrdal Hwang.

A tireless probe to discover who was, in Our Beloved's words, the "fucker" who "screwed up" and crushed the Penumbra Hotel with boulders.

Muckraking probes into the Risen and the Wolf Coven and the unbearable Our Beloved and the First Gombeenian Evangelical Anarchist Church of Escondido.

Missions to aid the oppressed, probes to find out the truth, and in particular to find anyone who had anything to do with Mara's suffering and death.

MONDAY, JUNE 8, 1998

Frightening news: I climbed up the arroyo this morning, as I do now every day. As I rounded the bend and got my first distant view of the bench at the top, I saw somebody by the bench, dressed in bright green, who waved at me and disappeared. The Chilean god, Kanaloa? I don't believe in him! *'Kanaloa' doesn't sound Chilean to me.*

Better news: Augustus got back from Oregon today with news that Glynda remains in love with Dr. Jezra and that she has agreed to a divorce settlement of $5 million. I told Gus not to conceal from her that I've gotten rich—partly because Glynda's not the money-grubbing type and partly because she'd find out sooner or later in the long run. *Why invent a wife at this late date?*

Meg, for the last time, *I'm not writing fiction.* I'm writing facts, as many as I can recall, so that some day I'll be able to dope out some of the mysteries of my life and maybe explain to future readers why I behaved as I did. Good fiction writers wouldn't think up something as gross, horrific and revolting as what I have to describe today, and if they did publishers wouldn't print it. *Meg, I warn you not to read this. It's too gross. Not to worry. I've read Stephen King and Anne Rice and so I'm ready for anything.*

—Or so you think. Anyway, back to my story:

Augustus, Wilbur and I set ourselves up at three desks on the otherwise-empty seventh floor of Duke's. Wilbur had a mild allergic reaction to the carpets, which were still in brand new condition, but he suppressed it with an inhaler. Over coffee I told them that I had authority to establish a large holding company as soon as possible, and that if they'd help me I'd give them a big one apiece for their trouble. I also said that even better things were down the road. *What's a 'big one'? You're not gay, are you?*

The drill was like this: Augustus and I made out the stock certificates in my name and new address, 800 Kingman Road, singing out the companies' names and addresses to Wilbur, who was preparing FedEx forms, separating carbons and stuffing envelopes. Because a lot of the certificates were from the same company, Wilbur kept getting ahead of us, which gave him time to proofread our work and his own.

We worked away like Zurich elves, until the envelopes were piling up two feet high and you could smell the sweat above the coffee. It wasn't long before my two new friends grasped the enormousness of what they were doing, and even though I didn't tell them about the other brief-cases, a kind of devilish hilarity rose up in them, and trying not to catch it myself I kept telling them to quiet down and write.

About an hour into it, I noticed Augustus working much slower than I was, and called for a break to compare notes. His handwriting was beautiful, and fancy like a diploma or an ancient valentine, and that's why it took him forever to write. When I asked him about it he blustered a little and then almost broke up. Turns out that when he was a poor black kid in Mobile, Alabama, in the 60's, his grade-school teacher, an old English lady named Miss Flora, who'd been a nurse in Africa during the First World War, singled him out as somebody special and painstak-ingly taught him elegant handwriting, because she said it would give him some standing in a world of white people. Augustus described Miss Flora so lovingly that I wanted to keep a piece of his work and frame it. But that would have been a wee bit pretentious, given that the certifi-cates weighed in at about $20 million apiece.

The work was so intense and precise and demanding that by 4:30 we were all ready to crash. We'd gotten through about a third of the brief-case but even so had processed enough paper to establish me as one of the richest men in America. It was OK for starters.

We carried the envelopes and briefcase up to Milly Beth, who phoned Fedex for a pickup. We visited Duke, who was well into his sec-ond bottle of Mumm's and rubbing his hands with glee. I asked to use his safe and take some cash, and he led us out into the foyer and keyed his way through the unnamed middle door between the office and the apartment. Duke and I went downstairs to a safe that was actually on the floor below but completely secure from it. The safe opened to a digital combination, followed by a cleverly set up voice ID (which if muffed would trigger an alarm on the ground floor). I set down the briefcase and told him I'd need the safe again before closing time. He said no problem.

I grabbed twenty thousand in cash and stuffed it into the side pocket of my jacket. *Shame on you! Even in fiction, you should be more careful with money.*

It was time to pick up the other briefcases and check out of the hotel. Augustus (lucky for him, it turned out!) was due home for dinner, and Wilbur needed a ride back to the hotel, where he'd left his bike. I paid them both and swore them to secrecy. Then we rounded up Paco and Sheehy and headed across town in the Mercedes. In the car I warned everybody that somebody dangerous was after me and didn't say why and gave them a vague description of Our Beloved. Shem pulled a .45 automatic out of a shoulder holster and released the safety, while Paco opened the glove compartment and checked the clip on what looked like a Berretta .32.

We pulled into the Tour d'Or crescent and parked. Paco got out of the limo and leaned back against it to watch the crescent and the street. The others came in with me. As I stood waiting at the front desk Wilbur offered to go up to Henri Quatre for my few belongings, and I sent Sheehy with him. The clerk got to me almost at once, and the computer printer was burping out my expenses, when I had a strange thought, and suddenly a chill went up my spine. The thought was that, if Glynda and I had had a son, he could be just Wilbur's age. Wilbur. *What the hell was I doing, sending him upstairs? That's what I'd like to know.*

I told the clerk to wait and I hit the Suites Elevator at a run. The damn elevator took forever getting down to me and forever opening its fat expensive pretentious door and forever hoisting its snob-loving bulk up to my floor. I bolted out of it and through the half-opened door of Henri Quatre and tripped over something and crashed to the floor.

The Most Amazing Thing

I raised my head and looked back. Doc Sheehy, whom I'd tripped over, was gazing at the ceiling with a dreamy look in his blue eyes, a hideous sight to behold, because the rest of his body was lying on its stomach. *Ugh.*

I raised myself to my hands and knees. Our Beloved was standing in the middle of the big shadowy room, facing me, and there were no woman's breasts now, and his leather jacket was bare of ornament. In one hand he held Doc's automatic and in the other an Uzi assault weapon like some I'd seen in the Risen arsenal. A sobbing from behind the bed must be Wilbur, and the open French doors suggested that the monster had let himself down from the roof. Evening traffic was noisy outside but couldn't compete with that atrocious voice:

"Arf! Arf! Little doggie! Doggie want a bone? Doggie's wetting his doggie-pants? Ba-a-ad doggie!" He tossed the gun onto the bed and with his left hand drew a machete from his belt. "Take your sportin' chance, Willy-Weeny. Go for the gun!"

I got to my feet and faced him. He must have been sizing me up, because he stopped talking, and for a moment, I thought the final moment in my life, I could hear trumpet music, maybe from the next suite over, a trumpet playing an old Fats Waller tune, and time seemed to slow down, and good old Fats, who always knew what he was about, was whispering to me, "He won't use the gun, Des, because he wants to have surprise on his side when he takes the hotel safe downstairs."

"Thanks," I said out loud, and Our Beloved must have thought I was talking to him, because he was just about to reply when I rushed straight at him. I thought I'd taken him off guard, but was dreadfully wrong, because as I reached for the machete he took a step backward and, with a lightning backhand move, struck at my right arm. It felt like he'd hit me with a baseball bat, but it didn't stop my blundering forward momentum, and as I crashed against him, all in the same moment, I realized that I had no hand and saw the blood from my arteries spurting into Our Beloved's eyes. He stumbled backwards and we fell to the floor with me on top, and as I came down on him his whole body stiffened under me and the great nasty mouth opened and a horrific war cry, a stinking sound fit to wake the dead and kill the living, blasted out at me like a tornado

BLAH!

I raised my right arm to smash him but was quickly reminded that there was no hand on it. All my hopes, my very being on earth, had dissolved into this impotent bloody gushing stump.

There was only one thing to do.

With all my might I rammed my stump into his mouth. *You sick bastard. I can't go on.*

The stump fitted snugly, like a dowel in its socket, with all my weight behind it, and suddenly the room was drowned in silence.

Our Beloved's sufferings were terrible but short. As Dr. Auchinleck later told me in his professorly way, "Few events are so immediately threatening to human life as a sudden and forceful intrusion into the mouth."

FRIDAY, JUNE 12, 1998, THE BELLOWS CLINIC

Mega Klein won't be reading this anymore. She should have told me she was being treated for panic attacks. I guess she was just too proud to let on.

Sorry to say this, but it's a big relief now that she's not looking over my shoulder. Her physical presence is a little offputting. She's less than five feet tall, and her body's shaped like an upright loaf of deli bread, and she's got a half-inch growth of black beard on her chin that she fondles when deep in thought, which is always, and she talks through her nose, looking at you cross-eyed.

Besides, writing correctly is a marvelous gift, but it's got to be hard on the glands. Maybe it's why so many good writers zone out on substances, hate everybody, look like dead fish and have fucked-up lives.

I might've bled to death if it hadn't been for Wilbur. I'd passed out and rolled over unconscious after finishing Our Beloved, and Wilbur fought off the dizziness of a concussion and the pain of a broken arm to dial 911 and alert the front desk. First thing I remember hearing is the sirens, and then they had me up on the wheely table and Paco was putting my severed hand on my belly and telling me to hold it with my other hand and not to let go of it.

They gave me a shot of morphine then, and the next thing I knew I was waking up in the city hospital the next morning with my arm in a jumbo sling that covered everything except for four black-and-blue fingers sticking out. Auchinleck presented himself at that point, a craggy donnish type who looked forbidding until his face broke into a teenage smile. He said I was still dangerously weak and shouldn't try fighting any more swordsmen for a while. He also said that Our Beloved had done the cleanest job he'd ever seen, and that the surgery had been successful.

He suggested that, when I got stronger, I convalesce here, at the Bellows Clinic in the Music Mountains.

The local police dropped in the next day. The interview wasn't very exciting. First off, they hadn't peeled away all of Our Beloved's aliases yet, but they knew he was wanted for murder in Colorado and aggravated assault in the I-15 incident (the cop survived with a fractured skull). They knew he'd killed Sheehy and in short they were downright embarrassed that he'd gotten into the Tour d'Or, and that it'd come down to his having to be stopped by a private citizen who'd lost an extremity in the struggle. They pieced it together from Paco and Augustus that Our Beloved's attack was the segue to an earlier drive-by incident in the hills. So far as I was concerned, they saw me as a victim and a hero, who'd saved Wilbur's life and snuffed out Our Beloved's with good old Nevadan ingenuity.

168

They hadn't checked up on my possessions in the safe, because Our Beloved had broken into my suite, not the safe. Our Beloved was a murderer and a certifiable loony, which completely explained why he'd tried to rub me out after a drive-by conflict.

Case closed. *We police know everything. Want to tell us we don't?*

I wasn't about to try.

And the reward! Coloradan lawmen had been through the wreckage of the Penumbra Hotel and discovered, among all the corpses, weapons and tools of sacrilege, bits and pieces of the stuffed sheriff and deputy. They got roaring mad and put $25 thousand on Our Beloved's head. I asked that this wad go to Sheehy's family, but it turned out he'd been a loner, so I told them to give it to Wilbur. Now he'll be able to finish his biology degree without killing himself in the process.

I told the police I'd been traumatized and didn't want to speak to the press for awhile. They said they'd do what they could.

Wilbur and Augustus showed up that afternoon, with Wilbur beaming through two black eyes and Augustus looking miffed because, he said, he hadn't been there with me in the pinch. With me propped up in my bed, the three of us sat through a few long periods of silence, each of us thinking our own private thoughts about what we and others had been through.

Then I dropped the blockbuster. I asked them if they could both join my firm for the summer, or at least until my arm was healed and I could get back to Duke's. I offered them outrageous wages. Augustus had no trouble deciding. His son Virgil could manage the gas station and do the towing, and the repair service more or less ran itself. But Wilbur was torn. He felt he'd made a commitment to the hotel manager, and that when his fracture healed he'd be needed again. I said I'd talk to the manager and try to get him off honorably.

That was all I could handle right then. On Friday I was transferred here, and that evening Augustus phoned in from Vegas that Crouse had gotten his payoff and kicked back over $4 million in change, that he was moving out of the office that weekend, and that I was now Duke. There were still the closing papers to sign, but since I couldn't sign a thing, I gave Augustus power of attorney on Monday, arranged for him to be able to pick up my satchels at the Tour d'Or and made him Acting Treasurer of Duke's, Inc.

That week Augustus had a rubber stamp made up, so he wouldn't have to break his ass using Miss Flora's elegant handwriting on every megabucks certificate.

I wanted to get the reregistration of the securities out of the way as soon as possible, because having the certificates in my name, as long as nobody else reported them stolen, was the simplest possible proof that they belonged to me.

None of this took much effort, and I had very little effort to give. During those early days I was flat on my back, weak as a kitten, doped up on drugs that kept me half-asleep but never left me feeling rested.

As I say, I had many visions of Mara during those days, and during some of them we kind of talked with each other, but we never seemed to get anything settled. I asked her to forgive me, and she said OK, but still my mind wasn't at rest because, you see, even though I saw her dead, I can't kill the Mara that's in my mind. You just can't do it with that sort of person.

I suppose that's why people believe in ghosts.

TUESDAY, JUNE 16, 1998, THE BELLOWS CLINIC

Wilbur just phoned to say that Paws has set up shop in the roof garden at Duke's. He's eating plenty of cat food, getting plump and sleek and stirring things up for the local lizards. He'll fall asleep on the bricks of the outer railings, with two legs dangling carelessly over the abyss. But when he's awake he likes to relax on an old hollowed-out cactus, with his one good eye just showing through a peep-hole near the top.

I had the most amazing dream last night. I dreamed I was visiting a

170

family, don't know who, in a nice white house in a valley. The parents asked if I'd like to see the family scrapbook, and they brought out a great red leather jobbie full of photos of them and their three kids—not your usual foolish snapshots but really dazzling scenes of the whole family, over many years, doing all sorts of exciting things all over the world. Some of the pictures seemed so deep that I could see into the space inside of them just like a window, while others seemed to move under my very eyes, as though the whole family past, all their years and madcap thrills and fascinations, was coming real for me. It was getting almost scary, but when I put the book down and got up to go, the dad said, "You ain't seen nuttin' yet," in precisely those words. He then pulled on a handle in the wall, and imagine my surprise when the whole wall opened up into an accordioned gallery array of mindblowing photos—not of the family any more but of all human history, and I saw at last what Moses and Cleopatra and Hannibal and Homer really looked like, with behind them the innumerable shadowy ancient faces of our whole parentage. Christ and Caesar, who were standing next to each other all buddy-buddy, looked so real that I wanted to talk to them, but my friend pulled me out of that room and down a long sunlit gallery, as he opened up wall after wall of pictures—the house was a giant scrapbook!—pictures of the animal kingdom from microbes up to blue whales, pictures of all the natural features of the earth and the other planets and the sun and the awesome ghostly stars, each with its own fascinating story to tell. It was all so incredible that this time I didn't want to leave the house at all, but for some reason I *had* to. After I said goodbye and got into the back seat of the car, I was suddenly a little boy again. My mother and father were in the front seat, just like the old days, and as he drove my father said, "Look back, Desmond, and you'll see an interesting effect." I looked back just as our car left the valley and cleared the next rise, to see the white house, and all its land, fold into the bosom of the valley like a page in a closing book.

What does this dream mean? Do dreams have to mean? Could it be an image of healing? Could I be healing *inside* as well as outside, I mean, could I be *growing*? But if I'm really growing, why did I dream about being a kid?

Maybe because kids are turned on by everything!

THURSDAY, JUNE 18, 1998, THE BELLOWS CLINIC

Wilbur phoned again. The news is finally in on Our Beloved. He was born Arcanis Valpudis, place of birth listed as Rest Area, CA, March 1, 1953.

LAPD liked him for his sister's rape and murder in 1976, but he beat the rap.

Starting in the early 80s, and in between prison stays for pimping, drug-selling and theft, he did odd jobs in Hollywood, getting a minor rep as a backstage jack-of-all-trades and even appearing as an extra in a few B-flicks. Around 1990 he gave up legit movies and drifted into hard porn and horrendous "snuffbox" S and M. The Vegas police have nothing else on him except that some time between fall '94 and summer '95 he was away for a few months in South America. But the Colorado authorities are still following some leads on members of the Lupus Coven or Crivellian Risen who might have survived the Penumbra disaster and escaped.

THURSDAY, JULY 16, 1998

TIME cover story:

AMERICA'S TALKING AGAIN!

I don't believe it! Seems that when news spread of America's 100 top talk-show hosts dying in the Escondido Inferno, the nation went into a state of clinical shock. Prozac sales skyrocketed, eating disorders ballooned, and the medical community reported treating 550,000+ cases

of withdrawal symptoms within a single week. But then something unexpected happened. As the reporter puts it, all over America—

rusty back doors began to creak open. Windows, long frozen shut, were pried free and pushed up. Cars were pulled to the curb and left empty, as the nation's streets, squares, parks, backyards and porches began to fill up with talking Americans. At first the subject was tragedy, as total strangers embraced each other, bewailing the loss of 100 cherished entertainers and the entire congregation of an American church. But then the subject turned to brighter things—to politics, sports, the movies, the weather, sports, trivia, gossip and everything else under the sun.

Quick to catch the entrepreneurial spirit, housewives started baking pizzas and hawking them in the street.

"It's a communications explosion," said Herb Warren, Professor of Communications at the Annenberg School, USC, "that is like to put the World Wide Web to shame." "They're still at it," reported Buster Fleem of KCRT from a helicopter over Critter, Idaho, at 11 PM Saturday night, while a source at CBS-TV noted that prime time ratings were hovering "just north of zero."

It's an ill wind, et cetera!

JULY 20, 1998

News item: the 213 children surviving the Escondido Inferno have been moved to a facility on the Pomo Indian Reservation near Sacramento and are up for adoption.

I think I'll adopt them all!

Book Two   **Rucking It**

• • • • • • • • • • • • • • • • • • •

Here follows *Rucking It*, the second volume of *The Most Amazing Thing*—the intimate, complete, unexpurgated and unabridged private journal of Desmond Ruck, the world's first and to date only trillionaire! Because *Rucking It* subsumes an even broader canvas than its predecessor, *Ruck's Run*—five years of time, three continents and large areas of the Pacific Ocean—and because it not only treats the many surviving characters of the earlier volume but also introduces scores of new faces, we have been obliged to increase the number and volume of explanatory notes. As a means of expediting this procedure, and additionally gaining knowledge and expertise from one of Mr. Ruck's most trusted companions, we have enlisted the editorial aid of Ethan Zoig, Ph.D., an administrator of the gigantic Ruck Estate and now president of the Free University of America. Dr. Zoig has not only provided invaluable insight into Ruck's private life, but also given titles to the chapters and written a crucial narrative.

As well as being a thoughtful, exciting, humane, sensational, profound, compelling, hilarious, evocative, sensual, faith-renewing and erotic

Editor's Note

book, *Rucking It* is likely to clear up not a few controversies. Of the countless volumes written, over the past years, about the landmark Salvage Defense in *The U.S. Government vs. Desmond Ruck* (2001) and the notorious "Floatifer Law" in the Arizona State Legislature (2002), of the seemingly endless dialogues conducted by the press over the mysterious events that brought the Bolgovnian Civil War to its sudden and tragic close, and of the prolonged and fiery debates about the real details of the Affair Known as Water Closet, no writer can speak with the firsthand authority of Desmond Ruck. He was a central figure in each of these historic events: the hero, or the villain, or the victim, or that strange combination of hero-cum-villain-cum-victim that only Desmond Ruck could be.

One happy note. Though numerous Ruckisms persist and our author continues to produce the occasional figurative nightmare, his literary style shows some improvement in the chapters that follow. Sometimes, indeed, his voice even approaches the level of poetry, of the simpler sort. I attribute this amelioration to the good offices of Prof. Mega Klein (U. Texas) although in fairness I must acknowledge Dr. Zoig's conjecture that Ruck is writing better "because he's fallen in love with life." Improvements notwithstanding, you will have no trouble recognizing his unmistakable voice.

—SIGMUND BAZOOM, *Editor*

Chapter Eight   A Hymn to Life

Composed by Desmond Ruck and dated "June, 2001"[6]

I love the morning smell of the desert, the herbs and the cactus flowers, the scent of dew wetting red earth, wafted on the day's first breezes as I lie waking.

I love the warmth of the down covers and the honey suffusion of sleep-hormones and body-warmth as I float in the wake of my dreams.

I love the big skylit bathroom, open through glass doors to a view of the White Mountains, with its blue and white Tlaxcala floor tiles, its black-walnut toilet seat warming under me, the inexpressible luxury of regular and smooth digestion, the big shower nozzle with its huge soft gush of sun-heated springwater, the baptism of the warming shower.

---

6. This prose poem was found among Desmond Ruck's papers. For reasons that will later be apparent to the reader, it seemed to me suitable for inclusion here. —Ed.

The Most Amazing Thing

I love the morning sunlight on my slated terrace, the oversized captain's chairs by the round oak table under the lilac and bougainvillea trellis—the trellis and furniture built with my own hands—the table now loaded by Catherine[7] with huevos rancheros and homemade hash and fruit salad and a crystal pitcher of iced tea, the delighted whish-and-clink of tea poured into the colorful wide-brimmed Mexican tumbler, the marvelous strange taste of food after the nightly fast, the strengthening warmth of the sun as I space out over the last sip of tea, the glow and edge of the beginning day.

I love walking down the alley of plumeria, cypress, boojum tree and royal palm to the shop, my dream-factory, where with my helpers I fashion things from wood and metal and clay, and fool around with chemicals and electronics. I love the feeling of taking, all by myself, an idea from a wordless glint to a completed object, of working what is shapeless into shapes, of beginning long projects and disappearing into them until I'm lost in them, of bosom closeness to material and tool and machine.

I thrill to the shock of blue pool water as I dive in just after noon and enjoy the low-level muscle pain as my limbs get used to the new strain and then the sense of ease and rhythm as I get well into my course of laps, the refreshing feeling of having a new center of gravity, and finally, as I tire, the peaceable separation from the world outside my pool and in the past. I savor my poolside light lunch of gazpacho or lobster stew or tuna salad, with bread grown in our fields and baked in our ovens, with butter and buttermilk from our own cows and dairy.

---

7. Catherine Vanya, who had been Ruck's favorite nurse at the Bellows Clinic (*Ruck's Run*, Ch. 7), later took charge of the household staff at Lomo Morado, a position she still holds. —Ethan Zoig

I drift into long afternoons, sitting in the shade of my trellis or my look-out gazebo, reading histories and novels and poems and books about nature and machines and businesses, and memoirs of people who, like me, have lived through tough days, though sometimes my eye will be caught by a handsome pile of cumulus clouds on the west side of Cabeza Blanca,[8] or a hawk wheeling over the desert and plummeting down at its prey, or sometimes I'll doze off for a minute, and like as not be wakened by Ranguma,[9] who's silently come out of nowhere and put her dear tired white head under my hand as it hung off the arm of the chair, and who looks at me with love in those undimmed eyes, and I'll realize that I've been dreaming of Mara.

At times like that I can't resist getting into the jeep with Ranguma and Paws and driving down the hill to the mouth of Marble Canyon, and walking up into it till we're 2000 feet deep in vertical rock walls, and (if it's not spring, when Seneca Creek really thunders), listening for the wildest noise I think I've ever heard, the kingfisher's cry echoing through the narrow canyon as he flashes upriver, and that cry will call to me of all the mysteries of nature, and of how, in Aldo Leopold's words, everything is interconnected. And then I may shout my great shout and Ranguma howl her eery howl, and as the echoes fade we'll stand silently marveling at the perfect desolation of the place.

I love the sunlight filtering down on grama grass through boughs of Apache pine, and the fiery light of a winter sunset on the snow of the Cabeza, and the soft gold of the reading lamp by my bedside. I love the orange, rose and purple evening clouds, and the table laid in white on

---

8. Ruck's mountain. See below. —Ed.

9. Readers of *Ruck's Run* will remember that *ranguma* is an Indonesian word for "sorcerer." For its new meaning, see below. —Ed.

the west terrace and the sounds of Sergei[10] at the keyboard heard from within the house, and the lantern-lit dinners and the taste of old wine and the sudden booming unanimous laughter of friends. I love the eddy of memory, the rush of insight, the glow of understanding. I love the sharing of joy or grief. I love the outstretched hand. I love the happy shouts of 213 children when they stream out of the buses from Pueblo Verde[11] and into the meadow for an Easter egg hunt.

I love all in man that talks to the patient roots that move stones, and to the stones that move but endure and to the water that feeds the roots and rounds off the stones. I love all in man that loves his world, all that hopes, all that remembers.

I love everything that women are and do, but I don't understand anything about them. I ache to find a woman who knows me, answers me, speaks to me across this void of wealth and wistfulness, who breaks the grip of Mara holding me even from the grave.

I love the mysteries of people. I keep one whisper-quiet BMW motorcycle at Duke's[12] and another at my house in Tucson, and weekday evenings or weekend mornings I'll glide incognito down suburban streets, slowly cruising along, watching people at work or play, catching glimpses of back yards, peering at porches, gazing into windows, and my imagination will fill in what the old man is dreaming of as he snoozes on a chaise lounge on the unmown lawn in front of his Craftsman-style

---

10. The now-renowned pianist Sergei Oistropovich was Ruck's guest while preparing for the Scarlatti Competition of 2001. —Ed.

11. Pueblo Verde is the school-cum-village near Lomo Morado that Ruck built for the 213 children who survived the Escondido Inferno of 1998 and whom Ruck subsequently adopted. —Ed.

12. Ruck's casino/office/residence in Las Vegas. —Ed.

house, or what issue Mr. Yuppy and his wife are arguing over at their bar-
becue, or what the two young boys are giggling about as they race out
the front door of the tiny clapboard, or who the stacked young woman is
going to meet when, with such a serious face, she strides down her walk
and gets into her Volvo. I cruise by, dreaming myself into their lives.

But I ache for the agonies of peoples. I hear cries of suffering from every
continent, agony caused by injustice and causing it all over again. I feel
the suffering of the roofless, the hearthless, the women and children,
the aged and the ill, the minorities and the oppressed. Give me time,
and God help me I will make things better for them.

Chapter Nine   The Troubled Trillionaire

It's all over. They've nailed me at last. I'm dogfood.

But at least I've had my day in the sun.

Gannett from my legal team called at 9:30 AM. He can't stall them anymore. An FBI motorcade, setting out from Vegas who knows when tonight, will arrive here at Lomo Morado some time around dawn, and I'm supposed to "surrender" to it, at which point we take a little drive back to the Federal Courthouse in Vegas.

The rap will be interstate transport of stolen goods (the frigging Imbratta van!), but that's just for starters. They'll throw the book at me. They'll put me away. They'll take everything.

Ranguma's been prowling around the house all day, moaning. She knows something's amiss.

I spent the day putting my things in order, in case the judge doesn't grant bail. It's just after sunset, and I'm holed up in the library with a bottle of Wharton's, a tray of tuna sandwiches and the samovar[13] going full blast.

I've got two jobs of work to do tonight. One is to run back through three years of this journal and delete everything that's humdrum, embarrassing to others or just plain chatty.[14] The second is to remember, remember and recount, the few things I've managed to achieve and the people who've meant a lot to me. How to begin?

The summer of 1998 was a time of healing, as life slowly came back to my right hand. Four, five hours at a stretch every day I'd be sitting on the skydeck at Duke's, poring through newspapers from seven states for clues about my mysteries, or watching birds at the birdfeeder, or just musing. During those peaceful times it occurred to me that I needed something like a game plan if I didn't want events to take on a mind of their own. I asked myself what my first priorities were, and came up with only two answers: personal freedom, and helping people who were in trouble. Personal freedom, I decided, required two things: a) to create privacy and security for myself, b) to delegate responsibilities. Helping people, I decided, had to be a focused job, rather than gadabout do-gooding.

With this in mind I began putting on staff.

I told Gus Randolph to hire the whole graduating classes of the University of Nevada's Law and Business Schools. I wanted young Nevadans who hadn't been ruined by corporate horseshit. Then, for my investment managers, I raided the presidencies of three of America's top

---

13. One of Ruck's inventions, jestingly named "samovar" by Oistropovich. Among other things, it roasted coffee beans and produced espresso. See below. —Ed.

14. We have no idea how much material Ruck deleted from his journal that night, because he copied the shortened version onto all of his backup files. —Ed.

retirement funds and got Vance Rousseau, Walter Clemens and Wallace Horowitz—three men who had superb track records for safeguarding other people's futures.

I put $200 billion worth of securities into their hands and told them to sell the lot of it and invest in Third World development.

They asked me, Why Third World development? I answered that I wanted my money to be of some use to the world.

They told me I was going to have one honey of a capital gains tax bill come April.

I said, So be it. I knew capital gains was going to open a can of worms (how could I establish the Imbrattas' securities' value at purchase?) but didn't want to let any of my employees in on *that* secret any sooner than I had to. Wasn't I afraid of screwing up their lives by making them accomplices after the fact? Not really. There's a golden parachute ready for everybody on my staff.

And why didn't I sit tight on my new-found investments so as not to attract attention? Because with that kind of money, there's no place to hide, especially when you're just about to adopt 213 Escondido Inferno orphans. You may as well just let it all hang out and do your own thing.

By the time I had everything shipshape it was September, and my right hand was usable again. I was the world's richest man, and it was time to start hoeing my row.

I had four projects, and none of them would be easy.

PROJECTS #1 AND #2: *Pueblo Verde and Lomo Morado*

First came the children. The State of California was finding them a royal pain in the butt. The Pomo Reservation, where they were "under care," wasn't really right for them and was staffed with green personnel and crawling with reporters nosing around for misrule and malpractice. I went straight to Governor Jimenez. I told her I was president (which I am) of the $29 billion dollar White Wolf Foundation. My offer of guaranteed world-class schooling and a $1 million trust fund for each child was too good to refuse.

To house the kids temporarily I flew to Bermuda, where I'd had such a good time at age eleven, and bought the House of York, a 100-room hotel right on Harrigan Sound. I staffed it with teachers that I had hired away from America's best private and public schools. I put Gus's wife, Rose Randolph, in charge of the whole thing, mainly because Rose was an experienced teacher and one of the few people at that point that I knew and trusted.

This worked out fine, except that Gus was always bolting to Bermuda for conjugal leave.

Of course I didn't want to pen up the kids in the hotel forever. I dreamt of building them a combination farm-school-village—a place where they could have education and community at the same time. That's how the idea for Pueblo Verde was born. On Saturday, October 3—I remember it clear as day—Wilbur and I saw on the local news that the Air Force was planning to sell off a block of 250,000 acres (including Mount Cabeza Blanca) in eastern Arizona. We got right on the phone, and Tuesday morning I was cruising over the parcel in a big chopper with a bird colonel. What dazzled me about the place was that the Cabeza's summit ridge made its own weather system by trapping westerly clouds, so there were about 4500 acres of green belt for crops and pasture on the gently rising lower slopes. The property had everything I needed, including a state road passing through its northwest corner and an air strip in the desert south of the mountain.

I bought the spread. No sooner had we closed the deal in November than I was down there with a planning team of about thirty architects, designers, engineers and teachers, crawling over the foothills in a little swarm of Hummers.[15] The experts stayed at a spa about half an hour

---

15. Four-wheel-drive vehicles used by the US Army during the Gulf War of 1991 and later made available to the public. —Ed.

away from the northwest entrance, but I spent my nights in the Vixen, on site. And it was during a sunset prowl in the Vixen that I discovered Lomo Morado. I'd been checking out the air strip—in fact, measuring its length with the Vixen's odometer—when I noticed about two miles to the north what looked like a graded road climbing a low promontory that formed the southernmost extension of the Cabeza. I made my way towards it and drove up a sagebrush slope to the ridge where I sit today: a table of land broad enough for a college campus and commanding a great view of the mountain and the desert.

What'd the USAF been doing up there on the ridge? There were bulldozed remains of a lookout tower and what might have been a heliport. In the evening quiet I looked around me. A vast sea of desert, bounded by snowy mountains, stretched to the east, south and west, and to the north the Cabeza towered like some kind of watchful god.

I had the most curious feeling, of being at peace.

Standing in the rosy glow and feeling the first cool night breeze, I pulled out my topo. The promontory was called Lomo Morado. The words had a lilt to them, and in that instant an image popped out of nowhere into my mind. I suddenly saw my house as it now stands: a broad-faced adobe, with big windows and tile roofs. Once that image was planted, I couldn't pull it out. I *had* to live on Lomo Morado, amidst all that solitude and beauty, near the kids.

I bedded down in the Vixen then and there, but couldn't sleep a wink for the excitement of it (and some other thoughts that I'll get into later). Next morning, when the planning team showed up, I told them they now had two jobs, not one.

Within a year the school-village of Pueblo Verde was ready for classes, and the house at Lomo Morado had risen in the exact shape of my dream.

It's 9 PM now and quite dark. With Ranguma limping stiffly behind me, I walk out onto the skydeck to stretch my legs. The stars are breathtak-

ing! I catch a whiff of dishwasher soap from the kitchen, but otherwise the ranch has gone to sleep.

Strange, I'm not all that worried about tomorrow. What worries me is whether I'll be able to write what I need to before dawn. Better stoke up on espresso and sandwiches.

How did the FBI get onto me? They came to the party sort of late, and might not be here at all yet, if it hadn't been for Molly Block. Back in the fall of '98 I'd managed, with the help of a few Vegas badges, to duck out of media interviews regarding the Our Beloved showdown, and I was doing my damnedest to displace all the Escondido Inferno adoption notoriety away from myself personally and onto the White Wolf Foundation. I'd have gotten away with both, I think—at least temporarily—if it hadn't been for Block. She was a junior reporter for the Vegas *Review-Journal,* and unlike most of her journalist colleagues she had a memory that went back more than two or three months. She put the two incidents together and realized that while a big foundation helping orphans was a Page One, lower-left corner story, orphans being helped by a foundation whose president had recently terminated an evil giant with his bare hands, or hand and stump if you will, was the kind of story the getting wind of which would make all the network news anchors jump onto an airliner and head for the scene, economy class if necessary.

Ironically, her editors at first wouldn't let her touch the story. They scoffed at it and assigned her to cover a dispute between two rival tribes over casino rights. Only when Molly Block threatened to quit her job, hock her Jetta and sell the story all on her lonesome, did they give in.

Even then, going was slow for her, thanks to me. I refused interviews and insisted on privacy, and when you have money, privacy means something. We turned her away, by her count, seventeen times. Other potential information sources, like the IRS, wouldn't give her access to their files on me.

As if this wasn't enough, she discovered she had breast cancer.

It was in the County Hospital, in the recovery room after surgery, that she met Viola Irving. Irving was a rare bird: a female computer hacker. Within hours they were in cahoots with each other. As they shook hands, bed to bed, Irving sang out, "If I live, Molly, I'll bag you a Ruck!"

How do I know all this? Because Molly Block works for me now.

Irving *did* live long enough (she died last year) to hack her way into the IRS files. Of course, the IRS wasn't interested in me as yet: it was February 1999 and I hadn't had to file my first big returns yet. What she found out, nevertheless, was just as incriminating. She discovered that my 1997 tax bill had been just over $2000 and, worse, she found out my home address in Eugene.

Molly flew to Oregon and interviewed Glynda. Within days she'd published the story:

RUCK'S BUCKS: TYCOON
CONCEALS SUSPICIOUS PAST

You guessed it, my friends. The FBI got onto me by reading about me in the newspaper!

The rest was a war of attrition. It's lasted just under 2½ years. The feds have kept coming back again and again. Each time they knew just a little bit more than before. What could I say or do? First I stonewalled. Then I stalled. Then I negotiated—all through Gannett and his legal team, of course. And that's how it came to this.

Not that these have been bad years. All and all, I wouldn't have missed a day of them. They were so full of thrills and new experiences that sometimes I didn't think about the feds for weeks at a time. I was rebuilding my life, if not inventing a new one.

But back to my projects:

PROJECT #3: *A Second Chance*

I mentioned four projects, the first two being the kids and the ranch. The third one isn't a cinch to write about, but if I don't, somebody else will, and get things wrong in the bargain, so I'd better down a slug of Wharton's and come clean with what happened. That reminds me. This project began on a night when I was hootching it a mite too heavily (I'm pasting in right from my journal):

OCTOBER 10, 1998[16]

What the hell's the matter with me?? Yesterday I was a sane man. Today I'm shaken, shrunken, possessed.

It started late yesterday afternoon. I'd just wowed Chris[17] by playing the scale of C, *vivace*, on the piano at Duke's with my right hand. Chris said he'd never seen such a fast recovery and (it being that time of day) suggested a celebration. That sounded funny coming from *him*, because he'd always struck me as a solemn kind of guy, but it seemed like a sensible idea, so I rang for Paco and asked him to stop doormanning and chauffeur us around for a while. While Paco was getting the Mercedes Chris and I grabbed one of those local nightspot-maps from a rack on the bar and plotted out a course that would take us to six of Vegas' plushest dives.

Not much happened at the first three bars. Chris seemed to get even sadder after a few drinks, and I wasn't in the mood for opening up about my past adventures or future dreams. It's amazing how dull things can get when you're trying to enjoy yourself in public. But at the Bull and Bear the mood suddenly changed. Chris let his guard down, and it turned out that he wasn't such a sour guy after all, but a jolly man in sad times. Wanna start looking sour? Just have your 12-year-old son die of leukemia, and your 15-year-old

---

16. The journal entries quoted in this chapter were apparently saved from material otherwise deleted by Ruck. —Ed.

17. Christopher Auchinleck, M.D., the surgeon who had reattached Ruck's severed right hand in May, 1998. —Ed.

marriage break up under the strain of caring for the poor kid in his declining days. Chris was getting into graphic details, and we'd just ordered another round of the bar specials, called Nadas—high-proof bourbon sours made with sugar and fresh lime juice, packing a velvet wallop—when he went silent and his jaw dropped and his eyes looked like Bugs Bunny's eyes, when Bugs sees that he's about to be flattened by an oncoming steamroller but can't do anything about it because he's stepped in a puddle of glue.

I asked what was the matter.

Instead of answering, Chris kept staring over my right shoulder. I twisted around to see behind me, and there was this shock of recognition. Two incredibly beautiful women had just come into the bar, and I recognized them as the Speed Sisters—the gals in the Dodge Viper who'd gotten between me and Our Beloved on the way to Nevada. They were done up to kill. The blonde was wearing a black, the brunette a silver lowcut clinging tube, and in the candlelight of the Bull and Bear I could see why the ladies had cut their straight hair short: to show off arms and breasts and necks and shoulders that would have driven the Dutch Masters to rut. As they moved towards their table a flash of candlelight from a big stone around the brunette's neck knifed into my eyes and transfixed the senses of my body and soul with every power that has ever driven man to woman and woman to man.

She glanced over just after sitting down and looked puzzled, as if trying to place me. After all, it'd been five months. To give her a hint, I raised my arms and did a hammy charade of holding and turning a steering wheel. That did the trick, and within seconds all four of us were up, laughing and botching our way through introductions. She (the brunette) was Rachel Muldoon, and her friend was Camilla Hoy. A waiter helped us pull our little tables together, and soon we were all tête-à-tête, sipping Nadas and bellylaughing uncontrollably at silly jokes. Close-up viewing did nothing to tarnish *these* girls' allure; in a word, they were exquisite, and they were lively and direct to boot. Of course, they were mad keen to find out what had been going on between me and the Death Bug on I-15 that day in May (they'd thought at first that the bug had been following *them*). They were amazed and (I saw with pleasure) a touch turned on when I told them who Our Beloved was and what had happened at the Tour d'Or the next day. Immediately they both wanted to look at my scar, and Chris managed to get light-years of mileage out of describing the nuts and bolts of how he'd reattached the hand.

The poor guy looked like a new man, and before you knew it he was pulling Camilla up for a dance.

I turned to Rachel, who was gazing at me all down-homey. I wanted to dance, to touch her and move with her and smell her hair, but instead I had to open my trap and pop the question, Would she like to join me for dinner?

Something went wrong with her eyes, almost as though I wasn't there any more. "Do you mean just evening or all night?"

Dope as I was, at first, I didn't take in what she was getting at. I just blinked at her.

"For the full course, dearie," she went on, "you're talking a thousand bucks."

That was a fist in the gut. I stuttered out something incoherent, threw a bill on the table, and bolted out of there. I know it was rude to Chris and even to the girls, but I couldn't control myself. I was in a snit.

Chris called me this morning. Turns out he'd been surprised too, but less so than I, because he's lived in Vegas so much longer. Also, Camilla had a nicer way of telling him, which started with a kiss on the cheek. Camilla agreed to spend a friendly evening with him: no money, no sex, just chatter, and Rachel had tagged along. Needless to say, the main subject of conversation had been me, and why I'd gotten so flustered by meeting a prostitute.

I fobbed it off to Chris as leftover trauma nerves, complicated by loneliness.

That wasn't exactly it. The long and short of it is, I'm sort of a mental case about sex. I believe that it's a special experience, like praying, and that it should be about as far from money as A is from Z. And my phobia goes beyond prostitution. I was stunned and for a long time made impotent when Glynda pushed me away in bed and told me I was a poor provider. Didn't she mean that, even though she was my wife, she too was on a meter?

Also I'm disgusted when a gal comes on to me (as they always are doing) because I'm rich. They're so interested in pleasing you that they can't even make love right.

The sex I've had with them just makes me lonelier.[18]

---

18. Ruck is alluding here to erotic relationships which, if he ever mentioned them in his journal, he subsequently deleted. —Ed.

The Most Amazing Thing

Sometimes I even wish I wasn't big and good-looking. I want love and sex to come from something essential, from the center of people.

But *is* there a center? Who can say?

OCTOBER 11, 1998

What makes somebody become a prostitute? Poverty? Lack of education? Are they all dropouts?

Women have this precious capacity, to hold another life within themselves, to bring it forth and feed it with the milk of their own bodies. What makes them throw this treasure away?

And what kind of creep does a man have to be, to pay for sex?

For me, it'd be like buying a depression.

These things were stewing in me during the time I was setting up at Lomo Morado, later that fall. On top of this, Chris was now *dating* Camilla and going crazy in love with her. He said that there was something intensely beautiful hidden inside her, a soulful beauty that answered her beautiful face and body, and that he wanted to bring this beauty to life and wanted to live with it.

It hit me that this might be the case with many women who are forced into prostitution by men's hunger and money. The thought of this tragedy began to haunt me.

Everything came to a head in November. Remember that sleepless night I spent in the Vixen after discovering Lomo Morado? Here's what I wrote the next day:

NOVEMBER 19, 1998

It's almost noon, and I'm in the Vixen, parked outside of Barrio's Bighorn Grill, where I've just eaten two Sheepman's Breakfasts and downed a pot of coffee. I'm on a roll. I'm as revved up as Big Daddy's Mongoose.[19]

---

19. This reference escapes me. —Ed.

194

Last night was the most important night of my life.

I didn't do anything. I didn't talk to anybody. I just lay in bed and thought. In a set of blinding visions, the future, my future, rampaged into me.

I see Pueblo Verde now: the school buildings, the cottages, the farm. I see Lomo Morado now: the house, down to its very doors and windows, and the hothouse and the inn and the shop. I see the lower slopes of the Cabeza green with olive groves and vineyards, grain and pasture.

Then something even more surprising happened.

The sheer excitement of planning Pueblo Verde and the ranch was keeping me wide awake. I don't know why—I guess just so as to keep myself from going manic—I started thinking about the Vegas prostitutes. Tossing and turning I rolled over on my back to look out the rear window at the night, just in time to see a shooting star (rare at that time of year) that burned its way across the eastern sky. In that instant everything was clear to me, and I knew what I had to do.

I would offer freedom and a better life, not just to Camilla and Rachel, but to all the prostitutes in Vegas!

My plan's really quite simple. You see, I learned last week that San Lorenzo College in Indiana (where Mara and I had almost gotten pickled by Dr. Hauck) has gone belly-up. Myrdal Hwang, the Korean billionaire, has withdrawn his support after the drug bust, but that isn't the half of it. Apparently the faculty and staff of the college, while praising Jesus with every breath, haven't exactly been practicing what Jesus preached. Males were sexually molesting females, females were sexually molesting males, males were sexually molesting males, females were sexually molesting females, and sometimes males and females were mutually molesting each other. What with all this, and the lawsuits and the protests and the publicity, the college has closed and the campus is up for sale.

I'll buy San Lorenzo and establish a college for ex-prostitutes! I'll offer a full four-year scholarship to any Vegas hooker who wants one!

And that's, in short, what I did. Magdalena College, which has just celebrated its second birthday, is like any other small college, with two exceptions: 1) its students are, all 723 of them, Vegas prostitutes who answered my ad in the *Review-Journal*, and 2) for every three faculty, there is one civic leader: that is, a person who's done service for society and can teach what that service is all about. I figured that hookers, who'd served society with their bodies and lost all their dignity, could serve with their spirits and regain it. But at that point I hadn't sorted out exactly how.

It's 3:10 AM. I'm roasting more coffee beans in the samovar and pouncing on what's left of the sandwiches. I've put out a can of special high-protein dogfood for Ranguma, who's off her feed (she's eating it, thank God!). I've taken another turn on the deck—the sky's clouded over now. From the deck you can look clear across Bañera Basin to the northwest entrance of the ranch, fifteen miles away, and at night you can see headlights as they come through the entrance. I can't believe that the agents would have started out after midnight, but I keep looking out there anyway. There's no time for any more diddling around.

PROJECT #4: *The Past Regained*

Three years ago I wrote in this book that I was going to hire information-seekers to do missions and probes into all the people involved in my 1998 adventures. I kicked off this project as soon as I started feeling strong again in September, but at first I screwed it up. In a word, I hired the wrong man. At the Bellows Clinic I'd run into Professor Michael Fenny, a visiting friend of Mega's[20] who was Dean of Journalism at her university. Fenny had knockout credentials, including a successful spell as a network investigative reporter and a best-selling muckraker book called *Facade: The Truth about American Foundations.* I gave him half a floor at Duke's and a blank check for staff and expenses. Then I buried myself in planning and construction for the Lomo Morado projects.

---

20. For the Bellows Clinic and Mega (Klein), see *Ruck's Run*, Ch. 7. —Ed.

When I came up for air three months later, I found out that Fenny'd put on a staff of 26 and sent half of them after Myrdal Hwang (they never found him) and the other half to research the Gombeenians: both projects (I suspected) that Fenny thought he could later turn into best-sellers. He'd skipped the Colombians and the Imbrattas (probably out of fear for his own skin) and was ignoring Mara and the Rev and the White Wolf and all of the other people I'd come to care about during my odyssey across the country.

I gave the good professor his year's wages and sent him back to his university. I recalled his staff and interviewed them one by one. They were a decent enough lot, but I didn't find anybody feisty enough to take the helm (like most managers Fenny hadn't hired staff for their leadership skills).

Then one morning I had a wacky idea.

FEBRUARY 15, 1999

10:44 AM. On a whim I've decided to call Molly Block right after lunch. Sure, you may say, she's done a pretty good job of blowing my cover, but just between you and me, I respect her for that.

8:00 PM. When I told her my name on the phone, she let out a whoop.

She was at the door of my penthouse atop Duke's fifteen minutes later, a disturbingly good-looking woman of thirty-five with red hair and blue eyes. Amenities were brief and clumsy. I took her into the living room, asked her to sit down, poured her a wine, sat down across the coffee table from her and just gazed at her. She might have thought that I was trying to mystify her or scare her, but it was different. I was simply admiring her. After what she'd done to me, and how she would expect me to feel about her, it took guts to be sitting there on the devil's own leather couch, and her courage became her.

"Molly Block," says I, "do you want the whole truth?"

She gulped. I'd managed to shock and excite her at the same time. Then, as if she saw through this gamesmanship, she came back with a move of her own. "How will I know it's the truth?"

The Most Amazing Thing

I turned and reached for a package on the piano behind me. It was a 250-page loose-leaf manuscript in a brown copy-shop bag. I reached forward and set it on the glass top of the coffee table between us, not roughly, but just roughly enough for it to make an emphatic little Thwack when it hit.

"Read this and decide," I said gently. It was my 1998 journal.

She shifted her position on the couch and readjusted her close-fitting tweed skirt. "Read it here?"

"Here and now, if you can. It's the story of how I got all this money. But there's a catch. It's off the record, OK?"

We shook on it. I looked her in the eyes, and they spoke volumes: the nervousness, the courage, the curiosity, and behind all these maybe a touch of mischief. I liked this woman.

Why was I spilling the beans to a reporter? Desperation? Lunacy? It may have been both of these, but in my own mind, I was playing the hunch that my journal, and the offer I had to make on top of it, would win her over.

That was about 2 this afternoon. I ordered Molly Block a pot of coffee, told her to buzz me when she was done reading, and hoofed it up to the ninth floor and the White Wolf Foundation. I've been spending lots of time there, interviewing staff hopefuls and reading up on social issues in the USA (I've even read Mike Fenny's book on foundations, which is very valuable in showing how some of these animals can eat up enormous amounts of income without achieving squat). Also I had a long phone chat with Chris Auchinleck, who's *proposed* to Camilla Hoy. She said yes, but they're both uptight about whether she should move in with him right now or finish her degree at Magdalena College first. Then I traipsed downstairs to the Weather Company, where Rousseau, Clemens and Horowitz, all looking damn proud of themselves, reported on my new Third World holdings, and how I was going to feed and clothe tens of millions while simultaneously making a mint.

Before I knew it it was 5:15, and folks were closing shop, and Molly Block was on the line. Her voice sounded sandy, and when I showed up in the living room I could see that she'd been crying. I asked her why.

"Because I can't publish the world's best story," she answered gamely, but I knew that wasn't it.

I'd made a friend.

I asked her if she now thought herself an accomplice after the fact. She answered that, from the journal, she wasn't sure that I'd committed any crime. As long as I didn't commit any crimes in the future, she'd have no trouble keeping mum.

I described Fenny's work and salary and the state of his division and asked her if she would quit the *Review-Journal* and take it over. Without batting an eyelash she agreed.

I'd say more about Molly, who's now a dear friend, but there's no time right now. Instead I'll record some of the things that she's discovered over the past two years, and how she's done it:

Hwang, the Gombeenians and What-all

Molly immediately hired Viola Irving, the computer whizz who'd broken into my IRS file. From her own bedroom in Vegas, Viola tapped into Freedom of Soul, International (Myrdal Hwang's front organization) and in minutes had Hwang's own mainframe working for her. FOSI's records showed that he'd bankrolled not only Hauck and San Lorenzo College, but a couple of hundred other American groups, including the First Gombeenian Evangelical Anarchist Church of Escondido. Hwang's list leaned heavily towards extremists, including militiamen and white supremicists. You'd almost have thought he was a North Korean agent, sent to sow discord in America, if it weren't for the fact that he was richer than the whole North Korean government.

More from Viola Irving: Hwang liked to keep mum about his own origins, because he wanted people to think he was some kind of god. But an international finance journal tabbed him as being half-Scandinavian (hence the strange name), 59 years old, educated in Paris, London and Heidelberg. His father built the family fortune blackmarketing military hardware and, no problem, Myrdal had laundered the loot into an investment empire. He was also "Archdeacon" of the First Umbilical Fundamentalist Church.

The Most Amazing Thing

South America: The Drug Connection
and the Search for Mara's Roots

Molly and I back-burnered the Colombian connection for the simple reason that we didn't think the Colombians would have much interest in my doings. But wire service records showed that there'd been a major bust in Colombia during the week of March 30–April 5, 1998—the same week that I took the van!—and that for months after this most of the druglords were either in custody or hiding out in the jungle. Among those mentioned was a family called Sturm—a name that Mara had passed on to me: a weird name for Colombia, until you remember all the Nazis who took refuge in South America after WWII. What happened down there after the bust? Molly hasn't discovered much as yet about the second half of 1998, except that by '99 the Sturms and some of their sidekicks were back in business.

Also we haven't yet begun a search for Mara's Chilean relatives. There just hasn't been time.

Our Beloved, the Lupus Coven and the Crivellian Risen

Wilbur, the bellhop who was in on my rumble with Our Beloved, bugged me for weeks to let him hire on with Molly, but I told him he had to finish spring term at college first. That summer Molly sent him up to Estes Park to research the Coven and the Risen and also to sniff out anything he could about the white wolf that saved my life. Wilbur took a room at the Stanley Hotel and at breakfast ran into none other than Axel Fanshawe himself, looking just like he does on TV. Fanshawe'd taken a six-month leave from "Twelve Hours" to write a book called *Christ and Satan: The Two Lives of Our Beloved, an American Cult Hero.* (I've declined to be interviewed.) This masterpiece is coming out next year, and Fanshawe has sold the movie rights for $6 million, so in short order we'll know all we ever wanted to know, and more, about Our Beloved and the other occupants of the Penumbra Hotel.[21]

Wilbur turned his attention to White Wolf. He rented a mountain bike and over weeks scoured the whole region for sightings. More on that later.

Titus Farnacle

Molly did some spadework on Uncle Titus while she was in New York, and Viola (just before she got too ill to work) infiltrated his corporate computer. Titus is still going strong, except that he's a few million deeper in debt than he was in '98. To cut costs, he's fired his whole credit-card staff (including men who were with him for up to thirty years) and replaced them with illegal female Cuban aliens who are almost slave-labor.

(I have plans for Uncle Titus.)

The Infamous Imbrattas

Guccio Imbratta is dying of throat cancer. He's holed up in a country place on Long Island, with a full-time nurse. (If I can beat this FBI rap, I want to find a way of seeing him myself.) Who was the poor old lady who took the first shot in the Imbratta/Calandrino massacre? Ironically, it was Lisetta Quirino, Guccio's widowed sister, who was coming home from the shop (as she did every day) to cook the old man's dinner.

Did any of the Imbratta or Calandrino boys survive that shoot-out? No. As I'd expected, Guccio had enough purchase with his local precinct to have the bloodbath hushed up. Molly (thanks to my having

---

21. In his haste, Ruck fails to mention that Fanshawe later abandoned this project, citing "death-threats." —Ethan Zoig

funded a new library in Harlem) got a royal welcome from the NYPD when she arrived in May, 1999. As far as they're concerned, Guccio's clean. They showed her their records of a bungled investigation they did in '97.

Molly turned up a lot of names, but oddly none of them was Mara Delano. (Was Mickey, maybe, trying to protect her?)

Mehbub Ali Shah

After getting as much dope as she could about Guccio, Molly set out from Manhattan in a rental car for Passaic, NJ. She found Ali Shah in a neat little house on Carteret Road. As it turned out, he wasn't alone. Molly phoned me from Manhattan that night.

"Desmond, I sort of messed up on this one."

"You mean, you couldn't find Ali Shah?"

"No! I found him all right, but he was—"

I got worried that Ali Shah was dead. "You mean, he was—"

Molly gasped, "*In flagrante.*"

"In what?"

"It wasn't really *all* my fault. I knocked on the front door and was sure—I mean I thought—I heard somebody shout 'Come in!' So I come right in. It's a cute house, but not, you know, all that big. The front door opens into the living room and the living room opens into the bedroom. I walk in and there's a whole police uniform, boots and all, lying all over the living room floor, and the bedroom door's open and there's this shouting and moaning—"

"He was doing it with a policeman?"

"A police*woman*, Desmond."

You'll never guess *which* policewoman! It was Georgia Fox—the policewoman of the fatal gunbattle with nephew Farrukh![22]

---

22. For this thrilling encounter, see *Ruck's Run*, Ch. 2. —Ed.

You can imagine it took a while for their mutual confusion and embarrassment to die down, but when they did, Molly was able to find out the whole story. This amazing turn of events had a very natural cause. After the shootout on April 3, 1998, Officer Fox went through the routine counselling required for police involved in fatal incidents, but for her it wasn't so routine. Fox had grown up in—and rebelled against —a devout Quaker family. She'd tried to tough it out as a pistol-packing street cop, but the Passaic shootout drove her back into a series of depressions in which her childhood upbringing came back to haunt her. As a last resort, the counselor suggested "healing sessions" in which Fox would commune with Farrukh's next of kin, Mehbub Ali Shah.

The friendship had started and grown from there.

They shared a love of gardening and a strong sense of family.

I'd told Molly to ask Ali Shah one question. I was still wearing Farrukh's taviz religiously (and wear it to this day). Though I'm not superstitious, I suspected that several times it'd saved my life. I wanted to find out if Ali Shah could tell us any more about it. Molly asked him, and he smiled a strange smile and replied that the prayers inside a taviz usually are aimed at something specific, and that in the case of this particular taviz it was back pain.

BACK PAIN! Maybe that's why my old back injury's never come back since that very day! But maybe it was something strange I did that day, like trying to pull my prong out from between those truck-wheels, that had a kind of chiropractic effect. We'll never know for sure.

In the spring of this year Ali Shah and Georgia took charge of the greenhouse at Lomo Morado. Now that construction's done on the big place, they're hiring staff. Yesterday, while I was strolling through, I noticed a strange new hand—a lanky dark guy who's all bent over and knit up. Georgia says his name's Salvador and that he can't speak a word of English but knows everything about growing organic vegetables.

The Most Amazing Thing

The Hauck Clinic

Molly briefed me about Guccio and Ali Shah and then flew to Louis-ville, rented a car, and retraced my path to the Honest Abe Inn. News of my buying San Lorenzo College had already hit the local gossip mills, so she got very helpful treatment from the police and fire departments in nearby Hagler. She found out that, as I thought, Bevan Slattery and Red Wind had died instantly in their fall onto the generator in the Hauck Clinic, as had Hauck himself. Poor Isobel, the silent girl with the eloquent eyes, passed away the very next day. Bessie van Ardsdale was in a catatonic state at the Crow County Hospital (if she recovers, she'll be tried for kidnapping). Two of Slattery's ward-mates, the stockbroker and the rabbi, were also recovering there, but they could tell Molly no more than we knew already. Hauck's staff, every last man-jack of them, disap-peared without a trace into the surrounding hills.

Blomsky, the Womuba Twelve, Schultzie, Keane, Heidi and the Thrumbles

After this I wanted Molly to take a rest. But Molly had, as I'd already seen, this quality, something like a bulldog, of never dropping a story once she was onto it. She'd been more gripped by the events near Pi-lotsburg than by any other part of my story, and she'd been saving it for last. We'd read in the news that Platinum Jayne's father, Fuzzy Blomsky, was under treatment at the San Francisco Veteran's Hospital with a new nerve-graft therapy that might help him walk again. We knew that the others of the Womuba Twelve had all somehow made it unscathed through their balloon flights. We knew also that Luke and Art Thrum-ble had both died in the truck-train collision, as had Washington Swift, the tow truck driver they collided with (I'm in touch with his family and have given them an annuity, and they've sent me a photo of him, to remind me of that tragic instant of my life when our eyes met from two doomed trucks).[23]

But what happened to Schultzie, the Rev, his beloved Heidi or the incredible Thrumble sisters remained a mystery.

This was partly because the town of Pilotsburg, KY, no longer existed. The Rev's beloved apple tree was gone. Only the steeple of his old church, rising absurdly from the hardened brown silt, was left of the whole town.

Molly had to set up shop in Henly, ten miles downriver.

Henly was itself a mess, owing to its having been just over the county line from flood relief. Half the stores had closed, and dogs were prowling among the garbage cans on Main Street. Molly moved into a downtrodden local motel that she renamed Psycho Four and promptly came down with the flu. When she told me this on the phone I decided that that was it, I had to come, so I buzzed Rick[24] and told him to fire up the 737 first thing next day. I asked Janet[25] to pack a bagfull of antibiotics and come along. We touched down at Quincy County Airport in Kentucky just after 10 AM EDT. I went aft, hopped on my BMW, motorcycled down the ramp I'd installed at the stern of the 737, and was on my way to Henly while Rick and Janet picked up their rental car.

---

23. For this riveting narrative, see *Ruck's Run*, Chapters 3 and 4. —Ed.

24. Most likely Ruck had spoken of Beauchamps in earlier entries that he since deleted. Hence it falls on us to introduce this important figure. Colonel (USAF, Ret.) Richard Beauchamps (pronounced "Beecham") was Ruck's pilot. Besides maintaining and flying a Boeing 737 and a Cessna, Beauchamps developed the new vineyards near Pueblo Verde and served as Ruck's government liaison and press representative. Regarding Ruck's first impressions of Beauchamps, allow me to quote an offprint from e-mail, dated 7/7/99 and provided by Augustus Randolph. "Dear Gus, I've just hired a prince of a man named Rick Beecham [sic]. He's an ex-Stealth pilot, built like a heavyweight boxer, very easygoing and jolly, excellent with machines but says he prefers farming. He looks perfect for a leadership position at the ranch." —Ed.

25. Dr. Janet Ballister, the resident physician at Lomo Morado and Pueblo Verde. Ruck, who is normally careful about introducing new names in his journal, was obviously writing in haste at this point. —Ed.

The Most Amazing Thing

I had quite a day. By evening I was able to write:

I'm dog tired but I've got to write this down. It's simply out of sight! I'll just type like crazy and correct the typos later.

Molly is really buoyed up by our arrival. We moved into three rooms next to hers in Psycho Four, and while Janet tended to Molly's flu, Rick and I began sleuthing. We hit paydirt right away. Our rooms came equipped with Chatham Ferry phonebooks, and Heidi Frederick was listed, with a Henly address.[26] Rick telephoned, and Heidi's voice-mail gave him a daytime phone number at the state mental hospital in Chatham Ferry. I phoned her there and in minutes was motorcycling south on 311, along the banks of the Sacannah River. It was a strange thrill to be back at the river that just about killed me twice only a year before, but things got a bit too realistic for comfort when I had a near-miss with a kid who was joy-riding in a vintage Mustang.

I guess you can't be too careful. Being alive is being in danger.

I was so muddled by the close call that I rode clean past the hospital. I slowed down, pulled a U and gunned it back to the gate. The guard was expecting me, and I was soon entering a big and spiffy new building (workers were still finishing off some of the trim) that must have come right off the top of the federal pork barrel after the old nuthouse at Pilotsburg had washed away. The lady at the front desk told me that Heidi Frederick was assigned to the Juvenile Ward on the third floor. I was sort of distracted in the elevator — in fact I was mentally girding myself up so as *not* to fall in love with Heidi as the Rev had — and so was absolutely bowled over by the first thing I saw when the doors opened.

I was looking into eyes I'd seen before and never expected to see again!

It was one of the Thrumble girls!

I've never seen such joy light up a person's face. She let out an piercing squeal of delight, which brought her sister to us at a gallop, and Sister let out

---

26. Chatham Ferry, the county seat, is four miles downriver from Henley and has a different area code from Pilotsburg. This would explain why Ruck had been unable to locate Heidi Frederick via telephone information earlier. — Ed.

an identical squeal and they grabbed me one from each side and squeezed me like a human vise right in between the pulsating elevator doors, as the elevator alarm went off and other patients came rushing and I stood there blubbering with pure joy.

Somebody was herding and gently nudging us out into the hallway, and when I'd rubbed the tears out of my eyes I realized it was Heidi herself. She had no easy time of it calming down the water nymphs, who were still well up in the decibels and apparently hadn't yet learned a single word of English. In the end she grabbed each by one wrist and spoke sternly to them, using one or two of the zany words of their own sisterspeak. They quieted down but absolutely refused to let go of me. She seated us all on a couch in the reception room, politely got rid of the other patients and sat down in the receptionist's chair across from us.

Heidi was dressed in nurse's white. She was as beautiful and warm as she'd been a year before, but absolutely flummoxed and amazed. You see, she'd had no idea who the Thrumble girls were, and neither did anybody else!

Heidi leaned forward and talked to me in hushed tones, and I soon found out why. The Thrumbles were a bone of contention at State Hospital. They'd fetched up, in some strange contraption of a boat, at Chatham Ferry the day after the Pilotsburg Deluge. The police and doctors couldn't make head or tail of them. They'd been penned up in the nearest psychiatric ward until the new hospital had been rushed through construction, at which point they'd been transferred there.

Heidi'd known the girls for about a month. She was convinced that the girls were healthy, intelligent young people who'd been victims of some kind of bizarre abuse, but she was a minority of one among the hospital administrators and staff, who all thought that they were hopeless idiots and unteachable. Heidi was hell bent to buck the system and go to bat for them, but she had to rein herself in for fear of getting the bum's rush.

I leaned forward and muttered to her that I had a plan that might save things, and that I'd like to discuss it with her soon, but first could she tell me how she'd gotten there herself, and what had happened to Schultzie and the Rev?

At this point Heidi started to cry herself. The two girls (who must have thought she was their good fairy) jumped up to stroke her hair and comfort her, and she repaid this with a look of love and a caress for each. Fighting back tears she told her sad story. On the day of the Pilotsburg Deluge she'd been assigned to help evacuate the old mental hospital, along with Schultzie and the Rev. They were supposed to bus the inmates to Chatham Ferry, which is on high ground and where the patients could be put up in the high school gym. But they only had two schoolbuses for the 120 patients who were left in the hospital. The Rev volunteered to stay with the 20 or so patients who couldn't fit in the buses and wait for help, but Schultzie pulled rank on him. He (Schulztie) said that if the bus didn't make it back in time, he'd take everybody up to the second floor and wait for help to arrive by water. The Rev shook Schultzie's hand and said he'd be back in an hour, but as luck would have it, the buses got held up in traffic—especially because of the snarl-up caused by the truck-truck-train collision that killed the Thrumble brothers and Swift. By the time they'd unloaded at the gym, Pilotsburg was under water.

It was out of their hands now. The National Guard would handle the water rescue in old landing craft. But when the Guard made it upstream to the hospital near nightful, Schultzie was gone. He'd jumped out a window to rescue a suicidal patient, and the pair of them drowned.

The Rev was inconsolable. He told Heidi it'd been *his* duty to stay at the hospital instead of Schultzie because Schultzie had a family and the Rev didn't. When Heidi tried to comfort him he all at once went mean and muttered something foul that she wouldn't repeat to me. He tore off his clerical collar and stomped on it and stormed out the gymnasium door. Heidi hasn't seen or heard hide nor hair of him to this day. Rumor had it that he'd tied one on and drowned himself and his sorrows in the Sacannah, but sometimes the thought came to her that he'd gone somewhere to make a better life.

I told Heidi that the Rev had cared for her very deeply.

"That's the bitter irony of it," she replied. "I fell in love with him *on that very day*—with his courage and anger and weakness. Desmond, I love the man, I burn for him."

Can you beat that? I pried myself loose from the girls and reached out and held Heidi's hands, just for a moment. I couldn't find words.

Before lunch the girls insisted on showing me their bedroom. It was a nice enough ward with eight beds in two rows, and their two beds were together next to the window with its river view. On the wall behind the beds, and just between them, was the Gable *Gone with the Wind* poster I'd seen in their room back at the Thrumble house. You could see from the stains on the edges that it'd been rolled up and gotten very wet.

That reminded me: Paws was the Thrumbles' cat! I tried to tell them that I had their cat, and that it was fine, but the trouble was, I'm no good at imitations, and soon had a lot of people wondering whether I'd be the next inmate at State Hospital. Heidi finally managed a pretty good cat charade, and I made like I had only one eye and pretended to be nestling something in my arms, and the girls jumped for joy.

I had to leave them then. I was hatching a scheme, and it was going to take a lot of long-distance calling. I told Heidi I'd be back next day, motored back to the motel, and managed to reach Cap at Nevil Castle . . .[27]

5:44 AM. It's just past dawn now, and I've just ordered a jumbo condemned-man's breakfast and gone out on the deck for a breath of air. The sun has turned the western range to crimson. I think I've just seen the feds coming, by the glint of the sun on their windshields fifteen miles away, and that will give me only half an hour before they're at my door. All I can say is, the girls seem very happy now, and they're writing me letters in good English already.

I've moved mountains to make sure that, no matter what happens to me, Nevil Castle will be bankrolled long enough to give Vi and Vicki a chance in life. If that happens I can rest easy.

---

27. "Cap" is Caspar Wickham, Ruck's international buyer. Ruck absent-mindedly interrupts the story of the Thrumble sisters in the middle, worried probably about having enough time to write down his final episode. The essential continuity is as follows: Ruck had authorized Wickham to buy and staff (among other properties worldwide) Nevil Castle, one of England's oldest and largest country estates. Ownership of the mansion was then conveyed to Ruck's White Wolf Foundation. Ruck's "scheme" involved the State Hospital's release of the Thrumble sisters (soon to become, via legal adoption, Victoria and Viola Ruck) into the custody of Dr. Janet Ballister. The girls were then flown to England with Heidi Frederick, who had agreed to accept the position of Foundational Director at the Castle and to supervise Victoria and Viola's education. Ruck's intention, conveyed in a letter graciously released to me by the Director, was to "take the two most abused children on earth and raise them as the princesses they really are." —Ed.

The Most Amazing Thing

6:17 AM. Oh God I'll miss this place. It's so beautiful in the early morning that it looks like a memory already! I've one more story to write before I'm ready for the fuzz.

Glyssom Hill

As I said, Wilbur spent the summer of 1999 biking and hiking the roads and trails in and around Rocky Mountain National Park, in search of the White Wolf. He also did nine of the highest non-technical climbs in the park. No matter where he climbed he carried his binoculars, to scan every vista for something white.

In early September he phoned me and told me that there was an Upside and a Downside. He said the Upside was that he was in better shape than he'd ever been before. The Downside was that he hadn't found scratch.

I told Wilbur it was time to get back in bad shape.

"What d'you mean?"

"You're 21 aren't you?"

"Since June 2."

"You've seen everything you can see. Now listen to what other men've seen. Try the bars around Estes Park. Not fancy places like the Stanley—just beer joints that mountain men might step into when they hit town. Ask about a white wolf. That's about all we can do, short of choppers. But whatever happens, don't drive when you're drunk."

He promised to nurse a single brew on each sortie.

Three nights later, Wilbur rang through to my private line at 2 AM. He sounded really odd, and when I heard what he had to say, I could see why. He'd struck gold at a dive near Lyons, CO, called the Broken Arms. The Broken Arms was a redneck beer barn, a big corrugated-iron hut off Route 36, with picnic tables overlooking the North Fork of the St. Vrain River. Wilbur stopped there because of all the Harleys parked in the lot. The picnic tables were packed with rowdy hobnail-booted bikers. Wilbur ordered a beer and sauntered over to the crowdedest and noisiest table, where the bikers seemed to be arguing about something.

Wilbur went right up to the head of this table, which suddenly went silent, with all the men glaring up at him, and asked politely if any-body'd seen or heard of a white wolf. To a man, they all gaped at him, thunderstruck (as though *that's* exactly what they'd been disagreeing about), and then a guy who looked just like Lee Marvin in *The Wild Ones* popped up and told Wilbur to butt out.

Wilbur had no choice and walked back into the parking lot until he was sure he wasn't being watched. Then he sneaked into the bar to phone me for instructions. But inside somebody caught his eye. It was one of the bikers, all by his lonesome, half-seated, half-sprawled over a table in the back. Even for a Harley-head this was no ordinary stud—the right side of his face was covered with hair, while the left side was hair-less and deformed with a terrible scar that looked like a burn, and the weirdo was quietly blubbering into his suds.

Wilbur had the presence of mind to put his pint down on the bar, go back outside, start his car and leave it running, in case he had to make a close escape. Then he went back into the joint and set his beer down on the man's table and asked him if he'd seen a white wolf.

It was like opening a floodgate. In near-gibberish, the creep (who had to be brother Herman of the Crivellian Risen),[28] let out a torrent of self-pitying, self-righteous, guilt-ridden drivel, the upshot being that he'd *shot the wolf* earlier that night at a place called Glyssom Hill, where he'd been led by a witch (Ould Chattox!) whose pet wolves had been "bit up by it real gude." The two old enemies both had it in for the wolf because it saved *my* life, and on top of this Herman wanted the pelt for (you guessed it) "Taxi Dermy." Equipped with his only remaining

---

28. Ruck's encounter with the Risen is tellingly conveyed in *Ruck's Run*, Ch. 6. —Ed.

gun, an old bolt-action Russian Army rifle, he followed Ould Chattox through the moonlight to the edge of a ravine, from which, madly working the rifle-bolt, he'd fired down on the wolf and her litter of cubs.

But Herman hadn't been able to take the pelt. He'd started down the trail into the ravine, out of the moonlight into the pitch-black shadow, when he was hit by a panic attack ("a chill of pure whore"), and he'd left the witch on Glyssom Hill and hot-footed it back into town for beer and consolation.

Wilbur was just asking Herman where Glyssom Hill was when he heard leather squeaking behind him. The Lee Marvin lookalike gave him a major shove, and from his flat-out position on the floor, Wilbur could see him and a mate dragging Herman out to the bikes. The gang was taking off. As soon as they'd gone, Wilbur made tracks back to the Stanley and phoned me.

I told him Louie and I would be there in the morning. He said fine, but that we'd have our work cut out for us. He'd been all through his Delorme topo book for Colorado, and Glyssom Hill wasn't listed in it.

(I forgot to tell you about Louie![29] For weeks, after my hand healed, I'd been trying extra hard to find him, but no dice. Turns out he was right under my nose, most of that time. For all his cactus-eating meditative wisdom, Louie had one weakness, and that weakness was for a Mexican lady who called herself Double Mocha and ran a topless bar at the crossroads next to Gus's gas station. Double Mocha advertised herself as having the world's premier pair of breasts—so gorgeous, they say, that one of her lovers, the Sultan of Glamistan, had given each of them a different name[30] and had each inscribed in his social register as a member of the Glamistani nobility. Now, as you might expect, I *hate* topless bars

---

29. Ruck's meeting with Pecos Louie, a scene replete with raw tension and mystical vison, can be found in *Ruck's Run*, Ch. 7. —Ed.

30. Nanda Devi and Nanga Parbat. —Ed.

and strip-joints, but Double Mocha's claim piqued my curiosity and I wanted to see how well she could back it up. So one evening I dropped in, and there plain as day was Louie standing at the bar, looking as before like a piece of shoe-leather but dolled up in a sassy storebought wild west outfit, from cream-colored Stetson down to alligator-skin boots. Louie was drinking rye whiskey from a row of lined-up shotglasses and watching Double Mocha's routine with the eyes of a foundling puppy. I followed his line of sight and, My God[31]

But I'm running out of time! I'll get back to this some day. The long and short of it is that Louie has won the object of his affections and is now the ranger and guide at Lomo Morado.

---

31. Ruck never saw fit to complete this story, which, if accurately recounted, would have done much credit to his generosity, compassion and understanding. He did, however, preserve with his "Hymn to Life" a poem which we here reprint for historical documentation:

Pecos Louie's Poem to
Double Mocha's Left Breast

how is it that a breast
can make a man feel blest?
why am I such a pest
to get you to divest
your ripe and fruitful chest
and cannot rest,
oppressed, possessed, obsessed
until I have caressed
—o happy, happiest—
your warm soft loving breast
and there my cheek to nest?
breast, breast, I do not jest:
forever be my guest
and you will have my best
unto my bounty's crest,
beyond all scope of test.
—Ed.

The Most Amazing Thing

At the crack of dawn this morning, Louie, Rick and I headed north in the Cesna.[32] From the copilot's seat I briefed them about the mission. As agreed, Wilbur rang us from the Stanley Hotel at 10 AM. He was trying everything but was still clueless as to the whereabouts of Glyssom Hill. But he did have one grim item from the morning paper: last night Herman had run his Harley off the south shoulder of 36 near Pinewood Springs and died instantly, 200 feet below, on the boulders of the St. Vrain river.

That left us up shit creek.

Or so I thought, until I glanced back at Louie. In the pitching, bucking Cesna (the flying's awful over the Front Range) he'd picked up the map on Rick's clipboard and was pencilling in a new route, slightly to the east of Estes Park. I asked him why.

"Country places ain't like city places," said Louie. "Up country you find two kinds of names for places, the names on the map and the names local folks favor. I reckon 'Glyssom' just ain't a map-name, and it don't sound like no injun name neither. Must be some paleface family."

"Why does that mean we change course?"

"I've a yen to see the plats[33] for those parts. That means we ought to head for Boulder, the county seat."

I phoned Wilbur, and he met us in a rented SUV at Boulder Airport. At the county courthouse Louie and Rick discovered that a Glyssom had owned land along Council Creek, which runs down into the Big Thompson Canyon. An hour later, we'd made contact with a deputy named Web, and he'd made it OK with the current owners, and we were all four-wheeling it up a jeep trail, past PRIVATE PROPERTY signs, alongside the creek. I was dead certain it was the right trail, because it'd rained two nights before, and there were two sets of motorcycle tracks in the dried mud. As we wound our way up and up, the great rock faces to either side converged on us, till we

---

32. Ruck's airstrip, still under refurbishment at this point, could accommodate only small planes. —Ed.

33. Regional maps showing ownership. —Ed.

214

were crawling up a huge alley of stone. Then the trail stopped with barely room to turn around.

We got out into bright sunlight and shouldered our packs. We puffed and sweated up the narrow path with Wilbur, who was eager to show off his fitness, well in the lead.

We never found a Glyssom "hill." It must have been the name of the trail and the little pass it led up to. Once we got to it, the pass packed a surprise. Instead of looking down a canyon or valley on the other side, it led us out onto a ledge of rock about half a mile across and slightly sloping down away from us.

Out beyond this snowpeaks were heaped up on all sides, glistering in the sun like a playland of gods. A fitting place for White Wolf to raise her litter.

The trail had petered out, but we had no trouble finding the ravine. Three hovering vultures told us where it was. When I saw them, something rose in my blood. In a flash I'd found the little trail that had frightened Herman so much, and was tripping and sliding down it.

If I hadn't caught myself on a boulder I would have fallen onto the wolf. She was lying smeared with blood amidst the remains of her pups. A dead vulture, its neck mangled, lay beside her.

White Wolf was alive.

I wetted my bandana with water and put it on her tongue and then, little by little, poured more water on it. She didn't complain then or when we gently loaded her onto a tarp and packed her out of the ravine and down Glyssom Hill. My arms were trembling from the weight when we put her down in the back of Web's Blazer. I tended to her and phoned ahead to the vet as, siren screaming and lights flashing, we raced up 34 towards Estes Park.

Two hours later the vet was telling me that she was going to make it, but that she'd never fully get back up to speed, because her heart'd been seriously damaged.

I named the White Wolf Ranguma, partly because of her mysterious powers and partly to keep the memory of Bevan Slattery and his beloved sorceress, Ranguma, alive.

If I can someday get her a heart transplant

The Most Amazing Thing

EDITOR'S NOTE: Ruck must have caught sight of the FBI motorcade at this point and left off writing in panic. Catherine Vanya, the housekeeper at Lomo Morado, tells me that he showered and shaved hurriedly that day and that he surrendered to FBI agents on their arrival just after 10 AM on September 4, 2001. Ruck's last act as a free man was to give Ms. Vanya his laptop computer (the same Ace Speedstar 50 that he had originally bought at the Essex Depot in New Jersey) for safe keeping. Among the few belongings he took to jail was a new Diké Cybermogul 1000 laptop with cellular e-mail capacity. On the evening of October 7, Richard Beauchamps received the following e-mail message at Lomo Morado, with instructions to pass it on to Ms. Vanya:

October 7, 2001. Clark County Jail
Rick, please tell Catherine to put this in the safe with my old laptop. Some day I may be able to paste it into my journal.

I've been suffering depression for the past few days. Vic Bellows[34] and Chris want me to take Prozac, but somehow I can't put the stuff in my mouth. I can't stomach cheap escapes. The knocks come with the party.

Of course I wasn't granted bail. Regis Bulstrode, a hanging judge if you ever saw one, cited "Mr. Ruck's recent acquisition of a Boeing Over-water 777" as evidence of "the wherewithal to outrun extradition."

Somehow I've wanted to be alone. Aside from Gannett, Chris and Vic, I've only allowed three visits. Molly came in and asked for my forgiveness. I said nonsense, and that we should all try to continue the good projects we'd begun.

Clemens, Horowitz and Rousseau dropped in last Wednesday to tell me that they'd finagled a way to keep the Feds from seizing my fortune (for now, that is). They also announced that, thanks to the huge success of most of my African and Indonesian investments, I'd just become *the world's first trillionaire!* Well, how do you like that?

---

34. Director of the Bellows Clinic. See *Ruck's Run*, Ch.7. —Ed.

216

I'll tell you what *I*'d like. I'd like to be a grunt day-laborer who sweats through his ten hours in the fields but then can walk up the hill in the evening and look around at the countryside and smell the memory of the day's sun in the earth and feel the breeze.

Speaking of laborers, Ali Shah is in town with that strange twisted dark man Salvador, whom somehow I don't trust. Ali wanted to try out a new taviz on me, with special prayers in it, that was just delivered from Pakistan. Trouble is, I like my old taviz. I told him to leave the new one, and I'd think about putting it on. He said that Salvador had simply pleaded to come along to the trial, on unpaid leave, and say a prayer for me, so that's why he brought Salvador. To say the least, Ali is bullish about his new friend: "Salvador's an excellent fellah, a splendid fellah, a very clever fellah, a gentle fellah, a devout fellah, a dependable fellah, and a most proficient hawticulturalist." I said OK.

The trial's tomorrow. Gannett did everything he could to cop a plea, but Barry Myers, the US attorney, is so damn sure of his case, and of getting my ass and trillion-odd dollars, that he won't hear of it.

Myers is so smug that he's already booked his flight back to DC Friday. He's also been making cagey comments to the press about making a big down payment on the National Debt.

The press will be at the trial in force, including all three network anchor people. Of course I'm guilty already, so far as they're concerned. Is it that having a trillion dollars is evil by definition? Or just that they can make more headlines and money by saying so?

A trillion bucks. Invest that tax-free at 6% and you get—I don't believe it! Over a billion a week!!

I hope I make minimum security.

A billion a week! It makes me not only the richest man in the world, but richer than most national governments. With that kind of money I could feed all the starving kids on earth.

I hear people get whacked in stir.

The Most Amazing Thing

That's, isn't it, $6 million an hour! In one hour I could turn around the future of a high school or small college!

Will they take it all away?

I could dig a thousand wells and turn the Sahara into a herbarium full of munching horses and happy Arab gals.

In stir you live in your own latrine.

I've accomplished the impossible, the end of the rainbow, the dream of limitless wealth and power.

Will I ever see Ranguma again?

Sorry for the self-pity, Rick. Take care of things, be good to people. When Molly gets there, try to cheer her up. After the trial there's something I want you to tell the kids at Pueblo Verde, but that can wait for now.

Desmond

Chapter Ten **Romantic Law**

PART ONE: NOMIKONS AND HAMBONES

Ranguma's herself again! She bounced into my bedroom this morning fresh as a daisy with this enormous wild hare in her mouth, and then she dropped the critter, alive! on the foot of my bed. She bounded onto the bed to give me a big wet schnuzzle that smelled of hare and desert, as the hare, in two huge hops, catapulted out through the north window. In ten seconds you could hear dogs barking all over the ranch, and Ranguma'd bounced off the bed again and was silhouetted in the doorway, fixing me with those sea-deep eyes. I blinked a moment, thinking of Mara, and in that instant Ranguma vanished. I threw on a robe and trotted out to the pool, which has a view of the mountain. I could just make her out, high-tailing it up the Cabeza.

I knew she'd go there when she got well, because I'd seen her ears go bolt upright when she heard wolves howling on the mountain. I'm just as sure that she'll always come back to me.

The Most Amazing Thing

Ranguma's heart surgery was four weeks ago. Janet Ballister, who'd been a vet before she took up internal medicine, flew to Houston to study the technique. Louie had a donor, a rogue male who'd run in front of Louie's pickup. Louie hefted the carcass onto his rig and got it down to the ranch infirmary in an hour's time. Janet rang me and I ran down and suited up to assist.

It went without a hitch.

How it feels to have her like new again, I can't tell you. *The happiness!*

It's as though, thanks to all my cares and sufferings, life is suddenly real to me.

It's as though I lost Mara and gained the power to love.

By the way, I'm not in jail! I'm at Lomo Morado, and I'm going to stay here. Why I'm not in jail is a whale of a tale, but also *some kind* of mystery.

1:47 PM. It's a gorgeous day, and I'm sitting on a chaise by the deep end of the pool. It's after lunch, and the day is slowing down, and I've asked to be left alone. I'll put down everything I remember, so as to someday solve, maybe, the new mystery that's been created.

The U.S. Government vs. Desmond Ruck

Bright and early on the morning of October 8 I woke to a tapping at my cell door. It was Roger Gannett, my chief counsel. Now Roger's a sharp legal mind and a decent sort, but he's got about seventeen different ways of conveying anxiety, which isn't so great for litigation, not to mention my morale. Today his pale and longish face was decorated with a round bandage from a shaving cut, and his jacket collar was half turned up. As I turned it down, he managed the throaty whisper, "They're all here."

He was right. Once I made it into the courtroom, I could see among crowded rows the familiar TV icons: CBS's Beeper Fennel, whose

220

beady Gotcha eyes were clamped on me like claws, NBC's Sam Cratch, with his look of permanent righteous outrage, and Brian Turbo of ABC, the biggest go-getter of all, just done with his own trial for spousal abuse. These three frontline correspondents were backed up chocka-block by a quiet horde of livid faces and ravenous eyes, the overall impression being of a pack of hyenas who'd just come upon a dying hippo. I scanned the rest of the courtroom: not a friendly face in sight, but everybody riveting on me in an orgy of voyeurism, getting their first gawk at the fabulous monster Ruck.

The jury, who looked politely scared to death, were all finding ways of not making eye contact with me, and there was no sign of Ali Shah or Salvador.

Somebody grabbed me from behind. It was Roger, who'd tripped over a wire and almost fallen. Would he be able to get it together? I glanced across the aisle at his competition. Bulky and florid under a Jamaica tan, wavy-haired US attorney Barry Myers was leaning over to confer with his backup team, the three young lawyers he called his Quiz Kids. In the near-silent room, I caught the phrase "thirty years."

Then if the bastard doesn't look up and wink at me!

The Judge came in and we all rose. Regis Bulstrode was a scrawny hook-nosed Van Burened old sod who looked like a cross between Uncle Titus and a show rooster. From the bench he squinted at counsel and the packed room with an expression that could have been boyish eagerness or sexual lust. Was this a control freak, or what?

What followed was a massacre. The Judge looked on with beaming fatherly approval as Myers presented an array of evidence and witnesses with machine-gun speed and Rolex precision. Such technique! And his manner! He went through his whole spiel without the slightest appeal to emotion. Facts were facts. He could have been a scientist summarizing his observations, a doctor stating his diagnosis. He established my presence at the shootout, my taking the van and the securities and cash.

The Most Amazing Thing

On top of everything, Myers managed to sound reasonable and humane. He said that only when my intention changed from self-defense to self-aggrandizement did my act become a crime.

And just for good measure he added that, if Guccio Imbratta hadn't owned the local fuzz and hushed up the bloodbath, I'd have been in the clink years ago.

By lunchtime next day, when we adjourned pending final arguments, everybody in the courtroom, including Roger and me, was convinced that Desmond Ruck was guilty as charged.

Roger and I sat speechless in the courthouse cafeteria, I munching apathetically on an egg salad sandwich, Roger unable to touch his lunch. The afternoon ahead looked bleak. We had no evidence, no witnesses, no arguments. Our entire strategy in not pleading guilty had been based on some slip-up the government might commit, some prejudice it might show; but Myers had conducted a prosecution made in heaven. I was giving serious thought to what jobs might be available, say in the year 2030, to clueless ex-con ex-trillionaires, when all of a sudden there was a noise and Roger almost jumped out of his chair. His pager'd gone off. He pulled out the thing and poked at it, and then hurriedly excused himself. As he exited the cafeteria into the hallway I saw him turn and suddenly look up, as though meeting somebody tall.

I sipped tepid coffee and thought about all the good books I'd be reading in stir.

A few minutes later Roger was back with a desperate kind of hope in his eyes. "We have a new pal," he said. "He's got an angle."

"Who the—"

"I'm not sure. But I think this guy's for real."

"But how—"

"I've just added him to our legal staff."

Court was reconvening. The mystery man awaited us just outside the courtroom door. As I approached him I was looking at a face that I knew, yet didn't know. It was Ali Shah's assistant Salvador, but he was transformed. His skin was two shades lighter than before, and he'd straightened up and gained half a foot in height. The twisted look was gone from his face, replaced by a disarming directness, chiselled features, piercing yet luminous brown eyes. His thick dark hair was perfectly coiffed, and he was dressed to a tee in a dark blue pinstripe suit.

"Your servant, sir," he said in a classy mid-Atlantic accent, handing me a business card that I clumsily thrust into my jacket pocket.

"Hi" was all I could manage, but it must have been more like "Ha," because my jaw had dropped.

Judge Bulstrode was majorly P-O'd by the change in counsel. There was big confusion up at the bench, with Mystery Man pulling what looked like a memo out of a black leather briefcase and showing it first to the Judge and then to Barry Myers, who looked alternately annoyed and curious. The jury (especially the women) were all eyes, and the audience was a-titter as Cratch, Fennel and Turbo twisted around to pow-wow with their legal consultants, and couriers scurried into and out of court.

After ten minutes or so, Myers left the bench to huddle with the Quiz Kids, who began excitedly haggling with each other, and just when it seemed that somebody would have to ask for an adjournment, Myers rejoined the bunch at the bench. You could tell from the way he first shook his head and then nodded that he was agreeing to something, but didn't much cotton to it.

Finally they all started nodding. I pulled the stranger's business card from my pocket. It said "Preston Vickers, Attorney." That's all.

Bulstrode smashed down the gavel and nasally announced that Vickers would "henceforth speak in Mr. Ruck's defense." The audience did a lot of confused muttering and chattering, and Bulstrode slammed down the gavel again and called for order.

THE SALVAGE DEFENSE

Preston Vickers (or whoever he was) faced the jury. He spoke. His voice was forceful but melodic, like some kind of American Laurence Olivier. It was totally without pretension. He carried no notes—precise references rolled out of memory as smooth as pinballs, bundling themselves into pithy conclusions.

Vickers's argument was simply this: no crime had been committed. The Imbratta van and everything in it belonged to me, Desmond Ruck, by right of salvage.

SALVAGE!

Myers rose to object, but Bulstrode told him to save it, there'd be time later.

So Vickers went on. He allowed as the law of salvage hadn't ever been enforced on land (Myers nodded his wavy head at this as if to say that *that's* what he was objecting about) but that in the landmark case of *Falcke v. the Scottish Imperial Insurance Co.*, the judgment had left the door open a crack for something like this:[35]

> . . . If the property of an individual on land be exposed to the greatest peril, and be saved by the voluntary exertions of any person whatever; if valuable goods be rescued from a house in flames, at the imminent hazard of life, by the salvor, no remuneration in the shape of salvage is allowed. The act is highly meritorious, and the service is as great as if rendered at sea, yet the claim for salvage *could not perhaps be supported. It is certainly not made.*[36]

Vickers then referred the court to Aristotle's distinction between *physicon* and *nomikon*, Justinian's distinction between *universalis* and *pro-*

---

35. Here Ruck seems to be using a section of legal records taken off the Internet. —Ed.

36. This judgment, made by L. J. Bowen, is quoted in William Rann Kennedy, *A Treatise on the Law of Civil Salvage* (London: Stevens, 1936), p. 7, and Martin J. Norris, *The Law of Salvage* (Mount Kisco: Baker, Voorhis & Co., 1958), p. 16. Ruck has altered, by italicizing, the final two sentences. —Ed.

pria, Gentili's distinction between *natura* and *gens,* and Jefferson's distinction between British imperial precedent and "the course of human events." What these distinctions amounted to was that there were two kinds of binding law, state law and natural law, and that natural law, or what Jefferson called "the course of human events" is sometimes a tonic or corrective for state law, and that salvage law existed in the "crease" between state law and natural law, and that my being caught in crossfire on Stuyvesant Avenue and ducking into the abandoned Imbratta van and driving away in it conformed in every vital way with the law of salvage, and that my having kept the money was not only a reward for my role as salvor but a reasonable act of self-defense, and besides, nobody'd ever reported it stolen.

Vickers wasn't done. He added that, by bribing the local police, Guccio Imbratta had turned his neighborhood into "a kind of moral ocean" —that is, a place where there was no state law but only natural law. He said that the Imbrattas had created "ocean effects"—that is, social chaos—which in turn made salvage law applicable.[37]

And he concluded that I'd be glad to return the fortune in full, with interest, to the rightful owner or the US Government.

Vickers presented this in tones of controlled passion, like a prophet so possessed by spirit that it scares him and he's got to hold it back. He was now standing right in front of the jury, whose seven women were looking at him like so many charmed snakes. I tell you, this guy had class.

When Vickers sat down, the Judge asked Barry Myers if he'd like a recess to consider the new defense argument. Myers rose and declined the recess and said that he'd speak briefly and that it should be construed as his summation. He told the jury that he had presented them

---

37. Vickers's line of argument, immediately christened the "salvage defense," has to date been the subject of 397 learned monographs and 21,776 academic articles, exploring its implications in law, ethics, politics, business, literary interpretation and erotica. —Ed.

with adequate evidence to prove me guilty of a federal offense. He said that Vickers's defense was irrelevant because by Vickers's own admission and the judgment in *Falcke v. the Scottish Imperial Insurance Co.*, there was no precedent.

The US Government rested.

The courtroom was silent.

The Judge, with a hideous graveyard smile, asked Vickers if *he*'d like a recess. Vickers respectfully declined. He stepped forward, facing not the jury but the full court. He spoke five sentences, that I can still hear.

"If all judgments required precedents, there wouldn't be any judgments yet. In every American legal judgment, there is not only the necessity to uphold the law but also the opportunity to renew the law. Fair juries and judges don't simply repeat legal history. They create it. The defense rests."

Immediately two hands went up in the jury, asking Vickers to repeat his summation. He did this, speaking more slowly but not changing a word.

Bulstrode, who looked like he'd swallowed his pencil, smashed down the gavel and recessed the court. I sat stunned, with Vickers's words ringing in my ears. But all around me the room exploded into debate and backtalk. Who was Vickers? An anarchist? A fascist? Who was Aristotle? What was a nomikon? Did all laws have precedents? America's been a pretty chatty place since all those talk-show hosts died, and the audience would have turned the courtroom into a real town meeting if the bailiffs hadn't kicked them out. As two guards whisked me out of court I looked around for my lawyers. Roger was following me faithfully, but Vickers had disappeared.

Back in my cell I crashed with a splitting headache. I OD'd on ibuprofen and slept round the clock. Roger dropped in just after I woke up. Roger was looking mildly worried, which meant he was in an upbeat mood. He said the jury was still out, which we agreed was good news, because if they all thought I was guilty they'd be back already.

I asked about Vickers. Roger said he'd been looking for Vickers, as were the networks and all the other media, but that Vickers had disappeared into thin air. He said that Ali Shah, who'd been as surprised as anybody else by Vickers's transformation, had poked into his things back at Lomo Morado, but he'd only found a few dirty old clothes.

Roger bowed out as my dinner arrived. I ate the musty meatloaf and washed-out string beans and reconstituted mashed potatoes, and had a gas attack and got depressed. It wasn't a sad-type depression, but more of an I don't give a damn, as though all spunk was bleeding out of me.

After supper I sat on my cot, looking at nothing, as my mind went blank and my muscles lost tone. All that I'd gone through, all that I'd tried to do, suddenly seemed meaningless, and my spirit ached for the sheer disgust of being inside my body.

I lay down and fell asleep and dreamed of Uncle Titus. He was very big, and I was very small. In one episode he was caning me because I'd dropped my scoop of ice cream on the sidewalk. In another he'd invited the Imbratta, Calandrino and Thrumble boys over, and they were all talking dirty about me, and I was supposed to wait on table and serve them reconstituted mashed potatoes, but they kept snatching at me and tripping me up, and when I went into the kitchen to get more food, I met this godawful witch . . .

THE SECRET ORDER OF THE HAMBONE

I woke in broad daylight. Gus Randolph was there, looking at me from a chair across the cell.

I blinked at him and rubbed my eyes. "Have they . . . ?"

"No," he said. "They're still out."

I was glad to see Gus. I hadn't wanted to see him before my trial, because Gus and I go way back, and he's sort of emotional, and I was afraid of losing it if I saw him. But the trial was over now and there was nobody, nobody living, that is, that I'd rather have seen.

My breakfast of coffee and hard rolls came in, and the guard was kind enough to bring a second cup for Gus.

Coffee awakened memories. Gus was soon reminiscing about his own time in jail, years back. As a buck private training to be a paratrooper, he'd been stockaded for almost a week for decking a drill sergeant who'd been needling him about his being black. He'd have been court-martialed if it hadn't been for a few of his white buddies going to the captain and setting things straight.

"I would have gone stir-crazy in that stockade," said Gus, "if I hadn't done a bushel of hamboning."

"Hamboning?"

Gus explained that hamboning was a way of making music by rhythmically slapping parts of your own body, thus turning yourself into a human percussion instrument. He said that when the slaves were first brought over to the States, the slave drivers tried to put down their prisoners' natural high spirits by taking away their drums. So the slaves, on the sly, turned their own bodies into drums and made music anyway.

I asked him if he could do some for me. Gus said sure. He started singing "Hambone, hambone, where yo' been?" and alternately slapping his own thighs and chest cage. I said it was amazing what a satisfying noise he got out of them, and how well it went with the music.

"But it takes a little practice," he replied.

I asked if he'd teach me. He said he'd come back that afternoon with some music and a real expert.

After lunch Gus arrived with a hambone Paganini—a mountain of a man named Bituminous Newton—as well as a boom box and a few CDs. I'm pretty musical, so the easier rhythms were a piece of cake, and within an hour Newton was teaching us a few of the slicker moves. After a while we were interrupted by shouts and banging. The drug runners in the cell across from us—two Russians and a Swiss—wanted to learn how to hambone, and so did the two Mexican alien smugglers in the cell to their left. Bituminous Newton got permission to go out and teach them, and we turned the volume up, and before long the jailhouse was rocking to a body octet.

"Hambone, hambone, where yo' been?

Aroun' the world and back agin."

Into the midst of this pandemonium rushed Roger, shouting for me to turn the ghetto blaster down.

Roger was so worked up he could hardly speak. "Th- th- they're coming back, Desmond. It's a hung jury!"

I was going to walk.

● ● ●

I spent the weekend and next Monday at the penthouse at Duke's to handle the legal hangover, which was considerable. Turns out Vickers's credentials were phony, and the FBI wanted to arrest me again, but Myers now had orders from higher up in DC not to press charges "pending further review of the case."

I soon found out what this pending business meant. One of the Quiz Kids phoned me Monday morning, and just after 3 I had a visit from Barry Myers, a couple of big shots from the FBI and US Attorney General's office, and a soft-spoken gray-haired man named Simon Palio, who turned out to be Undersecretary of the US Treasury. The subject: what Mr. Palio called a modest settlement. The U S Government would drop all charges against me if I would make them six equal annual payments of $50 billion. I asked where this money would go. Palio said, Public works and reducing the national debt.

I said, It's a deal. The biggest legal settlement in history was concluded with a handshake and a few bottles of Amador County zin.

I called in Gus and my three financial wizards. I wanted them to know that I was kosher again, and to ask their forgiveness for having kept them in the dark. I wanted to do this in front of the Feds, just so the Feds would know that my people hadn't been in on a conspiracy.

We all chatted over the wine. Like apparently everybody else in the

USA, the Feds were burning to know who Vickers was. I told them I would put Molly Block on the case.

I have, and she's so far come up dry.

By the way, I asked Myers if he had any dirt about the verdict, and he blushed under his tan. The six votes for Not Guilty had all come from women.

I flew here next day, and I've been here ever since. I'm here to stay, now, and I've got to get my shit together.

KEEPING ABREAST

While I was locked up, life went on. Molly came out here as planned, and romance seems to be afoot between her and Rick. Damn Rick! I told him to cheer her up, not chat her up. I'm crazy about Molly, and her smile so full of pluck and sweetness, but something, maybe Mara's ghost, always kept me from telling her so.

Maybe it's for the best. Rick, in his easygoing way, is full of heart. I wish them joy.

Sergei went to Rome and got himself a gold in the Scarlatti Competition (what a nice kid!).

My Third World businesses continue to groove under the leadership of my three Wise Ones, who tell me that my first $50 billion payment to Uncle Sam will barely scratch the surface of this year's profits. Gus is setting up a special roving team to make sure that foreign workers are getting a square deal, and the White Wolf Foundation (now the world's strongest) is opening a charitable branch in every nation where we have interests.

Viola and Victoria[38] have their hearts set on Cambridge University for next fall.

---

38. Formerly, the Thrumble sisters. —Ed.

Cap Wickham has bought me a Renaissance villa near Florence, a ranch in Kenya and a hideaway on the Big Island in Hawai'i.

On the education front I'm batting .500:

Pueblo Verde's in great shape. Rose Randolph turns out to be some kind of genius with kids, and I've made life for her and Gus more livable by moving him out to an office right here. The farm and dairy at the Pueblo are now in full production, and once Ali Shah has the hothouse up to speed, we'll be completely self-sufficient.

The kids' full day is taken up by school, farming and play, with no TVs or dead time.

But Magdalena College has a couple of problems. First off, the civic leadership people and the lit professors (who were all recommended to me by Mega Klein) are at each other's throats, because the litcrits say that civic leadership is "a cultural fiction." What they mean by that I can't quite fathom, but it sticks in my craw, so I've reassigned all of them (starting in January) to the White Wolf office in Ethiopia, where they can help out with famine relief. If they can prove that the Ethiopian famine's a cultural fiction, they're gonna save us lots of money. Zoig[39] can find replacements for them at the college, and he's agreed to run the college for at least a year.

Second, the gals at Magdalena College are getting uppity. They've turned the big chapel on campus into something called "the Ruckery" and are filling it up with begged, borrowed or stolen souvenirs called "Ruckiana." Somebody's hung a sign over the altar saying "GRATI-TUDE IS THE BEST ATTITUDE." They have meetings there at night, and faculty aren't invited. I don't like it, but I'm not about to pounce on something that started spontaneously.

Evening's upon us. 'Tuminous Newton's coming in tonight and will stay for three weeks, starting Sergei out on jazz piano. I can't wait.

---

39. Ethan Zoig, a writer and educator, had been hired out of early retirement by Ruck in September 2001 to become his cultural ambassador and occasional tutor. —Ed.

The Most Amazing Thing

As sunset reddens the Cabeza, a white form takes shape among the rocks. Ranguma returning. One of these days she'll bring home a new litter.

PART TWO: SHANA LADD

JANUARY 14, 2002

Dying from the heat.
This body-cast is choking me.
God damn it.
Can't talk today.

JANUARY 16, 2002

Much better this morning. Big clouds are backing up on the Cabeza, and we've got cooler weather and a breeze through the library doors. Janet's loosened my cast. The x-rays show the ribs are mending, but I'm not out of the woods yet. I won't be able to flex my torso for ten days or so.

My arms are free, but it hurts like hell to move them. I'm dictating this into a recorder[40] and will key it in when I can.

I've been busted up so many times now that healing feels real familiar. It's like a sea voyage from one inner place to another. It's a reminder, in spite of appearances to the contrary, of what a weak little mouse I really am. It's a holiday from health, when the big agonies, slowly easing up, teach me not to pay much attention to the little agonies of everyday.

---

40. A stereo cassette, labelled in Ruck's handwriting and dated "9/02," turned up at a garage sale in Grosse Pointe, MI, only a week before this volume went to press. But someone had recorded a Shag Craven concert over Ruck's original. So have the Mighty fallen. —Ed.

But it's also a pain in the ass!

I'll get the clowns that did this to me.

Thank God, I'm back on solids! Tonight Catherine will get Benedict[41] to make Contrescarpe Marseillaise, the dish Mara and I gobbled up in Louisville.

Mara of sweet memory. St. Albamara of the Sorrows. Shall I build her a church?

Molly Block's been reading to me. *National Geographic*, the *New Yorker* and the *Smithsonian*, novels by Dickens and Conrad, and (my favorite!) Homer's *Odyssey*. Molly's got a wonderful voice, low and soothing. The writing's so good, it sometimes makes me shiver. When I recover, I promise to write more. And better.

My toes itch and I can't bend over to scratch them!

I've got a grim tale to tell. But it's for another day. I'm off the painkillers at last, and now I'm going to have a bourbon and space out.

JANUARY 23, 2002

I can write again. Strength is seeping back into me.

Rose Randolph just dropped in from Pueblo Verde and said that the kids all wanted to pay their respects. I guess I've got to see them—after all, they have a right to see for sure that their stepfather's not dead, that he's going to make it. I said she could bring them tomorrow. But what kind of lie can I tell everybody about how I got crunched up? The truth is too gross, too shameful, disgusting, nauseating, unbelievable!

The truth is unnameable vanity and folly.

I'll tell them I flipped my BMW.

I'm especially uncomfortable in bed—I hurt no matter which side I lie on. I could use drugs, but that's not real sleep. I've got them working down at the Shop on a big silent air compressor with channels up to a

---

41. Benedict Goncourt, chef at Lomo Morado. —Ed.

bedroom they're building on top. À la some crazy neutral-buoyancy space simulator, *I'll lie down on air.*

I'll start by catching up on some old news.

After the trial in Vegas, I had one good and busy month. First off, I settled Uncle Titus's case. I'd thought long and hard about what to do with somebody who's in hock up to his eyeballs, corrupts the local police, makes his employees miserable, lives only for himself and is piss-proud and moralistic to boot. I decided to "liquify" him, to punish him by giving him what he wanted most, that is, loot.

I sent twenty Magdalena College volunteers (it was their Christmas holiday), all loaded with cash, to FARNACLE'S department store. They had instructions to buy everything in sight, as well as what was in the warehouse, which could be accessed by our rented trucks via the loading docks. They had a ball. By closing time they'd cleaned out the place, and Titus had almost $20 million in cash on hand. We'd clued in his leading creditors, who'd all won garnishment judgments against him long ago, and they simultaneously pounced. His home and office mortgagers followed suit.

We've donated all the inventory to local charities. Titus's slave-labor employees are having a chat with Immigration, but I've told the authorities that (unless they want to go back to Cuba) they can work at Lomo Morado or Pueblo Verde.

Uncle Titus is out in the cold, but not exactly. He's been informed that there's a job for him at the White Wolf Foundation.

What kind of job? Giving away money.

I'd loved to have seen and heard Uncle Titus as all this unfolded, but I had too many other things to do. Cap Wickham flew in to report on the properties he'd acquired for me and, because he's a stickler for detail, his reports—illustrated with his own videos—took the better part of a week. Cap's a very capable man: 6'6" and powerfully built, a Special Forces and CIA vet who was running a successful international real estate business out of Johannesburg, South Africa, when he saw my ad.

He's always dead serious, and his voice has a tone of command. He's got contacts you wouldn't believe, and he can make things happen.

While I was finding out all about Siena and Kenya and the Kona Coast, Rick was loading up the 777 for a trip to England. I wouldn't ride in the big plane all by myself because of the waste of fuel, but this time I had a few presents to deliver. Viola and Victoria have volunteered as part-time caregivers at Everham Grange, a large orphanage in the village near Nevil Castle, so we packed the plane with a ton or two of fruit and preserves from the greenhouse for the kids and staff at the Grange. But that took up hardly any space at all. Why we really needed the 777 was the schoolbus. I've designed the world's safest bus, with airbags not only in the seat-backs but in the side panelling and even the roof. I had a scaled-down version built especially for Everham Grange, and we drove it right onto the plane.[42]

The trip to England was pure delight. Molly, who's been taking flying lessons, flew copilot, and we all drove the new schoolbus from Heathrow to the castle, loaded down with goodies. While Rick and Molly were romantically exploring the rambling old castle and the local countryside, I was getting to know Vicki and Vi again. How they've changed! Heidi's taught them her own gracious manner, and they're not only speaking perfect English, but sounding as British as the Queen (whom, by the way they've been invited to meet!). TV news and the tabloid press have caught onto them as "Ruck's Cinderellas," and Heidi's had lots of trouble keeping the young gallants away.

When I arrived they were both wearing whipcord riding outfits, complete with dashing leather boots. They hugged me warmly but just a bit shyly at first. Heidi and the tutors have taught the girls presence, poise, bearing and composure—a marvelous frame for their super-vitality.

I posed the delicate question of what Vi and Vicki remembered

---

42. Like his Boeing 737, Ruck's much larger 777 was custom built, with a cargo bay aft. —Ed.

about their childhood, and they went into major detail about the house, the wildlife, the river and their solitary life. They said they'd not only talked their sisterspeak to each other, but also to birds, fishes and trees. Neither of them could remember having had a mother. When I asked about Art, they said he "bothered" them and beat them and that they were always glad when he went away.

Heidi later told me that the girls had relatively few of the traumatic symptoms she usually found in sex abuse victims. She reckoned that this was because, not knowing society or its language, or what a father was, or what sex was, the girls had come up with their own private value system for coping with their experience and supporting each other. Now that they've learned a new, socialized value system, I mean *our* system, their old days are behind them, like another life.

My last day there, standing with Vi and Vicki on the castle ramparts, I had a serious talk with them about their future. They both told me that their volunteer work at the Grange was very fulfilling, and that after college they'd like to do something of the same sort.

I see places for them at the White Wolf Foundation.

That day I took Heidi to lunch at the Hound's Tooth, a local pub. Luckily we weren't recognized (lately I've been getting mobbed whenever I step into public) and so could talk privately. Through her care for the kids, and her activities at the Grange, and her stewardship of the castle, Heidi's found a kind of happiness. But she still sorely misses the Rev. When his name came up, she gestured to the window on her right, which looked out on a pleasant garden bordered by a cobblestone path.

"I'd love to see him walk up that path right now," she said, "even if he's fighting mad and stewed to the gills." I followed Heidi's eyes, half expecting to see the Rev's red presumptious face thrust itself out from behind the yewberries. But that just ain't the way reality works.

Back at the castle, I promised the girls I'd be back in the fall for their first Cambridge Parents' Weekend. We flew here from Heathrow the next day, through some tricky weather over the Atlantic. "So as not to have an empty plane," as he put it, Rick brought along a 1964 Bentley S3 Continental Convertible, which he and Molly had found for sale on one of their jaunts. He means to restore it and use it on the 5-mile commute from Lomo Morado to his vineyards near Pueblo Verde.

It's dinner-time, and I've managed to avoid writing about the Horror for another day.

Next time.

JANUARY 25, 2002

The kids were all here yesterday. Sergei and Rose have been training them as a choir, and they ran through a wonderful medley of spirituals for me in the library. I'm glad I was able to stand up.

Word is that the Magdalena gals are cooking up some sort of visitation to me too, but they're keeping it under wraps.

It's time to bite the bullet. I'll just give the details, as they were revealed to me.

When I got back from England there was e-mail from Shana Ladd. I'd been in touch with her for about a year, on account of her being America's great authority on wolves, and in fact it was Shana who'd first recommended Ranguma's heart transplant. But we'd never met. Now she was coming to Vegas, on very short notice, as a kind of replacement for another speaker who'd gotten sick, to speak on "The Social Climate of Wolves," and she wondered if I'd fly up and attend and maybe go out for a drink afterward.

I wrote back that wild horses wouldn't stop me, and she quipped in return that in Vegas I might have to prove it.

Rick and I flew in by Cessna a day early. I had a few things to settle for Roger,[43] and Rick wanted some time with Molly. Rick, Molly and I had

---

43. After Augustus Randolph moved office to Lomo Morado, Roger Gannett became Coordinator of Ruck's enterprises at Duke's. —Ed.

a late lunch at what once was Duke's Casino but has now become what I wanted it to be: Duke's Brew, a high-class brewpub with a big menu of excellent Mexican food. No gambling, no smoking, no love for hire. After lunch I hopped on my motorcycle and buzzed out to UNLV for the lecture.

I got to the lecture hall with time to spare. It turned out to be a regular classroom, attended only by seven or eight seedy academic types. But when Shana Ladd appeared, the place lit up. She was in her thirties, slender and of middle height, with wonderful light olive skin and enchanting, almost hypnotic, dark green eyes. Her straight black hair was drawn into a chignon or bun at the top of the neck, which immediately reminded me of my favorite actress, Gene Tierney, who'd actually done up her hair in a chignon in one of her movies. Ladd was wearing a sleeveless black dress with a provocative V-neck, and a necklace of small pearls was the only jewelry on her body.

Nobody introduced her. She just started talking. And as she spoke, she caught and held me in her eyes.

Much of what she said's been flooded out by the insanity that followed, but at the end of her talk I remember something vibrating inside me, as if I'd already had a stiff drink. I was fascinated by Shana Ladd, in particular by her deep love of nature but also by the way this love awoke her body and sang in her words.

Before you knew it she and I were motorcycling back downtown, her arms gently around my waist, her body warm against my back.

I took her to the Bull and Bear and asked for a booth. In privacy and soft light, over rounds of Nadas, we eagerly unfolded ourselves to each other. In those two hours Shana spoke volumes. She told me of her house near Crested Butte, CO, of the mountains' changing colors over the day and the seasons, of the wildlife she saw during her long walks in a nearby canyon. She confessed being fascinated not just with nature but also with the world of machines and technology, and she spoke of her love of intense exertion and difficult, enthralling work. With singing eyes she praised the simple things—eating, sleeping, waking, laughing, building, communicating, as wonderful and almost religious events of life, and she admitted that she was keenly curious about people everywhere and their stories. I couldn't believe it! Every atom of her spoke to me. If souls are like orchestras, then Shana was playing every instrument of mine, in such rainbow harmony as left me breathless.

At one point we were talking about wolves, and I started describing Ranguma's unusual eyes, and was fumbling for words, when Shana brought me up short—

"Do you mean a fierce green fire?"

A *fierce green fire!* How dazzling. Those were the precise words used by Aldo Leopold, my favorite writer, in the most moving passage of his great book. I looked at Shana in astonishment and murmured "Leopold." Our eyes swam in each other. I'd never felt so in sync, so much on the same wavelength, with anybody else in my life.

We went on to discuss Leopold with great excitement, and John Muir and Enos Mills too, and I timidly let on to her my own hopes, that somehow, someday, I could be of help in saving the environment.

Neither of us wanted any food. She was staying at the Argus, just up the street, and as I walked her back to her hotel, around midnight, she walked brushing against me and in perfect stride, as though we were a single being.

She invited me in.

Shana's suite at the Argus had a sitting room done up rather like my digs at Duke's, which might have put me at my ease, except that I was suddenly aflame with desire. What with losing Mara and the run-in with Rachel Muldoon and all my doubts about why gals liked me, I hadn't enjoyed being with a woman in years. But Shana was something else. She'd blown away all my alienation. She was like another me, but with a marvelous difference. As I moved close to her lips and touched them with mine, I seemed to be discovering a lost part of myself. For an instant I remembered my first kiss with Mara, a moment that changed my life, but as I felt a wave of passion ripple through Shana's slender form, I lost all memory or awareness of anything but Shana's soft lips and sweet body pressing against mine.

With my arm around her we moved, without a word, into the bedroom, a large dim space lit only by light from the sitting-room doorway. I slowly undressed her, kissing and fondling each new area I uncovered, thrilling to the way her body would first throb with passion and then open itself passively, like a big unresisting irresistible flower. Fully naked at last she sighed and shivered and whispered my name and clung to me, and I then was on top of her and within her, and she was out-of-control panting and quivering under me, fully and fulfillingly doing the deed of love. The moment was so perfect, so equal to every yearning dream and aspiration, that I felt the sweet explosion coming and had trouble holding back, but as if knowing this she gently but firmly pushed me over and climbed on top. Then what had been delightful became unbelievable. I could look up at her and lose myself in her ardor. Panting, crooning lowly, swaying as though in a relentless wind of passion, she sailed on me like a galleon of spice. With soft cries she crested and then wilted onto me, inviting me back on top. I didn't need much persuading. In a moment I was all over Shana, kissing her deeply, and I was a guy on the verge of heaven.

But all of a sudden something felt wrong. Her arms, wrapt tighter and tighter around my back, were starting to hurt, I mean really hurt me. You know how it is when the nurse pumps up the blood pressure gauge on your arm, and you wonder just for a moment, *Is this thing going to crush me?* That's what it felt like, except it kept getting worse. I pulled my mouth free of hers, which had been sucking harder and harder on my tongue, and was about to shout something, when I suddenly became speechless with terror. Shana's legs were doing something that human legs aren't supposed to be able to do. They were moving up my body and wrapping around my rib cage just like her arms and doubling the pressure on my abdomen. On top of this she was somehow closing in on

240

my penis, which'd lost its erection and felt like a piece of dough going through a pasta machine.

Now I'm a big strong guy, twice her size, but my strength was nothing against the force that was crushing me. It suddenly dawned on me that Shana wasn't human. In the dimness I could see that the eyes and tongue had withdrawn into the head, leaving three black holes. A dull prolonged rumbling noise, like the lowest of low groans, was coming out of her, and I was about to faint from horror and agony when I was jolted back to life by huge inner CRACKINGS, one after another, that were the sounds of my own ribs snapping.

With the splitting pain the frantic impossible thought came to me: *If this monster is a robot, there's maybe a control somewhere.* The only part of her I hadn't seen or touched in lovemaking was her chignon. With one free hand I pulled up her head a little, while my right hand groped under her bun. My fluttering fingers touched a shallow knob, maybe an inch across. It didn't turn one way. My last conscious act was to turn it the other way.

I woke up, probably a minute or two later, reached for the phone and croaked a plea for help. When the medics found me I was lying on what looked like a deflated inflatable mannequin draped around an armature that could have been plastic or metal.

I'd survived.

But what a fool I'd been.

We're making progress, but we're nowhere near busting the case. The whole investigation's been hush-hush, of course. Otherwise imagine the scandal! I told the medics to give me a painkiller that left me conscious, just so I could tell the police to keep this thing quiet. My excuse? The truth: that it concerned an ongoing investigation (Molly's, that is) that was very sensitive.

But thanks to a call Roger made to Simon Palio at Treasury, the Feds are on the case, not investigating me this time but rather protecting me. After all I'm a major asset to the US government now, and they've got my safety in mind. I even got a personal letter from President Archie Carmichael, hoping I'll get well soon and visit him and his wife Smytha at the White House.

What we've learned of Shana Ladd is this:

The real Shana Ladd lives (just as the robot said) in Crested Butte, CO, and is the robot's spitting image, or vice versa. She was never invited to speak at UNLV, although she has appeared at UNevada, Reno.

The real Shana has heard of me, but never tried to contact me. She says she wants to meet me now, but I'm stalling.

Seeing her might scare me to death.

Checking in at the Argus, the robot used a forged credit card that accessed the real Shana Ladd's account.

A dittoed poster for the phony Shana's talk was circulated at short notice in the Zoology Department at UNLV, which explains the small turnout.

RoboGal is one of the most advanced contraptions that the FBI or I or anybody's ever seen. Her skeleton is pure titanium, articulated by muscles of aerospace elastic, and her skin is a porous polymer that we haven't identified yet. The eyes are elegant combos of glass and fluid that actually have little TV cameras in them, just as the ears have mikes. And her innards! Chris Auchinleck, who as a hand surgeon is good with robotics, and who was, coincidentally, contacted by the Feds as a consultant on this case, analyzed them as follows:

Unit Alpha: an air compressor inflating the body and empowering speech.

Unit Beta: a transmitter-receiver for exchanging information with Mission Control (wherever *that* is).

Unit Gamma: a humidifier for moistening skin, mouth, vagina, etc.

Unit Delta: A sack for holding materials eaten or drunk.

Unit Epsilon: an electric motor empowering muscle movement.

Unit Zeta: a computer for interpreting data and coordinating movement
and speech.

Some computer, too! It runs at 5 gigahertz, with 500 gigs on the hard
drive and 10 gigs of memory. With a computer so powerful, and smart
software and good communications, RoboGal packed a knockout bag
of tricks.

But still, too impressive to be an outside job. Shana's software was
just *too* smart for that. Somebody at Lomo Morado, somebody who
knows me, somebody who even might have been poking around in my
journal[44]

JANUARY 27, 2002

We've finished the airbed. I went down to the Shop yesterday morning and worked out the final design question: how to get the forced air to
"curl" at the height of about a foot, rather than racing up to the ceiling. I
did this by placing off-center freewheel propellors in all the floor-ducts.
They give the air a spin, sort of like a curveball, and this spin kicks in as
soon as it reaches parity with the upward lift (which diminishes propor-
tional to its height).

Thus you've got a bed of pure air that supports you without behaving
like Hurricane Andrew.

Even though I've dampened them for silent running, the props still
make a low F-F-F-F-ing sound, but then nothing's perfect. We heat the
air to 82, just like a day in Hawai'i, and because of this and the F-F-F-F-
ing noise I've named it the Honolulu Floatifer.

I tested it today. It was like flying! I'll sleep on it tonight and until my
ribs are all better.

Who sicced Shana on me? Why spend tens of millions on robotics

---

44. Ruck either left this entry unfinished, or finished it but forgot to save it on disk. —Ed.

when a $20,000 hit man could have done the job? Guccio Imbratta's too old and sick, and besides, even if he wasn't, he's more of an old-fashioned bread-and-butter bang-you're-dead type of guy. Myrdal Hwang? That's more like it. Molly's found a photo of him, taken at about age forty (that would be twenty years ago): a slender amigo with a touch of the Caucasian about him and a cruel elegant face.

I've got to know more—beginning with who the mole is at Lomo Morado. I think I'll put Cap Wickham on the case.

Whoever they are, they've hurt more than my body. To take the things I love—my dearest fondnesses, my aspirations, my very heart and soul—and then to bottle them up into a female-shaped automaton that seduces me with my own thoughts and tries to kill me—*that's* more than a physical assault. *It's a rape of the spirit. It's like making me naked, in every way, and then trashing me, in every way.* Can I look at a woman again, after this?

Chapter Eleven **The Unthinkable**

PART ONE: A JEWEL IN THE TIARA

At Lomo Morado the sun always shines. Looking north toward the Pueblo and Rick's vineyards at 3 PM, I can see pure white clouds sleeping like fat cats on the lower slopes of the Cabeza, but here it's always sunlight playing upon the house and the valley and the distant mountains, and while I'm sitting on the terrace reading, or writing, as I am right now, I'll sometimes look up with shock at the sudden newness of all those familiar sights, and the beauty of things seen, and this sense comes into me that the beauty is so ecstatic and painful, that it will kill me if I don't watch out.

That is, unless somebody else does me in first.

I'm counting on Cap Wickham to prevent that. If any man can, it's Cap.

We're gearing up for a quadruple wedding. Rick and Molly will be married on Sunday, as will Georgia Fox and Mehbub Ali Shah, Chris

The Most Amazing Thing

Auchinleck and Camilla Hoy, and Pecos Louie and Double Mocha. The ceremony will be performed by Gus (who's become a Canyon County J.P.) here on the terrace, and the reception will be inside so that we can hear Sergei and Bituminus on the piano. Things haven't turned out with those two as expected. Bituminus was supposed to be teaching Sergei jazz, but what we've mainly heard is Bituminus trucking through Chopin and the Goldberg Variations.

I've never heard such a big left hand.

I'll be in fairly good shape, I'd say about 85%, for the festivities. I can walk around easily now, but I can't exercise, and it still hurts when I laugh. But the Floatifer is a miracle-cure for me. It's literally like sleeping in mid air. (*Note to myself: build some more of them for hospitals.*) Rick quipped that he wanted to use it for his wedding night, which I can't allow right now, because it would slow up my healing.

But I wonder what it would be like . . .

Cap began his Shana Ladd investigation Tuesday. He set up shop in the living room without a secretary or tape recorder or notes (Cap's memory is that good!) and has questioned every person who might know anything. Later today he'll interview his last subject, that is, Yours Truly. So far he's spent the most time with Ali Shah, who says he hasn't seen the likes of Cap—for severity, that is—since his days in Pakistan. In fact, everybody Cap talked to came away slightly shaken. Cap's very well-spoken, but he doesn't miss a trick.

You may ask, in fact, I may someday ask, why I'm depending on a single retired major from Special Forces to save my neck, when I could afford my own private army. The simple, wacky answer is, running a private army isn't my idea of a happy life.

If you can't live well, what's the use of being a trillionaire?

5:10 PM. Cap and I sat out by the pool, so's not to be heard. He spent the first hour or so questioning me about who knew what and when. Then he asked if I'd written anything about myself. I told him about this

246

journal, which I keep in locked files. Also I said I'd written a kind of ode or hymn in hard copy last fall, but that I kept it in the safe. Who else had the combination? Rick and Catherine. Would I please show him the ode I wrote? I went and got the damn thing. Cap read it slowly and carefully as I sat biting my nails. When he was done he asked for a glass of whiskey. I rang for some Wharton's and ice and glasses.

After quaffing his drink Cap stretched out his long muscular form in his captain's chair, heaved a low satisfied groan and fixed me with piercing gray eyes. "I'm pretty sure who the mole was," he said.

Didn't he want to reinterview Rick and Catherine?

"I don't think so," said Cap. "I spent years in a combat command, and Rick Beauchamps is a man I'd follow into harm's way. That kind of officer doesn't rat on his chief. As for Catherine, whom I know you love, she's an unlikely suspect, especially since I've got a much better one."

"Who?" I shouted.

Cap brought his hands together and cracked his knuckles. "Salvador Savedra, alias Preston Vickers."

Salvador aka Vickers! Somehow that's been in the back of my mind too, but it seemed like an off-the-wall idea. I silently wondered, why then would Salvador go to court and beat my rap for me?

As though I'd said it out loud, Cap answered. "He defended you in order to keep the loot out of the government's clutches. It was a way of buying time."

"Then why would they immediately want to kill me?"

"I'm not sure. Maybe they learned something new, something we don't know. On the other hand, maybe there's more than one group out to get you."

"Have you got any idea who Salvador really is?"

Cap took a long pull on his bourbon, coaxed a French Gaulois cigarette out of his shirt pocket and lit up. He was obviously getting his thoughts together. "I'll make a guess, based on the following facts. Salvador had to be a kind of triple-threat genius. First off, a great con artist;

second, a brilliant legal mind; third, a cat burglar capable of busting a $100,000 safe and photographing or memorizing your hymn. This genius must also be enough of a sonofabitch to work for the Mafia or Myrdal Hwang. There's only one man in the world who's that good and that bad."

"Who's that?"

"His name's Mastho Jinn. He's respected and feared by the Intelligence community as maybe the most dangerous operative that ever lived. He's the son of a female Israeli spy who was kidnapped by a Nazi cadre that was hiding out in the forests of Brazil. She was a beautiful woman, they say—name of Sasha Jinn. She never gave up the information that the Nazis wanted, but information wasn't *all* these bastards wanted, and in the end she became the sexual property of their Kommandant, a cesspool of a man named Matthias Korm."

"About when was this?" I asked.

"Early 60's."

"Is this Korm still around?"

Cap scowled and momentarily looked away. "I'm told that he met— an appropriate end. But Korm's not part of our story, except to say that Mastho Jinn is his son. Sasha died of some tropical disease while Mastho was still a kid, and young Mastho escaped into the jungle and, incredibly, made his way through the bush and fetched up in the back streets of São Paulo. He learned all the rules of malice-management there—that is, what he hadn't already learned from the Nazis. That was the early 70's. Who knows what happened during the next few years, but by 1981 he was in Amman, posing as a Swedish art collector but really working both sides of the Mideast conflict. Since then he's surfaced here and there. Word is that he personally—solo, I mean—polished off a Siberian Secret Service chief, two African dictators and an Afghanistani warlord, and that once in Amsterdam he walked out of the Rijksmuseum, calm as you please, with a Vermeer under each arm.

"As for his sexual exploits . . ."

"Cap," I interrupted, "that can wait. Let's have some dinner." Somehow I didn't want an earful about Mastho Jinn's prowess in bed. Maybe I was thinking of those four weddings Sunday, and how I lie in bed alone.

FEBRUARY 5, 2002

I don't believe this.

Three into 714 is 238.

238 days—that takes us into October.

They say it's part of their mission.

Hey.

Can you break a Floatifer?

IT'S SHAMEFUL, ODIOUS, DEGRADED!

I'VE NEVER HAD SUCH FUN IN ALL MY LIFE.

Give it up now, so at least the world will know you had some shame.

I can't.

Why not?

I don't want to.

Gratitude! I went to church last Sunday, a little church in Tucson, between two bowling alleys, called St. Sigismund's. I went because I read in the paper that Father Feeny would give a sermon about gratitude.

Father Feeny said gratitude was a jewel in the Tiara of Faith.

Holy Father, I confess! It started on the night of my friends' quadruple wedding. I'd had a lot to drink and stupidly tried to dance, but the first time I flexed my torso, my rib-cage caught fire with pain. I tried to hide it, but folks couldn't help but notice. Janet ordered me back to my room, and Gus and Chris came along to the Shop to help me undress. With them I unsteadily made my way upstairs to my makeshift bedroom. The Floatifer, as always, was turned on, and when they'd dosed me with ibuprofen and helped me to go to the bathroom and take off my clothes and lie down on the Floatifer, the two men marvelled at my outrageous invention.

I confess, it must have been something to see. I floated in space a foot from the floor on a bed of balmy air. Immediately the pain went away, and I felt pleasantly sleepy. I thanked them as best I could and asked them to turn down the lamp and get back to the party.

As their steps and voices receded, I had the sweetest feeling. Eight people I cared about had just been united in marriage. Louie was building his own house on the north slope of the Cabeza and was beginning to blaze a 25-mile network of hiking trails for the kids at the Pueblo. Rick and Molly would be happy. Ali was serene and Louie delirious. Sleepily I looked around the bedroom, with its bare ceiling joists and carpetless floor and thrown-together furniture, and the place was suddenly beautiful to me, and the wonderful Floatifer-effects brought back circulation and soothed—

My eyes snapped open. Something was different about the room.

It had an angel in it.

Three angels, in fact, definitely female, standing white-robed between the lamp and me, so that their faces were dim, their silhouettes golden.

Suddenly it hit me that I was naked and floating on my back in the air. Somehow they didn't seem to find this strange.

The woman in the middle moved closer until she was just above me. It was Rachel Muldoon. There was a fragrance about her somewhere between lavender and woodbine.

Magdalena College had finally made its move.

As the other two approached to join her, Rachel opened a small parchment scroll, which she handed to the lady on her right. I've still got it in my safe,[45] so I can quote it verbatim, except I should add that the

---

45. No such document has been found. —Ed.

lady on Rachel's right, who was a tall shapely blonde with wonderful candid eyes, read the first stanza, and the lady on her left, who had light brown hair and a face that seemed to be looking at a sunrise, read the second, and Rachel read the third, except that all three joined in on the capitalized lines:

To Desmond Ruck, from the Magdalena College Class of '02[46]

> In gratitude and joy we three approach the Founder
> In thankfulness we kneel within the lamplit chamber
> To honor him we gladly doff the silken mantle
> *AMOR AMORI, AMOR AMANTIBUS*
>
> He found us peddling love in our expense of spirit
> He saw us leasing out the graces of our bodies
> He gave us back, with more, our bodies and our spirit
> *AMOR AMORI, AMOR AMANTIBUS*
>
> This gift was more than thrift, it was a spacious bounty
> Gift without thought of recompense or booty
> HE SHONE ON US LIKE SUN.
> We've now regained our dignity of body
> And we're inspired to grace him with our bounty
> LOVE GIVEN IS LOVE WON
> *AMOR AMORI, AMOR AMANTIBUS*

Unsure of what to say, I asked Rachel what the Latin meant.
"Love in return for love, love given to lovers," she almost sang.
"And you mean that the three of you . . . ?"
"Not just the three," said the blonde lady. *"All of us."*
"But I never—"
"That's exactly why," said the brown-haired gal, and kissed my hand.
I was overcome with awe.

---

46. The B.A. at Magdalena College was based on credit for three academic years and three summer sessions.

The Most Amazing Thing

And that explains why, in this great year of 2002, I have made, am making and will make love, in midair, to 714[47] grateful ex-prostitutes. I can't help it. There was no stopping them. Denying them would have been denying their right to love, dissing their dignity.

They come in the Magdalena College bus in groups of twenty-one. They stay in the Casa Morada, a big set of apartments across the grassy quad from the Shop. They visit me at the rate of three daily, one for bed-time, one for wake-up and one for afternoon nap.

My days are etched in love.

While not with me the ladies work with the kids at Pueblo Verde, or learn about wine-growing from Rick, or trail-blaze on the upper slopes with Louie and his people. That puts a kind of institutional face on their presence, but I know it won't prevent the awful truth from somehow get-ting out. Awful truth? The awful truth is that I'm so delighted that I don't care whether it gets out or not! The awful truth is an awesome truth.

They're wearing a path between the Casa and the Shop. They call this path the Magdalena Trace.

I'll pave it with marble and border it with roses.

It's often been said that even though guys boast about being crazy for sex, they get bored, even turned off, if a lot of good sex is offered to them. I'm happy to report that this isn't the case.

---

47. Of the 723 original matriculants to Magdalena College, two had dropped out, one had married and six were being treated medically for conditions that prevented their partici-pation. —Ed.

As I say, the bedroom above the Shop is a sort of primitive place. There's a staircase door downstairs for privacy, but no door or staircase railing up in the bedroom, so the first sight I get of each woman is a new smiling face coming out of the stairwell. I've got an espresso machine up here, a full bar, a chilled keg of Duke's India Pale Ale and a fridge full of snacks like smoked salmon, pickled asparagus, Vienna sausages, stuffed jalapeño shooters, muscat wine, paté de foie gras, deli rye bread, Black Forest ham, fresh buttermilk, shelled cashews, Almond Roca, Hawaiian potato chips, Gorgonzola cheese, fresh homegrown vegetables, lox and capers.

Sometimes we'll spend hours chatting. Rachel made each of them agree to tell me one special thing that's happened to them since entering Magdalena College. Many speak of the wonderful feeling of knowing where one is in history and being able to read serious stuff and meditate or dialogue over things and express their thoughts in writing. (*Damn it! I should go there myself!*) Many speak of what a genius teacher Ethan Zoig is, and how he's brought even more life to the place.

Before parting each lady signs a guest-book, leather-bound, that Rachel brought and left here, and there's space next to each name for a date and a yearbook-type comment. I'll quote a few:

"Remember the nightingale"
"lightning at midnight"
"tarantella at dawn"
"Sing 'Stardust' for me"
"Sprezzissimo!"[48]
"Kalepa ta kala"[49]
"A Floatifer for every family!"

---

48. Unknown word. —Ed.
49. "Good things are difficult to achieve." (Greek) —Ed.

The Most Amazing Thing

"To the Edison of Eros!"

"To the Napoleon of naps!"

"To the Caesar of Squeeze-her!"

". . . who was afraid of heights"

". . . who earned her wings"

". . . who flew the friendly skies"

". . . who brought peanut butter cookies"

". . . who brought oysters on the half-shell"

". . . who thought she knew it all"

". . . who thought she heard a train-whistle"

". . . who graduated magna cum loudly"

"Call me your cello"

"Appelle-moi ton oiseau."[50]

"Chiamami la tua Musa."[51]

"Aufwiedersehen im Leckerbissenthal."[52]

"Vidi, vici, veni."[53]

"Who the hell is Mara?"

"Think of me when you sneeze"

"To Desmond, soon to be a National Park!"

"Visit Old Faithful!"

"I brake for white wolves"

"I brake for kisses"

"The view's better up here"

"Play it again!"

"Call the firemen!"

"Don't make it stop!"

"I'll take a dozen!"

"Up, up and away!"

---

50. "Call me your bird." (French) —Ed.

51. "Call me your Muse." (Italian) —Ed.

52. "Be seeing you in the Valley of Tasty Snacks." (German) —Ed.

53. Misquotation of Caesar's "Veni, vedi, vici." ("I came, I saw, I conquered.") (Latin) —Ed.

"Where am I? Who am I? Was it a dream?"
"I'll think of you"
"Don't forget me"

Forget? In my mind's eye they wave like a sea of wildflowers.

What's it like making love on a Floatifer? Think of being a lark on a clear day in Eden. Think of dying and going to heaven. Then take out the part about dying.

Think of gratitude.

JULY 3, 2002

This is fun. This is commercial-free, nonpolluting, equal opportunity, sustainable, organic fun. This is the essence and nature of fun. This is too much fun.

Sex. A few nights ago we were hanging out together after dinner, and Ethan dumbfounded every one of us by asking us how to describe *seeing* to somebody who'd always been blind. It's possible, but it's damn hard, and it makes you sound like an out-and-out technician. Now, suppose Ethan had said, how do you describe sex to somebody who's never done it? *I mean, how sex makes you feel.* I've looked at dozens of books about sex, but none of the authors, not Freud, not Kinsey, not Joyce, not Philip Roth, not Henry Miller, takes a shot at it. So why don't I, with oodles of sex, an hour of time, and nothing to lose.

Sex is closeness, warmth, intimation, secret sharing, promiscuity, abandon.

Sex is variety, the fascinating variety of heat and warmth and coolness, the scintillating variety of smoothness and hairiness and dryness and moistness, the inebriating variety of muscle and bone and fat, the obliterating variety of all of these lovingly moving through time.

Sex is strangeness, adventure, discovery, the stranger suddenly close, the new sights and touches and smells, the gateway to mystery, the pro-hibitions and deprivations defied, the social norms upended.

Sex is circularity and the sweet coincidence of opposites: it's giving-receiving, it's submission-domination and top-bottom and over-under, it's tension-relaxation, it's remembering-forgetting, it's selfishness-un-selfishness, it's riddle and answer, it's a thighward insertion that's simul-taneously a spectacular ride and yet packs more security than all the cas-tles ever built by Arabs and Templars and Crusaders and Danes. It lives in contradiction and transcends philosophy.

Sex is the sight of a person at her best, with her looks reflecting your immeasurable liking of her looks and her delighted liking of yours.

Sex is rub stroke caress explore fondle squeeze embrace submerge.

Sex is a medley of moans and murmurs and sighs and whispers and squeals and snorts and lone words isolated like atolls in an ocean of passion.

Sex is the taste of lips and mouth and the flesh's freshness and pas-sion's misty sweat.

Sex is the smell of the skin's perfume, the hair's bouquet, the fevered panting breath, the secretions of the body's infallible honesty.

Sex is love and fondness and friendship, the friendship of two friends who all alone have opened the gate to a secret garden.

Regarding orgasms, I make out five classes: Class 1: Oops. Class 2: Yum. Class 3: Wow! Class 4: NASA. And Class 5: Vesuvius.

My god it's time to do it again! I've got to get my thoughts together. I'll get back to this tonight.[54]

President Carmichael and the First Lady have invited me to stay at the White House, in Lincoln's bedroom no less, for the weekend of Au-gust 16–18. I'm almost too shy to accept. But you can't turn down those types of invitation, because if you do, it comes back to haunt you.

---

54. We have no evidence that Mr. Ruck ever returned to this subject. —Ed.

There are other things I can do on that trip. I want to give the Bethesda Naval Hospital a Floatifer for burn victims. (Call Rick)

And why not give the Pueblo Verde kids a tour of the Capital! (Call Rose)

After that I'm going to try to see Guccio Imbratta. Molly finally reached him by phone last week and, excepting as he can barely speak anymore, he sounded almost friendly.

Cap's been after me to beef up security around here, and I've grudgingly agreed. We're blazing a 70-mile Jeep-trail around the ranch with four keeps (little castles) one at each corner, for the guards to live in while on duty. Cap wanted to bring in a garrison and a couple of Nighthawk gunships as well, but I drew the line there. There's no reason to expect a frontal attack.

Oops, I'm late for my nap!

JULY 30, 2002

News of the DC tour has put the kids onto Cloud Nine. Rose is having uniforms made for them—navy blue shorts with red borders and navy blue shirts with white collars (very understated), mainly so that we can keep track of the littler ones. I've invited Heidi to fly in from England with Vicki and Vi and join the tour. Of course there's no space in hotels, but Beatty Hood, the commander at Bethesda, has pulled some strings to put them all up in Annapolis dorms.

The President and First Lady will treat the kids to donuts and lemonade at 3 PM Sunday by the South Portico.

Summer updates:

¶ My three financial wizards, Rousseau, Clemens and Horowitz, whom I've put in charge of the White Wolf Foundation, dropped in for a pow-wow and rest cure last week; they're staying at a guest house we've built at Pueblo Verde, which keeps them a few miles away from the

Shop and events that might be misinterpreted. Clemens, who's been keeping tabs on Uncle Titus, reports that the old goat is doing well as director of our Moroccan office in Fez.

But in Ethiopia things aren't so groovy. The ex-Magdalena lit teachers transferred to famine-relief work have, all but one, flown the coop and come back to the States. They just couldn't take the grief. The one exception, a man named Rainer Maulwurf, wrote Clemens that he's at last found meaning in life, and that he wants to do this sort of work forever.

I asked for a copy of the letter.[55] Maybe that one conversion's worth all the rest.

¶ Some dunghole named Guvadich[56] has started a civil war in Bolgovnia, meaning that our relief-work there will be held up.

¶ Through swimming, jogging, weight-work and tennis, I've slowly gotten myself back in shape. I proved it yesterday in tennis with Wally Horowitz, a topnotch club player who was once ranked in New York State. He won in three sets, but I stretched him.

¶ Vicki and Vi (who leave for Cambridge University in a month) finally had their meeting with the Queen. Each of them wrote me a long letter about it, and they say she's a swell sort. The audience was followed by a gala international ball. Vi notes that the Crown Prince of Moldavia, who was a guest at the Palace, took a strong interest in Vicki and would dance with nobody else; Vicki writes that Vi was eagerly followed all night by the Grand Duke of Bohemia. Can't wait to see them![57]

¶ Last month I asked Gus if he and Rose would take a working vaca-

---

55. The Maulwurf letter has one sentence underlined in ms., presumably by Mr. Ruck himself. It reads, "I've at last discovered that Karl Marx's reading of society, while grand, consuming, awesome and quite irrefutable, has no relation to reality whatsoever." —Ed.

56. Correctly spelled Guradich. —Ed.

57. Ruck preserved these letters, together with Maulwurf's, with his most precious possessions in the library safe at Lomo Morado. While the Maulwurf letter is now framed and

tion in New York and buy me a pied-à-terre in Manhattan. They got a room at the Plaza with Central Park exposure (as Rose put it, for geographical reference) and right away started disagreeing, with Rose favoring an East Side apartment near the Metropolitan Museum and Gus pulling for a West Side apartment near the Museum of Natural History. Just so they wouldn't come to blows, I told them to look further downtown. They found me a wonderful old house on Gramercy Park.

¶ Georgia Ali Shah's pregnant! That means that Mehbub will finally have the child he always wanted and that Georgia can build her own nuclear family. Their hothouse, by the way, is far from full. As soon as I get the time, if ever, Rick and I will start crisscrossing the globe for specimens.

¶ What with Sergei and Bituminus, the piano in the living room never gets a rest. Sergei popped in at breakfast this morning and announced, "Desmond Petrovich, my friend! Get this, dawg! Dat 'Tuminus, he dona taught me da blues!"

AUGUST 1, 2002

Horrible interlude yesterday afternoon. The nap-time face coming up out of the stairwell was none other than Mega Klein's! and it had the same kind of look a hungry mosquito must have when it sees the Miami Dolphins getting out of the shower.[58] I almost fell off the Floatifer. Seems she'd caught wind of the Magdalena visits and somehow finagled her way into the sequence. As Mega stood there, fondling her little

---

on display at the Ruck Memorial Center in Las Vegas, the two others have been withheld by his administrators in order to protect the privacy of the Grand Duchess of Bohemia and the Princess of Moldavia. —Ed.

58. Mega Klein, a fellow patient of Ruck's while he was recovering from hand surgery at the Bellows Clinic in 1998. See *Ruck's Run*, Ch. 7. —Ed.

black beard and silently leering at me in what must have been a Come-Hither, I suddenly felt weak and dizzy, as though the condensed-air cushioning was just about to shut down and send me crashing to the floor.

I greeted her lamely and told her I was sick and couldn't see her.

Mega blew up. "Sick! *I* should get so sick! What you really mean is, I'm not good enough to be one of your 700 concubines!"

"That's just the point, Mega. They're not hookers anymore, and they're coming here to prove it."

Mega was huffing and puffing and brushing back the tears. "Fine way of proving it! . . . Fat lot of double talk! . . . Shagging hundreds of prostitutes in midair . . . You call that social work? . . . Mealy-mouthed Lothario . . . Desmond Ruck Desmond Fuck Desmond *Stück!*" In her rage Mega'd turned beet-red and was now doing a sort of spastic rapper's dance on the floor in front of me. Finally she pulled herself together and hissed, "Think you're something special, meatball? You're nothing, Desmond, nothing but *a worn-out American cliché!* Ever hear of a gal named Diane Ditt? You'll get yours." And with that she scuttled downstairs.

Worn-out American cliché! Those words cut me to the quick. An American cliché! How can there be an American cliché when everything American is so, so new? Newness can't be a cliché!

More to the point, who's this Diane Ditt? What's Mega going to do?

AUGUST 5, 2002

A perfect morning at LoMo.[59]

7:20 AM. I wake to sounds of the familiar chariot-scene played to the hilt by Ranguma and Paws. Ranguma has woken up and walked out onto

---

59. LoMo: Ruck's abbreviation for Lomo Morado. —Ed.

the terrace through the open bedroom doors and is doing her deep morning stretch when Paws jumps on her from the rim of a big potted plant. Ranguma lets out a low howl and takes off like a shot, racing round and round the terrace as caterwauling Paws rides her mane like a jockey. I jump up and stand in the doorway watching them, to see doors opening from the kitchen and guest rooms as a half-dozen other people pop out to cheer them on.

8:30. Breakfast—leftovers from last night really—by the pool in the morning sun. Catherine's crumb cake with a couple of canned peach-halves. A glass of iced spring water. Could anything taste better?

9:10. On my stroll to the Shop I peek into the living room where Sergei's giving a piano lesson to a kid from the Pueblo. Kid's none other than young Atlas Lockforth Ruck, originally son of Dominee the Gom-beenian minister. This kid's going to be a prodigy, which is a miracle, considering that, according to documents from the Escondido, CA, school system, he needed drug therapy for attention-deficit-with-hyper-activity-and-depression/anxiety disorder ("aggravated and with compli-cations").

What did Rose have to say when she read this diagnosis? "It's mind-boggling, how society can convert its own failure to educate kids into the kids' imaginary medical problems. Let's try giving young Atlas a few direct learning challenges, and see how he responds. And maybe a pi-ano lesson from Sergei."

9:20. At the Shop I work on a minor invention I call the TellTale: it's a screen that you can velcro to your office door. Wherever you happen to be, you can program this screen from your pocket organizer to let peo-ple know where you are and when you'll be back. Does a few other things as well. I space out for a minute imagining the messages my Tell-

261

Tale might have conveyed over the past few years: "CAPTURED BY WITCHES. WILL CALL LATER." "BURIED IN MUDBANK. PLEASE LEAVE MESSAGE." "PENIS CAUGHT BETWEEN TRUCK TIRES. HAVE A GOOD DAY."

10:40. I climb the Shop stairs to the Floatifer Room for a session of Magdalena Gratitude. Her name is Gypsy, and her gratitude is so tremendous, as is my gratitude to her, and our gratitudes are both so harmonious, and simultaneous, that for an hour I lose track of who and where I am.

12:05. Now I'm about to go to lunch at Pueblo Verde with the Wise Men, who are going to brief me about US Third World policy so that I don't look like a total dunce when I meet the President. They're also going to let me know what they've done to stabilize the Third World economies that we're pouring billions of dollars into. Vance Rousseau is the mastermind of this one. He's the only human I've ever met who can talk about economics and make sense.

Gypsy's guestbook entry: "A little twist at the end improves almost anything."

AUGUST 7, 2002

Mega's done her worst. She's leaked the Magdalena affair to the media. I'm all over the checkstand tabloids as Sardanapalus and Gomorrah. *Sixty Minutes* has been on the phone all day, leaving messages that they'll give me all 38 minutes.

In the end, Gus shut down the phone lines.

I'm a national scandal, a cultural embarrassment, a comprehensive goat, a vulgar sexual icon, a butt of ridicule, a paramount buffoon, a rampant leering idiot, a figure of shame. Was it worth it?

Yes.

PART TWO: THE AFFAIR
KNOWN AS WATER CLOSET

AUGUST 19, 2002

Alone in the living room at 17 Gramercy Park, New York, NY, with a case of terminal jitters and a headache that won't go away.

I think I've shot my bolt.

Mom always used to say, when I was in the dumps, "Eat something." Better see what's in the kitchen.

Feeling less suicidal now, after a beer and a turkey sandwich with a couple of hot peppers. Thanks, Gus and Rose, for being as ever thoughtful.

I've now got to describe one of the most disgusting and embarrassing events that ever happened to anybody.

It started out as harmless fun. On the 16th we bussed the Pueblo Verde kids down to the airstrip and put them on the 777. Rick and Molly were pilot and copilot, Wilbur was on the flight deck practicing navigation, and all 31 of the AV faculty were aboard as guides. It was a gorgeous morning, with feathery clouds still reddish from dawn, and a cool breeze across the tarmac. You've never seen as many happy kids! Although I couldn't be a kid again, I felt for them, and shared the thrill of a new world opening up in front of them with every minute.

We took off due east with a universal shout of delight and climbed steeply to 35,000 feet. During the four-hour flight, while the kids weren't wolfing down snacks and guzzling lemonade, the plane became an airborne school. Up front Mary Conover was telling the littler kids all about DC, while amidships Agnes Hackett lectured the older children about the terrain and settlement of the American West.

After visiting the classes I retired to the private apartment aft,[60] took a bath in my newly-designed tilt-proof tub and napped on the water-bed, next to the titanium-glass mix picture window that showed wondrous castles of thunderclouds high over the Mississippi Valley. I was feeling fine except for a mild stomachache; I'd been constipated for days.

I slept fitfully until Wilbur phoned me to belt up for the landing.

Vi, Vicki and Heidi's plane was two hours late, so Molly and Rick volunteered to wait for them, and then to limo them to Annapolis, before going themselves to their suite at the l'Enfant Plaza. Wilbur and I took a cab downtown to the Air and Space Museum, which he'd never seen before, and we gawked at the marvelous exhibits till closing time.

Then we went to Old Town for an excellent Indian dinner. The hot curry, laced with chutney and washed down with New Zealand beer, jostled my stomach but did nothing for my constipation.

Maybe my stomach was quirky because I was excited. After I'd dropped Wilbur at the l'Enfant and headed towards the White House, I started getting goosebumps. No matter what you may say about Archie Carmichael—about his arrogance and self-righteousness, I mean, or his obsession with golf—he's still President, that is, a symbol as well as a man. It was the symbol part that was getting me uptight in the cab. Would the Chief of State be miffed by my recent scandal? And what about Smytha Carmichael?

Smytha, as everybody knew, was the Conscience of the Nation, if not the whole world.

---

60. The interior design of Ruck's 777 was completely modular, enabling its use as a cargo plane, a passenger plane, a flying luxury apartment or any combination of these things. —Ed.

Smytha, they say, could put anybody to shame with an angry flash of her fine eyes.

The cab drops me at 1600 Pennsylvania Avenue, and at this moment, I guess because of my nervousness, life pops into overexposed technicolor, and time starts moving very fast. I'm suddenly through Security and in an elevator with a spiffy female aide who's explaining, it sounds like for the 677th time, how elevator's been in use since the days of FDR, who needed it in the worst way; and she continues as we toddle down the 2nd floor hall and into the Lincoln Bedroom suite. There she rambles on about how this was never really Lincoln's bedroom, nor the towering rosewood bed his bed, and on into Bess Truman's restoration and Emily Spinach, Alice Roosevelt's pet snake, until perhaps noticing my glassy eyes she wishes me good evening and disappears.

Uneasily trying to stifle curry-burps, I case the joint. A table by the windows has been set for tea. The bed, though humongous, is kind of hard and bumpy, and on the table beside it are two sheets of paper: one a room service form and the other a calendar print-out announcing that the President and First Lady will visit me for tea tonight at 10 (earlier events of the day include no less than 36 holes of golf), that he and I will meet over coffee at 11 AM tomorrow to "discuss world affairs" and that I'm expected at the South Portico festivities on Sunday.

I'm on my way to my overnight bag for a few gulps of travel-bourbon when the door cracks open and my God it's Carmichael himself, followed by the First Lady, both in evening dress (her silver gown coordinating with a diamond necklace and her steel-gray hair), both of them shorter than they looked on TV, both beaming regally, both talking nonstop about how glad they are I've come. Faced with this mutual babble I'm not sure which of them to look at, so I try a tennis-match oscillation, my head bobbing up and down en route to signal approval. This stops being necessary when we sit down at the tea table and start noshing cinnamon toast and sipping our tea.

The Most Amazing Thing

About then I get my first taste of Smytha's fabled eyes. Flanking an elegant slightly-arched nose and abutting eyebrows of youthful black, these dark-brown beauties aren't down-putting at all. They're frankly curious.

To defuse embarrassment I glance back at the President just in time to catch him looking distrustfully at his wife's looking at me. Pitfalls of greatness. But in an instant he's grabbed the ball again, or rather my left thigh, which he gives a cronial attention-getting pat and says, in a kind of secretive voice, "Tell me, Mr. Ruck—pardon my frankness—is it true that, what with your wilderness reclamation and homeless relief and farm reforms,[61] you're going to give away $100 billion this year?"

Not exactly, I say. A good deal of that amount would be long-term small-business loans.

"Do you plan to give at that rate every year?"

My stomach rumbles loudly as I answer, "Yes, that is, until I can increase it."

The Chief Executive looks bemused, almost irritated. "Increase it! But how can you give at that rate, and as an encore pay Uncle Sam $50 billion a year, without turning yourself into a sieve?"

Smytha is all eyes as I describe Vance Rousseau's idea of Entrepreneurial Giving: investing in Third World areas that develop so fast that they speedily cycle back into industrial profits. She repeats "Enpreneurial giving! How fascinating. Give me another example."

I quote Vance again, that the simplest example is a village family business where the parents give the children food, clothes and business education, which the children will repay by taking over the hard work and enlarging the business and ultimately running the show and supporting the parents when they retire. I explain that what we do is just extend that family-business idea.

---

61. Reluctant to subject the reader to a lengthy footnote at this exciting juncture, I recommend the Addendum footnote at the end of this section. —Ed.

Smytha likes this topic. "But how can you be sure," she asks, "that pumping so much money into developing countries won't result in the kind of chaos that hit the Asian markets in 1998?"

I reply that in every country where we invest, my Three Wise Men have put in place a system of buying-curbs and selling-curbs that they call "Panic Insurance."

The Fine Eyes wander waifishly over my head and shoulders as she ignores my explanation and asks, "Did you ever stop and think that maybe you were the world's most powerful man?"

"So what?" I answer.

The Eyes fix on my lips as Smytha sighs a throaty sigh, like a leopard purring. She asks, "Don't you feel powerful just knowing what people would do *in return* for all that giving?"

"No, it just makes me feel, er, complete."

"But what if," she croons knowingly, "what if people want to show their *gratitude*?"

Gratitude! Everybody's got the skinny on me! I burn and cringe. Smytha cackles, and the President clears his throat and averts his eyes.

Flushed with success at embarrassing me, Smytha leans towards me and softly announces, "Desmond, excuse me for saying so, but as far as power-mongering is concerned, I think you're still a novice, and you possibly could use a lesson or two."

At this moment a Navy captain has materialized out of nowhere and is murmuring into the President's ear. Carmichael, suddenly looking done in, rises and excuses himself, telling both of us it's that goddamn Bolgovnian ethnic separatist, Jazeps Guradich, fanning up all kinds of shit in Kharkharsk again—this time by taking hostages. The President's on his way to the Oval Office to say a word to General Benton Froehling, chairman of the Joint Chiefs—but he'll be right back.

The door's no sooner shut than Smytha's pulled something out of her evening bag and in short order is sploshing whiskey of some sort from a silver flask into her tea and then mine. We both giggle. "Archie's such a bear about spirits," she confides, her Fine Eyes flashing. She wrestles her chair an inch closer to mine and whispers, "But he can't see this from the . . . *Oral Office!*"

At this moment my lower intestine growls like a cornered grizzly, and as I try to mask the noise with a lame guffaw at her unholy pun, Smytha's left hand has casually moved to my right forearm. "Here's to good times, Desmond," she murmurs, raising her cup in a toast.

As we drink, America's Conscience first rubs, then holds her knee against mine.

What do I do now? I feel like I'm a captured finch being toyed with by a Maine cooncat. How is it that women can get so much mileage out of such crude moves? And why the hell does it feel so damn good? Why doesn't some PC professor write a book about *that?* My mind gropes for alternatives. Should I pull my leg away like an offended virgin? Should I grab the First Inner Thigh and give it an unmistakably erotic squeeze? I decide to take the middle course, leaving my leg where it is and gulping my spiked tea, which promptly starts dribbling down on my chin.

As I grab my linen napkin the President is striding back in, and the First Lady's hand and knee have returned to home base. The Commander-in-Chief is obviously heated up by what he's just done, which turns out, he lets on, to be ordering naval maneuvers in the Baltic. He pours himself another cup of tea (said tea being a gift, Smytha inserts, from the Nehru family) and launches into a blustering harangue about what it means to be, as he puts it, Police Chief of the World. This set-piece is about as fresh as Martha Washington's wedding flowers, but Carmichael enlivens it with tosses of his thick white shock of hair and territorial eye-contact.

As he plows on through anecdotes about Sitting Bull, Emilio Aguinaldo and Matahari I experience two feelings, neither exactly pleasant.

The first feeling is that, ablaze with spousal testosterone, the Pres is trying to put me down as a hedonist who practices dreamy philanthropy and seamy you-know-what while real men have to mind the universal shop (my offending knee begins to burn with shame).

The second feeling—and it's an even uglier feeling—is my bowels telling me that it's time for big business. I haven't had a shit in two days, and Smytha's Long Island Tea has broken up the logjam, and something Godzilla-like is moving down through me with a will of its own.

I constrict my colonic muscles and start sweating like a pig.

The President doesn't notice my agony. Warming to the task, he kicks off a lively disquisition on Lend Lease. There's a disaster coming. My stomach is singing *Lohengrin* and I feel like a woman in late labor with septuplets. I'm going into shock.

If he makes it to the Marshall Plan, we'll all be knee-deep in guano.

At what seems like the last moment I glimpse Smytha, in undisguised homicidal boredom, looking at her diamond watch. Guessing that His Nibs has glimpsed this too, I consult my own watch, touch his sleeve and, with the air of a deeply concerned citizen, intone, "Mr. President, I'm keeping you up."

Carmichael looks at his watch and decides it's true. He mumbles something about evening prayers and rises from the table. As the First Couple simultaneously chirp about the Lincoln Bedroom and good times to come this weekend, I escort them to the door, carefully avoiding bows or bends. At the door she gets up on tiptoe and whispers, I mean *whispers to me* something I don't fully catch, sounding like "Enjoy the *Income Bedroom*.[62] Expect the unexpected."

I let that one fly by as she leaves and stick my hand out to the President, who won't let go of it and fixes me with a steely stare. "Ruck, the world we live in is full of risk and opportunity. Look at this mess in Bolgovnia—some nobody strongman ready to start a war, and it's the USA

---

62. Here as before, a rather questionable witticism concerning Presidential uses of interior architecture. —Ethan Zoig

that's called in to mediate. We need big men in the White House, men big enough to—to compass the sweep of the times. Now you know I came to office on your white bread, family values platform, but that's not necessarily gonna be true of my successor. A fellah may have a scandal or two—big guys almost always do—but the public will usually forgive them, especially since you're single. But it's time to get serious and get your eyes on the prize. As you know, Vice President Lehrer's older than I am. There's going to be a gap in GOP leadership when I'm gone. Think of the clout you'd have if you were a trillionaire and Chief Executive to boot. You'd have both reins of power in your hands. It's yours to lose, Desmond." And Carmichael has turned and stalked off down the hall.

So that's it. He wants me to run for President.

I run for the toilet.

The Lincoln bathroom. The Lincoln toilet. Think how many illustrious hindquarters, including maybe Abraham's own, have been lowered onto it! But such thoughts aren't on my mind as I sit down on this seat—just pure agony. There's no immediate relief, only ominous tremors. The monstrous thing inside of me moves slowly, unstoppably, excruciatingly downward. It's the non-me moving in the me. Or it is an unknown part of me, menacing, frightening, loathsome, but commanding, coming to light. It seems to be slamming against vertebrae, crunching vital organs, ripping my insides out as it moves inexorably down and down. I feel it begin to exit, but there seems to be no end to it. Will it pull my life out after it? Will Desmond Ruck, body and soul, be douched away into the DC sewer system?

Then, with an accelerating rush and a heavy, wooden-sounding thud, it's gone. I've never felt such relief! I wipe myself and sit there panting for a minute, then, without rising, reach behind me to flush the toilet. I don't want to see the foul thing I've produced. But something sounds funny. Instead of a flush, there's a kind of lame gurgle. Something's blocking the flow.

Guess what.

I rise and look at it, gripped with horror. It's grotesque. Jet black, a good foot long, stone hard and wide as a baseball bat. It's too big for the equipment! It's not going anywhere.

There's something awesome, almost majestic about it. It glares up at me, this hideous creation of mine, and it defies me. It's realer than I am.

This is where I panic. This is where I make a bad mistake. At this point a Voice should be saying to me, "Desmond, calm down. It's not the end of the world. It's only a very large piece of shit. Call the help. Tell them you've been ill. People will understand." But instead I'm thinking, "This is foul, this is gross. I'm dying from shame. This is an insult to the White House and a slap in the face of American dignity. This is how I answer the President, who had faith in me? *At all costs I've got to destroy it!!*"

I pull up my pants and look around the bathroom for an appropriate tool. Nothing doing there. I frantically ransack the sitting room, the bedroom. Any decent-sized rod or post or hammer or even large screwdriver would do, but there's nothing. Intent on foraging out into the hall, I go to the door and open it a crack. I'm greeted by an unbelievable sight.

Approaching, halfway down the hall is the First Lady, buff naked except for a black, broad-brimmed Spanish hat and Flamenco boots. She's got a champagne bottle in her left hand and a bullwhip in her right hand, and she's headed my way, and there's a spring in her step.

Holy shit. I quietly pull the door shut. I race for the sitting room, which also opens onto the hall. I hear Smytha knock on the bedroom door, then turn the knob. As she lets herself into the suite, I let myself out. I figure I've got about a minute while she checks out the bedroom and sitting room, knocks on the bathroom door (which I've left closed), enters said bathroom and discovers the USS Toilet Turd, deciding maybe to launch it with her champagne bottle. I speedily and stealthily make my way down to the other end of the hall. My prayers are answered. The President's *golf bag* is propped against the wall next to what has to be their bedroom door.

I choose my club carefully. A driver will mash, an iron will slice.

I select the putter.

I'm about a third of the way back to the Lincoln Bedroom when I see Smytha coming out of it. Even at this distance, she looks visibly shaken, and her bullwhip is at half mast. I've got no choice but to grab a door-handle on my right, silently let myself in and hide until she passes.

But I've let myself into the antechamber of a room that's occupied! Two men are kneeling by a table near the window, about twenty-five feet away. Neither has noticed me enter. One of them is the President. The other man I've only seen in a photograph, but his exquisite, arrogant face is unmistakable.

The President is praying with Myrdal Hwang. The table next to them is piled high and green with US currency.

I want out of there. I silently count to ten once, then twice, and open the door which thank God doesn't creak. The hall's empty.

Thirty seconds later, I'm back in the Lincoln Bathroom, using the putter to full effect. The golf club works like magic, almost as though it was made for the job, but my thoughts are troubled. The First Lady as a dominatrix coming to teach me the Ways of Power—that doesn't bother me so much—think of Cleopatra! But the President taking money from Hwang and praying with him—*that shouldn't be*. Hwang's an international criminal, and the President should know it. What kind of god were they praying to? An evil god like Kanaloa? But I'm jolted out of these thoughts by major noise. It's a handheld radio at high volume, and just after I hear it two big Secret Service types dart into the bathroom and each of them grabs one of my arms, while the Navy captain I've seen before shouts from the doorway, "Don't let him flush it! Somebody bring a plastic bag."

● ● ●

My shit and I were taken to a washroom next to the White House kitchen and thoroughly examined. Captain Fosbert (who turns out to be Carmichael's military attaché and confidential assistant) found my story a bit hard to swallow, but my large size and the large bag of evidence made it in the end, as he put it, "compelling." How'd they discover me? The putter, like all the President's other clubs, was bugged, so that the President could move about freely on the golf course without getting into trouble. Secret Service men listened in to that and other bugs from a converted cupboard near the kitchen.

When I went to work with the putter in the bathroom, strange noises, that (they said) sounded something like the Baghdad bombing raid, started coming out of their receiver.

The Secret Service boys thought it had to be a break-in, and raced upstairs to defend their leader.

During the questioning I kept mum, both about Myrdal Hwang and, of course, about the First Lady.

When he was finally sure I didn't pose a threat to national security, Captain Fosbert escorted me back to my room. On the way, he assured me that the President's putter would be thoroughly cleaned and returned to its bag.

Fosbert even tried a few lame gags to patch things up, like "all this soon will just be water under the bridge." But though he was trying to calm me down, he himself seemed more worried and distracted than my ridiculous situation deserved to make him. *Could he too have seen the President and Hwang?*

It was 2:10 AM. I went to bed but couldn't sleep, and so I heard the note being slipped under the door at dawn. I turned on a light and opened the envelope. It was from the President himself. He would be holding emergency meetings with Bolgovnian envoys and representatives of the upstart warlord, Jazeps Guradich, that weekend.

He regretted that all other appointments had to be cancelled.

In the morning I left the White House without seeing him or Smytha again. I had the awful feeling that everything, including the Bolgovnian conflict, was my fault.

I bought a ride to Annapolis and got to work trying to patch up the weekend for the children, who were all sad to be missing the President.

This morning, Monday, I saw the kids off at Dulles and caught a New York plane. A cab took me to this marvelous old house on Gramercy Park.

● ● ●

LATER, TYPING IN BED.

Tomorrow I visit Guccio Imbratta.

What a kaleidoscope life is! Good things and evil, miracles and monstrosities, spring up out of nowhere! And nothing stays where you've put it.

Yesterday, while the Pueblo Verde kids were off touring the Mall in DC, I took Vi and Vicki to Paca House in Annapolis and then to lunch. How strange—a little preposterous but also dazzling—their British accents sound! They were babbling ecstatically over their crab cakes about their romances with European royalty, but I'm afraid I was something of a bear. I told them to look sharp, because the highest places sometimes held the worst secrets. The girls listened politely and then started peppering me with questions about the White House.

That's not really what I needed at the moment. Without answering any of their questions, I told Vicki and Vi that they were both filthy rich, and that the world knew it. I said that wealth alone, and everything and everybody that wealth could buy, wouldn't by itself make them happy, and that they'd be happy only if they set goals and values for themselves and worked like hell for them, and that the men they loved should also be working towards goals and values, or else they wouldn't be worthy of the girls' love.

But then the girls stoutly defended their men. Vi asserted that Ferdinand, Crown Prince of Moldavia, was a young scholar whose great ambition was to scour the countryside with a tape recorder, collecting Moldavian folktales from the storytellers themselves. Then he wants to preserve these folktales both on CDs and in a set of books. Ferdy's also an avid sailor who trained on the HMS Rose[63] and now sails his own trimaran out of Genoa (*that* one got to me, because I've developed a real yen to learn sailing).

And then Vicki, who could hardly wait to begin, reported that Rudolf, Grand Duke of Bohemia, is studying in Berlin *to be a doctor*, that he hopes some day to do research into new treatments for sports injuries, and that he plans to open up free clinics in the poorer sections of his country.

I had to admit I was impressed.

I've got to talk to Cap about Myrdal Hwang. What does that monster want from Carmichael? Power, certainly, but power to do what? Does Hwang have an angle on Jazeps Guradich? Whatever he wants to do, paying off the President's illegal! Whom do I turn to? Folks in the administration won't rat on their leader. Folks in the opposition have too much of their own dirty laundry hidden away to risk a face-off. The only thing for it, I guess, is to get Molly to beef up her secret investigation.

Getting sleepy. Strange, isn't it, that if I hadn't laid that enormous turd and been stupid enough to try to destroy it, I wouldn't have been able to avoid Smytha or discover the President and Hwang and the money.

Makes you stop and think.[64]

---

63. A sail-training vessel run by an American nonprofit corporation. —Ed.

64. ADDENDUM, EXPLAINING N. 54 ABOVE: So as not to interrupt the witty, fast-paced dialogue in the Lincoln bedroom, we have delayed an explanation of President Carmichael's remark concerning Mr. Ruck's public projects. Here the Chief Executive is referring to a variety of philanthropic enterprises that Mr. Ruck was apparently too modest to mention himself. Augustus Randolph has passed on to us a photocopy of the typescript "shopping list" that Ruck presented to him on January 1, 2002:

> buy all privately-owned old growth redwood, Douglas fir and spruce groves and deed them to the federal government on the condition of wilderness protection

The Most Amazing Thing

Lomo Morado. Days of killing heat. Ranguma and Paws have become night creatures, lazing around or downright asleep dawn to dusk.

The Floatifer's down for repairs and cleaning. The Magdalena College visits—those few that are left—have been put off.

Activities at Lomo Morado go on, much as before.

But everything is changed. The buildings have a new look, a strange feel. The landscape is an unfamiliar world. Even my body feels bizarre, as if I'd left my own somewhere and put on somebody else's.

Things won't ever be the same again, at least until I've[65]

But let facts speak.

At 9 AM on August 20 I woke from a deep sleep in the front bedroom of 17 Gramercy Park and walked out onto the balcony to check the weather. It was already in the 80s, but darkly cloudy, with grumbles of thunder from the east. I went back in and phoned for the limo and showered.

The hot water with its New Yorky chemical smell, gushing out of the

---

buy all parcels of 50,000 acres or larger and all uninhabited islands in U.S. waters and deed them to the government on the condition of wilderness protection

establish a shelter at every community college where the homeless will receive support on the condition that they take courses and assist in college maintenance

buy generic software for America's public libraries, so that said libraries are not subject to a Microsoft monopoly

establish an American Farmers Cooperative that will lease equipment to farming families, provide them with high-volume low-priced supplies and represent them in pricing disputes

establish a $1 billion scholarship fund for the first state that passes anti-handgun legislation

The rest is history. —Ed.

65. Ruck did not complete this sentence. —Ed.

huge old brass showerhead, couldn't wash away a brooding sense of guilt over the Lincoln Bedroom fiasco.

I was going to visit Guccio Imbratta—the source of my wealth—the man I'd robbed.

I shaved, dressed, pocketed my maps and the Berretta .32 I'd brought along just in case (not that I'm much of a hand with guns), and walked out to the corner of 20th and Third, where I picked up a papaya juice and a bagel. The limo was late, so I keyed my way into the private park and breakfasted on a bench, as white-frocked nursemaids with baby-carriages passed under a threatening sky.

I had to wave down the limo because the driver had forgotten my street address. He was a dipso named Ryan Riley, a wild-eyed man with three days of beard, and we hadn't wandered and screeched our way six blocks up Third Ave when I told him to pull over because he was too blotto to drive. He protested when I said I was going to take the wheel, but I lied that I knew his boss Mr. Gocksel, whose name I'd picked up from the logo on the door, and at that point all the fight went out of him.

As I moved through traffic I checked the mirror. For an instant—talk about déjà vu!—I seemed to see Mickey Imbratta's corpse, just as he'd looked in the van that awful April day four years ago, but it was only Riley sprawled across the back seat, fast asleep.

In the tunnel the tired old TownCar showed a tendency to wander, which would be tie-rods, and now and then would be shaken by low vibrations, a possible main bearing. Leaky manifolds, loose muffler, squishy brakes, ping, knock and four dead shocks added finishing touches to this epic of deferred maintenance. I lowered both front windows and opened both vents to fight the smell of stale tobacco, B.O., assorted beer-burbs and bean-farts, rancid hamburger droppings and cheap hootch.

In this death machine I fought my way to exit 61 and Patchogue. As I swung the loose steering wheel right and left to keep the old crate on track, I more than once asked myself, "Why am I doing this? Why take the slightest risk?" But the answer always came up the same. Imbratta knew things that I didn't know. He could tell me things about Mara. He might know something about RoboGal or Mastho Jinn. Knowing these things might save my life. Knowing them might ease a nasty feeling I'd been having, of being caught in an invisible, tightening net.

The driving calmed and focused me a bit, and I passed through a spell of better weather, but when I hit Patchogue the skies were threatening again. I'd escaped the Manhattan thunderstorm but driven into another—no rain yet but a great angry darkness, alit with flashes and ominous grumbling, that moved towards me from the sea.

The Imbratta abode was set aways back from the coast road on a little rise facing the ocean. You drove up past a big plush lawn to a picture-perfect English cottage from the 30's, set between two old yew trees. You parked to the right of the house in an area by the garage that fairly recently had been repaved and probably enlarged to make room for the doctors and other care-givers to the sick old man.

There was only one other car in the lot: a sleek silver-gray Porsche Boxster.

In increasing rain I hurried around the yew and up the walk to the front door, which was shielded from the weather by a little portico. After hefting the massive iron knocker I glanced around and was treated to a view of the sea, where a whole navy of whitecaps was marching towards me under lowering clouds.

I checked my watch. It was 12:25.

As the door opened I was hit with a blast of hot moist cigar-laden air and found myself looking down at a small ageless woman in a dark shawl who sized me up very cautiously and closed the door in my face as she took my name back into the bowels of the house. The rain was coming down in earnest now, hard and from the east, so hard that even though I was roofed it was catching me with little ricochets from the front and sides.

The door opened again and she beckoned me in. She led me from the dark entrance hall back through a large living room to a glass-roofed conservatory opening off it to the rear. Guccio, propped up in a wheelchair, was sitting smack in the middle of this space, while just to his left stood a dark-haired young man—not much more than a kid, really—in a high-fashion black warm-up suit.

In one hand this kid had a big green cigar, lit. In the other was a .45 automatic, pointed my way.

I raised my hands above my head and shot the kid a helpless worried look. He gave the old man a quick sideways glance and then lowered the gun. The gun was an old Army-issue number, the kind that look really mean when they're cocked, and you could tell that this one wasn't.

As the room shook to a big clap of thunder, I looked over at the old man. This was no healthy dude. His face was dead white, his neck blotched with red (from radiation?), his body a skeleton shrouded with an old shirt and vest many sizes too big. A bowl of lemon Jell-O, untouched, lay in his sunken lap. But there was light in his watery eyes, and across the room I could hear his labored rasping in and out of breath.

Incredible how life fights for itself! Guccio must have loved his life. Maybe that's why the kid was smoking the stogie (which looked like it was going to make him puke)—so the old dog could have a whiff of his own past.

I said how-do-you-do, and if Mr. Imbratta had time, I had only a couple of questions to ask him. Guccio tried to answer, but all that came out was a horrible rattle—the cancer had eaten away that much of his throat. *Poor Guccio—keeping secrets all his life and now condemned to silence.* I looked at the kid.

"Grampa don't talk real good no more," he said, stifling a cough. "Like, he's not feelin' so good these days." The boy introduced himself as Berto, an Imbratta grandson—the spiffy Porsche Boxter must belong to him. Berto brightened a little and apologized for treating me suspiciously ("You can't be too careful anymore these days"). He said that just before Grampa lost his power to speak, he'd told Berto that he had no hard feelings for "the Rocco," which was Grampa's name for me. Summing it up that "the Rocco stole the money feya and squeya," Guccio'd told Berto that it should be a lesson to the kid. Berto was going on about this when there was an harsh rasping sound from the old man.

"AL-BERTO!!"

The woman, who'd been hovering among the plants, scurried up to help Guccio, who was coughing and spitting, but the old man convulsively pushed her away. He looked up at Berto and gestured to the right-hand side of his own vest.

"Shit! I forgot," said Berto. He gently stroked his grandfather's trembling head with one hand, while with the other removing a post-card-sized white envelope from the vest pocket. A nearby flash of lightning caught the old man's eyes, which were fixed on me either in friendship or maybe a touch of mischief.

Berto strode over and handed me the envelope. He said something, but his words were lost in the thunder.

The silence following the thunderclap was broken by a loud knocking at the front door. As the nurse went to answer it, Berto was back at Guccio's side, his gun drawn. I thrust the envelope into my left pants pocket and fingered the pistol in my right. You could hear the sound of torrential rain as the front door opened. Then almost instantly a cry from the nurse and a thud.

"Duck!" I yelled at Berto, pulling my gun, but instead Berto put himself in the line of fire, pointing his useless automatic at something in the living room and out of my line of sight. Then the shooting happened. Two shots only. I didn't see where they went because my eyes and gun were aimed at the door to the living room. A man in a raincoat was suddenly through the door, sweeping the room with his pistol, but at that moment my Berretta went off. I must have winged him or scared him at least, because in a flash he wheeled and disappeared.

I ran after him as far as the front door, but decided not to step into the rain and become a target.

The woman was lying on the floor just inside the living room. It looked like she was just shaken up, so I helped her to a chair and rushed back to the conservatory. It was a slaughterhouse. Guccio was sprawled in his wheelchair, his head slightly thrown back, with a bullet-hole just over his left eye. His sorrows and memories were over. Berto was lying on his side, semi-conscious, and blood was gushing from his neck. He was alive, but couldn't live long with a wound like that.

Ripping off my shirt, I roared for the woman, who staggered in. I held the kid up as she wrapped the shirt around his neck, just firmly enough to let him breathe. We both knew there was no time for an ambulance. She told me Brookhaven Hospital was in town, off 27, on Hospital Road. I snatched the boy up and told her to call the ER and describe the wound, and then to call the police.

I trotted out of the house and through the cold splashing rain, breathing hard, with the bleeding kid in my arms. Bypassing the limo, which might have killed him a second time, I put him in the Boxster, grabbed his keys and fired her up. The car handled well in the rain, and I expedited things by turning on the brights and blinkers and sitting on the horn as I swept by traffic in the flooding rain.

I got to the Brookhaven ER in ten minutes that seemed like forever. They were waiting for me at the curb. Because of the nurse's call, they were ready for him.

After Berto was wheeled into surgery, the receiving nurse came out of her booth and towelled me down—I was shivering—and found me a sheet to wrap around myself. This nurse, a sweet Asian lady named Scotty, plied me with hot coffee, but I couldn't hold the cup straight and spilled it on my sheet. I wasn't myself again until the ER doctor came out and said that they'd sewn up Berto and he was responding and he'd be OK. I was so relieved, I cried a little. Somehow I'd gotten to like the kid.

The Most Amazing Thing

Scotty and I filled out a few forms with info from Berto's wallet. After that I sat down on one of the waiting-room couches for a breather. Sirens and flahing lights outside announced the arrival of the local law. They asked me a few polite questions and left. The woman, who turned out to be Guccio's cousin and nurse, had told them who I was and what I'd done for Berto.

Alone for a moment at last, I suddenly remembered the envelope from Guccio.

I pulled it out of my pocket. It was soggy from the rain, and I had trouble pulling it apart without turning it into a useless wad. Very carefully, very gently, I extracted a press clipping, or rather a photograph, that looked as though it'd come from the *New York Times*. It showed a small group of civilians being threatened by three soldiers with automatic weapons. The caption read "Bolgovnian separatist militia took an international peace group into custody yesterday in Kharkharsk, Bolgovnia." The Jazeps Guradich hostages! But what interest would Guccio have in Bolgovnia, and why would he give the photo to me?

I studied the faces of the prisoners. I saw something I could not believe. My vision began to fail, my blood ran cold, the hairs stood up on my forearms and every joint tingled.

Have you ever seen a group photograph or painting where one face alone looks directly out at you, appealing to you, challenging you, speaking to you, almost as though it could see you right from the paper?

There was such a face in this photo.

It was Mara Delano.

Mara's alive.

282

Chapter Twelve **Bolgovnia. Klaiprenska. Khakharsk.**

I'm lonely.

I'm lonely and not feeling very strong and, to tell the truth, I'm a little confused. The sort of confused where, if you're using something like a calculator or electric drill, and you've just put it down somewhere, you can't find it again, or you come on it and don't know what it is, or if you do know, you can't remember what you were doing with it. The sort of confused that's like being delirious when you don't have a fever at all.

How is it that the ranch I've built, Lomo Morado, the stuff of dreams, full of joy and harvest and production, floating in sunlove on its mountain like some sort of Camelot, can be as bare and lonely as a desert ruin? How is it that the lines of my adobe mansion, designed on my own easel, set up under my own eyes, can look like a confused heap of Pick-up-sticks?

Maybe I'll feel better when these stitches are pulled out of my tongue tomorrow and I can talk to people again.

Bolgovnia. Klaiprenska. Khakharsk. I've left my soul there somewhere, like an overcoat left on a clothes-tree in an inn, and to get it back

283

The Most Amazing Thing

I must return there, mentally I mean, and snatch it from the den of horror.

By telling my story.

I'll pick up where I left off.

My first impulse when I saw the photo of Mara, which is lying right now on the desk beside me, was to fly to Khakharsk on the next plane, walk straight into Jazeps Guradich's arsenal and buy the turkey out. It wouldn't have cost more than $100 million or so, and the Bolgovnian government could have taken that out of his hide if they arrested him later. I have a clumsy blundering way about me, which *Time* magazine has called "rucking it," of walking into situations with a red-tape-cutter and a big wad of money.

Sure, that's what I would have done, say, two years ago. But if I had, I wouldn't know what I know now. In fact, I'd probably be dead.

Instead I decided I needed expert help. When I returned from the hospital in Patchogue to my house in Gramercy Park, there was voice-mail from, among others, Cap Wickham, who said he'd be back at LoMo in a couple of days. Of course Cap was the perfect choice. He was a man of action, with all kinds of secret service and diplomatic connections, and he'd really blown me away with his identification of Salvador aka Preston Vickers as the infamous Mastho Jinn.

Cap made Tucson Airport by the night of the 27th and found Rick there to fetch him in the Cessna. He strode towards me across the tarmac at LoMo radiating his patented mix of coolness and macho power, and shook my hand with a mit that felt big and powerful enough to choke a bull.

At midnight we powwowed around the big table by the library window, over bourbon and cigars. Gus was there, and Rick and Molly, together with Ethan Zoig, who joined me here after finishing up at Magdalena. The talk was frank and sometimes heated. Rick and Gus insisted that we kick the tires and light the fires of the 777 and hit

Khakharsk in force, backed up by a platoon of our own border guards and packing heat (he could pull strings to get us permission to land at a Bolgovnian military airfield). Zoig disagreed, saying that I should do exactly what I'd originally thought of doing: go alone and spend big. Molly agreed with Zoig, except that she wanted to come along as my aide.

Then Cap, who was seated opposite me at the other end of the table, cleared his throat loudly and stared everybody down. He outlined what he called a redundancy approach. Sure, I could use diplomatic channels to offer Guradich a payoff for releasing the hostages. But also he and I should fly to Khakharsk in low profile, just like tourists, to see what we could finagle through undercover channels.

"No!" shouted Ethan. "That's insanely dangerous! What if Desmond Ruck became a hostage?"

But I was in no mood to worry about *that*. If taking risks meant seeing Mara a day sooner, I'd take risks. Besides, what was the risk in parleying with Guradich out of a suite at the Hotel Oriental in Khakharsk? Cap would inform the Bolgovnian government in advance, so that I'd have their cooperation.

That was that. The next night, that is, September 28th, Cap and I were squeezed together in the two last available tourist class seats on Aeroflot Flight 237. Now that I'm a celebrity of sorts, there was no way to keep from being recognized by other passengers on the plane, but after a couple of hours the whispering and tittering around me died down. Then Cap touched my arm. Over the next ten minutes, in tones nobody else could hear, he briefed me on the Bolgovnian crisis, which went back hundreds of years. The civil war, he told me, was the result of an age-old religious dispute. The Tiempskga (ruling party) and the Separatists were both Catholics, but with a difference. The Tiempskgaians believed in papal infallibility, and that was that. The Separatists believed in the Lutinian Heresy, which stipulated that Christ as a baby wasn't nursed at the breast. As the heretic Bishop Lutinius roared out in

The Most Amazing Thing

1490,[66] *"Almighty God does not suck ANYTHING!"* The Pope hearing of this sent Lutinius a missive to the effect of "Thanks for sharing this. You're excommunicated." Lutinius in turn left Khakharsk and set up an armed camp in the remote province of Uchdhuk. Soon afterwards the carnage began, and it's gone on more or less ever since.

Except under Guradich things had gotten worse. Guradich was no run-of-the-mill religious extremist; he was a thoroughgoing scoundrel if ever there was one, who'd been compared, at one time or another, to Pinochet, Stalin, Milosevic, Mao, Hitler, Himmler, Rasputin, Cesare Borgia, Saddam Hussein, Idi Amin, Ceauşescu, Franco, Marcos, Peron, Herod, Nero, Batista, Macbeth, Robespierre and Papa Doc. His government, if you could call it that, was rife with martial law, curfews, quarantines, alienation, commodification, balkanization, reigns of terror and scorched earth; with palace guards, lackeys, flunkies and mandarins; with ruling juntas, troikas and cliques; with secret police and masked inquisitors; with fifth columns, deportations, executions, assassinations, mutilations, immolations, strangulations, lapidations, cremations, defenestrations, disappearances, patricide, matricide, fratricide, infanticide and genocide; with spin, propaganda, misinformation, hidden agendas, lies, fraud, paste, varnish and doublespeak; with conspiracy, graft, kickbacks, payoffs, bribes, extortions, pork barrels and hanky-panky; with seduction, perversion, prostitution, sadomasochism, sodomy, pederasty, infamy and abomination. He was treated like a god by the locals.

Why? Maybe it was because he kept all the adult males of Khakharsk shot up on drugs.

After this peppy briefing Cap inflated his rubber collar and promptly went to sleep, and I was left alone with my thoughts. These thoughts were troubled. After nine months of peace I was suddenly wrapped up

---

66. 1590 is the correct date. —Ed.

in mysteries again. There was Myrdal Hwang—a living menace to the whole world—but at least I was doing something about *him*. Before leaving LoMo I'd briefed Molly and Rick confidentially about what (the Hwang part, anyway) I'd seen at the White House, and told them to make getting all the dirt on Hwang and exposing him to the press their only priority: *sparing no expense*. Once we had Hwang's dirty linen on display, we could either smoke out the President or at least force him to dump Hwang and behave like a good little boy again. But what were the two of them up to anyway? Could it be something nasty that would be fait accompli before we got to them?

But Mara troubled me even more. How could she have survived that knife wound and the flaming collapse of the Penumbra Hotel? Why hadn't she contacted me in the four years since then? How was it that after getting brutalized by her sadistic husband in Chile, leaned on by the Imbrattas in the Bronx, anesthetized by the nasty Dr. Hauck and cut open by Our Beloved in Colorado, she was now again the captive of ruffians?

As I drifted towards sleep on the big plane, it struck me that there was something legendary about Mara, that maybe she was born to live out the suffering that men, with their gross-out obsessions and pure cuss-edness, have always loaded on women. At that moment my heart went out to Mara, and I woke up struggling with my seat belt to get up and help her, as though she was on the plane, or I wasn't.

Six hours later, after being slammed every whichway in a drafty old twenty-seat puddle-jumper out of Moscow, we were smacking down on the runway at Kharkharsk. As the ancient taxi careened past bombed-out houses up the hill towards the city, I could now and then make out its skyline, prickling with arabesque turrets and dominated by a big structure that hunched over everything like a dragon's spine. "What's that monster building?" I asked.

"The fortified church called Klaiprenska," said Cap, who was sitting next to the driver. "That's where your friend Guradich is holed up." The cabbie turned his florid face around at me and shouted in a barrage of spit and garlic, "I'M YAYFGAYNEE! I SPEEEK EENGLISH!"

Khakharsk is built on a hill, or rather a foothill of bigger mountains beyond, and the Hotel Oriental is right at the top of town, facing the Klaiprenska across a big cobbled square. The two buildings balance each other strangely. The Oriental looks like some degenerate old Neopolitan palazzo, a fading, bullet-pocked pink facade with a forest of gray shutters. The Klaiprenska, if only in front, is like a hulking Roman temple, its colossal columns all blackened by age, and behind this an even taller medieval-style wall with a huge artillery shell hole through what must have once been the rose window.

The rest of the square is bordered by threadbare shops, down-at-the-heels hotels and chintzy eateries.

The square was a mess. It was so crowded that we had to exit the cab and, with the cabbie's help, tote our valises across the square to the hotel. Crowded with whom? In the first place, there were the soldiers. A company of crimson-uniformed Bolgovnian Army troops had set up two .50-caliber machine-gun emplacements behind piled sandbags just in front of the hotel, while on the other side, in between the church columns, you could make out an unknown number of Castro-capped separatist guerillas in fatigues packing assault weapons.

But these forces wouldn't have crowded the big square at all; it was the newsmen. All over the place, and in all sorts of languages, TV correspondents were filing their reports. These newshounds were so busy reporting that nobody noticed my arrival, which was probably the only real news that day. The cobbles were a nest of power cords, and the Babel of news was crowned by the shouts of technicians cursing loose connections or cameramen backing into each other.

But that's not all that was weird about the place. It *smelled* funny, though I couldn't say of what, and wherever the newspeople and soldiers weren't, there were hordes of pigeons—big, loud and dirty pigeons—milling around on the cobbles. Yefgeny the cabbie told us that the birds were sacred to the memory of St. Fragatrud, and that whatever atrocious things the Khakharski did to each other, nobody was allowed to touch a pigeon. *HELLO!* These birds were concentrated on raised sections of the cobbles, about four feet square, that had mean-looking black vents in them. What was underneath all this, the sewers?

As we passed the Bolgovnian emplacement, Cap, who'd been joking with Yefgeny, asked him, "Why do your soldiers have to wear bright red? To make them better targets?"

"Nossr," beamed Yefgeny, "I theenk eet ees to deesgwise the bleeeding."

The hotel lobby was awash with reporters waiting for telephones, locals who were gophering for the reporters, a few prostitutes and some off-duty military. We registered and were shown up to the Potemkin Suite—the only rooms that were too expensive for the press. It was about 7 PM, Bolgovnia time. In the worn-out opulence of our drawing room, we uncorked some Wharton's and made plans. Cap had some connections in town, "friends of friends" he called them, who already knew that I was coming, and he didn't think he'd have much trouble fixing up a meeting between me and Guradich the next day, but all of the local phone lines that worked were tied up. We could wait till morning, but that didn't satisfy Cap. After dinner he'd go out and "see what he could rustle up."

We ate at a street stand in the square—the Khakharsk restaurants all having closed at 6 PM "for dinner." The only grub for sale in the square was *blukies*, pungent pancakes made with flour, garlic and ground pork. Cap surmised that blatant consumption of blukies by the press must have caused the heavy atmosphere around the square, which he described as stale blech. Although he was famished, Cap refused to eat a blukie, contenting himself with beer and *slutska* (Kharkharski unleavened bread). "I'm a born hunter," he explained. "Hunters don't leave smells."

The Most Amazing Thing

"Good hunting then," I said to him, and he smiled and turned and disappeared into the milling crowds in the square. I drank two more beers, looking up at the dark and troubled face of the Klaiprenska. Then I found my way up to my bedroom and hit the sack.

What it was—maybe biorhythms, maybe pure exhaustion—I don't know, but I slept like a stiff. I didn't even hear Cap knocking on the bedroom door, and I didn't wake until he'd opened it and his large form was standing in the doorway, blocking out most of the drawing-room light. "Desmond, get dressed."

I jumped into some clothes, managing to wrongfoot my trousers and reminding myself along the way who and where I was, but it was like trying to sweep away a puddle; the sleep kept trying to flow back into me, almost as though to say, *"Friend, don't be a fool. Don't go anywhere. This is where you want to be."* I stumbled into the drawing room, my shoes still unlaced. Cap was standing by the windows, facing me. He wasn't alone. A stranger, heavy-set, in civvies, overgrown with jet black hair and beard that showed little more than a pair of angry dark eyes, was slouched in one of the armchairs. Both men were smoking Gaulois cigarettes.

"Mr. Ruck," said Cap, getting formal, "this is Karrel Barda, General Guradich's chargé d'affaires. Mr. Barda, this is Desmond Ruck."

I nodded at Barda, but he didn't bat an eyelash. What a nasty stare! What sort of dope was he on?

"Mr. Barda's arranged a meeting with the General," Cap announced.

"*Right now?*" I looked at my watch. "But it's 2 AM."

"We keep our own time in the Klaiprenska," said Barda, in English that could have come right out of Chicago. He had a high, dry, cackling voice for a man his size.

I turned to Cap. "You mean we're going in *there*?"

Cap took a last drag on his Gaulois, crushed it in an ashtray and exhaled with a grimace. "It's the only way. Guradich is negotiating with

290

Talmar Ajka[67] for the independence of his home state of Uchdhuk. If and when that happens, the General can walk out of the Klaiprenska a free man. But until then, he's a renegade in the eyes of the law, with a murder warrant on his head. Ajka's still playing with the idea of bringing in the tanks and blowing him away. Guradich can't come out to you. Desmond, I know this presents a risk. Why don't I go it alone, as your envoy?"

I was wide awake now, the adrenaline pumping. "No way, Cap. The sum we'll be talking about is too big. He might not trust you." I'd read up a little on Guradich. Around Russia and Eastern Europe he was known as "the little Satan." He didn't trust anybody, probably with good reason.

Cap grinned. "In that case, welcome aboard. The risk isn't that great anyway. Guradich wants his own breakaway state, and harming you won't get it for him. Besides, we have some extra insurance." He picked up the phone and dialed the desk.

In two minutes somebody knocked on the door. I let in a slight, dapper, olive-complexioned young man in a neat crimson Bolgovnian Army jacket and cap. I couldn't remember ever having seen this guy before, but there was something familiar about him.

"This is Major Bassilly Sklov of the Bolgovnian Presidential Guard. He comes with President Ajka's best wishes and is your guarantee of immunity and safe passage. The Major doesn't speak English, but he and I can patch things together in a couple of languages." Cap checked his watch. "We'd better be on our way."

Sklov flashed a reassuring smile, and we shook hands. His hand was warm and soft, suggesting that the Presidential Guard must have a pretty easy time of it, but like Barda's, his eyes had a glassy, preoccupied look. What were these turkeys popping?

---

67. Ruck has failed to note that Balmar Ajka was at that time President of Bolgovnia (1999–2003). —Ed.

The Most Amazing Thing

We took the lift down to the hotel basement and exited into the darkness through a service entrance behind the kitchen. The air was cold, the sky overcast with dark clouds tinged with a sickly pink. Silent as thieves, we hurried up one dark alley and down another, in the general direction of the fortress-church. Along the way I tripped on a raised stone and, lurching, grabbed Cap by the shoulder. He turned and, off balance, supported my bulk with his left arm. My God, the man was strong as a tree!

I was thoroughly lost by the time we got to a high, windowless, gray wall that had a little door in it.

Barda, who with Sklov was leading the way, stopped at this door. "It's the old Bishop's Palace," he said. "It's right next to the Klaiprenska, and connects to it by a secret passage." He pulled a gun from his jacket pocket and hit the door three times—so hard that I could hear the metal bite into the wood—then after pausing, twice again. Immediately an old lock began complaining, and after about a minute the door creaked open, into the pantry of a large kitchen. Whoever opened the door was female by her voice, but I could tell no more about her, because she turned and switched on a flashlight and led us through the disused kitchen and into a hallway and up a broad stone staircase and then over uneven flooring through several huge unfurnished reception rooms, and from them into what must once have been the Bishop's library or office, a paneled room with a musty-smelling fireplace. To the left of this fireplace, in the wainscoting, was a concealed door opening into a passage—the Bishop's private way into his cathedral. The passage was so low that Cap and I were all stooped over, and mercifully it soon ended in a staircase up.

At the top of the stairs was a landing with a table that had an oil lamp burning on it. Beside this table was a tiny door. I was the last to squeeze through it.

I thought I'd entered Hades.

The door opened into the nave of the Klaiprenska about ten feet above floor level, almost exactly where the nave met the transept, so I had a full view into every corner. At first the whole place seemed to be exploding, until I realized that it was only a lot of reddish strobes going off irregularly, like Christmas tree lights, all over the huge interior. So whenever you could see one part of the church, most of the rest of it would be black. But every flash revealed men heavily armed. There were a dozen sandbagged machine-gun nests, two on each side of the nave, facing the main doors, and the massive altar, which looked to all four extensions of the building, was a thicket of machine-gun barrels. Snipers crouched on ledges high above the floor, which teemed with maybe five hundred paramilitary troops, most of them shouting or arguing in Bolgovnian. There was a mist in the air that wasn't incense, because the place reeked of crack cocaine. The blessed and sanctified Cathedral of Klaiprenska, home of the blessed St. Fragatrud and seat of the holy Bishop of Kharkharsk, had gone mad and become a killing machine.

Cap, who was already on the steps down to the floor of the nave, tugged at my sleeve to follow him. I asked him, why the strobes? "Late Soviet-era misdirection technique," he muttered. "Not very effective."

We were walking, among the snarling soldiers, up the nave now, skirting the arsenal-altar around towards the choir. Barda led us towards a marble staircase leading down, and we took it.

This would have to be the crypt.

The stairs, which pivoted forwards and backwards on big stone-floored landings, seemed to go on forever. We easily lost 75 feet of elevation.

At the bottom of the staircase, Barda tugged on a rust-covered metal door that must have been twelve feet high. As it grated open I was almost felled by a blast of stink. It was the same smell I'd smelled in the square, concentrated twenty times over. Instinctively I reached for a handkerchief—all I had was a kleenex—and put it over my nose. The iron door clanged shut behind us. We seemed to have entered endless dark space.

293

But this space wasn't empty. There were cries and groans, as though in hundreds. Some sounded very near, some very far. They weren't cries of fear or pain — *that*, I could have handled better — they rang with misery, despair. I tell you, it sickens me even to remember them.

I've never seen such suffering.

As I say, some sounded very near, some very far, and as my eyes got used to the dimness I could see why. The dungeon, which was lit by widely separated paraffin torches, seemed to go on forever. It stretched almost the full length of the Klaiprenska and extended beyond it under the square. The gigantic room was wall-to-wall a torture chamber. Human beings were chained, racked, even impaled. They were dehydrated, emaciated, like death camp inmates. Some were conscious, some comatose, others stone dead. The prison guards wore surgical masks. Most of the prisoners were male, but quite a few were women, and of these the younger ones had been stripped and chained to the floor, their legs pulled apart in a V.

Was this what they did to Mara?

I stopped next to Cap, who had paused, looking down at the dead body of a woman who'd been savagely mutilated. Cap's face was as usual impassive, but he was making a compulsive tsk-noise with his cheek.

"Are these the hostages?" I asked him.

"No," he barked back, coughing. "These would be MIAs and POWs and captured civilians from the civil war."

"But that was spring of 2000."

"I know," said Cap, walking on again. "There must be fewer of them now."

"Cap," I gasped from behind, "why do they bother torturing these people?"

He shot back, almost angrily, "The separatists are poor, frustrated, barbaric, doped-up idiots. They commit atrocities just to remind themselves that they have balls."

Bolgovnia. Klaiprenska. Khakharsk.

At the far end of the dungeon, under the square from which the tireless pigeons could still be heard cooing and fluttering, the prisoners were all long dead, some bespattered with feathers and droppings that came down through the grates. Rats were working among them. I saw one pop its head out of a person's mouth.

As I looked away in disgust, something caught my eye on the wall above the bones. It was an old fresco, triple-life-size and half-obscured by grime, of a haloed saint in female garb. St. Fragatrud herself. She was easy enough to identify. Who else would have a pigeon's head?

At the end of the aisle Barda led us to the right and through another metal door. We walked four abreast down a bare, electrically lit corridor that must have been the basement of the Bishop's Palace. As we walked, I wondered how Guradich would explain this away when we met him. I wondered what all those quacking news correspondents would say if they could see what was right under their feet.

An ugly thought came to me then—that Guradich didn't plan to let us go at all! But why would they want to kill me, if—I touched Cap's arm, but just at that moment Barda herded us into a room to the left. It was some sort of chart room or briefing room, about 40 feet by 40 feet. It was fluorescent lit, and its ceiling was supported by four massive pilings of hewn wood, set evenly in a square and about ten feet apart. Towards the front of the room, six or seven men were standing around a table, examining a map. They all turned to face us as Barda led us in. Barda gave the salute, and placed Cap and me, as though to introduce us, just in front of one of the forward pilings. The men we faced were all in camouflage fatigues except for the tallest one, who was in the hooded black garment of a monk.

You'd have no trouble picking out Guradich. Instead of a Castro-cap like the others, he wore a rakish beret, à la mode de Saddam Hussein, and he was old and fat, with a deeply lined face and a big gray moustache that looked like it'd been vacationing in his soup. Everybody except the monk was fawning on him.

295

Recognizing me, Guradich smiled a deeply satisfied smile, and then glanced over at the monk.

From my angle I couldn't see much of the monk's face. He was looking directly at Cap, who stood a few feet to my right with his back to a piling. Cap stared back at him.

But Cap didn't look the same. His body had stiffened, his face gone white. His left hand made a sudden move for his jacket pocket, and from the corner of my eye I saw the monk move too, and I heard the strangest noise, like "*fluTTT!* At first nothing seemed to change: Cap still stood facing the priest, whose right hand was now diagonally across his body. Had Cap shot the man? I looked back at my friend. A bare metal knife handle was sticking out from his neck, right at the Adam's apple. *That* had been the noise; the knife went through his neck and spine and drove into the piling behind him.

Cap's knees slowly gave. The knife howled in the wood as the dead body dragged it down.

In disbelief I glared back at the priest. Now he was holding a gun pointed at me, and the others, including Basilly Sklov, were drawing weapons too.

But at this point only the priest mattered. His hood had come off, and his face was tearing my soul to shreds.

It was the face of Salvador Savedra the gardener and Preston Vickers the lawyer.

It was the face of the killer Mastho Jinn.

Guradich was clapping his hands and shouting with glee. "Veery good, Fadda Angelo! Veery good! You do bik boy here for an encore, Fadda, no? Here, I fetch for you da needle." Guradich waddled forward to Cap's body. He reached down and pulled an automatic out of the dead man's jacket pocket. Then with his left hand he yanked out the throwing-knife. The body pitched forward, its left shoulder still twitching. Guradich wiped off the blood on his fatigue trousers and made his way over to Jinn.

"Do eet for Jazeps, Fadda," he said, handing Jinn the knife. "Or you vant him to pray fust?"

"In nomine Domini!" said Jinn, grinning. "I'll do Mr. Ruck at ten paces, General, first thing in the morning! You can enjoy it over your morning tea. But his attendance is necessary somewhere else first." He winked at Guradich, who smiled and sent him a mock salute. I was almost dumb with shock at the death of my friend and protector. And I, condemned to death! "G-general," I stuttered, but to no avail. Without another glance at me Guradich slouched out of the room, followed by Jinn and Basilly Sklov, who stopped in the doorway with his back to me, took off his red officer's jacket and cap, folded the jacket and exited with them under his arm. As Barda was tying my hands behind me, it occurred to me, in a flash, why Sklov had looked familiar—where I'd seen him before. It was that night, so long ago, in the drug factory below Hauck's clinic, giving instructions after the fire.

But he'd looked familiar even then![68]

Barda and his men marched me out of the room and down the hall to a darker hall, not back the way we'd come but in the opposite direction. They pushed me, almost threw me, down a steep staircase, into a torch-lit corridor flanked by old cells walled with irregular cemented stones.

They locked me in one of these dank cells and cursed me and spat on me and called me Ruckovich Fuckovich and did nasty little dances and mooned me, until it bored them and they went away.

I was dog tired. There was a straw mat on the floor, next to what looked like a grating. I squatted down and managed to sit on it. With my hands tied that way it would have been no fun to lie down.

I was about to die, but that's not what was on my mind. First, I had to deal with Cap's death. Sorrow for Cap and self-pity rose up in me, but giving in to them would have meant total collapse. More impor-

---

68. See *Ruck's Run*, Ch. 5. —Ed.

tantly, Cap's death had pulverized my self-confidence. I'd completely depended on the man—his strength, his alertness, his knowledge, his contacts, his ability to get the job done, his incredible poise. Now I felt naked, impotent, abandoned—just the way I felt in the old days with Glynda.

I had to reach down into myself. I had to reach down for some spark of strength, or there was no hope for me at all.

One way of doing this was figuring out why things were happening like they were. I could understand why Cap and Jinn would want to kill each other—they were two soldiers of fortune on different sides—but everything else was puzzling. Why was Guradich going to execute the world's richest man, when he could have bargained for or ransomed me for a fortune? Even self-consumed kooks like Guradich aren't that spacy. I examined every possibility, but still it didn't figure.

I decided to stop torturing myself and try getting my hands free. That meant standing up, which wasn't all that easy, and working my forearms together, up and down, to establish a little give.

I'd just begun to work on this when I heard the sobbing.

It was coming from the next cell, through the grating by the mat. I crouched down to listen. It was low, female, achingly miserable, yet almost musical. It had to be Mara.

With my head at the grating, I called her name. The sobbing stopped, and I heard her unmistakable whisper. *"Can it be you?"*[69]

My heart stopped for a second, but then started beating like crazy. Strength welled up in me. "It's me! It's me! I'll try to get to you!" I hissed, and went at the rope like gangbusters.

I don't think those robes could have resisted me if they'd been stainless steel. I was out of them in minutes, a few square inches of skin the

---

69. *As in Ruck's Run*, Ruck sets some of Mara's dialogue in italics, to distinguish between her emphatic whispers and her ordinary speech. —Ed.

worse, and on my knees I worked the old grating with quiet fury, till it popped out in my hands.

"*I'm coming,*" she fiercely whispered. In a minute she was in my arms.

I felt the warmth of her body, then held her at arm's length to look at her. She was OK, unharmed, as beautiful as ever.

It must've been about 4 AM. Morning was only three hours away. You'd think that, with Guradich and Mastho Jinn waiting to kill me at dawn, Mara and I would sit down, set up a few parameters, and cook up some kind of game plan. That's not at all what happened. Our conversation, such as it was, went sort of like this:

"Mara, why did you leave me thinking you were dead?"

(Kiss) "*Darling, darling, I wanted to contact you in the worst way. But it would have brought you danger, mortal danger.*"

"From Jinn?"

(Kiss, Kiss) "*No, darling. Jinn is just their tool, their puppet. There are terrible men, darling, in Colombia, in Korea, in America, and here. They are very powerful. I had to work secretly for you. I had to tell lies, make compromises. I had to sacrifice myself, in endless suffering.*"

"But what are we gonna do now?"

(Kiss, Kiss, Kiss) "*Dearest heart, we are going to die tomorrow. Jinn has betrayed me. Guradich is at last aware of my true identity. He has sworn on his mother's grave. Nothing will stop him. We will die together, my darling, our souls united. But first we must be married in our hearts, and our union must be engraved into the stone of time and consummated in the most exquisite passion.*"

I tried to reason with Mara but there was no stopping her. She was like a force of nature. The next half hour was the most passionate experience in my life. Talk about no tomorrow. I forgot the cold of the granite floor and its hardness. I forgot the dictator Guradich and the assassin Barda and the fiend Jinn. I forgot the death that seemed to wait inevitably at the next opening of my cell door. My one thought, my utterly enveloping occupation, was Mara, who beyond being a thought had become a universe and an eternity. In the act of love, deliriously sensuous and strangely brutal, I gave up all I had planned, dreamed of, wanted to be. I laid my future as sacrifice on the altar of her body.

And then, unbelievably, I fell asleep.

I woke with Mara shaking my arm. *"Wake up! Get dressed! They're coming!"* I'd no sooner pulled on my clothes and gotten to my feet than an officer was in the cell and behind him two soldiers with drawn pistols and blinding flashlights. The two soldiers were part of the bunch that'd razzed me. The officer was a big red-faced dude that I hadn't seen before. He smiled broadly at Mara, who was beside me facing him, and said something in French that sounded like "Ancient Ted Boudoir, Mademoiselle."[70]

Then Mara did the strangest thing. She hauled off and hit the guy so hard with her open right hand that his red skin went all white from the impact of it. I thought the man was going to shoot her, or at least lay her out. But what he did surprised me again. He reached for the hand that had walloped him, brought it up to his lips and kissed it tenderly.

It raced into my head that this bastard was Mara's lover!

Mara brushed by him and flounced to the open cell door. She turned and looked back at me. Her face had a deathly set to it that I'd never seen before. For the first time, I saw that she had aged in the four years since I'd last seen her. Her voice was cold and flat.

"Desmond, you're hopeless. But at least you won't die a total idiot. You've now read one page in the book of life." She disappeared by herself down the corridor.

---

70. The officer probably said, "Enchanté de vous voir, Mademoiselle," but we cannot be sure that he pronounced it correctly. French is not taught in Bolgovnian schools. —Ethan Zoig

My world fell apart.

I've never felt so alone.

Lobsterpuss was just standing there, leering at me, grinning his stupid arrogant grin and fingering a knife in a scabbard on his belt. You could read in his hungry blue eyes that he was waiting for Mara to get out of earshot. Then he would whip out the shiv and cut off some kind of human souvenir before taking me to the real butcher.

I didn't care about anything anymore, so what the hell?

I leaned forward just a bit and smashed his red forehead with my fist. He didn't exactly roll with the punch, and as his heavy mass bowled over backwards it took the two soldiers, who were much smaller than he was, to the floor with him, and while the knaves were on the floor scrambling for the guns they'd dropped, I grabbed each of them by the back of the neck, snarled "Ruckova Fuckova" and bashed their heads together smartly. They fell like stones.

I pocketed a pistol and lit out down the corridor for the staircase. I had it in my head that not all the separatist bozos would know I was a prisoner, so if I could just avoid the men close to Guradich I had a chance to escape.

As I jogged down hallways towards the torture chamber, I saw no soldiers, which I found strange. I didn't discover why until I got to the big crypt itself. Everything had changed. A weak light of morning filtered down from the grates above, but instead of pigeons you could hear the unmistakable loud heavy grinding noise of tank treads in the square.

It was showdown time. President Ajka was going to take out the Klaiprenska.

The guards had all fled. There were keys all over the floor. I quickly freed a few of the stronger prisoners, but told one of them who understood English that until the shooting stopped they'd be safer down here than above.

I took the marble stairs two at a time to the cathedral nave and, in the weird red strobe light, made my way among the armed men towards the little staircase we'd all originally come in by. No one paid me any notice because they were all fussing over their machine guns and ammunition.

I looked down at them from the doorway to the Palace corridor. These separatist idiots were going to give it their all. As though those machine guns could do squat against the armor-piercing shells of heavy tanks.

Guradich was nowhere in sight. He was feeding his men to the slaughter and likely was fixing to escape via the Bishop's Palace.

Unfortunately, that was *my* only escape route too.

I pushed through the corridor door and froze in my tracks. In the lamplight I was face to face with Mastho Jinn, and his knife was at my throat.

He forced me onto the lamp-lit landing just inside the door and frisked me, pocketing my pistol. "You've saved me some time, Mr. Ruck. I was on my way to get you." His voice was jaunty and the handsome brown eyes twinkled with mischief.

"Rot in hell, you motherfucker," I hissed. I thought of going at him, knife and all. But the thought filled me with dread.

"Who needs hell, when we have Kharkharsk?" he answered archly, and motioned me to walk down the corridor towards the Palace. I obeyed, stooping low, and he lit us from behind me with a flashlight. About halfway to the Palace, the passage met with another from the right that I hadn't noticed the first time, and Jinn made me turn and take it. This new passage became a ramp upwards, obviously to a higher floor of the Palace.

At last we reached a landing with a door, where he told me to stop. I turned to face him.

Jinn's voice was suddenly gentler, almost confiding. "Mr. Ruck, I can possibly save your life, but you've got to obey my every instruction."

"But why would Mastho Jinn try to save my life?" I shot back. "Didn't you kill my friend and plan my execution?"

Something in what I said struck him as funny, for he stifled a laugh. "I don't think you'd believe the truth right now if I told it to you, so let's just say that I'm in it for money. Let's say you escape, more or less in one piece, and I get a million bucks in a Swiss account. Sound like a reasonable idea?"

I looked at him. True, *that* made sense. I nodded.

"OK," said Jinn. "A deal! Now just stick out your tongue."

"My tongue?"

"Your tongue, Mr. Ruck. Nothing else will do."

I stuck out my tongue and with a deft downward stroke of his knife he laid the flesh open near the tip. I doubled up in pain. Jinn touched me lightly on the shoulder. "Quiet, man, quiet. We'll make it right again. You'll see why this had to be."

What was this devil going to do next!

Jinn turned and opened the door quietly. He led me into a room that blinded me with morning light. Gradually I could make out windows and what looked like a hospital bed. Somebody was lying on the bed with his back to me. It was a very big man, fully clothed in a blue peasant's shirt and lederhosen. Jinn led me around to face him. The man was unconscious. The man was

ME.

The likeness was incredible!

My mouth was slowly filling with blood, and I was so thunderstruck that I must have staggered. Jinn caught my upper arms in grips of steel and shook me. "Ruck, get a hold of yourself. You have to see one more thing."

He led me to the head of the bed. Reaching down he gently pulled down the man's jaw, which hung slackly as the sunlight streamed into the mouth.

Where the tongue had been was a hideous crude bloody stitched scar.

Jinn closed the mouth. "Mr. Ruck, this is Boris. Isn't he a knockout?

It took the Sturms and Guradich three years before one of their people —it was Barda—found him down in the Caucasus. Beginning to catch on? Boris was going to be the transitional figure in their takeover of your financial empire. They were going to kill you and destroy your body. But they hadn't a prayer of ever getting Boris to speak American the way you do. The surgery was yesterday. They were going to announce that Ruck—I mean Boris—had been injured, by extremists quote unquote, and hospitalize him over here for a few months, while on his bogus authority they fired, reassigned or murdered everybody in your organization who knew you well. And once they'd taken charge they were going to get rid of Boris, too."

I went to the sink and spat blood. Jinn was at my side in an instant.

"Hey, we need some of that. Let it ooze over your lip and down your chin. Haven't you caught on yet? I'm going to take you out of here as Boris, whose recent incision is bleeding and who has to find his doctor. But I can't appear to have been in this room. Change clothes with him while I go around and come back the other way."

A thunder of artillery fire opened up from the square, and the walls started shaking. Jinn gave me a stern look and disappeared into the back corridor.

As flakes of old paint started coming down from the vibrations of the cannonade, I struggled with Boris's massive body, at one point almost dropping him to the floor. I got all I needed, the lederhosen and the shirt, then pulled the covers over him, got dressed and stuffed my own clothes under the bed.

Suddenly Jinn was in through the other door, looking very priestly.

"Boris has a slight limp, a stiff left knee from an old tractor accident. When he feels confused, which is quite often, he lowers his head to the left and reaches for his eyebrows with his left hand and slowly shakes his head, like this." He demonstrated Boris's gesture of confusion. Then he gave me back my pistol, which I stowed in my lederhosen pocket, and motioned for me to come along. Slurping and dribbling blood, I followed him out the door.

We went down a short hall that opened directly into a briefing room. There Karrel Barda, his face white with dread, was giving hurried instructions to a small group of armed men who looked like the remains of Guradich's private guard. Barda looked across the room at me with surprise. Would he catch on? As Jinn jawed away at him in Bolgovnian, I gave Barda a pleading look, then made Boris's gesture of puzzlement. Barda sharply looked away, guilty I bet about the surgery. Everybody else, after the first glance, had turned away from me because of the blood.

Jinn was moving again. Behind him I limped between rows of men and through the far door. The noise of battle outside grew more deafening, as though Bolgovnian tanks were now approaching the Palace itself.

Walking faster now, our guns drawn, we crossed two large and empty sitting rooms on our way to the front of the palace and the main staircase, with Jinn explaining to me that the only way to escape without encountering crossfire was via the roof, where Guradich was awaiting a helicopter. As Jinn put it, we'd "have a word" with Guradich and commandeer the aircraft.

We'd reached the second-floor landing of the main staircase, Jinn was already bounding up the next flight of stairs, when I was frozen in my tracks by a blast of automatic fire from the bottom of the stairwell. Bullets hit the wall a few feet in front of me and traced a line back towards me close enough to nick my lederhosen. I turned raising my gun and almost without aiming fired a round down at the red-jacketed Basilly Sklov, who had me in his sights from the front hallway.

Sklov toppled backward and fell spread-eagled on the green and white tiled marble floor.

Jinn called to me, and I raced up to him on the next landing. "What was that?" he asked, but then realizing that I couldn't speak, he turned and climbed on.

The flat roof was reached by a ladder behind a little door at the top landing. The trap door at the top was open and I could hear all hell breaking loose above me as I climbed. The roof I climbed onto was like a picture of fear. The air seemed to be exploding, and under a cloudy sky big winds were blowing clouds of black smoke from the Klaiprenska directly towards us, as tank cannon and smaller arms went off incessantly.

Across the roof, through the smoke I could make out the lone figure of Guradich. His beret was gone, his gray head thrown back, and he was dancing a little dance of rage and gesturing with his pistol above him, where about 100 feet up a little chopper was hovering. Obviously the chopper pilot'd lost some visibility from all the smoke, and was having some qualms about whether to come down at all, and Guradich was furiously commanding the copter to land and helplessly threatening the pilot with his gun.

Jinn left me and strode across the roof towards the General. In that grim setting Jinn in his monk's habit moved like an avenging angel, an emissary of Death. With all that racket Guradich didn't hear him coming, or see him till they were face to face. For just a second they stood that way, as though it was an instant of recognition, and then without warning Jinn delivered the most crushing head-butt I've ever seen. The General crumpled to the rooftop and was no sooner down than Jinn had lifted him up in his arms, like a feather, and was carrying him towards the front of the Palace. Reaching a declevity in the battlements, Jinn stepped onto it, paused a moment, braced himself under Guradich's weight, and pushed up with incredible strength until the unconscious man was almost at arm's length above his head.

For a few seconds he held the General there, as though on display. Then with a barbaric cry he hurled him four stories down into the street.

Even in all that noise, you could hear the cries of victory and terror from the soldiers below.

Jinn trotted back to me. "That may end the bloodletting" was all he said.

From Jinn I glanced to the chopper, which'd now descended to eye level. We raced for it and scrambled aboard at once. Inside the cockpit, Jinn pointed me to one of the two back seats and himself sat next to the pilot, who seemed delighted to see him. As we hovered there, Jinn leaned over to the pilot and shouted a few words, and the pilot nodded excitedly.

The craft skimmed the city skyline and gained altitude after crossing the town walls into the country. At about 500 feet we headed for the valley floor and turned right. As soon as the pilot had the thing on course, he turned to me and smiled and said Hello in English. "Mr. Ruck, this is Gleb," said Jinn. "He's agreed to take us across the Russian border and seek asylum in Tzinsk."

The chopper maintained its low altitude as it climbed up the long green valley toward a distant ridge. You could count the sheep peacefully grazing, as though Guradich and the civil war hadn't ever happened.

Jinn was shouting to the pilot again, and the pilot pointed to a place under Jinn's seat. Jinn pulled out the first aid bag and rummaged in it. He handed me a white pill. I had to stick it into my mouth behind the cut in my tongue, which hurt like hell, and wash it down with blood. I began to feel better almost right away. In minutes, just as we hit the top of the pass, and I heard Jinn talking English with somebody on the radio, I felt my head lolling, and blacked out and woke with Jinn shaking me. I'd choked on my own blood. He shouted at me to spit into his handkerchief and leave my mouth open. He propped my head sideways against an old knapsack. Then I lost consciousness altogether.

● ● ●

The Most Amazing Thing

Just before waking I dreamt of tongues. Big powerful cows' tongues steering like ships' prows through five-pound mouthfuls of fresh grass, rough loving tongues of lionesses cleaning their cubs, friendly slobbery tongues of golden retrievers and labs, Ranguma's tongue, Mara's tongue. I finally woke up dreaming that *I* was a tongue, huge and fat and beefy, and that I had a big, big problem.

I woke up in a kid's room, looking up at a life-size Kobe Bryant poster that was pinned to the ceiling, and so in my grogginess I went from thinking I was a tongue to thinking I was a kid, in my parents' old frame house in John's Landing, Portland, OR, in my room with its Bill Russell poster.

Could I go out and shoot hoops with my buddies? No, I was sick, something to do with my mouth. Mom said I couldn't play today.

For some reason I then began to cry, and when I cried my mouth stung. My memory started coming back. I stuck out my tongue and touched it gingerly with my right hand. It had some sort of waterproof bandage on it. I realized it must've been stitched up and bound for stability.

Oh God, I thought. What I've been through. And still alive?

I started mentally placing myself in space and time. This would be Tzinsk, Russia. Why a kid's room? Well, maybe the US Consulate in Tzinsk was small, and the hospitals in Tzinsk aren't so good, so they had a doctor in to treat me and then carried me over to the Consul's private residence, and the Consul had a kid or two.

(This turned out to be right on. Except he had six.)

Still flat on my back, I started working on questions. Some I could answer, some not. I was clear at last, more or less, on why Mara'd lured me to Khakharsk and why she and Guradich no longer needed me alive. Why'd Basilly put his red uniform and cap back on? I figured he'd decided to find a secret way out of the Palace and leave it, as he'd come in, in disguise.

Why had Jinn mentioned the Sturms? The Sturms were that Colombian drug-lord family. Had they brought in all the drugs for Guradich's men?

Sunlight, late afternoon probably, filtered in through a window to my left, falling onto an old cowskin rug. I felt no desire to move.

Why'd the showdown between Cap and Jinn been so sudden? I guessed, because Cap had recognized Jinn and caught on to the double-cross.

Why hadn't they settled my case right then, the way Guradich wanted? Because Mara wanted to see me? She must have pulled some weight around there.

But why'd she want to see me if she wanted me dead?

I needed to pee. When I got up, I found I was dressed in one of those sky blue patient's gowns that are so embarrassing because of the way they hang open in back. I was heading for the door when a blond kid in his early teens popped his head in.

"Hi," he said shyly. "Mom made you a smoothie." He put the big glass on the night table. In his other hand he had a small pad and a felt-tipped pen which he put down on the bed. "You can write down anything you need."

Instead of writing, I said, "UHHHH" and pointed at my crotch. He got the picture.

Back in bed I propped myself up on pillows and sucked in gulps of smoothie through a straw. I couldn't taste anything but I needed the liquid and the sugar. Because my tongue couldn't measure the coldness, I got one of those awful cold burns in my throat and had to wait ten minutes before I could suck in more.

During this time the Consul knocked and came in to see me. He was a white-haired guy in his fifties, very clean cut, with piercing gray eyes, and he introduced himself as Winslow Walker. He told me I'd be flown to Moscow the next day, and that my people knew what'd happened, and that my 777 would be waiting for me there, to take me stateside to Vic Bellows's clinic, and that Vic would be expecting me. He said that the world press would be jumping sky high about the shoot-out in Khakharsk, and my role in it, but that the Bolgovnian government had everything under wraps, and the American government was keeping mum until they could establish the details. He asked if I had any questions. I grabbed the pad and pencil.

I scribbled, What happened in Khakharsk after we escaped?

"It was a massacre. The Bolgies came in and machine-gunned everybody."

Nobody survived?

"One man only, uh, a very big man, scared half to death and without his tongue. He'd apparently jumped out of his window and landed on a lower roof and broken a leg in the fall. The Bolgies didn't know he was there."

Then Mara was dead. Or had escaped.

I had just one more question, though I was already almost certain of the answer: Where's my friend the monk?

"Oh, him," said Walker, smiling. "He's down at my office faxing. He'll be back for dinner."

For dinner, no less! Did Winslow Walker have any idea whom he was going to be eating with? I'd have thought Jinn would be well away by this point, and that the only hide or hair I'd ever have from him again would be a phone call telling me the number of his Swiss bank account. Should I warn Walker? Somehow I decided no. Jinn was a barrel of surprises, and I wanted to see this one play out.

Dinner that night was a fancy spread. The Consul had a big dining room, and the oak table was expanded to hold Jinn, Gleb and me. The Walkers' four resident kids, three boys and a girl, showed up bright-eyed and bushy-tailed, eager I thought to see me. But, oddly, when Jinn appeared at cocktails in his borrowed Marine fatigues, carrying a slender leather portfolio, they all flocked around him. What was this dude, a magician? A mover of spirits?

On top of this, he had the Consul in his pocket. Jinn excused himself

310

from the kids to sidle over to Walker, who was standing with his wife, and show him the faxes (presumably) that were in his portfolio.

As they examined these, Walker began to beam boyishly and Mrs. Walker, a tall blonde lady with fine features, went pale with emotion.

I couldn't take it anymore. On top of everything, this conniving asshole was making me jealous! Still a bit unsteady from my drugs, I lumbered over to them, glared menacingly at Jinn and dumb-showed to Walker that I wanted to see him alone. Walker shot Jinn a glance, then announced, "Mr. Ruck, there's something you need very much to know. Come with me."

Walker and I headed for the study, which was just off the dining room. Amazingly Jinn came with us.

The Consul, who was now carrying the portfolio, shut the door behind us and motioned us to two seats across from his desk. Just after we both sat down, Jinn eyed me evilly. In the soft lamplight he looked like some dark figure of legend. Yet there was a maddening spark of humor in his eyes.

"Mr. Ruck," said Jinn, "you're laboring under a misconception. Since you wouldn't believe anything I told you, and since, I must admit, the truth is hard to believe anyway, I asked some friends in DC to send these along."

Walker opened the briefcase and pulled out a few papers. "These are from classified CIA files and can't go beyond this room. They concern a man named Mastho Jinn."

I examined them. The CIA files looked just like the ones in the cloak-and-dagger movies, full of vital stats and hypothetical accusations. They listed Jinn as a bigger man than he actually was, but otherwise they weren't very exciting.

I pulled out my pad and wrote.

What are you trying to do, Jinn? Make us believe you aren't yourself?

I handed the note to Jinn, who smiled and handed it on to Walker.

"Please look at the last page, Mr. Ruck," said Walker.

311

I turned to the last page, which had two photos on it. The top one had obviously been taken with a long telephoto lens and afterwards enlarged. It was of three men in uniform, with a circle crayoned around the middle one, who was almost a head taller than the other two, but the features were very blurry. The lower photo, on the contrary, was crystal clear. It was a socialite snapshot of Jinn as a young man, probably taken when he was posing as a Swedish art collector in Amman over twenty years ago. He was at a black-tie event and again his height and mass dominated a social group, which this time included a couple of ritzy dames. Even so many years away, there was no mistaking his identity.

I started feeling dizzy.

It was Cap Wickham.

My reality crashed.

I looked up at Walker and the mystery man. Walker had all the beaming glee of a delighted voyeur, and Mystery Man was looking at me with bemusement.

I tore into my writing pad.

Well, if Cap Wickham is Jinn, pray tell, who then are you? I scrawled and tore off the sheet and thrust it at him. He stifled a laugh and replied, "Mr. Ruck, it's almost as though you were born to be surprised." He reached out for the pen, wrote five words in broad strokes and handed me the paper. Under my question I read

Mordecai MacCrae, at your service

The name roared through my memory like a locomotive: Mordecai MacCrae, the Rev's buddy in Iraq, the war hero, the most capable man in the world, the super-sleuth on Death Row in Kentucky.[71]

I wrote

But MacCrae's dead!

---

71. See *Ruck's Run*, Ch. 3. —Ed.

The man crumpled the paper and grimaced. "As a matter of fact, I *am* dead. Officially speaking. Thanks to a wicked narcotic, I passed muster for death by starvation at Eddyville.[72] They sewed me into a body bag and passed me on to next-of-kin. But next-of-kin turned out to be two CIA men and a medic who had me on IV as soon as they'd cut the bag open in the hearse. Why was the CIA so worried about my health? Not just because they've gotten kinder and gentler. No, they had a special job for me, a job I'd accept only if they let my poor suffering wife in on the secret. So special that over the past four years I've sometimes wished to be back with my Death Row cronies in Eddyville."

Walker broke in, "But wasn't it worth it, MacCrae! When you threw Guradich from the battlements you broke the separatists' spirit and ended a reign of terror! You're going to go down in history with Sergeant York and Jimmy Doolittle!"

The man grunted and pulled more papers from the portfolio. He shot them in my direction along the glass-topped desk. These were three xeroxes of *Los Angeles Times* photos showing LAPD Lieutenant Mordecai MacCrae as the chief investigator in the $21 million Butterfield jewelry robbery that happened in '89, casebreaker in the St. Janusa Nunnery sex-for-drugs scandal of '91, and tracker-down of the serial killer Charlie Walsh in '94. The likeness was unmistakable.

I looked at MacCrae and nodded dumbly.

"And those aren't phony photos, like the *New York Times* photo that the so-called Basilly Sklov cooked up and fed you through Guccio Imbratta. You can fax these back to your people and have them verified. Is that proof enough, Mr. Ruck? Care for a spot of DNA?"

I lowered my head with my hands on my brow. There was a silence.

When MacCrae spoke again, it was as if he'd read my mind. "I understand, Mr. Ruck. It's a bummer to be thoroughly and almost fatally betrayed. But don't blame yourself. By anybody's standards, Mastho Jinn

---

72. The Kentucky State Penitentiary. —Ed.

was pretty hot stuff. I had to laugh when you called me Jinn back in the Klaiprenska, because deceiving you like that was Jinn all over: *the imagination, the arrogance.* Among intelligence operatives he was billed as the baddest man in the world, and he kept living up to it. I'd have had lots of trouble with him in single combat on a level playing field. But I had the drop on him, because he didn't expect to see me as part of Guradich's cadre, while I *did* expect to see him."

I shook my head. His eyes went soft again.

"Of course. Somebody else betrayed you besides Jinn. I'll have *much* more to say about her."

I suddenly felt zonked. Can you visit me in the States? I scribbled.

"Not right now. There're a lot of loose ends to pick up, including what to give to the press and how to do it. Also the CIA wants Boris, for keeps, and that'll take some doing. Should keep me til mid-October. Then I need a week at home. I'll come to your ranch after that."

I excused myself, waved goodnights as I walked through the dining room and dragged my ragged ass upstairs.

OCTOBER 22, 2002

My dreams long ago were prophetic.

I sit in the warm sun on the Lomo Morado terrace, looking out at the western mountains, and eveything looks desolate and dead.

MacCrae arrived last night. I was with Mehbub in the hothouse when we heard the Cessna. We jumped in the Jeep and were waiting on the tarmac when Rick and MacCrae taxied up. The two of them were already fast friends, discussing varietal grapes to beat the band. Mehbub recognized his old mate Salvador, and there was much laughter as MacCrae went into his Salvador routine one more time. I was feeling better, happier. My tongue was working again.

There's no solace like talk among friends.

It being warm and starry, I suggested that Rick and Ali Shah take

MacCrae's gear back in the Jeep, while MacCrae and I walk up to the house.

You can bet we had things to talk about. MacCrae was burning to hear the story of how I'd come by my fortune and whom I'd met along the way, so I promised to let him read the journal. I could barely get in a question till near the top, when we were both puffing a bit.

"Why weren't Guradich and the others shocked when you suddenly killed Jinn?"

He looked at me grimly. "Guradich needed Jinn's expertise to bring you in, but after that he needed Jinn like a hole in the head. Over vodka with Barda, me and Sklov, on the night before you came, Guradich put a hit on Jinn, and left it for us to arrange the time, place and manner. We agreed to play it by ear. Of course this fitted *my* plans like a glove, because it meant I'd get a shot at him before he could finger me to the others."

I asked how he and Jinn came to know each other.

He put me off. "That's part of a much longer story. I'll tell you tomorrow, or whatever day we get to it."

"Well, if you can't tell me that, can you tell me who the alleged Basilly Sklov really was?"

MacCrae paused a moment. "OK, but this may hurt. Basilly Sklov was an alias for Klaus Sturm, or Klaus von Sturm, as he liked to call himself."

"You mean the Colombian drug lord?"

"The same. He hatched the plot against you and took Guradich aboard by giving drugs to Guradich's army and promising the General a share of your wealth."

"How ironic!" I shouted.

"What do you mean?"

"I mean that Sturm's the man I shot in the Palace."

MacCrae stopped in his tracks, his shocked eyes flashing. "*It couldn't have been.*"

"Why not?"

He and I were both standing still now, facing each other, about ten feet apart. MacCrae spoke with some effort. "Because I killed Klaus Sturm myself the night before. He was on to me, and letting him live would have cost my life, and yours, and who knows how many others. I can't imagine whom *you* shot, unless it was Sturm's sister. She was about his size and could have taken his uniform in an escape try. It would have been just like her."

"Sister?"

"Thea Sturm, Klaus's sister and partner in crime." He paused. "I'm sorry, Ruck. It's the woman you called Mara."

I stood there, silent, motionless.

My dreams long ago were prophetic.

I've killed Mara.

Chapter Thirteen   The Gathering Storm

Containing, among Other Things

Sting of Memory

Doom and Diane

The Other News

Sex on Trial

The Human Sandwich

Shana Redux

The ?-Billion Dollar Man

STING OF MEMORY

OCTOBER 30, 2002

"You've been had, duped, tricked, fooled, misled, cheated, betrayed, gulled, deceived, deluded and led down the garden path," said Mordecai MacCrae, his long legs crossed and feet propped up on my desk in the library as he sprawled in the leather chair across from me.

He rose, walked to the window and took a powerful draw on his cigar. "You've been lied to, fed a line, conned, played, bilked, diddled, hooked, rooked, swindled, snowed, stroked, soaked, snookered and scammed," he pronounced, disappearing into a huge cloud of his own smoke.

He strode back to my desk and faced me, smiling bitterly, arms akimbo and slightly out of breath. "You've been foxed, flimflammed, flummoxed, hornswaggled, humbugged, boondoggled, bamboozled, stuffed and served, chewed up and spat out again, washed and hung out to dry. Additionally, you've been sold down the river."

I didn't know whether to laugh or to cry. Without thinking, I did a Boris.

"Ruck, cut that out!" MacCrae barked. "Come to your senses! You can't start living again till you've looked hard at the truth."

It was just shy of 8 this morning, and frankly I don't have much stomach for cigar smoke at that time of day. Lucky for me, there was also the smell of coffee beans roasting in the samovar, and precisely on the hour of 8 came the pleasant sound of them sliding down into the grinder, whose motor buzzed into life, activated by their weight. The air exploded with the smell of newly ground coffee. As the machine proceeded to pat the grounds firm and express the steam through them, I walked to the window and let in the first morning breeze.

All of a sudden Ranguma was beside me. She nuzzled her head into my right hand. Something smiled in me. I'd survived everything else. I could take this, too.

"OK," I said. "Get on with it."

Ranguma curled herself up on the floor by the window.

As I poured the espressos MacCrae placed a big computer monitor on my desk. He rolled his leather chair around the desk, so we both could face the screen. He put a cut-glass ashtray on the desk and rested his cigar on it. He switched on the computer, turned on the remote keyboard on his lap and double-clicked through a few menus.

Suddenly I was back on Stuyvesant Avenue in the Bronx, on April 2, 1998. You see, I'd given MacCrae my laptop three days ago. He'd taken the journal off the hard drive onto a Zip drive and then put it in one big file in the computer. He'd spent hours and hours poring over the file. Now we were going to revisit my wild days with Mara, or I should say, Thea.

MacCrae used his touchpad to race through long alleys of text. "Let's start here, Desmond," he said.

I looked at the screen. April 3, 1998. Mara and I were in the Vixen, together, racing west through Pennsylvania after the Ali Khan shootout.

> Mara asked me to tell her about myself—what I did, that sort of thing. I said, I'm a Nobody from Nowhere who did Nothing. Up ahead the overcast had relaxed into broken clouds, and the low sun was making sly remarks from the southwest.
>
> Mara smiled mockingly and said, "That can't be. It takes more than a nobody to pull a solo job like this."
>
> I told her I hadn't planned the job. I asked, How could I have? That made her think a minute. I looked up, and she looked different, like somebody who'd just read a letter.

"Notice that?" MacCrae asked.

"What?"

He turned to me. "OK, let's go back a step. As you've probably guessed by now, Thea was in the Bronx that day to take delivery of the fortune that the Imbrattas had put up for the Colombian operations. Thea wasn't lying to you when she told you that it was a brokered buyout. The brokers were the Calandrinos, but she omitted a few key details about her own involvement. She also didn't tell you how the firefight between the Calandrinos and the Imbrattas really got started."

"How did it?"

"Thea stirred it up herself. She'd been going to bed, secretly, not only with Michelangelo Imbratta but also with Xavier Calandrino."

The back of my neck caught fire. "THAT'S A LIE!" I boomed out. "How the hell can you say that?"

The Most Amazing Thing

MacCrae looked at me as calmly as if I'd asked him for a match. "Thea told me herself. As Father Angelo I took confession from her more than twenty times at her compound near Mirasoles in Colombia."

I gaped at him.

He kept looking straight at me. "I've got a number of surprises for you, most of them unpleasant. Except for one, which can wait till after lunch. Thea Sturm was, how should I put it? a sexual entrepreneur. Who knows what the psychological factors were? By her own account, she'd been sexually molested by her father, and after that always feared men, and started giving herself to them sexually in order to cathart her fear. Somewhere along the line it dawned on her that, thanks to male psychology, this act of submission could become an act of domination, control. She started taking advantage of her own neurosis. She exploited her sexuality in business, politics, crime. And she enjoyed her work. In this case she'd worked Mickey Imbratta and Xavier Calandrino into uncontrollable hatred for each other, and the final spark was touched off just at the right moment, that afternoon in the Bronx."

I cut in. "But she can't have banked on their all killing each other."

"Not all at once," he answered. "But she figured that, if at least one man died, the vendetta-effect would account for most of the others within a year or so. Then she and her brother could move in and steal back the operation they'd sold to the Imbrattas."

"That's Satanic!"

"Curious," he said. "That's exactly the word Thea used, describing herself, more than once in confession. But then Thea in confession was a different Thea. When she confessed she was moralistic, contrite, agonized—as if the whole world's guilt weighed down on her shoulders. But once out of the capilla, she'd immediately default back to her old ways, as if confession had made her free to sin again. And what sin! Thea had a rare combination of gifts: great beauty, control of several languages, near-photographic memory, creative imagination and above all the magic power of holding a listener in her thrall. But even with all that, she didn't bargain on you."

"Me?"

"You, Desmond. You interrupted her plan. As Thea lay there under Mickey's body in the van, her mind was racing madly—"

"You mean she was *conscious?*"

"Of course she was conscious! Thea was like a beast in the jungle: she even *slept* conscious. She had no idea who you were or what you planned and was counterfeiting unconsciousness in self-defense. When you undressed her in the motel to clean her off, she thought that her apparent helplessness might cause you to touch her sexually, a move that she could then exploit. When you didn't do that, she remained immobile as a way of buying time."

"Until?"

"Until she had you pegged, knew who was with you and what you were about. Then she could telephone Klaus in Colombia, and he'd take action." MacCrae scrolled upscreen again:

> I told her I hadn't planned the job. I asked, How could I have? That made her think a minute. I looked up, and she looked different, like somebody who'd just read a letter.

MacCrae cleared his throat. "This opened the way for her. At the coffee-stop, she didn't go to the bathroom at all. She nipped around the corner to a pay phone, and dialed up brother Klaus in Colombia. But she didn't like the news she got from him. The Colombian government, with help from our FBI, was moving in on him. His forces had abandoned ship. It was all he could do to save his skin."

I sighed and sipped my coffee. I remembered Lewis Carroll's *Through the Looking Glass,* where somebody walked right through a mirror into a strange new world. Listening to MacCrae was like somehow walking through a mirror, into the weird world of what wasn't me.

The Most Amazing Thing

MacCrae stood up and stretched. I went over to the samovar and pressed a button for more coffee. As I checked a few of the gauges, he walked over and stood beside me.

"Imagine it for a minute, man. Just *think* about the fix Thea was in at that point. I can hear her this very moment, in that inimitable hushed tone of hers, telling me about it. Thea Sturm, accustomed to comfort, to command, suddenly thrown back upon herself, without support. Far from home, the great prize literally in her hands—yet she was helpless. Suddenly, ironically, this great drug-czarina was totally dependent on you, but she could depend on you only as long as she held your male attention and kept you in the dark about who she really was."

"But couldn't she have—What about Pilotsburg, anyway? When I'd disappeared over that cliff, and was in jail, why didn't she—"

"Escape with the money? Quite simple, Desmond. Thea was a piece of work, but she wasn't Supergirl. She knew zilch about finance, and on top of that she was night-blind, machine-illiterate and scared to death of highways. Her own Camry in Colombia, as she put it, was a *mass of dings*."

I couldn't help giggling at Mordecai's imitation of the unforgettable whisper.

He gestured for silence. "She spent that Sunday night in the Vixen and in the morning hired a hippie to help her drive to Pilotsburg. In town she found out where you were in jail. She got through to Luke Thrumble's cellular (he was in Art's truck) and offered Luke money for you. He refused to give you up in town, so they agreed that he'd deliver you to her on the banks of the Ocalona. And so, as she put it, *almost soiling herself* out of pure funk, she nursed the Vixen at idling-speed downriver to the meeting place. The river was so loud that she didn't hear your truck-train crash at the junction. When you showed up at the Vixen on foot, she was truly surprised and overjoyed."

"You mean she really liked me?"

"*Needed*. And if I may add, desired. When I told you that Thea indulged in sexual politics, I left out one detail. She only fancied big, tall men. Under 6'3″ or so, and you didn't make the cut with Thea. Desmond, you're one of the biggest dudes around, and I assure you, that feature wasn't lost on her. So your muddy reappearance on the Ocalona made her glad as a kid at Christmas."

I asked him why didn't she tell me the truth about bribing Thrumble to drop me off.

"I suppose, because her dishonest version of the story made her look more helpless, and that's how she was controlling you. Besides, Thea was no normal con artist or liar. Most liars will tell you the truth whenever they can, to buffer their credibility. But Thea once told me that she *lied whenever possible*, because the tension of it added *zing to life, like some powerful spice*."

MacCrae paused to relight his cigar. I found myself staring at the computer screen, but there was, like, this confetti storm in front of it. I was really confused. I'd always thought that when women exploited men, or vice versa, they didn't really *like* them, and when they liked them, they didn't exploit them. This sure added a new wrinkle. I was fuzzily trying to phrase another question when Ranguma volleyed out a loud bark, and at the same instant Ethan Zoig burst into the room. MacCrae (thanks to the pressure of his recent days in Khakharsk) wheeled around like a shot, only to see Zoig staggering under the wolf's friendly weight and holding up both hands in apology. "Damn!," he said. "When I stay here I start behaving like a kid again. Sorry. Desmond, there's news. I mean, news."

"You mean, bad news," I said.

"Yeah," said Ethan. "Bad news."

DOOM AND DIANE, *THE OTHER NEWS*

It was bad enough news that we had to have a conference about it on the terrace at lunch. Molly, Rose and Gus were there, and Ethan and

Mordecai, and Heidi Frederick, who'd come from England for a few viticulture lessons from Molly. Rick was off delivering medicine in Melanesia. The council was rounded out by financial gurus Vance Rousseau and Wally Horowitz, who'd come up from Vegas for a week of R & R.

I seldom drink wine at lunch, or even offer it, but this time I asked Catherine to decant several bottles of cave-chilled *auslese* into porcelain pitchers and set them out.

Ethan's news was none other than the Governorship of the State of Arizona. The election's next week. Nobody's paid much attention to it, as we've all counted on Mo Stretorian's tacking on a second term and, as Wally put it, there was nothing the matter with Mo that a good state legislature couldn't cure. But Stretorian's suddenly behind in the polls. The front-runner's Diane Ditt. So that's who Mega Klein was talking about! According to Ethan, this Ditt is a nightmare. She's so PC she shits icecubes. She nailed Mo for having a fling with his secretary in 1975, years before he even got married. She's written a book called *Serpent in the Cupboard* accusing American big names from JPJ[73] to JFK of being sexual ghouls who hit on less powerful women and gorged themselves on control. She's written another called *Nature's Little Joke*, which basically says that male heterosexuality is an obsolete biological nuisance, that should be fixed. They say she's allergic to the human touch. Ethan says, "She's got a mind like a steel trap: it's always snapping shut."

And Ditt's buddy-buddy with Mega! It was Mega who ratted to her about me last August, and Ditt has now decided to make a witch hunt against me one of the big deals in her campaign.

How come we weren't alert to Ditt sooner? She's come up in the polls very suddenly and, besides, we had bigger problems.

Anyway, what *can* you do? It's a free country. People can say what they please.

---

73. Ruck refers here to the naval hero John Paul Jones, 1747–92. —Ed.

We lunched around the big table on the terrace, which was beautiful in full sunlight and a mild breeze. Catherine served cole slaw and a scrumptious potato-and-sausage casserole, and the tone of emergency didn't spoil anybody's appetite. Except, maybe, Molly Beauchamps'. I remember glancing at the way her lovely red hair caught the breeze and sunlight and noticing how gaunt she looked. *Can the cancer be coming back?* I'd better buzz Rick.

I called the group to attention and asked for a briefing on Diane Ditt. Seven people started up at once, but I turned to Vance Rousseau, who had his hand raised. Vance addressed me. "Desmond, you've got your priorities skewed. Diane Ditt isn't out to kill you; Myrdal Hwang *is*, and on top of that he's a threat to the whole country."

Molly stood up. "Mr. Rousseau, that's my portfolio. I've got enough dope on Hwang right now to make him a national outrage, but he's bought himself so much influence everywhere that the media are afraid to touch it."

"Which means?" asked Vance.

"Which means that I start my own national newspaper, right in DC. Wilbur Lapham, I think you've met him, is coming with me. My husband Rick, as soon as he's back from the Pacific, will come to DC and serve as publisher until we've hired a permanent staff. We'll call it *The Other News* and feature emerging stories that the rest of the media don't want to touch. We're hoping to kick it off by early January. The whole first issue will be devoted to Myrdal Hwang and his dealings with everybody, including President Carmichael and Jazeps Guradich."

"*GURADICH!*" I burst out.

Molly turned to face me. "Sorry Desmond! That came in just this morning, while you were in conference. A source in Belgrade, very reliable, is ready to document Hwang's simultaneous backing of the General and his Bolgovnian adversaries, as well as his collaboration with the Sturm cartel in drug trafficking. I'll brief you on that this afternoon, if you've got time." She looked back at Vance. "Anyway, after the first issue of *The Other News* hits the street, we figure that Hwang will have so many enemies to cope with that he'll back off of Desmond."

"And so will the Chief Executive," added Vance. "If he's on Hwang's payroll, our President's a candidate for impeachment."

Everybody started yakking like crazy. Molly sat down again, looking exhausted.

This time I stood up and waved my arms to be heard. "Listen, everybody! I know this is heavy news, but Carmichael isn't the first President to have traded influence for money, and exposing him may be the kind of kick in the tail that the system needs. You can talk about Carmichael all week as far as I'm concerned, but right now we need to sort out a worst-case scenario for Diane Ditt as Governor. What can she do to us?"

There was silence for a second, until Ethan Zoig, facing me across the big table, said, "Everything."

"OK, Ethan," I answered. "Sock it to me."

Ethan took a sip of wine and put down the glass and pushed it a few inches away. "First off, it's not just that Ditt is coming in. The polls now show that she's dragging in a bunch of hangers-on with her. With a little luck they're going to control both houses."

"So?"

"She's already got a squad of staffers drafting new legislation. Some of it concerns you."

The table went so quiet, I could hear the hum of cicadas in the desert brush a mile away. I grabbed for my *auslese*. I asked Ethan, "Concerns me how?"

"It makes sexual harassment a felony offense, with jail time and fines that could eat up your entire fortune."

I heaved a sigh of relief. How could Ethan bring up something so irrelevant? "Ethan, whom have I harassed?"

Ethan's eyes went sad. "Desmond, maybe we'd better discuss the rest privately. Personally I don't think you'd harass a housefly, much less a human being, or that you ever did. But sexual harassment is a legal category that can have different meanings in different jurisdictions. The Ditt legislation, I'm afraid, will stretch it to cover, uh, I mean, events here on the ranch after the Magdalena graduation."

Everybody gasped. I gulped my wine and almost choked. I got dizzy. No, I hadn't harassed those ladies, but suddenly, almost like somebody'd cast a spell, I felt *the deepest sense of guilt*. I stood up convulsively, knocking down my chair. I glanced round the table, but nobody except Ethan and Mordecai was making eye contact. I signaled the two of them, and they both followed me across the terrace and back into the library.

But in the library there was new business to attend to. Rick had phoned us from Melanesia, in midair between Vanuatu and Guadalcanal. I sat down at my desk to take the call, gently pushing Paws off my chair. Rick, barely audible, said he'd run all his errands and asked if he should come home or fly to Morocco for an International Red Cross congress.

"Come home, Rick," I said. "Molly's not looking so good. I want her to see Janet."

"How's that again?"

"Molly's looking sick!" I shouted.

I heard a faint grunt, and the line went dead.

I pulled out some bourbon and glasses and told Ethan and Mordecai that we were going to set up a mock trial. Ethan, with his knowledge of Diane Ditt and his acquaintance with the scandalous harassment cases at the now-defunct Saint Lorenzo College, would play Ditt. Mordecai, with his brilliant legal mind, would play my counsel, and either of them could call me to the witness stand. We were just setting up the chairs when Rick called again. This time he sounded even farther away.

"My right [static]'s overheated, and I shut [static]."

"You've lost an engine?" As I spoke, I switched on the speaker-phone feature and turned it up.

Rick's voice boomed out, "I can't hear you. I've shut down my right engine, copy?"

"Copy! How far to the airfield?"

"Half an hour. But my left engine's heating up. And with [static] I won't have the reverse thrust to land this [static] mother on that short runway."

"How can this happen with a new 777?" Mordecai asked.

"Don't know. Can't rule out [static]"

"Sabotage!" we all shouted.

"Copy," said Rick.

Then for about a minute I couldn't hear him. Ethan ran across the room to get an atlas. Mordecai calmly filled an ice bucket and poured three glasses of bourbon.

The radio came alive again. "Desmond!"

"What are you going to do?" I shouted.

"Desmond, if I don't make it, will you take care of Molly?"

"I'll goddamn marry her, you turkey!" I roared. At this moment Paws staged a war game and dug his claws and teeth lightly into my right calf. I jumped and yelled.

The line went dead again.

The three of us were standing there like clowns, gawking at each other. Almost to myself, I asked, "What do you do when you've lost an engine and you've got a short runway to land on?"

"Use the other three," offered Ethan.

"777's only have two," I said. Ethan turned beet-red. That man hates to be wrong about anything.[74] Mordecai growled, "Hmmm. My dad

---

74. Ruck is in error here, but fidelity to the text prevents me from deleting his comment. —Ethan Zoig

made a wheels-up landing in the sand on Midway once, but that was in a B-25."

"Yeah," I added. "those old bombers had tougher skins. The fuselage on a modern jet is so light that it's almost sure to—"

"I've got it!" shouted Mordecai. "Alternate engines until just before landing, so neither gets too hot. Then use both of them to land."

"Right on!" I said. "That's sort of what I did once with the Vixen."

"That's where I just read it," he replied. "The Ruck fan-belt procedure."[75]

We sat down and drank and lit up cigars. There was no way to go on with the trial. I kept trying to reach Rick but not getting through. The tension of it all was beginning to wear me down. I had to share things. I told Mordecai and Ethan about Molly's bout with breast cancer three years ago. Ethan said he'd heard of a clinic in Canada that saved people who'd been thought beyond hope. Mordecai said you only hear about those places from the patients who survived. They asked me about Molly's new newspaper, and when we got talking, I started to feel better. They asked about Hwang and Magdalena Force[76] and the famous Thrumble sisters, and the talk gave me a little relief.

It's good to remember, now and then, that I haven't screwed up *everything*.

At 2:27 the phone rang. It was Rick, loud and clear. "Don't marry her yet, chief. I'm on the ground." He'd hit on the same idea as Mordecai's

---

75. See *Ruck's Run*, Ch. 3. —Ed.

76. In his haste Ruck omits mention of one of his own greatest achievements: the foundation of the Magdalena Force. In the spring of 2002, pursuant to Ruck's developing master plan, Magdalena College closed its doors (its faculty and staff being reassigned to international education programs in the White Wolf Foundation). That summer the campus was refurbished as graduate school for a fast-strike global rescue and assistance force. Skilled in techniques as varied as wilderness survival, nursing, agriculture, nutrition, communications and urban renewal, Magdalena Force teams have since made their presence felt in every corner of the globe, and MF has become the byword for innovation in global assistance. —Ed.

and made a perfect landing. But he'd be delayed while they fixed up the plane.

"No," I said. "Hop on somebody else's plane and let them fly you home. We need you."

After that we all decided it was time for a walk on the mountain. Not that we got very far up it, being sodden with wine and whiskey. But we made it up to one of my favorite spots. Louie calls it l'Espalda. It's a shoulder of land just south of a switchback in the trail, and it looks down at Lomo Morado from about half a mile away. It's flat and grassy and shaded by pine and oak. Louie's dug a well there and capped it with an antique hand-pump. He's built a couple of big benches out of oak and set out a miniature oaken half-barrel for hikers to drink out of. After a hot climb, the taste of the spring water up there's quite unlike anything else I've ever drunk.

Ethan and Mordecai'd never been up there before. As we sprawled on the benches, passing the barrel among us and savoring the pine-filtered afternoon breeze, my two friends looked down, admiring the ranch I'd created and commenting on this feature and that. My old good spirits started coming back.

Later on, after a longish silence, Ethan had one of his typical inspirations, and Mordecai popped one of *his* typical big surprises.

"Mordecai," says Ethan out of a clear blue sky (and in fact the sky *was* clear and blue). "I've been thinking about your three aliases: Salvador, Vickers, Father Angelo. Salvador means savior or rescuer. Vickers comes from the English 'vicar.' And of course there's Father Angelo. They're all religious names. Excuse me, but is this a coincidence?"

Mordecai smiled broadly. "Well, the Father Angelo part is self-explanatory," he said. "But I chose the other two names to remind myself that even though I'm a gross military type, I was on a mission of mercy. And maybe to remind you, Desmond," he eyed me sharply, "of an old friend you may be too busy to remember."

I sat bolt upright. "You don't mean the Rev—that is, Howard Keane!"

Mordecai nodded gravely. "Himself. The Rev is alive but, let's say, in reduced circumstances. He's cooling his heels in a maximum security prison near Bogota."

"He isn't! but how—"

Mordecai waved me off as he took a swig from the barrel. "It's a long story, but the nutshell is this: two days after the Sacannah flood, Keane came to see me on Death Row. Of course he had no trouble getting in, and the guards let us talk privately. Briefly put, I recruited the Rev for my mission to Colombia. The sense of excitement and danger in it gave him a new lease on life. He came with me into the jungle, to the Sturm compound, dressed up as a monk—no big deal for him. I must say, for a complete novice, he wasn't at all bad at the spying game. He's so bright, you know, so intense. But what went, in the end, was his self-control. We'd gone for a rare night out in Mirasoles, a foul jungle rat-hole that was swarming with dealers, thugs and police. We were dressed in civvies, partly to attract less attention, partly because the Rev had evening plans of, uh, a social nature. We swilled some rum, not much mind you, but enough it turned out to get the Rev's engine started. I went to the loo and came back two minutes later to find everybody in a tither and him in custody after punching out a plain-clothes cop. In the squad car the police must have planted some drugs on him. The Colombian anti-drug campaign needs a yearly quota of convictions and sentences, and he was one of them. They billed him as a big fish. There was nothing I could do for him and still keep my cover. Nothing, that is, till now."

I was grinning uncontrollably. "Let's go!" I told them. "I'll spring him. I'll start tonight."

But on the way home my friends gently convinced me that this particular mission of mercy could be made more effectively on the telephone.

Back at the ranch I started making phonecalls. Before dinner I called Molly and told her about Rick's close escape. She was overjoyed when I let her know he was on his way back to her. I also told her she had to see

Janet and get examined tomorrow. She balked at first, then stalled, but finally gave in. Then I called Janet and put her in the picture.

Just before dinner I took Heidi aside and told her to sit down. I announced that the Rev was alive and that we were going to bring him back. She burst into tears.

And after dinner Mordecai and I put in a call to Winslow Walker in Tzinsk. We told him we needed to contact somebody in the State Department who could pull strings to liberate a US operative who'd come a cropper in Colombia. He told us to call Thurston Hale, Assistant Secretary of State. He said that Hale's been crowing to the world about the Khakharsk caper and that he'll move mountains for us.

We'll do the mock-trial tomorrow morning, and in the afternoon Mordecai will finish briefing me about Mara. It's after dinner now. I'm in bed, bushed.

SEX ON TRIAL

OCTOBER 31, 2002

Another exhausting day. I'm writing in bed again, at least in the part of the bed not occupied by Ranguma and Paws. If I ever get married again, I'll kick them off the bed.

Married! What a thought. But at least I can think it again.

Rick's back, though I haven't seen much of him. He'd caught a redeye into Vegas and was out here by 8:30 AM. He bounced off the plane, gave me a bear hug and rushed off to Janet's, where Molly was waiting. I trudged back up the hill dreading what was to come.

At 9 Ethan, Mordecai and I set up in the Library, locked the doors and turned off the telephone.

I'll skip the preliminaries, except to say that over the first hour and a half Ethan sketched out a brief history of sexual harassment issues, including the cases of Anita Hill and Paula Jones. He then chatted about some recent decisions he'd researched, and summarized the substance of a conference call he'd had with Roger Gannett and his staff; and after that he quoted the most telling sections from Diane Ditt's books and articles, so the three of us would all be on the same page.

Then the trial began.

Ethan, speaking as the Judge, kicked off by announcing that I'd been arraigned on 694 counts of sexual harassment, crimes for which the maximum punishment was 3,470 years in prison and, calculating from an estimate of my current worth, sixty-eight trillion eight hundred forty-four billion three hundred ninety-one million five hundred fifty-seven thousand [here he stopped to catch his breath] one hundred six dollars and seventy-seven cents in fines. He arrived at these figures because the estimated prison term per infraction according to Ditt was five years, and the estimated fine per infraction would be 5% of the defendant's net worth.

I asked if I could pay in installments.

■ **PRE-TRIAL MOTIONS**

MORDECAI: I move to have the case thrown out of court because none of the alleged victims has filed a complaint.

ETHAN (as Judge): Denied. Because the 694 ladies have had sex with Mr. Ruck, they are potential victims de facto and de jure.

MORDECAI: I move to have the case thrown out because none of the women are willing to testify against Mr. Ruck. They're all going to testify in his defense.

ETHAN (as Judge): Denied. As you'll see, even testimony in Ruck's defense can be taken as evidence of his crimes.

MORDECAI: What!

ETHAN: Hold your horses— I mean, silence in the Court!

■ **WITNESSES FOR THE DEFENSE**

MORDECAI: Your honor, I've now questioned all 694 witnesses. Down to the last woman, they all avow that they initiated sexual relations with Mr. Ruck. They assert, moreover, that they were not in his employ or in any way under his authority when these relations occurred. They attest that they initiated these advances of their own free will, and contend, additionally, that they wouldn't have known what free will was if it hadn't been for the education offered them by Mr. Ruck. In conclusion, they declare that having sexual relations with Mr. Ruck was a liberating experience, and maintain that it was more fun than anything they'd ever done in their lives before.

ETHAN (as Prosecutor): Allow me to contest that avowal, refute that assertion, confute that attestation, repel that contention, dispel that declaration and mitigate that maintainance in order:

¶ As for the avowal that the 694 ladies initiated sexual relations with Mr. Ruck, the State of Arizona is indifferent to who initiates what, the sexual relations in and of themselves constituting a state of harassment in which the more powerful of the two parties is (if one of the two is indeed more powerful), de facto, culpable.

¶ As for the assertion that the 694 ladies were not in Mr. Ruck's employ or in any way under his authority when these sexual relations occurred, the State of Arizona makes no distinction between the status of employer and coequivalent statuses, such as protector, educator or benefactor. Authority, though not asserted, may be imputed under these circumstances.

¶ As for the attestation that the 694 ladies initiated these advances of their own free will, the State of Arizona accepts Governor Ditt's avouchment, in her important book *The Serpent in the Cupboard*, that so-called free will is not more than a fiction or figment of the deformed paradigm of reality created jointly by victims of dysfunctional power relationships and by their oppressors.

¶ As for the contention that the 694 ladies wouldn't have known what free will was if it hadn't been for they education offered them by Mr. Ruck, the State of Arizona accepts Governor Ditt's inference, in her seminal work, *Nature's Little Joke*, that the concept of free will erected by humanist educators at Magdalena College is itself a false construction figmented by the Western capitalist power-driven model. The word "freedom" itself is no more than a cipher in the text of harassment.

¶ As for the declaration that having sexual relations with Mr. Ruck was a liberating experience, the State of Arizona questions the reliability of any individual who would relate the concept of philosophical liberty to the frictional arousal of the genitals.

¶ As for the maintainance that having sexual relations with Mr. Ruck was more fun than anything they'd ever done in their lives before, the State of Arizona has identified "fun" during sexual relations as evidence of a power disparity and hence a harassively dysfunctional interaction.

¶ Finally, as for the Defense's averral that the 694 ladies have come here to protect Mr. Ruck rather than accuse him, the State of Arizona interprets this act as profound, conclusive and irrefutable proof of their victimization.

The State of Arizona rests.

MORDECAI (as Mordecai): You goddamn well better rest, you fictional frictional hypocritical hypothetical unctious autocratic sophist!

ETHAN (as Ethan): I'm famished. Let's get some lunch!

We discussed the trial out on the terrace, over bagels and lox. Mordecai and I both kudoed Ethan over his presentation, which was awesomely putrid. Then we got down to business. All three of us were of a mind that the Ditt law was tyrannical and wouldn't hold up, but none of us could pinpoint chapter and verse to that effect in the US Constitution. I trotted into the Library for the *Columbia Encyclopedia* and brought it out, opened to the document in question.

"Amendment One guarantees the rights of religion, speech and assembly," Ethan pointed out. "Is sex assembly?"

"If so, then murder is, too," growled Mordecai. "I think we've got to face the fact that individual states can make laws regulating sexual behavior. In the old days these were called blue laws, and some of them, though unenforced, remain in the books to this day. Now Ditt is aiming to pass one with teeth in it. And it's an ad hominem law aimed directly at you, Desmond."

Ethan half-choked on his bagel and I smacked him on the back. Clearing his throat, he said, "Ditt means not only to ruin you but to disgrace you. If she has her way, you'll rot in jail through the whole appeal process."

Mordecai leaned back in his chair, closed his eyes and pressed his hands together with only the fingertips touching. "This is how I think the appeal process will play out. The lower courts will support the state. After all, a state law is a state law. But higher courts will begin asking whether the law itself is constitutional. They'll begin asking whether 'imputation' of harassment gives the state too wide a range of interpretation, and thus whether, more generally, the law erodes the individual liberties guaranteed by the Bill of Rights." He opened his eyes and looked at me. "But I'm talking long haul. In the short run, Desmond, you're in a major pickle."

"God," I moaned. "Will it ever end?"

"Don't worry," said Ethan. "We'll see you through this."

I felt soiled and sweaty. "Suppose we break for a swim or whatever and meet here again at 2?" We still had to finish that horror show about Mara. I asked Ethan to join us, for moral support.

THE HUMAN SANDWICH

After swimming, at poolside, I made three short phone calls: to Rose Randolph at Pueblo Verde, telling her I'd like to visit next week and asking her what day would be best; to Robby Grauer[77] at Magdalena Force, setting up a date for him to fly in and update me on his progress; and to Vi at Nevil Castle, locking myself into a week of trimaraning with her and Ferdy out of Hilo in November. These were all pleasant calls, and necessary, but I had ulterior motives for making them. I needed steadying, centering. I was sandwiched between two unbelievable impossible unbearable women, Diane Ditt and Mara/Thea, and I needed being reminded that there was a world out there where people made sense.

Trying to restore this world of sense and reason, I invited Ethan to

---

77. Robert MacDoughall Grauer, Jr., currently junior senator from South Dakota, served as the first director of the Magdalena Force from 2002 to 2005.

join Mordecai and me in the afternoon for the continuation of Mordecai's disclosure about the Sturms et al. We set up a triangle of easy chairs in front of the desk in the library. Before Mordecai began, I briefed Ethan about what had been revealed that morning. Then Mordecai booted up the computer and began.

"It may have surprised you, Desmond, to learn that you didn't run into Thea on the banks of the Ocalona by chance. But if Thea Sturm could help it, nothing ever happened by chance. Your adventures with her were all tailored, in a rough-cut way, by Thea and her gang. Her whole presentation to you—I mean, the character she assumed for you—was a diabolical work of art, orchestrated to a strategy of seduction and control. How did she know which strategy would work? Let's start at the beginning."

He scrolled up through the text.

"Here you are in the hotel, just giving the seemingly unconscious Thea a bath. Thea described me this scene in great detail. She said she'd never been treated with this care and tenderness by any of her lovers, or anybody, since her mother'd dressed and undressed her as a tiny tot. She could read your character in the touch of your hands. "

"What character?" I asked.

Mordecai volleyed out an uncontrollable laugh. I looked over at Ethan, who was stifling a giggle.

"What's with you guys?" I asked. "If I'm gentle with somebody, does that make me a freak or something?"

Mordecai was about to answer but Ethan waved him off and said, "Quit it, Desmond. Don't you know that your compassion is legendary around here? People love you for it and even make the odd little joke about it."

I hadn't known!

"It's true. Compassion is one of your strong suits, Desmond," added Mordecai. "But Thea exploited it as a weakness. Her mind, her whole being, was so attuned to issues of control that straightaway she was inspired *to take charge of you by playing the victim*. Remember those days with her, man. Again and again, when she moaned with sadness, or lost consciousness, or played dead, or even just looked wistful, it would drive you into agonies of compassion. Remember the life-story she told you — a total fabrication, of course — about how'd she been victimized first by her husband and then by the Imbrattas and on top of that by Kanaloa, God of the Ocean. Now, Desmond, look at the other side of the ledger. How many times did Mara joke or laugh?"

Rather few.

"How many times did she offer you substantive help?"

Precious few.

"How often did she express optimism or gusto?"

Hardly at all.

"Of course not. Any of these shows of strength would have broken the spell, would have loosened, if you will, the reins of her weakness."

"That's nicely put," said Ethan. (*I wish somebody'd ever say that to me!*)

"By the way, what was this Kanaloa thing?" I asked Mordecai.

"I'm just getting to that." He scrolled ahead. "Remember this?"

Grim news: I climbed up the arroyo this morning, as I do now every day. As I rounded the bend and got my first distant view of the bench at the top, I saw somebody by the bench, dressed in bright green, who waved at me and disappeared. The Chilean god, Kanaloa? I don't believe in him!

"Sure," I said. That happened to me at Vic Bellows' place."

Mordecai chuckled. "That's something of a story in itself. In the first place, when Thea told you her life story in the Vixen, she was inventing as she went along, borrowing story elements from her reading and from South American folklore. It occurred to her to add a supernatural pitch — so as to increase your sense of her as doomed and thus enhance her control over you — but the only name that popped into her head was

338

of an Hawaiian god, Kanaloa. She called it the weak link in her whole story. But you bought it lock, stock and barrel."

I winced.

MacCrae went on. "Now when brother Klaus fled Colombia, he used one of his phony passports and came straight to the States. His goal was simple: to intercept the Vixen and get his hands on the securites. Of course he wasn't sure where Thea would be, but she'd promised to call him as soon as possible at Dr. Hauck's clinic. Hauck, don't you know, was one of the Sturms' best customers. In San Lorenzo Klaus picked up the VW you call the Death Bug, and when she called he hopped in it, drove to Louisville and started tailing you."

"But how in blazes did they steer me to Hauck's clinic?"

"Think back. Klaus started tailgating you just before the San Lorenzo exit, and that's also about when Thea announced her tummy-ache. You'll remember also that the San Lorenzo offramp led only southward and that the Honest Abe Inn was the first eatery on it. Because Thea knew that you were a sucker for helpless women, Klaus had told Betty van Ardsdale to drag some basket case down to the Honest Abe as a means of entrapping you. And get this:

> Before I knew it, and despite a warning glance from Mara, I'd asked how far away the Institute was, and Bessie said only a mile, and we'd packed ourselves into the Vixen, which was parked nearby.

Thea mentioned exactly this scene to me, calling it her finest hour. Pardon the expression, but Thea had you so deep in her pocket that she could use negative English, like the warning glance, as a means of confusing you and confirming her credibility. Check out this later passage:

> the whole thing seemed no more to me than a bizarre coincidence, but Mara thought otherwise. She thought that the VW bug was a plant to get us to leave the freeway at the San Lorenzo exit.
> I said, No, Mara, that plan's got too many loopholes.

> She looked at me reproachfully. *"What do loopholes matter if the plan succeeds?"* I didn't quite follow this and told her so, but that didn't phase Mara in the slightest. In her mind the whole deal at Skythorpe was part of an Imbratta plot to nail us.

A subtle piece of dishonesty. Here, where you're not suspicious at all, she arouses your suspicion and misdirects it, keeping her position on the moral high ground. But the psychology of all this is interesting: it's almost as if, from time to time, she was teasing you, challenging you to suspect the truth."

Still unbelieving, I asked, "But how did they get me up to the Penumbra Hotel?"

Ethan cut in. "Wait a minute, you're ahead of me. I haven't read the journal, but it seems to me that if I were the unscrupulous Dr. Hauck and I had Desmond in my power, I'd finish him off right away."

"Hey that's right," I said. "What was with the clinic routine?"

Mordecai thought for a moment. "Thea didn't tell me about that in so many words, but she *did* say that she, Klaus and Hauck couldn't agree about what to do with you: that she wanted to spare your life, and the others didn't, and that they'd finally convinced her that you had to die. This temporary difference of opinion must have caused the delay. Of course, Thea only pretended to drink the mickey-finn that put you under. You may be wondering why she went to the Women's Ward, got into a patient's robe and sat down with the others. Well, she knew your huge size and staying power, and she needed an out in case you escaped. But once she was in the ward, she took a shining to the big albino guard and began a dalliance with him that you interrupted."

"You mean—" I blithered.

"Thea loved impulsive sex with strangers. She couldn't resist this opportunity to cop a feel."

"So that's what poor Isobel wanted to tell me!"

Mordecai went right on. "As far as Freda's Foods and the Penumbra are concerned, it was an even sloppier job. You see Klaus Sturm—"

The terrace door had opened and Catherine was striding towards me with a portable phone in her hand. "Desmond, this is important. It's Thurston Hale of the State Department."

I needed a bit of relief and called time out. While the men got some coffee, I walked out onto the terrace, under high clouds, sat down in a captain's chair and, in easygoing conversation with a well-spoken Foggy Bottom powercrat, settled the Rev's case. It would cost a bundle, but the release would be immediate. Since Rick was unavailable, I asked Hale to make sure the Rev had enough scratch to buy a ticket here.

As I was saying goodbye, Ethan and Mordecai strolled out on the terrace to stretch and take a breather.

I went to the terrace door and shouted, "Mordecai, I've sprung the Rev!"

"Right on!" Mordecai turned and came back to me. "What'd it cost?"

"An arm and a leg." I didn't mention a figure because I couldn't risk the Rev's finding out how much I'd paid for him—it might trigger another guilt attack. (Is guilt the American Disease?)

"That reminds me." Mordecai pulled out his wallet, probed into it and handed me the million-dollar check I'd sent him.

"But you earned that," I protested.

"Irrelevant. I don't save a good man for money."

A *good man.* Had I finally made it? I let him force the check on me, and we ambled back into the library. By now I was feeling a bit wrung out, but I wanted to hear the end of the story.

"Where was I?" asked Mordecai when we'd sat down in the library again.

We all struggled to remember.

"Was it Klaus?" asked Ethan.

"Klaus it was!" MacCrae exclaimed. "Let's dispose of Herr Klaus as fast as we can. He had good looks and what passed for a pleasantly eccentric manner, but at heart he was a lowlife asshole with a multi-billion dollar chip on his shoulder. He had no education to speak of. He'd inherited the drug operation in '96 from his dad Friedrich, who was I hear a real hot number. But Klaus had no feel for the business. He was awful with people and always changing his mind. He was also a compulsive tinkerer, a failed inventor, an addict, a pervert, and, if you don't mind my saying so, a poor excuse for a criminal. By 1998 he'd totally messed up the whole Colombian operation, of course, without telling his friends the Imbrattas, who unbeknownst to them were about to buy $200 billion worth of pure grief."

I asked, "But how did he get it all back later?"

"He didn't get it back. Rather, he and Thea charmed Myrdal Hwang into bankrolling a new operation. Thanks to Hwang's dough, connections and savvy, the business took off again. But I'm ahead of myself. It's Klaus you have to thank for the Penumbra Hotel disaster. Klaus, that is, and that colossal piece of shit, Arcanis Valpudis, alias Our Beloved. Do you remember finding out (where is it?) that Valpudis had been in SA? Here,

> The Vegas police have nothing else on him except that some time between fall '94 and summer '95 he was away for a few months in South America.

That's where Valpudis met the Sturms. It was love at first sight, especially for Thea. And that's how the Sturms first met Hwang, who'd known Valpudis in Los Angeles and had been grooming him as a future right-wing rabble-rouser. When Valpudis went back to the States, he started peddling drugs for the Sturms.

"Let's segue now to May Day, 1998. Back at the Hauck Clinic, Thea and Klaus had agreed on the Penumbra Hotel as a failsafe, because Thea knew that she could put Denver on your itinerary. Once she got you to Estes Park, Thea phoned him, and they arranged the fake kidnap. But Klaus, who planned that caper, was too drunk that morning to pull it off, so Valpudis went into town and dynamited the restaurant and picked up Thea. Back at the Penumbra Hotel, while you were in custody in the Lupus Coven, they revived Klaus and had a pow-wow. The

Sturms offered Valpudis a share of your loot if he'd join them in getting rid of you and laundering the securities in L.A. Valpudis was happy to oblige—but he had problems of his own to solve. As you'll remember very well, Desmond, the Lupus Coven and the Crivellian Risen were at each other's throats, and Valpudis's power base was crumbling.

"With these various challenges in mind, the three of them got high on coke together, and Klaus proposed a makeshift plan to kill a number of birds, in a manner of speaking, with a number of stones. Klaus' reputation for bungling had preceded him, so Valpudis, even though in his cups, had some reservations about the project, but the Sturms assured him it was a piece of cake, and Klaus was off like a shot up the mountain in a pickup truck full of dynamite and detonators. Thea and Valpudis were going to stay in the hotel and kill you and grab the Vixen keys.

"But here's the crazy part of the story: after Klaus left, Valpudis and Thea sniffed some coke and started making love. Thea, monumental flake that she was, told me that for sexual kicks, nothing could beat love-making with a giant deranged cult-figure on a taxidermy table at the top of a hotel that was about to be crushed by giant boulders, while witches, wolves and rednecks had at each other one floor below. They thought they had more than an hour to spare before Klaus kicked off his version of the Apocalypse. But that's not the way things worked out. Valpudis, in flagrante with Thea on the table, spotted you crossing the roof in the moonlight. Thea, bless her departed soul, saw a chance for one more neurotic control trip, so she doused herself with ice water (that's what you later slipped on). Valpudis, who'd been a makeup artist in Hollywood, decorated her throat with canned spaghetti left over from their dinner, before he sallied forth to meet you. She said she wanted you to die '*remembering her as something pure.*'"

I was starting to feel whacked out and dizzy again. "Mordecai," I said, "that's enough dementia for a day. Maybe for a lifetime. Let's knock off."

Mordecai smiled sadly and rose.

"Wait a minute!" cut in Ethan. "How did Thea get out of the Penumbra Hotel?"

"She grabbed some clothes and went out the same exit Valpudis used. There was a fire escape around in back. They managed to escape in the Death Bug. But they smashed the Bug into a rock on their way out and damaged the front end. Otherwise they'd have gotten to the Vixen before you, Desmond. Valpudis trudged up the mountain road and after a while met Klaus on his way down. Together they pushed the Bug out of sight of the road and walked into Estes Park as police and fire engines raced past them to the burning hotel. In two days they'd had the Bug towed and repaired and were in Boulder. At that point they decided to cut their losses. They had a few thousand cash from the Crivellian kitty. Thea and Klaus flew to L.A., where they could get more money and a phony passport for her. Valpudis set out in the Bug to find you. He lucked out."

I asked, "Did Thea ever ask Klaus what went wrong with the explosives?"

Mordecai laughed bitterly. "Simple. The nut had forgotten to turn back his watch for Mountain Time."

I asked who was responsible for RoboGal.

"Klaus and Jinn!" barked Mordecai. Klaus was certain that RoboGal would frighten you so thoroughly that you'd lose trust in all your friends and blow your cover. Jinn, who was adept in all forms of spying from sneak-thievery to computer hacking, got into your personal journal. He stole all your innermost thoughts and aspirations and passed them on to Klaus, who programmed them into RoboGal. That's how she got so thoroughly onto your wavelength."

"Then why did she almost kill me?"

"That wasn't the idea, Desmond. She was supposed to loosen up after you passed out from the pain, and then escape. Just another of Klaus's slightly faulty plans."

Ethan had one more question. "Who killed Guccio Imbratta?"

Mordecai sighed, like some exhausted laborer. "That was all Thea's work. Using Barda as her emissary, Thea convinced Guccio that if he gave you the doctored photo, you'd fall into their clutches and he'd get his money back. Then, so's not to have to share the loot, she put out a contract on the old man through the Calandrino connection. The idea was to make the hit before you came, so you'd find the photo clutched in Guccio Imbratta's dead hand. But the hit-man got stalled in New York traffic and arrived late. That's how *you*, Desmond, got there first and lost another of your nine lives."

Shortly after that we quit for the day. Mordecai has reams more to share, but I know enough already about the forty-odd times I've been gulled and outwitted. It's midnight now, and I lie in bed tortured, confused. How can two women be as different as Diana Ditt and Thea Sturm, and there still be such a thing as a woman?

SHANA REDUX

NOVEMBER 1, 2002

I saw the *real* Shana Ladd for the first time today. She phoned from Tucson, said she had a couple of days free and asked if she could visit.

It's good she did, because I don't know when I'd have summoned the courage to meet her face to face. We lunched by ourselves in the library. At first she was full of questions about Khakharsk, but once we'd eaten and the coffee was poured, we relaxed, and the talk wandered here and there. I was still struck by her incredible similarity to RoboGal, but the makers of RoboGal, whoever they were, had missed something, a girlishness, that came over her when she got excited. They also missed a robust, almost horsy laugh, that totally demolishes her image as an ultra-serious environmentalist.

At last I told her about my new interest in sailing, and she really lit up.

She's staying two more days. I'm going to take her around the whole ranch.

The Rev is due in tonight. I don't know what sort of mood he's in, so, rather than throwing a party, Mordecai, Heidi and I will meet him at the airstrip by ourselves.

Molly's tests are back, and they're not good. Rick and I want her to go for treatments right now, but she insists on setting up in DC first. There's no moving her. Publishing the truth about Hwang has become her crusade.

Just had a call from Winthrop Walker in Tzinsk. He's been having fits trying to get any news out of Khakharsk, because the government has imposed secrecy on everything concerning the Klaiprenska Massacre. But the grapevine says that poor Boris has been arrested and is going to be tried for espionage. What bullshit! I said I'd discuss this with Thurston Hale.

1:22 PM. News from Guadalcanal has shown up on my Vegas voice-mail. The 777 *was* sabotaged. The draining cocks on the cooling systems of both engines of the 777 were left slightly open.[78] Hwang?

1:30 PM. Called Hale. He said he was good friends with the Georgian President (Boris is a Georgian citizen) and would get on it right away. He also's going to contact the CIA, who want to bring Boris to the States.

While I was on the line with Hale, I asked if he knew a good oncologist in the DC area. He told me that the best person he'd heard of, named Murtagh, was at the NIH, working on some wonder drug that cut off tumors' blood supplies.

Edgar Murtagh, 202-779-3435.

Time to take Shana to Pueblo Verde!

---

78. Col. Beauchamps has altered this technical detail in order to deter future sabateurs. —Ethan Zoig

NOVEMBER 3, 2002

Just got back from Marble Canyon with Shana. Everything is fun with that woman! She's full of questions when we talk, and every subject seems to have a laugh somewhere inside it, and she can disagree without getting uptight. Sometimes when we walk we don't talk at all, but there's still this sense that she enjoys being with you.

Yesterday morning we were sitting alone in the library, and we both fell asleep! We'd been up late the night before at the Rev's party and were sipping coffee and having a quiet chat, seasoned with peaceful pauses, and all of a sudden it was past noon, and I woke after the sweetest sleep, to see her stretching.

She left for Tucson today. She shook hands with me in LoMo's parking lot and walked to her rental car and was just about to open its driver's door when she turned around towards me, as though to take one last look at me. I wanted to kiss her then.

THE ?-BILLION-DOLLAR MAN

The Rev's homecoming was something to remember. The Learjet taxied right up to us, and when they'd killed the engines he came through the door and just froze, looking at Heidi with wide open eyes. She froze too, as though time had stopped. The Rev was in Colombian Army fatigues. He was gaunt but looked strong, and as he gazed at her the flush came back to his cheeks. Then they rushed into each other's arms.

I put the Rev in a bedroom in my wing of the house. Mordecai and I left them to themselves for the afternoon. Mordecai stayed with me for a couple of hours as I ambled around the ranch, visiting people and catching up on their projects. In between stops we chatted, mainly about his family and his home near Morro Bay, CA. His wife Barbara writes mystery novels, and his kids, three boys, are all away at school.

347

Mordecai and Barbara have their own stable and can ride right from their back yard into Los Padres National Forest.

I left him in the greenhouse with his old buddy, Ali.

That evening we partied. It was no formal thing. I grilled tuna steaks on the terrace. The Rev showed up, looking even gaunter after an afternoon in bed with Heidi, but quietly jolly. Even though he's grateful for my having sprung him, he couldn't seem to swallow my being such a rich man. He gripped me by both arms and asked me, "Where's my historian of the times? Where's my poor pilgrim?" and then started singing a snatch of song from Prokofiev that went, *"Peregrinus, expectavi."*

Mystified, I asked to talk to him alone. We walked off a few paces and stood at the north edge of the terrace. "What's all this," I asked him, "about my being a historian, a pilgrim?"

The Rev gave me a portentious look, as in *You mean you don't know?* but he didn't say anything. Then his eyes went vague. He looked as if he couldn't wrap words around his own metaphor and needed a measure of bourbon to get his vocabulary back in trim (but he's on the wagon for good now!).

Finally he spoke as though in pain. "Remember when we first met, years ago, in Pilotsburg Jail? You'd saved Platinum Jayne's father's life and gotten yourself arrested for it? Well, when I heard that, I thought, if that doesn't beat all! It's an image of modern times! I mean, your average Joe Six-pack, he's not a pilgrim at all, but *you and I,* Desmond, we were seekers! Seeking, seeking . . . perhaps something nameless and new, perhaps something ancient and forgotten, but inevitably colliding with guilt in the very sweat and violence of our search."

"What kind of guilt?" I asked.

"*What kind?* Call it guilt of renewal! Thus the pilgrim becomes the hunted, and the seeker is sought for his seeking. I've looked in Scripture . . ." The Rev went on to talk about Abraham and Job and Jacob's wrestling match.

I stopped him. "What about Mordecai?" I inquired. "He's done his share of killing, but you called him a good man. How does he deal with his guilt?"

"Maybe you better ask him," sighed the Rev, and went on, "If there's such a thing as goodness at all, maybe it's a special way of looking at guilt."

After that he found Heidi and they excused themselves. By midnight Sergei had brought down his electric guitar (which he's learned to play in no time flat), and Tuminous was hamboning and Double Mocha was dancing (but with clothes on). Somewhere along the line Catherine appeared, pushing a cart of liqueurs, and I caught her and danced with her. She was flushed with embarrassment at first, but then a look of sweetness came over her, as though she'd finally come into her own, and I looked up from her face to see everybody dancing.

I saw Ditt on TV last night! She's pulling national coverage by making me the goat of her campaign. Goat indeed. She calls me the Satyr of Canyon County and talks about maybe having me surgically altered. It's the first time I've ever seen the woman. She's very tall, gaunt, gray, raw-boned, almost cadaverous, with jutting eyebrows over half-closed eyes, like Frankenstein's monster, and she accompanies her comments with sudden almost spastic hand gestures that have everybody around her jumping. Is something wrong with her health? She looks haunted, possessed, but it's as though these spooky qualities are what makes her so popular. My flesh crawls!

NOVEMBER 6, 2002

The election was yesterday. Ditt won by a healthy margin.

My goose is cooked.

The inauguration's January 19. Until then her supporters won't be able to swing a majority for the sex harassment legislation.

That gives me until about February 1.

Guilt! why am I smothered in guilt, all of a sudden? More to the point, why am I such a phenomenally easy mark? A con gal feeds me a line, and I tail her like a puppy. A robot sings my song, and I turn into the robot's robot. An army of ladies hits on me, and I promptly become a human geyser. Then Diane Ditt calls me a heel, and Old Faithful is reborn as a dribbling prison cell faucet. *What am I anyway, some kind of cross between a puppet and an echo chamber?* Is this how I manage my rights and liberties?

I think I'll leave the country. I've got to spend some time alone.

Chapter Fourteen The Merlin Box

A Postscript by Ethan Zoig

I really hate to do this. I feel like a stranger, walking by surprise into your home, with news of irreparable loss. I must tell you that Desmond Ruck's journal, which I have just finished reading for the first time, breaks off after the last line of the November 6, 2002, entry. Mr. Ruck would write two more fragments, but they are undated and must be read in context.

My name is Ethan Zoig. For over a year I was privileged to have Desmond Ruck as my employer, colleague and friend. It was the most exciting year of my life, though, thanks to Ruck, there may be other exciting years to come.

Because of my close contact with Ruck during his last year, I have been asked by Cuthbert Nelson and Sigmund Bazoom to prepare the conclusion of this book, as well as adding a few notes to Mr. Bazoom's explanatory comments. I'm also responsible for the book and chapter titles, which I tried to invent conformable with Ruck's exuberance and sense of humor. I can't compensate you for the loss of Ruck's voice, which was uniquely expressive of his character. I can only assure you that no one is more sensible of this loss than I.

Let me begin with a narrative that I know Ruck himself would have put first. Alex Fanshawe's new book about Molly Block Beauchamps, *Destiny of Truth*, tells it in detail, so I'll be brief. Beauchamps and her husband, Col. Richard Beauchamps, arrived in Washington on November 14, 2002. That same day they leased the offices and presses of the recently defunct Washington, DC, *Courier-Post-Dispatch*. Early next morning they began interviewing job candidates whom they had recruited via the Internet. Successful candidates were housed in the nearby Hotel Creighton, which had been purchased by White Wolf Enterprises (Ruck's for-profit corporation) in late October and would be managed by Ruck's protégé, Wilbur Lapham.

The next week, development of *The Other News*—including the nuts and bolts of journalistic design, style and protocol—began in earnest. Training sessions and policy conferences ran well into the night seven days a week. First-rate investigative reporters, including Warren Heinz, Marian Daguerre and Axel Fanshawe himself, were attached as correspondents.

But from the start the project faced two besetting emergencies. Molly Beauchamps's health was failing rapidly. Dr. Edgar Murtagh of the NIH insisted that she begin treatments immediately, but instead she stuck to her desk until she was almost too weak to talk on the phone. In late November Col. Beauchamps e-mailed Ruck to say that he'd just dragged his wife to the NIH for her first treatment of a new drug that Murtagh was testing. After this treatment she regained strength, but refused to enter the rehabilitation program prescribed by Murtagh. Her health began to decline again.

As if this were not enough, the White House was using every measure available to prevent *The Other News* from ever appearing. In *Destiny of Truth*, Fanshawe details a calendar of licensing delays, break-ins, surprise searches, buggings, court restraining orders, computer viruses and mysterious power outages, all orchestrated by a White House dirty tricks team under the President's personal command. Molly and Richard Beauchamps endured these interruptions, and occasional threats of much worse, with teeth-grit determination. And when, on the night of January 2, 2003, the eve of publication, the *Courier-Post-Dispatch* building was ravaged by explosion and fire, Molly Beauchamps coolheadedly downloaded the entire issue onto *The Other News's* website. Coverage of the fire by all the major TV networks instantly turned this website into a global mecca. Within a day, the contents of the website were on the front pages of newspapers worldwide.

The word was out. In the journalistic canon devoted to the exposure of high-level corruption, the Beauchampses' website must rank as a classic. Its accusations were focussed and lucid, its evidence detailed and voluminous. And the documentation was impeccable: no less than a 59-page affidavit from Captain (USN) Phillips Fosbert, President Carmichael's military attaché and longtime factotum. Fosbert enumerates seven visits made to the White House by Myrdal Hwang in the invented persona of Sung Tree, a Eurasian philanthropist—each visit preceding an important juncture in US-Bolgovnian relations. He vividly recounts the night of Water Closet (August 16, 2002), when, on his way to warn the President of a possible White House break-in, he and Desmond Ruck separately discovered Carmichael and Hwang praying beside the now famous Table of Dollars.

Within hours of the website's publication, the House of Representatives was in special session, debating the impeachment of Archie Carmichael, 43d President of the United States.

The cold and stormy night, which brought closure to that notorious day, gave way to another that was yet more infamous. The events of January 3, 2003, rocked the nation and left it trembling. It is no boon to American self-confidence, or tonic for the national morale, when an incumbent President jumps to his death from the roof of the Federal

Office Building. Nor is it especially reassuring to discover, a few hours later, that the 76-year-old Vice President, on hearing the news, has been hospitalized with cardiac arrest. America, which four years earlier had been "talking again," was now suddenly silenced, muffled under a blanket of shock that would soon give way to outrage and recrimination.

It was a week when shock waves travelled in minutes around the world, disrupting precarious balances and impelling chain reactions that boomeranged back to their point of origin. President Lehrer's first act after recovering consciousness was to break diplomatic ties with Bolgovnia, which was allegedly harboring Myrdal Hwang. The Hong Kong stock market, which had been towering giddily, plunged 42% on Friday the 4th, touching off by Monday a global frenzy of selling. Only the international borrowing, buying and selling curbs, put in place by Ruck and his Three Wise Men, Clemens, Horowitz and Rousseau, saved the global economy from collapse.

These daunting occurrences, and their ramifications, which held public attention in thrall for weeks, all but obliterated from view the two events to which we must now turn our attention: the recovery of Molly Beauchamps and the disappearance of Desmond Ruck.

On the 4th of January, 2003, only a day after her towering journalistic achievement, Molly Beauchamps suffered a grave relapse of her cancerous condition. Certain that her number was up, she refused the hospital, opting instead to spend her last hours in bed in her DC apartment. Col. Beauchamps urgently telephoned Dr. Murtagh, only to discover that Murtagh was vacationing at his retreat on Jekyll Island, Georgia. Within an hour Col. Beauchamps was in the air in the Ruck Learjet; within three hours he had flown the good doctor back to the nation's capital.

The pair stopped at Murtagh's NIH lab on their way back to the Beauchampses' flat, where they found Mrs. Beauchamps weak almost beyond speech. Then and there Murtagh rigged up an IV administering the same experimental drug that he had used before. He told the Colonel that, despite present appearances to the contrary, if Molly Beauchamps survived the night and promised to be a model patient in the future, her prognosis was good.

The two men spent the night in the patient's room. Beauchamps tells me that towards dawn he must have fallen asleep, for he was wakened by his wife's voice, calling for the morning newspaper.

But to return to Ruck. When Desmond got back from Hawaii on November 20, 2002, he was tan and healthy but seemed withdrawn and distracted. The infectious smile, the thunderous laugh, the friendly hand on the shoulder were still there, but less frequent, as he spent hour on hour in his library, writing notes, drawing charts, talking on the phone. Ranguma[79] missed their walks in Marble Canyon, and though Ruck would occasionally seek out Pecos Louie, or the Reverend Keane, or Mehbub Ali Shah, to discuss matters of a philosophical nature, he seldom joined our larger evening get-togethers. It was as though the pressures of his life had finally caught up to him, stretching a subtle net of tension that ensnared his being.

He confided in me only twice. The first time was just before Thanksgiving, when I'd half-cajoled, half-tugged him out of the library for a late afternoon stroll up to l'Espalda. We'd begun by discussing minor matters, but halfway up the trail, when we were sweating and breathing more deeply, he opened up. He said he was beside himself, with guilt, anger and frustration, over the Ditt legislation and the prospect of going to prison. He said he'd been imprisoned three times in his life—in Kentucky, Nevada and Bolgovnia—and that nobody was going to get him back in there again.

"But what can you do," I asked, "disappear?"

"No," he said. "I mean, even if I wanted to, too many people depend on me. But at least I can buy some time."

It was then that he told me of the *Iwa* scheme. At Hilo, he said, he'd

---

79. Paws the cat had already been flown to Hawaii for pet quarantine.

bought a big trimaran and renamed it the *Iwa*.[80] He was now having it provisioned and fitted out for one-man navigation. In January he would fly to Hilo, set sail, and lose himself in the South Pacific.

"For how long?"

He shrugged, a bit helplessly, and said, "I don't know."

I asked him how big the *Iwa* was (he said 100 feet) and then how he'd possibly sail so large a boat alone.

"Piece of cake, Ethan. At the club in Hilo I met this wonderful guy named Helgo Strummer.[81] He's soloed around the world twice. He runs a cutting-edge computer think-tank on Maui. He and I are brainstorming on the phone and the Net. We're putting together a robot-skipper that'll see to every angle of navigation. It's loaded! Fail-safes, redundancies, fuzzy logic, manual override, voice commands, built-in location-finder, 19″ readout, remote access—the works! We're calling it the Merlin Box. And *that's* just for starters. We've also got a Kai'la—"

"A Kai'la?"

Ruck hemmed and hawed. "Sorry, Ethan, shouldn't have mentioned it. I promised Strummer I wouldn't discuss it till the patents went through. I mean, it's just too revolutionary."

In our absorption Ruck and I had reached l'Espalda and turned back without stopping to enjoy the view. On the way down he went on and on about the *Iwa*, waxing ecstatic and running through dozens of technical details that I've since forgotten.

In fact, I wasn't listening all that carefully. *I* was the worrier now, brooding, as Ruck spoke, over my friend's boundless faith in machines and his radical confidence in his own inventiveness. This time, I fretted, he may be going too far.

In the end, the conversation shifted to Molly. As we strode off the

---

80. Hawaiian for frigate bird. —Ed.

81. Norwegian-Swiss engineer-adventurer. His memoirs *Windward Memories* (New York: Cardanom, 2004) contain a chapter entitled "Three Days with Desmond Ruck." —Ed.

grade and back onto the ranch, Ruck brought me up to date about her progress with *The Other News* and the backup resources he was creating for her at Lomo Morado.

I didn't see Ruck again until two days later, when he'd scheduled an early-morning meeting with Augustus Randolph, Mordecai MacCrae and me. After minimal formalities Ruck asked us all to sign on, with Richard Beauchamps, who could not be present, as administrators of his last will and testament. This request seemed to echo in a shocked silence. It's not that anybody was surprised at his making a will. I guess it was just that at that moment, we all suddenly realized how much we depended on Desmond Ruck for our enthusiasm and confidence.

Without waiting long for us to respond, he went on. Of course, he said, we wouldn't be responsible for the immense White Wolf Foundation or any of the other Ruck enterprises. That job would remain with his Three Wise Men. *Our* responsibility would be to put together a permanent agency that would administer, from Ruck's inestimable and still-expanding private funds, his bequests to almost two thousand separate beneficiaries, including the students and staff at Pueblo Verde, the tutors of Magdalena Force and the denizens and associates of Lomo Morado. This agency, which would be sizeable, would handle investments and the tracking of and correspondence with beneficiaries. We four (that is, including Beauchamps) would meet quarterly as a board of directors to oversee the agency's affairs. The estate would cover all our expenses and pay us exorbitant salaries.

Ruck then patiently and carefully laid out the full details. I was impressed by the care with which he'd worked everything out.

We all agreed. Instead of shaking hands, Ruck disappeared into his walk-in liquor closet and emerged with a bottle of Calvados and four glasses. For the next two-and-a-half hours, right through lunch, he was his old self again, and the room repeatedly rang with laughter as he and Randolph teased each other about the old days in 1998 and '99, when things were just getting started.

The Most Amazing Thing

After lunch Ruck asked me to come back into his library alone. I remember glancing at my watch in the doorway and noting that—though I'm not much of a believer in luck—the digital readout, 1:23, looked portentous. Ruck had a talent for pulling surprises—even for surprising himself. What enormous Ruckery was in the making now?

In five minutes I knew, and those five minutes changed my life, and, if I and my successors can do our job decently, will change the history of American culture.

We sat down in two leather chairs near his desk, and he eyed me squarely. "Ethan, some time ago, last spring, was it, you mentioned that what this country needed was a free university. You said that, didn't you?"

I said yes, that was during one of our long phone conversations about Magdalena College, and I had told him that it was about time the U.S.A. stole a page from the great European free-education tradition.

"Well?" Ruck asked, looking as though he expected me to know the answer of some as-yet-unasked question.

"Well, what?" I shot back. Now I could feel it coming.

His eye caught an impish twinkle as he asked, "How much do you think such a university would cost?"

Trying to suppress a quaver, I told him that I thought, at current rates, you could build and run a world-class university for about a billion a year, but that the endowment would have to be large enough to allow for bad years and the periodic deflation of interest rates.

"How big an endowment would that be, Ethan?"

"Don't rush me, Desmond!"

I thought for a few seconds.

"Check my calculation," I said. "$25 billion at 8% brings in $2 billion a year. I think that that much, barring catastrophes, would be adequate for construction, yearly expenses and inflation. You might want to add a few billion for emergencies and spinoff projects. But are you really going to build this university?"

358

"No," he grinned. "*You* are! That is, if you're willing to take it on."

I couldn't respond, being suddenly choked and blinded by tears. A free university, grounded on principles of social responsibility and engagement, had been my dream for decades. I nodded my head, and managed, "Yes, yes."

Ruck went to his desk and hand-wrote and signed a memo to his Troika releasing $50 *billion* to me out of his General Fund. He then phoned Roger Gannett, his chief counsel, and asked him to make it his first priority, on receipt of these funds from me, to set up a private endowment with them, of which I was to be Chair and CEO. Finally he punched in the White Wolf's Chairmen's office phone number in Las Vegas, got Wallace Horowitz on the line, and put him in the picture. He hung up, laughing. "Wally says don't spend it all at the same joint."

Ruck put the Learjet and a pilot at my disposal, so that I could begin my project in Las Vegas that very day. Before leaving, I pleaded with him to abort his Pacific sailing voyage. I reminded him of all the projects he had in hand, how much he had to live for, how much he was needed. He shook his head. "Ethan, I feel shot. I won't be worth a hill of beans to anybody till I've seen this thing through, stayed the course and put it behind me."

"Then at least take along a crew!"

In the end he took one shipmate: Paws the cat.

I was fairly well occupied for the next few weeks. How do you build a great university? How do you manage a $50 billion endowment? I spent much of December in Las Vegas under the tutorship of the Wise Ones and their gnomes, learning the first principles of endowment management and nonprofit law. But I came back to Lomo Morado for weekends. With Rick Beauchamps in the nation's capital, Mordecai Mac-Crae with his family in California and Augustus Randolph in Hilo overseeing work on the *Iwa*, I thought Ruck needed some looking after.

During those weeks Ruck spent almost every weekday at Pueblo Verde, the school-village he'd built for his adopted children, the or-

phans of the Escondido Inferno. Of the 213 children originally en-
rolled, there were then, I think, about 175 left, the others having graduated and gone to college. Ruck had arranged for Rose Randolph to free
up groups of five of them for hour-long walks on the surrounding slopes
of Mt. Cabeza Blanca. This way he managed, over three weeks, to have
personal time with each of the kids. Mrs. Randolph insisted that each
group be photographed on their return from the slopes, and now these
thirty-odd photos hang all over the three unwindowed walls of the
school library, each showing a different assortment of children, proud
and happy, clustered around their giant stepdad. A duplicate set hangs
in the library at Lomo Morado.

This marked an exception for Desmond Ruck, who generally dis-
liked being photographed.

Recently I asked Rose what Ruck had talked about with the children
on those walks. Many things, she replied; but the one topic he never
missed was the need for each of them to create a life that mattered, not
just to others but to themselves. When asked how to do this he answered that different people would do it in different ways, but nobody
without hard work, for it took years of practice and apprenticeship before you could gain the technical and social skills necessary to be of real
service to others.

Weekends he'd return to the ranch and Shana Ladd, who was now
flying in every Friday. Saturday nights they would join Heidi, the Reverend and a few others of us for dinner. Otherwise they kept much to
themselves.

On December 21, Ruck and Ms. Ladd took off for Louisville, his
Boeing 777 loaded with recently designed rescue and medical equipment. They spent the Christmas week on the Magdalena College campus, now the training facility for Magdalena Force, which was then,
under the directorship of Robert Grauer, on its way to becoming the
world's premier rescue and relief organization. Grauer informs me that

Ruck examined every training procedure in detail and made some apt suggestions regarding both strategy and on-the-scene tactics.

Ruck returned to Lomo Morado on the 28th. It was his wish to sail out of Hilo on the 31st, before the publication of the first edition of *The Other News*, because he could not stand the shock of another scandal. He said goodbye to Ms. Ladd, who was off to see her mother in Montana, on the tarmac of the landing strip at sunset on the 28th.

This left Ruck two days to prepare for his voyage. I saw something of him during this time, of course, but we were never alone together. He actually had little enough to do, since Augustus had taken charge of things at Hilo. I'd see him strolling here and there in the company of the Reverend Keane and Heidi Frederick. Ruck was friendly, as ever, but restless, stopping to chat but then, after just a few minutes, setting forth towards some other part of his ranch, almost as though he was afraid to have seen that place or person for the last time.

An undated journal entry, probably from the night of the 30th, gives an index of his state of mind:

> Mehbub's putting in a back door for the hothouse, and a slated area outside it, so that pots can be prepared out there and won't have to be wheeled through the whole place in case they're to be put near the back.
>
> Ranguma needs a friend. Tell Catherine to find a labrador pup.
>
> Has Gus bought catfood?
>
> Tell Louie to build a 20' round tower, with a 15' diameter open platform on top, on the site of the old observation tower. We'll put a telescope up there.
>
> The Floatifer's got to be dismantled. I don't care how many hospitals want one, or how many the world needs. I just don't want it there. It gives me dreams. They're too sweet dreams and too bad dreams, and right now I can't separate the sweet from the bad.
>
> Winter here's not a cold time, but a quiet time. Nature's gone back into herself, the land is dreaming. Music. Sergei's in the living room playing Tchaikovsky. When is his family coming over? February. Everything here's

in good hands. No foul-ups, no emergencies. From that point of view, I've done OK.

Brian Turbo had a segment on me on network news tonight. He said the harassment case would be the biggest in history. He didn't have any real films of me so he showed low-quality camcorder footage from the Vegas trial. The man can't seem to get his facts straight. He called San Lorenzo Saint Lorenzo and the Floatifer a fuffle. To my credit he billed me as a philanthropist and a hero of Khakharsk, but even that's inaccurate.

Larry Flynt's published an article about the Lincoln Bedroom affair in *Penthouse* titled "The Turd that Saved Its Nation."

It's ironic that no matter how much I go through and feel and suffer, I always come across publicly as a clumsy, lucky nit.

I suppose I could live with this notoriety, if I didn't have to watch it from stir.

Shana keeps insisting to come on the boat with me, and I keep saying no. Why don't I let her ship on? Maybe it's because, if she came, it would be fun.

Am I doing penance or something?

NB, read up on GUILT. Sigmund Freud, maybe? Last December I followed up on the Rev's suggestion to ask Mordecai about guilt. When I asked him, he grinned wickedly.

"Guilt," he said, "comes in many different strengths and vintages. It's to be savored like fine wine."

"Damn you MacCrae!" I boomed out. "Talk straight to me! How does a good man think about guilt?"

He grinned. "Think of it as the shadow left by sunlight."

"*Sunlight*," I mused. "Sunlight suggests life, happiness. But how can you feel happy about things you're sorry you did?"

Mordecai caught me with riveting eyes. He meant business now. "Who says I'm sorry I did them? I'm *sorry* about things I did wrong. I'm *guilty* about things I did right. Guilt, damn it, is the residue of justice!"

This took me back to Square One again. "But why," I asked, "feel guilty about what you did right?"

He paused a moment, then entoned, "Because any powerful deed, however well meant, does damage by disrupting an established state of affairs. And because, no matter how much we know and how well we do, we're ambivalent presences in an ambiguous world."

362

I burst out, "And sleeping with 600-odd grateful ex-prostitutes, is that just? Is that powerful? Is that benevolent?"

Mordecai's brown eyes twinkled. "That depends," he said, "on whether we're talking nomika or physica." And with that he was up and out of the room.

Will I ever fathom this man? I think I'll try Freud.

On December 31, 2002, Desmond Ruck flew as a private passenger on an airline flight from Las Vegas to Hilo. On his arrival that evening he was met by Augustus Randolph. Mr. Randolph has kindly agreed to provide in his own words a record of what followed:

Narrative of Augustus Randolph

Forgive me in advance. I'm no writer. But I reckon I can tell a simple story, same as the next man. As many of you will know, I've been close to Desmond Ruck from the very day he fetched up in Las Vegas in a beat-up motor home, to the last day, maybe, he was seen by anybody on earth. I honor Desmond Ruck, I love Desmond Ruck and, most important, I miss the man. I've hoped, even to this day, that somehow he'll come back alive, and walk right into my office, and say "Gus, let's scare up some dinner." But each day that seems less about to happen.

At 4:15 PM on the last day of the year 2002 I met Mr. Ruck at the airport in Hilo. He was wearing a faded peach-colored knit tennis shirt, olive safari shorts with lots of pockets and Nike light hiking boots (though personally I feel tennis shoes give you a solider stance on deck). He greeted me warmly but didn't say a lot as we walked to the car. I'd reserved a room for him at my hotel, but he insisted on spending the night afloat in the *Iwa* on Hilo Bay, to get his sea legs as he put it.

He did though agree to have dinner with me. We drove north on Rte. 19 and found a simple place overlooking the sea. We ate Portuguese sausages and sipped microbrew. I expected Mr. Ruck to talk of old times or such-like, but instead he asked me, very politely, if I could find a paper and pen, and then he started giving me these crazy instructions—not crazy like nonsense, but crazy from the point of view that people on the ranch knew them already. Like how often the kids at the Pueblo liked field trips, and what Sergei's family would need when they came over from the Old Country, and what to do when Ranguma was off her feed, and even how the plumeria and royal palms along the path needed watering more often than the cypress and Joshua trees.

"But Desmond," I finally said, "people *know* these things already. There's no need to worry."

Then his face went so sad. "Write them down, Gus. Make sure they happen. Put my mind at rest."

It was as if he knew.

An hour later we'd picked up Paws at my hotel and were in the launch on our way out to the *Iwa*. The cat, who had bad memories respecting water, was not exactly your happy camper and took to cowering under a canvas tarp by the engine box. We drew up to the big sailboat, and Mr. Ruck climbed the ladder, and I reached him up the cat. Then I climbed aboard too, and we lit up the boat, to do inspection. Mr. Helgo Strummer, who'd done the instrumentation, was in Samoa that week, but Mr. Ruck was up to speed on those matters. He made straight for their invention, that Merlin Box, which was installed just behind the mainmast, and switched it on and put it through all its paces, though what he was doing is more than *I* can say. Then he went all through the rest of the boat and checked everything out, like a pro, right down to the diesels and the sea water conversion system and the cat-door I'd put in the main cabin. I'm not allowed to mention *everything* he checked out, but I can tell you, it was all in good working order.

When he'd finished inspecting he came up to me and put his hands on my shoulders and said I'd done a good job. I asked if I could come down in the morning to say goodbye, but he said no, that he'd be weighing anchor just after sunrise, but I could wave to him from my hotel terrace, which was just above the bay.

I didn't sleep so much that night. I turned on the TV, which had only a local channel, and kept waking up to the same show, over and over, about how brave men were digging up all the unexploded rounds of artillery ammunition on the sacred island of Kaho'olawe.[82]

Next day it dawned cloudy. I'd been dozing, and I woke because the wind started rattling the venetian blinds by my bed, just like somebody batting at

82. Kaho'olawe was used for target practice by U.S. armed forces during World War II. —Ed.

364

it with his hand. It was 7:15 AM. I got dressed, grabbed my binoculars and went out on the terrace.

Down on the boat, I could see Mr. Ruck moving here and there on the deck, making sure of things. Near 8 AM he checked his watch, went back to the cockpit and started his diesels. Then he fiddled with the Merlin Box and went off and stood by himself on the deck. What a thing! The Box took over, and the boat headed out for the ocean. Mr. Ruck looked around till he could see my motel. He raised his right hand to wave, but he held it steady, almost like somebody'd painted him there, as I waved back and the boat moved away.

Dated December 27, 2005

Augustus Randolph stayed on the island of Hawaii four more days, visiting Ruck's property there and arranging for the shipment to Lomo Morado of several indigenous plants that had been requested by Mr. and Mrs. Shah for the Lomo Morado hothouse. Then he flew back to Arizona.

The events that follow are best conveyed in calendar form:

January 2, 2003, 9:17 PM. Citing "security reasons," Desmond Ruck breaks off radio contact with the outer world.

January 3, 3 PM. At my request, the Ruck Estate administrators (Beauchamps, MacCrae, Randolph and I) meet via conference call. All are concerned about Ruck's safety. We agree that I will update them via the same medium on a weekly basis. (This conference ended with Beauchamps giving us extensive coverage of the national crisis developing out of the Carmichael suicide.)

January 8, about 10 AM. The *Iwa* is sighted by fishermen off the coast of Christmas Island. This makes Ruck heading due south at a surprising speed.

January 10, 3 PM. At the Ruck Administrators' meeting I report the sighting. MacCrae suggests that he and Beauchamps locate and "tail" Ruck's boat, shift by shift, in two planes. Beauchamps thinks this a good idea but cannot go because of the crisis and his wife's health. Randolph thinks it's a not-so-good idea, because tailing is precisely what Ruck doesn't want. I'm of two minds. The suggestion is tabled.

The Most Amazing Thing

January 12, 11:17–21 PM. Ruck's radio sends an SOS that is repeated once and then abruptly terminated. I organize a massive air-sea search, coordinated by Robert Grauer of Magdalena Force.

January 13–15. A freak typhoon of enormous size sweeps across the Pacific in Ruck's path, delaying the search.

January 16. The search begins in earnest.

January 20, 12 noon. Cuthbert Nelson discovers the *Iwa* dismasted, drifting about 1000 miles west southwest of the Galápagos Islands. Paws the cat is aboard and alive, but there is no sign of Ruck.

January 26. The search for Desmond Ruck is abandoned.

January 29. MacCrae and I fly to Panama City to examine the wreck. Before leaving I contact Strummer, who has returned from Samoa to his home on Maui. Strummer reports that his last word from Ruck, on January 10, recorded on voice mail, was the curt declaration that the *Iwa* was turning east. No explanation.

Why had Ruck turned east? MacCrae and I conjectured about this as we flew to Panama, but there were simply too many open questions.

A few of these were answered when we saw the boat. Captain Nelson (who was helpful and courteous in spite of his own injury and the loss of a crewman) had had the *Iwa* hoisted onto a drydock. As we walked around it and then over its shattered deck, the hulk spoke volumes. Desmond Ruck had not left the *Iwa* by choice, nor had he abandoned it in a storm. The upper hull on the port side was laced with bullets from automatic weapons. On deck we worked our way through the jungle of tangled lines that the storm had made out of Ruck's elaborate automatic navigating system. There was a blackened hole, about six feet wide, in the deck directly in front of the mainmast, from an explosion that toppled the mast directly aft, crushing and destroying the Merlin Box. Looking down through the hole you could clearly see right through the hull to the drydock floor.

Only its packing of flotation material had prevented the *Iwa* from sinking to the bottom of the Pacific.

We examined the main cabin and the rest of the boat. The *Iwa* had been ransacked, gutted. And theft hadn't been the motive. Valuable pieces of equipment lay scattered among the clothing, toiletries and cookery.

It wasn't until almost dark that MacCrae discovered Ruck's laptop. He'd pulled a rubber mat from the floor of the carpet and noticed a faint indentation in the decking which, when pried up, revealed the receptacle of our friend's last words. More on that shortly.

Paws, Nelson told us, had "come out of the woodwork" two days after the towing began. Nelson's mate, Honus Stout, retrieved the animal from the sailboat and took it under his special care, feeding it canned chicken soup.

But all this is two years ago. Two years have passed since we left the wreck of Desmond's dreams and brought Paws back to Lomo Morado. It's almost a year since Mordecai MacCrae gave up his intensive search of the Pacific Islands. Shana Ladd continues her own independent search, and was last heard from in Kwajalein.

I return to Lomo Morado quite often, and indeed have not far to go. The walls of the Free University of America are rising on a 2000-acre campus just north of the Cerveza Blanca. Aside from the absence of its genius loci, Lomo Morado is not much changed. As it ages, in fact, the place seems even more beautiful, a tribute to the unified vision and stylistic intuition of its founder. As Ruck wished, Richard Beauchamps has taken charge of operations. He and Molly left Washington, DC, after handing over the reins of *The Other News* to its new editor, Beeper Fennel, and its new publisher, Smytha Carmichael (whose decision to do investigative reporting was made shortly after the successful publication of her memoirs, *My Other Life*). Wilbur Lapham has returned to the ranch to assist Col. Beauchamps in his administrative duties.

Last May, at his own suggestion, the journalist Axel Fanshawe arrived at Lomo Morado with the intention of writing a definitive biography of Desmond Ruck. He remains here, busy with his research and interviews.

The Most Amazing Thing

Though Myrdal Hwang is on the Most Wanted list in 93 countries, his whereabouts remain unknown. Some rumors have him conducting his affairs from the control deck of a U.S.S.R.-era atomic submarine, while others—though these are barely credible—put him on his own spaceship.

Let me update a few more records, with apologies if I omit anything of importance:

Shortly after MacCrae and Ladd left on their trans-Pacific searches, Helgo Strummer visited Lomo Morado and spent several days aiding us in our inquiries. Now in his early seventies, he has sailed many seas and is rich in lore. He enlightened us about the intricacies of solo sailing and impressed all with his learning and compassion. When we asked him about the mysterious "Kai'la," he would respond only that it was a "conveyance still under development." A conveyance! And missing from the wreck! This means 1) that Ruck and the machine were taken together, or 2) that he was killed and the machine taken, or 3) that he escaped alive on the machine and was later lost at sea. After a telephone conference with MacCrae, we agreed that 3) was most likely. After all, if Ruck's assailants had him and the machine, why would they ransack the *Iwa*? And if they took him for ransom, why wouldn't they have offered him back for sale?

The Reverend Howard Keane and Heidi Frederick were married at Lomo Morado in April, 2003, and are living happily at Nevil Castle, where they engage in charitable activities.

Ruck's large-scale acts of philanthropy, implemented both abroad and at home (see the note at the end of Chapter 11, Book 2) are in the process of changing the social face of the world.

Pueblo Verde is down to 53 students, the rest having graduated. Richard Beauchamps has OK'd a proposal by Rose Randolph to open the school-village to disadvantaged orphans from all over the world.

Ruck's financial enterprises continue to flourish, driving his net worth to heights that even he would gape at. His Three Wise Men,

Rousseau, Horowitz and Clemens, were awarded two Nobel Prizes (Economics and Peace) in 2004 for their role in the economic stabilization of the Third World.

Ruck's notorious invention, the so-called Honolulu Floatifer, has been adopted (with certain modifications) for the treatment of burn victims by 301 major hospitals. Sales to private parties are rocketing.

Ruck's wards, Vi and Vicki, the infamously abused daughters of Art Thrumble and an unknown woman, are now, respectively, the Grand Duchess of Bohemia and the Crown Princess of Moldavia.

The Beauchamps vineyards on the slopes of the Cabeza Blanca have begun producing a highly touted cabernet sauvignon grape. Richard and Molly are enlarging their adobe house by the vineyards in anticipation of the birth of twins.

Pecos Louie and Double Mocha, now known as Louis and Celita Powell, are the proud parents of a baby boy, Desmond Ruck Powell.

Sergei Oistropovich and Bituminous Newton are on a world tour as a jazz-classical combo. Sergei's wife and two children live at Lomo Morado.

Rescue workers recovered the bodies of Klaus Sturm and Karrel Barda from the ruins of the Bishop's Palace in Khakharsk, Bolgovnia. No trace of Thea Sturm was found.

Boris Karachayeffsky, the Georgian peasant who had been kidnapped by Jazeps Guradich to act as Ruck's double, was released from Bolgovnian custody after the intervention of the Georgian consul. He later emigrated to the United States and now assists the Shahs in the gardens and hothouse of Lomo Morado.

Glynda Jezra, the ex–Mrs. Ruck, has filed suit for the rights to the Ruck Journals. She claims that her husband, Dr. Frank Jezra, ran away with all her money and that she is indigent.

Ranguma is alive but hardly well. The glaze of her eye, the slouch of her gait, the very droop of her ears bespeak clinical depression. The only glints of her former joie de vivre appear when she sports occasionally with Paws the cat, or when Rick Beauchamps takes her on walks up Marble Canyon or to l'Espalda, which I sometimes join.

After the presidential crisis and world financial turmoil of early 2003 had died down, the media turned their attention to Ruck's case. Hundreds of articles and TV segments devoted themselves to the possible identity of his attackers. These were followed by the predictable documentaries and—I've lost count how many—feature films about his life and disappearance. But amidst this flurry of speculation and reenactment not a single shred of valid evidence as to Ruck's whereabouts, alive or dead, has been uncovered; and of the hundred-odd reported Ruck-sightings on every continent, none has yielded substance.

Finally, a word, and no more than a word, about the draconian Governor, Diane Ditt. Her maniacal crusade against Ruck, which caused him to flee the continent out of panic and guilt, was itself cut short by her sudden death, and most of her followers in the Arizona state house quickly turned coat and abandoned her legislation. I refuse to dignify her memory with further comment.

I will leave you with Desmond Ruck's poignant last words, retrieved from a computer file dated 1/10/03. Note that the change in course he decides on at the end of this passage would have left him facing north. My guess is that that course brought him into view of a craft that had been following him, and that, catching sight of it, he took evasive action by heading for the eastward fog bank now on his starboard side.

Noon. I sail over long swells on a sea that looks like molten lapis lazuli and feels like God's meadow. For an hour this morning I stood in the bow, with nothing in front of me but the buffeting beckoning sea. The view ahead was majestic. To my left and within about ½ mile was an immense bank of haze, soft but impenetrable, seeming to hold a universe of mystery, while to my right, the west, the sea stretched forever in an endless cavalcade of living valleys and hills, under the tremendous sun. Standing there I must have gone into a zone. Was I travelling in space, or in time? In space, for sure: I was headed south at about ten knots. But in a spacy way I was traveling in time too, not forward or backward, but more like into the very heart of time, into the sun and wetness that make all life and action on earth. You could feel, even *taste*, the sun and water mating in the air.

My soul started gulping it in. I began to heal. The healing didn't come in words. Au contraire. The healing came right out of the sun and sea and air, and the sudden sensation, the awareness that I was *part of them*, came not from the brain but flooded up through my body. I was part of this, and living was a joy.

Now I sit writing in the cockpit. The sun is right overhead, I cast no shadow. I'm nothing. I'm nothing but a tiny droplet of sea evaporating, in no time at all, into the sunny air. Thank you, Mordecai. I accept my guilt. What's important? *The beauty.*

I'm going back. I've made big mistakes, and almost died for them, but I'll be born again to laughter and make others smile too. I'm turning around and sailing home. My children are missing me, and the trellises need tending to, and I want to see Shana and have my own children with her. I understand at last. Life isn't about how much you matter to people. Life's about what matters to you. And everything matters. *Everything has a story.* It's the most amazing thing. Heidi, I've done it! Ditt, put up your dukes! I'm coming about and heading north.[83]

---

83. I appreciate the strength of Dr. Zoig's sentiment but nonetheless feel it incumbent on myself to offer at least a few details about the sudden death of Governor Ditt, who was after all a famous person of her time. She passed from us while attending a governors' conference in Florence, Italy. While on a guided tour of the famous Piazza della Signoria, she suffered a massive stroke and dropped to the pavement. She was rushed to the emergency room of the Florence Hospital, but efforts to revive her were futile. Diane Dorothy Ditt was forty-nine. Her loss was acknowledged by many testimonials from the great and famous. Admirers wishing to pay their respects in Florence will find a small brass cross set into the pavement at the spot where she fell, which is near the southeast corner of the Piazza, directly in front of Michelangelo Buonarotti's famous statue, the *David*. —Ed.

INDEX

Index

Index

Estes, Mr. and Mrs. Founders of Estes
Park, Ch. 5

Estes Park, CO. Ruck breakfasts in,
Ch. 6, Part 1

Ethiopia. Location of Ruck charity,
Ch. 10, Part 1

Everham Grange. Orphanage near Nevil
Castle, Ch. 10, Part 2

Facade. Book about US foundations,
Ch. 9

*Falcke v. the Scottish Imperial Insurance
Co.* Case referred to during Salvage
Defense, Ch. 10, Part 1

Fanshawe, Axel. Journalist researching
Our Beloved, Ch. 9

Farnacle, Titus. Ruck's uncle, Ch. 1

FARNACLE'S. Titus's department
store, Ch. 1

Farrukh. Ali's nephew, Ch. 2

Father Angelo. Guradich associate, Ch. 12

Father Feeny. Tucson divine, Ch. 11,
Part 1

FBI. Pursues Ruck, Ch. 9

Fennel, Beeper. Network anchorwoman,
Ch. 10, Part 1

Fenny, Michael. Scholar who assists
Ruck, Ch. 9

Ferdinand of Moldavia. Courts Viola
Ruck, Ch. 11, Part 2

Fez, Morocco. Site of Ruck's Moroccan
offices, Ch. 11, Part 1

First Inner Thigh. Body part, Ch. 11,
Part 2

First Umbilical Fundamentalist. Group
connected with Myrdal Hwang, Ch. 9

Flatirons Park. Colorado location visited
by Ruck, Ch. 6, Part 2

Fleem, Buster. Radio reporter, Ch. 7,
Part 2

Flo. Member of Womuba Twelve, Ch. 3

Floatifer. Ruck's famous invention,
Ch. 10, Part 2

Floatifer Law. Anti-Ruck Arizona legislation, Book 2, Introduction

Flora, Miss. English teacher who helps
Augustus Randolph, Ch. 7, Part 2

Florence, Italy. Location of unfortunate
event, Ch. 14

Flynt, Larry. Magazine publisher, Ch. 14

Fosbert, Capt. Phillips. White House
aide, Ch. 11, Part 2

Fox, Georgia. Police officer, Ch. 2

Franco, Francisco. Spanish dictator, Ch. 12

Freda's Fresh Feeds. Estes Park restaurant, Ch. 6, Part 1

Frederick, Heidi. Social worker, Ch. 3

Freedom of Soul, International (FOSI).
Myrdal Hwang's organization, Ch. 9

Free University of America. Founded by
Desmond Ruck, Ch. 14

Freud, Sigmund. Founder of psychoanal-
ysis and authority on sexuality, Ch. 11,
Part 1

Froehling, General Benton. Chairman,
Joint Chiefs of Staff, Ch. 11, Part 2

Fuck, Desmond. Mega's term of abuse,
Ch. 11, Part 1

Gable, Clark. Star of *Gone with the
Wind*, Ch. 4

Galapaga. Chilean princess, Ch. 2

Galápagos Islands. Vicinity of a maritime
sighting, Ch. 14

Gannett, Roger. Ruck's chief legal council, Ch. 10, Part 1

376

Index

Index

Los Padres National Forest. Horseback riding in, Ch. 13

Lothario. Any unscrupulous male seducer (from Nicholas Rowe's play, *The Fair Penitent*), Ch. 11, Part 1

Louisville, KY. Vixen repaired there, Ch. 4

Lutinius, rebel bishop, Ch. 12

Lyons, CO. Vicinity of The Broken Arms, Ch. 9

Macbeth. Legendary tyrant immortalized by Shakespeare's eponymous play, Ch. 12

MacCrae, Barbara. Mystery writer, married to Modecai, Ch. 13

MacCrae, Mordecai. Policeman, Ch. 3

MacPherson Road. Ruck bikes along it in Ch. 6, Part 1

Madonna. Actress, Ch. 3

Magdalena College. College for ex-prostitutes founded by Ruck, Ch. 9

Magdalena Force. International rescue and relief force founded by Ruck, Ch. 13

Magdalena Trace. Slang name for a trail between Casa Morada and Ruck's shop, Ch. 11, Part 1

Maine cooncat. Toys with finch, Ch. 11, Part 2

Mao Zedong. Chinese dictator, Ch. 12

Marble Canyon. One of Ruck's favorite haunts, Ch. 8

Marcos, Ferdinand. Philippine strongman, Ch. 12

Marshall Plan. Post-WW2 US assistance to Europe, Ch. 11, Part 2

Marvin, Lee. Movie actor, Ch. 9

Marvin Gardens. Valuable property in the game Monopoly, Ch. 1

Marx, Karl. Political philosopher, Ch. 11, Part 1

Matahari. Famous female spy, Ch. 11, Part 2

Maui. Hawaiian island, Ch. 14

Maulwurf, Rainer. Professor at Magdalena College, Ch. 11, Part 1

Melanesia. South Pacific area, Ch. 13

Merlin Box. Automatic navigating and sailing contraption, Ch. 14

Metropolitan Museum of Art. Rose favors area, Ch. 11, Part 2

Michelangelo. Renaissance artist, Ch. 14

Microsoft Corporation. Potential monopoly, Ch. 11, Part 2

Miller, Henry. American author noted for explicit sexuality, Ch. 11, Part 1

Mills, Enos. Founder, Rocky Mountain National Park, Ch. 10, Part 2

Milly Beth. Curtis Crouse's secretary, Ch. 7, Part 2

Milosevic, Slobodan. Serbian strongman, Ch. 12

Mirasoles, Colombia. Site of confessional, Ch. 13

Moake Mountains, New Guinea. Scene of Dr. Bevan Slattery's strange adventure, Ch. 5

Mobile, AL. Where Augustus Randolph went to school, Ch. 7, Part 2

Mohammed. Founder of Islam, Ch. 3

Moldavia, Princess of. Ruck relative, Ch. 13

Monsieur. *See* Imbratta, Michelangelo

380

Index

Olivier, Laurence. British actor, Ch. 10, Part 1

Omnium, Ltd. Stock used to buy business, Ch. 7, Part 2

Oral Office. Smytha Carmichael's mocking term for Oval Office, Ch. 11, Part 2

Other News, The. Beauchamps newspaper, Ch. 13

Ould Chattox, Member of the Lupus Coven, Ch. 6, Part 1

Ould Demdike, Member of the Lupus Coven, Ch. 6, Part 1

Ould Redfearn, Member of the Lupus Coven, Ch. 6, Part 1

Paco. Driver for Duke's, Ch. 7, Part 2

Paganini, Niccolo. Famed Italian violinist and composer, Ch. 10, Part 1

Pakistan. Birthplace of Ali, Ch. 2

Palio, Simon. Undersecretary of the US Treasury, Ch. 10, Part 1

Panama City. Home port of Cuthbert Nelson's *Vettie*, Publisher's Introduction

Papa Doc. Haitian strongman, Ch. 12

Passaic, NJ. Home of Mehbub Ali Shah Happy Motors, Ch. 2

Patchogue, NY. Site of Imbratta residence, Ch. 11, Part 3

Patrice. Farnacle servant, Ch. 1

Patterson, Floyd. Heavyweight boxing champion, Ch. 6, Part 2

Pavarotti, Luciano. Operatic tenor, Ch. 3

Paws. Thrumble cat, Ch. 4

Pecos Louie. Hermetic poet, Ch. 7, Part 1

"Pecos Louie's Poem to Double Mocha's Left Breast." Work of literary art, Ch. 9

Pedro. One of the Womuba Twelve, Ch. 3

Penthouse Magazine. Refers to Ruck, Ch. 14

Penumbra Hotel. Coloradan retreat, Ch. 6, Part 1

Perón, Juan. President of Argentina, Ch. 12

Phil. Physician-patient, Ch. 5

physikon. Aristotelian term used in Salvage Defense, Ch. 10, Part 1

Piazza della Signoria. Square in Florence, Ch. 14

Pick-Up-Sticks. Children's game, Ch. 12

Pillar of Fire Church. Hackensack landmark, Ch. 1

Pilotsburg, KY. Ruck jailed there, Ch. 3

Pinewood Springs, CO. Scene of accident, Ch. 9

Pinochet Ugarte, Augusto. Chilean dictator, Ch. 12

Platinum Jayne. Rock star and religious thinker, Ch. 3

Pomo Indian Reservation. Temporary home for Escondido orphans, Ch. 7, Part 2

Portland, OR. Collections agency housed there, Editor's Note

Potemkin Suite. Ruck's rooms in the Hotel Oriental, Ch. 12

Powell, Desmond R. Their child, Ch. 14

Powell, Louis and Celita. Ruck friends, Ch. 14

Prokofiev, Sergei. Russian composer, Ch. 13

Index

Index

Index

WITHDRAWN

THE WILD WEST

GUNSLINGERS AND COWBOYS

ARCTURUS

ARCTURUS

This edition first published in 2015 by Arcturus Publishing

Distributed by Black Rabbit Books
P.O. Box 3263
Mankato
Minnesota MN 56002

Text: Frederick Nolan
Design: Chris Bell
Cover design: Akihiro Nakayama
Original concept design: Keith Williams
Project editors: JMS books
Project manager: Joe Harris

Cataloging-in-Publication Data is available from the Library of Congress

ISBN: 978-1-78404-078-9

Printed in China

SL003858US
Supplier 29, Date 0514, Print Run 3421

THE WILD WEST

GUNSLINGERS AND COWBOYS

A Bad Hoss (*Charles Marion Russell, 1864–1926*).

"A decent cowboy does not take what belongs
to someone else and if he does he deserves to be
strung up and left for the flies and coyotes."

Judge Roy Bean.

CONTENTS

INTRODUCTION

WHEN THE UNION Pacific Railroad was formed by the connection of the existing Central Pacific and Union Pacific railroads in 1869, the West truly opened up. As more and more Euro-American emigrants poured in, homesteaders staked their claims for land to farm and live on, and new towns were founded, including the so-called cow towns that served as centers for the cattle industry. With the expansion of the cattle business came the cowhands or cowboys, the men who worked on the ranches and drove vast herds across the country for the cattle "barons." After spending months on the trail with only cows for company, they were more than ready to spend their hard-earned wages in the saloons and dance halls of the new frontier towns.

Some of these towns, like Dodge City and Tombstone, became notorious,

Meeting of the engines on the completion of the first railroad to the Pacific in 1869.

acquiring a reputation for crime and lawlessness—places where disputes were settled with a gun in typical "shoot first, ask questions later" fashion. It was not always easy for the elected town sheriffs and marshals to keep law and order and "decent" citizens were sometimes forced to hire "gunfighters" or "gunslingers" to keep the peace. They could be experienced lawmen, like Wyatt Earp and Bat Masterson, or known "man-killers" like John Wesley Hardin—and sometimes the line between the two began to seem a little blurred.

As rancher and gunfighter Clay Allison said, when accused of the murder of fifteen men: "I have at all times tried to use my influence toward protecting the property holders and substantial men of the country from thieves, outlaws, and murderers, among whom I do not care to be classed."

RAILROADS AND COW TOWNS

Railroad building on the great plains.

THE RAILROAD COMES TO TOWN

IT WAS AN EVENT THAT TOOK

PLACE ON MAY 10, 1869, NORTH OF THE GREAT SALT LAKE AT PROMONTORY SUMMIT, UTAH, THAT GENERAL WILLIAM TECUMSEH SHERMAN PROPHESIED WOULD "BRING THE INDIAN PROBLEM TO A final solution": the completion of the transcontinental railroad. Four celebratory rail spikes, replicas of those that actually secured the rails in position—two gold, one silver, and one a blend of gold, silver, and iron—were tapped in place. Then a fifth, iron spike was hammered down by Leland Stanford, formally joining together the two great railroads—the west–east Central Pacific of which he was president and the east–west Union Pacific—to form the Union Pacific Railroad.

"GOLD, SILVER, AND Other Miners!" the advertising flyers screamed, "Now is the time to seek your Fortunes in Nebraska, Wyoming, Arizona, Washington, Dakotah, Colorado, Utah, Oregon, Montana, New Mexico, Idaho, Nevada, or California!" And they came, fortune seekers and sodbusters, adventurers and vagrants, fighting men and fools. Now, more than ever before, America

☞ *Railroads meet at the Golden Spike ceremony.*

was moving west. Even as the Union Pacific line was completed, its eastern division, renamed the Kansas Pacific, was already spearing across the plains toward Denver, Colorado. From Topeka, Kansas another line, the AT&SF (Atchison, Topeka and Santa Fe Railway), was aiming southwest toward Santa Fe and down the valley of the Rio Grande to El Paso, Texas. Others would follow: Northern Pacific, Denver Pacific, Texas and Pacific, Denver and Rio Grande, Burlington and Missouri.

William F. Cody.

and bring in the meat, and the problem was solved. Soon buffalo hunting to supply food for the railroad workers had become a full-time occupation and many frontiersmen made it their living, among them Wild Bill Hickok, Wyatt Earp, Bartholomew "Bat" Masterson, and the young William F. Cody, who killed around four thousand animals in just over a year, earning him his famous nickname "Buffalo Bill."

The workers hired to build these lines were a tough, rowdy crew, many of them Irish, men who lived hard, drank hard, and needed a good square meal three times a day. The farther west the railroad went, the more difficult it was to ship food to the laborers (the first refrigerated railroad car was not built until 1869). A solution was soon found. Out there on the endless plains were millions of buffalo, prime meat on the hoof. All the railroad builders needed to do was hire men to kill them

The need to feed the graders and surveyors, the sections gangs, navvies, and gandy dancers, along with those involved in the buffalo hide trade that resulted from the wholesale slaughter, was more damaging to the Native American peoples than any disease or war. It deprived them of their major food source. A further step in the eventual containment and repression of all the Native American peoples was made in 1871 when Congress passed the Indian Appropriation Act, which invalidated all existing treaties with the Native Americans and made them wards of the federal government.

BUFFALO HUNTERS

THE U.S. GOVERNMENT MADE

NO FORMAL COMMENT ON THE KILLING OF THE BUFFALO HERDS AND IT MADE NO EFFORT TO CONTAIN OR CONTROL IT. YEAR BY YEAR, THE SLAUGHTER ACCELERATED. IN THE EAST OF THE COUNTRY, manufacturers developed techniques for converting buffalo hides into soft leather for shoes, belts, and carriage hoods. Men who could use guns—and most could—did the math: if there were twenty million buffalo and a hide was worth three dollars, then $60 million was wandering about on the plains. All you needed was a buffalo gun and some cartridges—an investment of around $100 that could earn twenty times that in as many weeks. Big money in a time when a hired hand was paid a dollar a day.

THE BUFFALO HUNTERS altered their methods accordingly. Now only the hides were taken from the dead buffalo: the rest of the carcass was left to rot on the prairies. It was said that the Kansas Pacific was lined with buffalo carcasses on both sides for two hundred miles. The new railroads inching westward across Kansas provided an easy service for getting the hides to the eastern markets quickly and cheaply. In the year 1872–73, following the introduction of a new, powerful, heavy bullet that could drop a buffalo dead in its tracks, it was estimated that around 1,500,000 buffalo hides were sent east on the Kansas railroads alone. Right alongside them, as part of a new industry, went thousands

Buffalo lying dead in the snow, left behind by the hide hunters.

Shooting buffalo on the Kansas Pacific Railroad.

of Texas cattle on their way to the slaughterhouses of Kansas City to provide prime beef steak for the dinner tables of the eastern cities.

Cut off from the prewar markets by the Union blockade of southern ports during the American Civil War, Texas ranchers had become established on the Gulf of Mexico and the number of cattle running wild in Texas had multiplied, so that by 1865 there were around six million of them in the country around San Antonio, Corpus Christi, and Laredo. Fully grown steers fetched such a cheap price that it was hardly worth the expense of rounding them up and driving them to market.

As early as 1866, Charles Goodnight, the son of a dirt farmer who had served as a scout for the Texas Rangers during the war, had realized the only way to make any money with these unwanted cattle was to try to take them north to better markets, to the new reservations where the army had to provide food for the Native Americans who lived there, and to the booming mining towns where fresh beef brought a decent price. He enlisted the aid of Oliver Loving, a man nearly twice his age who had taken Texas cattle north as far as Chicago before the war. Together they blazed a long trail from Texas to the new reservation at Fort Sumner in New Mexico, then beyond that to the mining camps in Colorado, and later still, as far as Wyoming.

BOOM OF THE COW TOWNS

THE REAL REVOLUTION IN THE

CATTLE BUSINESS BEGAN WITH A FARSIGHTED ENTREPRENEUR NAMED JOSEPH G. MCCOY—THE ORIGINAL "REAL MCCOY." HE REALIZED THAT IF THE TEXAS CATTLE THAT WERE NORMALLY DRIVEN TO Missouri or eastern Kansas were brought to the new railhead towns on the plains, they could be shipped directly by train to the huge eastern markets crying out for supplies of fresh meat. McCoy went to St. Louis to get backing for his scheme. The Missouri Pacific threw him out, the Union Pacific was no more than lukewarm, but the Hannibal and St. Joseph Railroad proved more positive, a reaction that resulted in Kansas City's displacing St. Louis as the major market for Texas cattle.

IN 1867 McCOY purchased the townsite of Abilene for $2,400. He won over local opposition to Texas cattle, laid out stockyards and loading facilities, and built a hotel that could sleep eighty guests. After distributing adverts to dozens of towns in the southwest announcing the new facilities, he sent a stockman down to Texas to persuade more drovers to come to Abilene. In the region of forty thousand cattle arrived in the town that year and would soon be followed by hundreds of thousands more.

Abilene was the first cattle town—"cow town" was the more usual term—but there would be

The Texas cattle trade: cutting out a calf from the herd.

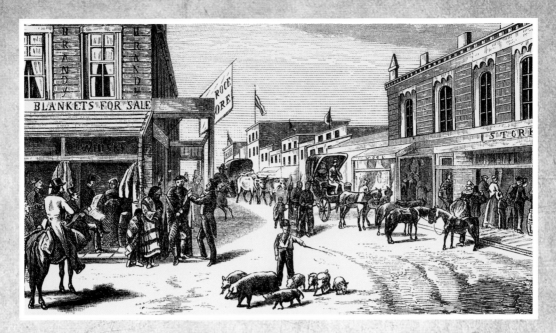

👉 *A street in Wichita, Kansas, in around 1880.*

plenty of others, with names that still resonate today: Ellsworth, Newton, Wichita, Caldwell, Hays, Ogallala, Cheyenne, and most memorably of all, Dodge City, the "cowboy capital." Each attracted merchants, businessmen, bankers, and "decent" families. And in every city, on "the wrong side of the tracks," were gamblers, saloon-keepers, and prostitutes, all waiting to separate the cowboys from their hard-earned wages.

Each of these towns became busy hubs of activity until the railroad—and the cattle—moved on, when they collapsed into rural backwaters once more, in a sort of boom-and-bust pattern. The story of Abilene is a perfect illustration of the rise and fall of the cow town. After the first trail herds arrived, it began to grow and kept growing. Where there had been a scattering of log huts and a few outlying farms, larger buildings began to appear. By 1870 there were four hotels, ten boarding houses, five general stores, and ten saloons. With a couple of exceptions, they were all one story high in the style peculiar to the frontier town—they had a "false front," a wooden facade designed to fool the onlooker into believing the building was two stories high.

The town's principal meeting place, favored by the Texas ranchers and the local movers and shakers, was Drover's Cottage on Main Street. Built by Joseph McCoy and run by J. W. Gore and his wife, it was three stories high

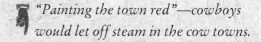 *Drover's Cottage, Abilene, a popular meeting place.*

later known as "The Gun that Won the West"—or similar weapon holstered on their right hip. After months on the trail with only cows for company, they were ready to have a good time and spend every cent they had earned on the drive in the shortest possible time. Their order of priorities was simple: get cleaned up, go out on the town, and get drunk. They drank their liquor straight and were prone to settling arguments with bullets (no self-respecting cowboy ever fought with his fists). And waiting for them—and their cash—was the cow town, an oasis of color in the drab landscape of the cowboy's life.

with a hundred rooms and an adjacent barn that could hold up to a hundred horses and fifty carriages if required.

At first, the cowboys who came in with the herds virtually took over the town, riding from saloon to saloon (no self-respecting cowboy ever walked across a street), wide-brimmed Stetsons—the large, high-crowned cowboy hat of choice—thrown back, their big Mexican spurs jingling, a Colt .45 revolver—

"Painting the town red"—cowboys would let off steam in the cow towns.

WILD BILL, "PRINCE OF PISTOLEERS"

Cowboys Coming to Town for Christmas
(Frederic Remington, 1861–1909).

THE LAW MEN

ALTHOUGH COW TOWNS WERE

NOT AS VIOLENT AS MYTH HAS PAINTED THEM—THERE WERE NO VIOLENT DEATHS IN ABILENE DURING THE FIRST TWO YEARS, FOR EXAMPLE—THERE WAS AN ABSENCE OF LAW AND ORDER. THE ONLY WAY "decent" citizens could contain the worst excesses and "tame" the cowboys was to employ "man-killers"—gunfighters with the reputation of shooting first and asking questions later, men whose mere appearance on the scene could avert an impending gunfight or quell a drunken mob.

THESE LAWMEN— town police chiefs— walked a fine line between keeping the unruly element under control and the merchants and saloon-keepers happy. Some of them were fine men, honest and brave. Others were much less fine and a few of them would probably be described as psychopaths today. Their lives have been frequently portrayed in print, and in films and on TV—grossly inaccurately, more often than not.

"Bear River" Tom Smith.

and then to Tombstone, Arizona; men like Wild Bill Hickok, who kept the law in Hays and Abilene; and others like the Masterson brothers, Henry Brown, Mike Meagher, Billy Tilghman, "Mysterious" Dave Mather, and Charlie Bassett. It was men like these who gave birth to the modern legend of the gunfighter, the lone lawman facing a killer on a dusty street at high noon. That this kind of movie-style confrontation never happened is irrelevant: as one historian observed, if enough people are prepared to believe something—true or false—it's a fact.

Men like Wyatt Earp and his brothers Morgan and Virgil, for instance, who moved from Wichita to Dodge City

Abilene got its first taste of law and order in September 1869, when a law was passed by the town council making it illegal to carry a deadly weapon inside the city limits. Signs prominently posted to this effect were very quickly shot to pieces by the very cowboys who were meant to obey them and when a jail was built, it was torn down.

Abilene's next marshal was Patrick Hand, a gunsmith; he was replaced by Smith's deputy, James McDonald. Before long, however, to quote the Abilene *Chronicle*, "every principle of right and justice was at a discount. No man's life or property was safe from the murderous intent and lawless invasions of Texans." With a new cattle season

 The saloon, a popular place for cowboys to let off steam.

The city fathers decided that Abilene needed someone with a firm hand and in June 1870 hired "Bear River" Tom Smith, who had earned his nickname in a skirmish with vigilantes in mining country. Born in New York in 1840, he had worked for the Union Pacific Railroad in Nebraska and later at boom-and-bust Bear River City, Wyoming, where he became the town's first law officer. In October 1870, Smith was shot through the chest while trying to arrest two men accused of murder.

imminent, the city fathers decided to fill the law-enforcement vacuum by bringing in the most famous gunfighter of his day, James Butler "Wild Bill" Hickok. "The law-abiding citizens decided upon a change, and it was thought best to fight the devil with his own weapons," said the *Chronicle*. "Accordingly, Marshal Hickok, known as 'Wild Bill,' was elected marshal."

WILD BILL HICKOK

JAMES BUTLER HICKOK BEGAN life on May 27, 1837, on a farm in Homer (later Troy Grove), Illinois. At nineteen he joined James H. Lane's "Free State Army" in Kansas and served for a year, reportedly as the general's bodyguard. Already becoming known for his skill with firearms, he was elected constable of Monticello, Kansas, in March 1858, but left later that year and worked as a teamster for stagecoach and mail firm Russell, Majors and Waddell. In 1861, while assigned to Rock Creek Station, Nebraska, he was involved in a fight with David McCanles in which McCanles and two other men were killed. The encounter was grossly exaggerated in an article in *Harper's New Monthly Magazine* and it went on to make Wild Bill Hickok famous.

DURING THE AMERICAN Civil War, Hickok served as a wagonmaster, scout, sharpshooter, and spy; there are almost as many legends as facts surrounding this period of his life. After the war he settled in Springfield, Missouri, where in 1865 he killed Davis Tutt in a duel in the town's main square. The following year he made his way to Fort Riley, Kansas, where he worked as a scout and guide and also served as deputy U.S. marshal.

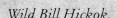

Hickok also became acquainted with General George A. Custer at Fort Riley and scouted both for Custer and General W. S. Hancock on the latter's campaign against the Plains peoples in 1867. Custer took a liking

Wild Bill Hickok.

An illustration from the Harper's Magazine *article that first made Hickok's name.*

to Hickok and Custer's wife said he was "a delight to look upon." Hickok's appearance was certainly eyecatching. He was handsome, tall, and lithe, with long hair, and an impressive handlebar moustache, after the fashion of the times.

By the time he had been appointed Ellis County sheriff, in Kansas, at a special election in August 1869, cheap novels describing his fictional adventures were encouraging would-be badmen to test him. In August 1869, he killed a cavalryman named Bill Mulvey, and the following month teamster Samuel Strawhun, who was creating a disturbance. Both killings were considered justified. The following year he killed a soldier, John Kile, and wounded another in a saloon fight in Hays City and hastily quit that locality.

THE HICKOK–TUTT DUEL

On July 21, 1865, in the town square of Springfield, Missouri, Hickok killed former Confederate Army soldier Davis Tutt after an argument about gambling debts. This stand-up, quick-draw gunfight was later popularized in fiction as typical, but it was in fact the first on record in the gunfighting era. Rather than the face-to-face, fast-draw fight commonly portrayed in movies, the two men faced each other sideways, about seventy-five yards apart, drawing and aiming their weapons before firing simultaneously. Tutt missed, but Hickok didn't and Tutt was killed instantly. Two days later, Hickok was arrested for murder (the charge was later reduced to manslaughter). He was released on $2,000 bail and stood trial on August 3, 1865. At first, the jury was told that a conviction was the only option, but were later informed by the judge that they could vote under the unwritten law of the "fair fight" for an acquittal, which they duly did.

On April 15, 1871, Hickok became marshal of Abilene where, on October 5, 1871, while breaking up a drunken brawl outside the Alamo Saloon, he mortally wounded gambler Phil Coe. During the shoot-out, another man brandishing a pistol ran between the two opponents and the edgy Hickok killed him, too. Later it was discovered that the unfortunate man was Mike Williams, a special policeman hired to keep the Texans from pestering the dancers at Abilene's Novelty Theater. Hickok is said to have never fired his gun at another man again.

Hickok's grave in Deadwood, South Dakota.

Bill's Wild West show. He settled in Cheyenne, Wyoming, where he guided hunting parties, and on March 5, 1876, married Agnes Lake. After their honeymoon he joined a mining party going to Deadwood, South Dakota. There, on August 2, 1876, he was shot in the back of the head by drunken gambler Jack McCall while playing poker. Unusually, Hickok had not been in his habitual position with his back to the wall. The cards he was holding at the time—black aces, black eights, and the jack of diamonds—have been known as the "Dead Man's Hand" ever since.

How many men did Hickok kill? According to his biographer, Hickok himself claimed "only thirty-six." That "only" alone would seem to entitle him to his formidable reputation.

At the end of the 1871 cattle season, Abilene decided it no longer needed the expensive services of the so-called "Prince of Pistoleers," and accordingly, on December 13, Hickok was dismissed as city marshal. The railroad had moved on and so had the cattle trail drives and the men who worked them.

In 1873 he capitalized on his fame by appearing, briefly, in *Buffalo*

"Dead Man's Hand"— black aces, black eights, and the jack of diamonds.

DODGE CITY GUNFIGHTS

Dodge City peace commissioners. From left to right, standing: W.H. Harris,
Luke Short, Bat Masterson. Seated: Charlie Bassett, Wyatt Earp,
Frank McLain, Neal Brown.

QUEEN OF THE COW TOWNS

A NEW STAR WAS RISING IN

THE WEST, A TOWN THAT WOULD BECOME INFAMOUS FOR ITS LAWLESSNESS AND REMAIN SO FOR TEN UNAPOLOGETIC AND UNREGENERATE YEARS: DODGE CITY, THE "BEAUTIFUL, BIBULOUS Babylon" of the Kansas plains. Its fame began as the railhead of the AT&SF, the "hell on wheels" where the railroad's track crews spent their weekly wages, then it became the center of the buffalo hunting and hide trade, and finally, when the stockyards were completed in 1875, the greatest and longest-lived of all the cow towns.

PRETTY SOON, DODGE City had a population of about a thousand people, most of them making a living from the buffalo trade, which in 1873 generated 1,617,000 pounds of meat, 2,743,100 pounds of bones (for making fertilizer), and 459,453 hides. Then in 1875 the trail herds began arriving in Dodge, diverted by the barbed wire being strung across the plains by settlers who were fencing off tracts of land. Over the next two years

☛ *Rath & Wright's buffalo hide yard in 1878, showing 40,000 hides, Dodge City, Kansas.*

Dodge City expanded to welcome them. The Dodge House, a fifty-room hotel offering a daily menu of delicacies and imported wines, blossomed on Front Street. The famous Long Branch Saloon opened farther down, and across the plaza the Lady Gay Saloon and Comique Dance Hall and Theater were erected. Two more dance halls followed—one of them run by "Rowdy Kate" Lowe. Ham Bell, former marshal of Great Bend, built the Elephant stables, so large they covered three city blocks.

Cowboys and young Texans flocked to the town in their hundreds. The Santa Fe rail tracks marked the "deadline." To the north of them, you minded your manners and checked in your guns at one of the places designated by the law. South of the tracks, there were no rules: saloons, gambling houses, and brothels

A View of Dodge City, Kansas, published in 1880.

never closed, and pistol shots rang out day and night, sometimes in celebration, sometimes in anger. The city also has the distinction of having given rise to two terms used in the English language: "red light district," from the Red Light House, a house of ill repute that stood south of the tracks, and "Boot Hill," as Dodge's cemetery, and many another in the West, was dubbed. Nobody knows for sure how many men died violently during the city's heyday. Mayor Robert L. Wright said there were twenty-five killings during the first year of the cattle drive and it may even be true. The story was told of a conductor on a train heading west asking a man where he was going. "To Hell, I reckon," the man said. "Okay," said the conductor, "give me a dollar and get off at Dodge."

GUNFIGHTS AND GUNSLINGERS

THE NOTORIOUS FRONTIER

TOWN HAD MORE THAN ITS FAIR SHARE OF GUNFIGHTERS. DOC HOLLIDAY, CLAY ALLISON, "MYSTERIOUS" DAVE MATHER, BAT MASTERSON AND HIS BROTHERS ED AND JIM, WYATT EARP and his brothers Morgan, Virgil, and James, along with Luke Short, "Longhaired" Jim Courtright, Billy Tilghman, "Cockeyed Frank" Loving, and Wild Bill Hickok all patrolled its streets on one side of the law or the other. With such a volatile cast of characters, it's not surprising that gunfights took place. They were at their peak during a ten-year period shortly after the city's founding in 1864.

MONDAY, DECEMBER 23, 1872

Former stagecoach driver and marshal at Newton, Billy Brooks, gets into a quarrel with a Santa Fe yardmaster (also from Newton) named Brown. Each man fires three shots at the other. Brown's first shot wounds Brooks; but Brooks's third shot, after nicking one of Brown's assistants, kills the yardmaster on the spot.

SATURDAY, DECEMBER 28, 1872

Matthew Sullivan, saloonkeeper, is shot dead when someone fires into his saloon through a window. Billy Brooks is widely believed to be the assassin, but no action is taken against him.

THURSDAY, MARCH 4, 1873

Billy Brooks comes under fire from a man named Jordan. However, he manages to take cover behind a water butt and escapes unhurt.

24

TUESDAY, SEPTEMBER 25, 1877
Riding his horse, a drunken cowboy, A. C. Jackson, fires his gun into the air outside Beatty and Kelley's Saloon on Front Street, and Sheriff Bat Masterson orders him to surrender his gun. Jackson refuses, fires his gun a couple more times, and gallops off. Bat and his brother Ed open fire, wounding the horse. The cowboy escapes.

MONDAY, NOVEMBER 5, 1877
During the afternoon, a quarrel erupts between "Texas Dick" Moore and Bob Shaw, owners of the Lone Star Dance Hall and Saloon. Ed Masterson, the assistant city marshal, orders Shaw to surrender his weapon, but instead Shaw takes a shot at Moore. Masterson clubs Shaw over the head with his pistol, but Shaw opens fire on Masterson, who is hit in the chest. His right arm paralyzed, Masterson drops his gun. Snatching it up again in his left hand, he puts one shot into Shaw's left arm and another into his left leg, knocking him off his feet. During the fight, a random bullet hits Dick Moore in the groin and another wounds bystander Frank Buskirk. All the participants recover.

FRIDAY, JULY 26, 1878 Around 3 a.m., some drunken cowboys begin firing into the Comique Dance Hall, creating panic among the revelers inside. Constables Wyatt Earp and Jim Masterson arrive and shots are

SALOON SKIRMISH
It's Tuesday, April 9, 1878, and Marshal Ed Masterson has spotted that Jack Wagner, one of a party of noisy cowboys in the Lady Gay Saloon, is carrying a pistol. He disarms Wagner and hands the gun to Wagner's boss, Alf Walker. When Masterson and his deputy Nat Haywood leave, Walker gives Wagner his gun and the two cowboys follow the lawmen outside. Masterson grapples with Wagner. Walker tries to shoot the deputy but his gun misfires. Wagner shoots Masterson, but in spite of the wound Masterson receives, he fires four shots—one hits Wagner, the other three Walker. Walker falls outside the rear door and Wagner staggers into Peacock's Saloon and collapses on the floor. Bleeding heavily, Masterson walks two hundred yards to Hoover's Saloon and tells bartender George Hinkle "I'm shot," before collapsing on the floor. He dies within half an hour. Wagner dies of his wound the next day.

exchanged. One cowboy, George Hoyt, is wounded in the arm; infection sets in and he dies on August 21.

SATURDAY, AUGUST 17, 1878
Drunken cowboys attempt to take over the bar at the Comique. Policemen (probably Charlie Bassett, Jim Masterson, and Wyatt Earp) bend a few heads with their revolvers and although shots are fired no one is seriously hurt.

FRIDAY, OCTOBER 4, 1878
Resentful of the rough treatment he had received at the hands of James "Dog" Kelley, mayor of Dodge City,

who threw him out of his saloon, cowboy Jim Kenedy decides to kill Kelley. He goes to Kelley's house and fires four shots. One of them hits and kills Dora Hand, a singer. A posse led by Bat Masterson, now sheriff of Ford County, and including Wyatt Earp, Billy Tilghman, and Charlie Bassett, sets off in pursuit of Kenedy and catches up with him the next day. He puts up a fight in which his right arm is shattered and his horse killed. He is later unaccountably acquitted of the killing—some money may have changed hands between Kenedy's father and the city officials.

FIGHT AT LONG BRANCH

On Saturday, April 5, 1879, gamblers "Cockeyed Frank" Loving and Levi Richardson are in a dispute over a woman. Richardson is about to leave the Long Branch Saloon when Loving comes in and takes a seat at a gambling table. Richardson sits down too, but in moments the two are back on their feet shouting insults at each other. Both men draw their guns, Richardson firing first and missing. Loving's gun misfires and he runs behind a stove as Richardson fires two more shots. Loving then begins firing and Richardson is hit in the chest, side, and right arm. Still firing, he falls back against a table and bystander William Duffy grabs the gun. Richardson is dead within minutes, Loving's only injury is a scratch on the hand.

MONDAY, JUNE 9, 1879 When a group of cowboys refuse to surrender their weapons on entering town, two lawmen (probably Wyatt Earp and Jim Masterson) engage them in a gunfight in which one of the cowboys is shot in the leg as the rest gallop away.

SATURDAY, APRIL 9, 1881 Jim Masterson and A. J. Peacock, co-owners of the Lady Gay Saloon and Dance Hall, get into a quarrel, aggravated by bartender Al Updegraff, who supports Peacock. All three start shooting but no one is hurt and the quarrel is (temporarily) patched up.

SATURDAY, APRIL 16, 1881 Following receipt of a telegram from his brother describing his difficulties with Updegraff, Bat Masterson arrives in Dodge by train from New Mexico. As he arrives he sees Peacock and Updegraff across the street and shouts "I have come over a thousand miles to settle this. I know you are heeled [armed]—now fight!" Although the street is crowded, all three draw their guns and begin firing, Masterson from behind the railway embankment, Updegraff and Peacock from the jail. As the bullets fly, two more men (probably Jim Masterson and Charlie Ronan) join the fight, firing from a nearby saloon. Updegraff is shot through the chest and a bystander is wounded slightly. The fight is stopped by Mayor A. B. Webster

and Sheriff Fred Singer. After paying a small fine, Bat Masterson leaves town, accompanied by his brother and Ronan.

MONDAY, APRIL 30, 1883 Three women working at the Long Branch Saloon owned by Will Harris and gambler Luke Short are arrested. Meeting city clerk L. C. Hartman (a special constable who had helped to make the arrests) on Front Street, Short pulls a gun and fires twice at Hartman, who falls. Thinking Hartman dead, Short turns and walks away, whereupon Hartman fires a shot at the retreating gambler. He misses as well.

SUNDAY, JULY 6, 1884 After experiencing serious provocation, gambler Dave St. Clair shoots and kills Bing Choate, who has just boasted, gun in hand, that he is fastest gunfighter in town.

FRIDAY, JULY 18, 1884 Near the opera house, Assistant Marshal Tom Nixon fires at ex-marshal Dave Mather. He misses, but the shot leaves a powder burn on Mather's face.

MONDAY, JULY 21, 1884 At about 10 p.m., Tom Nixon, "on duty" at the corner of Front Street and First Avenue, is shot dead by Mather, who leaves his saloon in the opera house saying, "You have lived long enough." A cowboy named Archie Franklin is wounded in the leg by one of the bullets which passed through Nixon's body. When arrested, Mather says, "I ought to have killed him months ago." The fight is believed to have been caused by Nixon's part in getting a saloon operated by Mather closed. The following year Mather is found not guilty of murder and walks free.

TUESDAY, OCTOBER 16, 1884 At about 10 p.m., Marshal Billy Tilghman confronts a rowdy bunch of cowboys near the bridge over the Arkansas River and when they pull their guns, empties his pistol at them. "About twenty-five or thirty" shots are fired, but when Billy switches to a Winchester rifle, the cowboys fire a couple more defiant shots, then gallop off unhurt.

BULLETS FLY

In an argument over a card game in the Junction Saloon on Sunday, May 10, 1885, bullets fly as Dave Mather (or perhaps his bartender brother, Josiah) shoots and kills David Barnes. Mather himself is wounded along with two others. Further casualties are avoided when Sheriff Pat Sughrue breaks up the fight, grabbing Barnes's brother John as he reaches for his gun and also arresting Josiah. Neither stands trial: they both skip town. Dave Mather remains "Mysterious" to the end: the date, place, and manner of his death are unknown.

"Mysterious" Dave Mather.

In 1885 and 1886, as the ten years of lawlessness came to an end, a series of fires destroyed most of Dodge City, but it was the steady influx of settlers drawn by the promise of free land that really tamed the town—an offer made by Congress in the Homestead Act of 1862. Anyone who filed a claim, paid a ten-dollar fee, and agreed to work the property for five years was given 160 acres of land. It was originally thought that the settlers would not be able to farm successfully on what had once been dubbed "the Great American Desert," but the late 1870s and the early 80s were unusually wet years, resulting in bumper crops wherever the ground had been plowed.

At first, most of those who came were farmers from the Midwest, but when the railroad companies, desperate for passenger traffic, sent agents to Europe to recruit more settlers, the great exodus really began. Between 1863 and 1890, nearly one million people filed homestead applications. A stream of emigrants began to arrive, bringing with them the windmill, the plow, and barbed wire fencing. Soon over one hundred thousand acres of Ford County were under cultivation, a fifth of which were fenced off. Domestic cattle took the place of longhorns and winter wheat that of prairie grass. While the day of the cowboy was not yet over, the day of the homesteader had come. And they had come to stay.

HOMESTEADERS AND FEUDING CLANS

An American homestead in summer.

HOMESTEADERS

THE FACT THAT THEY HAD THE

RIGHT TO FILE A CLAIM FOR HOMESTEAD LAND AND BEGIN FARMING DID NOT MEAN THAT HOMESTEADERS WERE WELCOMED EVERYWHERE WITH OPEN ARMS—IN FACT, IN MANY PLACES THE OPPOSITE WAS VERY much the case. Once a claim had been staked, the homesteader was there for good: in these circumstances, possession was nine-tenths of the law. Should someone try to take the land back—no matter how sound the legal basis—there would be war.

BY THE 1880s, many of the cattlemen who had once herded half-wild longhorn steers along the dangerous trails to the markets in the east of the country had become sophisticated breeders of pedigree cattle, providing the high quality beef now in demand. Men like Charles Goodnight in Texas, Alexander Swan in Wyoming, or John Chisum in New Mexico owned—by right of possession and determination (backed up

by well-armed cowboys)—vast tracts of land on which their stock roamed. They were extremely hostile toward any homesteaders who wished to file claims upon this land. For the cattle industry to operate effectively and profitably, the countryside needed to remain open, rather than be fenced

☞ *Freeman homestead in Gage County, Nebraska, the first claim under the 1862 Homestead Act.*

off. The math was simple: each cow needed up to ten acres of open range and access to water to thrive. A herd of eighty to a hundred thousand head of cattle required between half a million and a million acres to forage upon. The cattlemen would oppose strenuously the arrival of settlers of any kind, but especially "nesters," who would fence off water, build houses, and, when times were hard—which they frequently were—turn to stealing cattle for food or money or both.

As a result, feuds—sometimes called "wars"—flared up: in Montana between cattlemen and homesteaders; in New Mexico between cattle-owning businessmen seeking to maintain their monopoly of army beef contracts and newcomers trying to unseat them; in Arizona between cattlemen and sheepmen; and in Texas between warring families—feuds that went on for so long that the men fighting them were never entirely sure what had started them in the first place. One such was the Taylor-Sutton feud, the longest and bloodiest of a dozen or more in Texas history, which emerged during the South's Reconstruction era.

In Texas, "carpetbaggers" (financial adventurers from the north whose name derived from their ability to carry all their possessions in a single valise or bag) had flooded in. Edmund J. Davis, who was governor and virtual dictator of Texas at the time, was one of them, "elected by popular ballot" in 1870 to administer what was referred to throughout the state as the hated "Carpetbag Constitution." And no more bitter controversy marked Davis's regime than his establishment of a state militia and a state police force, both answerable to him.

Many Texans, who perceived them as having been created solely to enforce "carpetbagger law," hated the police with a vengeance, none more so than outlaw and gunfighter John Wesley Hardin, who killed two state policemen in Gonzales later that year.

THE TAYLOR vs. SUTTON FEUD

THE ORIGINS OF THE FEUD ARE

SWATHED IN UNCERTAINTY AND CONTROVERSY. THE TAYLOR CLAN, COMPOSED OF LARGELY STAUNCH CONFEDERATES, WAS LED BY PATRIARCH JOSIAH TAYLOR, A VIRGINIAN WHO HAD SETTLED NEAR Cuero in DeWitt County, together with his five sons, Pitkin, Creed, Josiah, William, and Rufus, and their sons, nephews, in-laws, and friends. The Sutton faction was composed of relatives or followers of William (Bill) Sutton, who had also moved to DeWitt County.

THE GENERAL public perceived the Taylors as cattle thieves and rustlers, while the Suttons—despite their brutal methods—were seen as embattled vigilante-style lawmen. The rules of engagement were viciously simple: in a feud, anyone who harmed a member of your clan harmed you. Whatever you did to achieve revenge and whatever means you employed to remove a dangerous enemy were acceptable.

Early in July 1869, special officer Jack Helm arrived in the cattle region between DeWitt County and the Gulf of Mexico at the head of a posse of around fifty men, with the stated aim of arresting rustlers. According

THE BACKGROUND TO THE FEUD

According to some, the trouble began when two of Creed Taylor's sons, Hays and "Doboy" Taylor, were involved in the killing of two African American soldiers in Mason County in November 1867. Their names now on a "Wanted" poster, they were also accused of killing two bounty hunters who came after them. In March 1868, in his role as deputy sheriff of Clinton, Texas, Bill Sutton killed Charley Taylor while trying to arrest him for stealing horses. Nine months later, on Christmas Eve, Sutton killed Buck Taylor and Dick Chisholm in a dispute about the sale of some horses. The Taylors, for their part, were not inclined to let these killings go without some form of retaliation.

to newspaper reports, by the end of August, Helm's Regulators had killed twenty-one men and arrested another ten; many of those killed were shot "trying to escape." A number of the Taylor family's friends and relatives featured among them. One month later, on August 23, 1869, another posse led by Special Officer C.S. Bell laid an ambush that resulted in the death of Creed's son, Hays Taylor.

When on July 1, 1870, the Texas State Police was established by Governor Davis, Jack Helm was elected one of its four captains and was sent to continue his "war" on rustlers. Bill Sutton was among the men he recruited, along with some DeWitt cattlemen who had already demonstrated their loyalty to

 Cattle raids on the Texas border were commonplace.

the Sutton faction. The rest of Helm's men were or would inevitably become Sutton sympathizers.

On August 26, 1870, Helms's men arrested Henry and William Kelly, sons-in-law of Pitkin Taylor, on a trivial charge. They were taken a few miles from home and shot, while Henry Kelly's terrified wife, in hiding, watched helplessly. Helm was dismissed from the Texas State Police when his misconduct came to light, but he continued to serve as sheriff of DeWitt County.

In the summer of 1872, Sutton sympathizers shot Pitkin Taylor and he died six months later. His sons Jim

Cowboys on the range, the wagon carrying their food in the background.

and Bill, and their friends, swore to avenge him and wash their hands in Bill Sutton's blood. Their first attempt on Sutton was made on April 1, 1873, when three of the Taylor clan fired through the door of a Cuero saloon and wounded him. He survived and in June escaped from an ambush, this time without injury. By now the Taylors had enlisted a major ally to their cause: gunfighter John Wesley Hardin. Hardin and Jim Taylor were responsible for killing Jack Helm in a blacksmith shop in Wilson County.

The day after Helm was killed, a group of Taylors surrounded the stronghold of one of Helms's men, Joe Tumlinson,

near Yorktown. After a brief siege, the local sheriff and a posse appeared and miraculously talked both parties into signing a truce, but it lasted only until December, when Wiley Pridgen, a Taylor sympathizer, was killed at Thomaston. Enraged, the Taylors attacked the Sutton faction and besieged them in Cuero for a day and night, until they themselves were besieged, in turn, when Tumlinson appeared with a larger band of Sutton followers.

By this time the county was in a state of open war. More killings followed: in just one week in January, a man named Johnson in Clinton and another named McVea in Cuero were killed, and John Krohn was seriously wounded. Bill Sutton finally decided to leave the area, and on March 11, 1874, had boarded a steamer at Indianola when Jim and Bill Taylor arrived at the dock and killed him and his friend Gabriel Slaughter in front of Sutton's pregnant wife.

The Sutton faction soon got even. Kute Tuggle, Jim White, Scrap Taylor, and three other men were driving a herd of cattle up the trail for John Hardin, who had just killed a deputy in Comanche and was now on the run. Tuggle, White, and Taylor were arrested and charged with stealing the cattle, and brought back to Clinton. On the night of June 20, 1874, a mob of thirty men took them out of the jail and hanged them.

The feud dragged on, despite Bill Sutton's death, with Reuben H. Brown, marshal of Cuero, now the leader of the Suttons. Bill Taylor was in Indianola jail, charged with killing Sutton and Slaughter, but he managed to escape during a hurricane. He went on the run and on November 17, Brown was killed in a saloon by five men, whose names were linked to Bill Taylor. One month later, on December 27, there was a big gunfight in which a gang of pro-Sutton men ambushed and killed Jim Taylor. He was not yet twenty-four years old.

With Jim Taylor's death the feud might have ended but, just a year later, the Sutton sympathizers—many of whom were peace officers—were implicated in the murder of Dr. Philip Brassell and his son George, who was said to have been involved in the earlier killing of Sutton factionist Jim Cox. Eight men were eventually arrested and held for trial, but no one was willing to testify and after years of legal maneuvring, only one man was convicted and even he was eventually pardoned.

The Taylor-Sutton feud was over, but there would be plenty more. In fact while the Suttons and the Taylors were killing each other in Texas, a new war was starting up over in Lincoln County, New Mexico, and this time it was not a dispute about land, honor, or revenge— although all three were certainly involved—but money.

☞ *Cattle rustling was considered a serious offense. Those caught were often subject to vigilante-style punishment.*

THE GRAHAM vs. TEWKSBURY FEUD

NO FEUD IN THE HISTORY OF

THE WEST HAS BEEN BLOODIER, MORE RUTHLESS, OR MORE TRAGIC. THE GRAHAM-TEWKSBURY FEUD ERUPTED IN A REMOTE MOUNTAIN AREA CALLED PLEASANT VALLEY, NORTH OF GLOBE, ARIZONA. What started it and why it generated such intense hatred and revenge, no one can say: most of the leading participants died in the feud and as a result were never able to set down for the record what actually happened. To this day, outsiders are discouraged from asking about certain aspects of the Pleasant Valley war. It may have been a dispute over who should have control of the range—sheepmen or cattlemen; but like all feuds it was also about jealousy, hatred, pride, and revenge.

THE EARLY SETTLERS in Pleasant Valley were cattlemen, with ranches on the high mountain plateau. Bostonian James Dunning Tewksbury came to the valley in the late 1870s with his four sons, their Shoshone mother having died. In November 1879, he married Lydia Ann Shultes, who had three children, and set up house in a cabin on Cherry

Edwin Tewksbury.

Creek and should have lived happily ever after. But in 1882 ex-miner John Graham arrived in Globe, looking to get started in the cattle business. He met Edwin Tewksbury, one of James's sons, who invited him to Pleasant Valley. Before the year was out, John Graham and his brother Tom had staked out a stretch of land farther up the creek from their new friends.

One January day in 1883, absentee cattle rancher Jim Stinson's foreman, John Gilleland, rode over to the Tewksbury place accompanied by his sixteen year-old nephew, Elisha, and Epitacio "Potash" Ruiz to look over the cattle in their corrals (one version) or to go hunting nearby (version two) and rode into trouble. The four Tewksbury boys were there, along with Tom and John Graham. Somehow, harsh words were spoken and shooting started. Gilleland was killed by Ed Tewksbury and Elisha was wounded as he and Ruiz fled the scene. However, the Grahams and Tewksburys presented a united front and the charges against them were dropped.

At some point the Graham boys double-crossed the Tewksburys by registering the cattle in their name alone. The Grahams then swore affidavits accusing the Tewksburys of rustling and in a gunfight at the Stinson ranch, John was wounded. To cover their backs, the Grahams formed an alliance with Jim Stinson and teamed up with the five sons of another new arrival, cattleman Martin Blevins.

Feeling increasingly persecuted, the Tewksburys withdrew and Cherry Creek now became a demarcation line: Grahams to the west of it, Tewksburys to the east. In the fall of 1886, the Tewksburys leased some of their land to prominent northern Arizona sheep

HATFIELDS vs. McCOYS

The Hatfield and McCoy feud raged for years. The warring families lived mostly on either side of Tug Fork in the Big Sandy River region, on the Kentucky-West Virginia border. They were led by Randolph "Ole Ran'l" McCoy and William Anderson "Devil Anse" Hatfield. As with many such feuds, the spark that set if off is unclear, but it may have been a simple dispute about the ownership of a pig. Whatever the cause, it soon escalated into a full-blown blood feud. The situation was exacerbated when Roseanna McCoy began a relationship with Johnse Hatfield, although Johnse eventually abandoned Roseanna for her cousin Nancy McCoy. In 1888, on New Year's Eve, a band of Hatfields attacked the McCoy cabin, burning it down and killing two of Randolph's children, and beating his wife Sally and leaving her for dead. A number of Hatfields were eventually arrested for their part in the massacre; seven received life sentences and one was hanged.

The feuding began to ease and after more than a dozen deaths between the two families, a truce was finally agreed in 1891.

The Hatfield clan, 1897.

farmers and herds of sheep were driven into what had been exclusively cattle country. Word soon went round that a certain cattle baron was offering $500 for the head of any man who herded sheep south of the demarcation line. Then in February 1887, a sheepherder was murdered.

By summer the sheep were gone, but although the cattlemen had won that battle, the game was anything but over. In July, Martin Blevins disappeared and his fate remains a mystery to this day.

Despite sporadic attempts by lawmen to calm things down, the fighting and killing continued in a series of standoffs and ambushes. During the next eighteen months, Hampton and Charlie Blevins were killed, as were Sam and Andy "Cooper" Blevins; Billy

and John Graham and John Tewksbury were also killed. Jim Tewksbury eventually died of tuberculosis in December 1888, and with only Ed Tewksbury, one Graham (Tom), and one Blevins brother still standing, it appeared the feud might be at an end. Tom Graham even moved out of the valley to avoid further trouble, but further trouble came anyway: in September 1891, George Newton, the only cattleman known to have joined the Tewksburys, disappeared en route to his ranch from Globe; no body was ever found.

Finally, in June 1892, Tom Graham returned to Pleasant Valley to sell his ranch. He was ambushed and mortally wounded near Tempe, on August 2, by two assassins who, before dying, he identified as Ed Tewksbury and John Rhodes. Only Tewksbury stood trial; he was found guilty of murder and sent to prison, where he served two years; the charges against him were dismissed on appeal in 1896. He then became a deputy sheriff in Globe where he died on April 4, 1904, in a strange footnote to this bloody tale.

A likely member of Sheriff Mulvenon's posse, which pursued and killed John Graham.

THE LINCOLN COUNTY WAR

Branding cattle on the Texas prairies.

EARLY SKIRMISHES

THE LINCOLN COUNTY WAR

WAS ONE OF A NUMBER OF OUTBREAKS OF CIVIL UNREST OR DISTURBANCES—A SERIES OF SO-CALLED "WARS" THAT RAN FROM THE EARLY 1870s TO EARLY 1883. THE FIRST OF THESE, WHICH TOOK place in 1872, might have been termed the "Horsethief War"— incoming American settlers (many of whom would figure in the later conflict) waged war on indigenous Hispanic horse thieves, ambushing or lynching them without compunction.

John Simpson Chisum.

HARD ON THE heels of these killings, another "war" broke out between the Horrell brothers—a tough clan of Texans who had left Lampasas County when the law there got too hot for them—and the local New Mexican population, whom the Texans looked down on. The Horrell War raged out of control for almost a year, including assassinations, ambushes, and an attack upon a wedding in which three men were killed and two others seriously wounded. When even the Horrells began to find things out of control, they fled back to Texas, leaving a trail of violence as they went.

A year or two later, the Horrells become embroiled in another blood feud in Lampasas, which ended with brothers Mart and Tom Horrell in jail and charged with murder. The jail was then stormed by a vigilante mob and the brothers were killed.

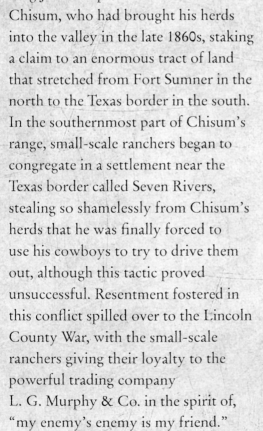

☛ *The hanging of a horse thief.*

In 1876 it was the turn of the Pecos Valley in New Mexico to act as a backdrop to unrest. This was the "Pecos War" or "Chisum's War," since it was waged by Texas traildriver and cattle king John Simpson Chisum, who had brought his herds into the valley in the late 1860s, staking a claim to an enormous tract of land that stretched from Fort Sumner in the north to the Texas border in the south. In the southernmost part of Chisum's range, small-scale ranchers began to congregate in a settlement near the Texas border called Seven Rivers, stealing so shamelessly from Chisum's herds that he was finally forced to use his cowboys to try to drive them out, although this tactic proved unsuccessful. Resentment fostered in this conflict spilled over to the Lincoln County War, with the small-scale ranchers giving their loyalty to the powerful trading company L. G. Murphy & Co. in the spirit of, "my enemy's enemy is my friend."

"The House" as the Murphy firm was known, had become the dominant economic and political force in Lincoln County. It was bolstered by the patronage of a powerful political clique of lawyers and land speculators known as the Santa Fe Ring. Some Ring members acquired the lucrative contracts to supply food to the Mescalero Apache Native Americans on their reservation at Fort Stanton, near Lincoln. Members of the Ring also controlled the law, which they did not hesitate to use for their own purposes. They were able to run Lincoln County the way they wanted, controlling the local sheriff and maintaining a "buddy-buddy" relationship with the military.

Chisum stood alone against these factions until 1876, unable to stop the small ranchers and the outlaws employed by the House from stealing cattle from him and selling them to Lawrence Murphy, who in turn sold them to the government at prices Chisum could not compete with.

THE REGULATORS

AT THE END OF 1876, A YOUNG

Englishman named John H. Tunstall arrived in Lincoln County and with the aid and encouragement of Chisum and his attorney, Alexander McSween, established a ranch, a general store, and a bank in Lincoln, making it clear that the intention of the three men was to overthrow the domination of the House and take over its monopoly. By the time Tunstall's challenge materialized, the founders of the House were no longer in charge of its destiny; Lawrence Murphy was dying of cancer and his partner, Emil Fritz, had died in Germany. Murphy's protégé and—some said—adopted son, James Dolan, took the reins, with the help of another Irishman, John Riley.

MANY OF THE small farmers and ranchers in the Lincoln area—especially the Hispanics who had suffered under the domination of the House for years—switched their loyalty to McSween and Tunstall. To begin with, Dolan used his connections to manipulate the law so that legal proceedings against Tunstall caused the Englishman constant harrassment, but when he refused to buckle under the pressure, a warrant was issued to seize

👉 *The Torreon, a 20-ft (6-meter) tower, built in the 1850s. Dolan's sharpshooters were stationed here during the Five-Day Battle (see page 44).*

all his property. On February 18, 1878, Sheriff William Brady sent a posse to Tunstall's ranch to carry out the order, turning a blind eye to the fact that known outlaws with a grudge against Tunstall had joined it. The men caught up with Tunstall and killed him. It was at this point that the situation escalated into a shooting war.

When lawyer McSween managed to have warrants issued for the arrest of Tunstall's murderers, Sheriff Brady not only refused to recognize them, but arrested the men (one of them was young William Bonney, who would later be known as "Billy the Kid") deputized to serve the warrants. Supporters of the McSween-Tunstall faction took this to mean that the law would not help them and dubbing themselves "Regulators," banded together to effect their own brand of justice.

Two weeks after Tunstall's death, two of the men suspected of having killed him were executed by the Regulators; a bystander who tried to intervene was also shot down mercilessly. On April 1, Sheriff Brady and his deputy George Hindman were killed on the street in Lincoln. Three days later, in a gunfight at a sawmill near present-day Ruidoso, the Regulators killed Dolan supporter Andrew Roberts (who also went by the name of Bill Williams), but not before

1878 TIMELINE

FEBRUARY 18: Rancher and merchant John Tunstall is killed by the Murphy-Dolan faction. Warrants are issued for the killers. Sheriff William Brady arrests the men trying to serve the warrants (including William Bonney).

MARCH 1: The Regulators are formed from McSween-Tunstall sympathizers and small cattle ranchers.

MARCH 9: The Regulators execute the men suspected of killing Tunstall.

APRIL 1: Sheriff Brady and his deputy are killed in a gunfight with the Regulators.

APRIL 4: Dolan supporter Andrew Roberts kills Regulator leader Dick Brewer and is then himself killed by the Regulators.

APRIL 18: Several men are charged with Sheriff Brady's murder, including William Bonney.

APRIL 29: A shoot-out at the Fritz ranch leaves new Regulator leader Frank McNab dead and several others wounded.

APRIL/MAY: The violence continues, resulting in more deaths.

JULY 15: The Regulators gather at McSween's house, which is besieged by the Dolan faction.

JULY 19: The house is set on fire. McSween and several of his supporters are killed as they try to escape the burning building.

he'd had time to shoot the leader of the Regulators, rancher Dick Brewer, and severely wound two others.

Lincoln County now became a war zone as armed bands of Dolan and McSween sympathizers hunted each other down, occasionally colliding in

General Lew Wallace.

One of the survivors was young William Bonney. He had worked for Tunstall and played a prominent role in every gunfight that had taken place. In the anarchic lawlessness that followed what the Dolan side called "the Big Killing," what was left of the Regulators stayed alive as best they could. But at long last intervention by the U.S. government resulted in the dismissal of the pro-Dolan governor of New Mexico, Samuel Axtell. He was replaced by American Civil War general, Lew Wallace, who instituted a campaign of military-style warfare against the Regulators, now regarded as violent outlaws who were terrorizing Lincoln County.

His policies seemed to work, but just when it looked as if the war was over, it flared up again in February 1879, when lawyer Huston Chapman was murdered in Lincoln by a drunken gang. Lew Wallace met secretly with William Bonney, who had been with the gang, and promised him a pardon if he testified against the men who had murdered Chapman, one of whom was Jimmy Dolan. Bonney kept his word and Dolan was charged with murder. But when the pro-Dolan district attorney refused to honor Wallace's deal, Bonney, who had been charged with Brady's murder, decided to take no chances and went on the run.

shoot-outs and skirmishes. Finally, in July 1878, the feud came to a blazing climax with the "Five-Day Battle" in the town of Lincoln, when the Dolan faction laid siege to the McSween house where the Regulators had gathered. After four days of inconclusive fighting in which at least two men were killed, troops from nearby Fort Stanton were marched into town, ostensibly "to protect women and children." In fact their commanding officer, Lieutenant Colonel N.A.M. Dudley, supported the Dolan side and stood by without intervening as they set fire to the McSween house and killed four men—one of them McSween—as the occupants tried to escape the building under cover of darkness.

WYATT EARP, TOMBSTONE & THE O.K. CORRAL

Main street, Tombstone, Arizona.

WYATT EARP IN TOMBSTONE

THE NAME OF WYATT EARP,

THE CELEBRATED LAWMAN WHO KEPT ORDER IN TOMBSTONE, ARIZONA, ECHOES DOWN THROUGH AMERICAN HISTORY. HE ARRIVED IN THE CITY WITH HIS BROTHERS MORGAN AND VIRGIL AND their wives at the end of 1879, leaving behind a good, if somewhat patchy, record of police work in cow towns such as Wichita and Dodge City. But it was in Tombstone that he made his name.

TOMBSTONE, IN THE San Pedro valley near the Arizona-Mexico border, was founded in 1877 and flourished when prospector Ed Schieffelin discovered rich silver deposits and founded the Tombstone Mining District. When the Earps arrived, it was still "a hodgepodge of shacks, adobes, and tents" with perhaps a thousand inhabitants. Within a year the population had doubled and by 1881 it had multiplied by ten.

Wyatt Earp.

To begin with Wyatt, who had declared himself "tired of lawin'," worked as a security guard for the express financial company Wells Fargo, then quit to become deputy sheriff for the Tombstone district of Pima County, with Morgan taking over his job with Wells Fargo. At the same time, Wyatt and his brothers began staking mining claims and buying small properties, in a serious effort to establish

themselves, financially and politically, as responsible businessmen. When Cochise County was formed on February 1, 1881, with Tombstone as the county seat (administrative center), Wyatt ran for sheriff but was defeated by John Behan. He acquired

Old facades on Frémont Street, Tombstone, Arizona.

an interest in the gambling tables at the Oriental Saloon and encouraged Dodge City cronies like Bat Masterson and Luke Short to work them. In June his brother Virgil was appointed chief of police and in October Morgan was appointed special officer.

The Earps were consolidating their position and might even have succeeded had it not been for the hostility they aroused among the "cowboy" element, personified by local cattle ranchers like N. H. "Old Man" Clanton and his three sons, Ike, Phin, and Billy. There was also a crew of hangers-on, including ranch hands and the McLaury (or McLowry)

Bat Masterson (standing) and Wyatt Earp in Dodge City.

local tough "Buckskin" Frank Leslie. Three days later, they arrested Luther King, who confessed to having been one of the stagecoach robbers and named three others as his partners in crime. King was taken to Tombstone and jailed, but a couple of weeks later he escaped and disappeared.

Annoyed at losing an opportunity to boost his chances in the coming election for sheriff, Wyatt Earp cut a deal with Ike Clanton: if Ike agreed to betray the three stagecoach robbers that King had named, he would settle for the publicity of arresting the killers and turn the Wells Fargo reward money over to Ike. The deal fell apart when two of the robbers were killed in New Mexico. Then in July, Wyatt's friend, John Henry "Doc" Holliday—dentist, gambler, and tuberculosis sufferer—fueled suspicion that the Earps might be involved in illegal activities and might not be not the upright lawmen they professed to be.

The reputation of the Earps was somewhat restored after Virgil stepped in as acting marshal when Tombstone's chief of police, Ben

brothers—Frank and Tom—and Johnny Ringo, "Curly Bill" Brocius, and others. This gun-toting gang did not like the Earps at all and were not afraid to use their weapons to defend or assert any of their rights that they felt might be threatened by the Earps.

In March 1881, the two factions became sworn enemies after a stagecoach was ambushed near Contention and driver Eli "Bud" Philpott and another man were killed. Wells Fargo agent Marshall Williams assembled a posse that included Wyatt, Morgan and Virgil, and Bat Masterson, and set off in pursuit of the attackers. The next morning they were joined by Sheriff John Behan, his deputy Billy Breakenridge, and

Sippy, left town under something of a cloud. Big, tough Virgil enforced the law with vigor and arrested violators without fear or favor, and by midsummer the Earp brothers were pretty much in control of what took place inside the city limits. Another stagecoach was held up by masked men on September 9. Virgil led one posse in pursuit of the thieves and John Behan another: Virgil's posse caught up with and arrested Pete Spence and Frank Stilwell—who also happened to be Sheriff Behan's deputy. During the robbery, the word "sugar" had been used to refer to money. It was a term that Frank Stilwell was known to use.

Although the charges were dropped, the arrests caused a lot of bad blood. Frank McLaury, Ike Clanton, Johnny Ringo, and some others told Morgan Earp they would kill him and his brothers if the Earps ever came after them. Tom McLaury told Virgil the same thing. So, in early October, when Virgil rearrested Spence and Stilwell and the latter was held for trial, the situation became tense. At around the same time, Marshall Williams let Ike Clanton know he was aware of the deal Ike had made with Wyatt, and Ike threatened to make the Earps pay for revealing their secret.

Cochise County Courthouse, Tombstone, built in 1882.

GUNFIGHT AT THE O.K. CORRAL

ON THE COLD, CLEAR MORNING

OF OCTOBER 26, 1881, THE EARPS LEARNED THAT A VERY DRUNK IKE CLANTON WAS PROWLING THE STREETS, ARMED AND LOOKING FOR A FIGHT. WYATT, VIRGIL, AND MORGAN WENT IN SEARCH OF HIM. When Virgil found Ike, he disarmed him and marched him into court, where he was fined $27.50. As Wyatt left the courtroom, he encountered Tom McLaury who began making threats; Wyatt knocked him senseless with his gun and walked away.

IKE AND TOM

were joined by Frank McLaury and Billy Clanton. After being warned repeatedly that the cowboys intended to kill the Earps, Virgil asked Sheriff John Behan to help him "disarm these parties," but Behan refused on the grounds that if the Earps went after the cowboys there would be a fight. Instead, he promised he would persuade the McLaurys and Clantons to leave town.

About half an hour later, not knowing how many of them would be waiting,

Doc Holliday.

Virgil "called on Wyatt and Morgan Earp and Doc Holliday to go help me disarm the Clantons and McLaurys." He handed Holliday his shotgun, telling him to keep it under his coat and the four men set off up Fourth Street and turned onto Frémont.

Six men were gathered near the O.K. Corral, on a vacant lot between Mollie Fly's boarding house and the cabin of former mayor, William Harwood: Frank and Tom McLaury, Ike and Billy Clanton, John Behan and Billy

Claiborne. As the Earps and Doc Holliday approached, Behan intercepted them. "For God's sake don't go down there or they will murder you!" he said. Virgil shook his head. "I am going down there to disarm them," he replied.

Seeing the Earps advancing, the cowboys backed farther into the empty lot, almost in line abreast. "Boys, throw up your hands, I want your guns!" Virgil boomed, and within seconds the shooting started—and was over inside half a minute. When the smoke cleared, both McLaurys were dead and Billy Clanton was mortally wounded; Morgan and Virgil had minor wounds and Doc Holliday just a nick. Ike Clanton had grappled with Wyatt for a moment before running for cover; Billy Claiborne also fled. Afterward, Sheriff Behan tried to arrest the Earps but Wyatt refused to submit.

The O.K. Corral; the gunfight actually took place in a vacant lot on Frémont Street near the rear entrance of the corral.

The gunfight—contemporary writers called it a "street fight"—was over, but the controversy still rages today. Although a justice of the peace declared the Earps had been acting as officers of the law, and later a Cochise County grand jury refused to indict them, many others muttered that the Earps had shot down men who had had their hands in the air. The bodies of the three dead men were put on display in an undertaker's window with a sign that said:

> ## MURDERED ON THE STREETS OF TOMBSTONE

The aftermath of the gunfight was equally violent. On December 28, Virgil Earp was the victim of an assassination attempt that rendered his left arm useless. In March 1882, Morgan Earp was shot dead while playing pool—Pete Spence and Frank Stilwell were named as the killers, among others. On March 20, Virgil and his wife left Tombstone for California under heavy guard. Wyatt, Warren—the youngest of the Earp brothers, who had just arrived in town—and Doc Holliday escorted them as far as Tucson where they believed Stilwell would be waiting to kill Virgil. That same night, March 20, Stilwell, was found dead in the Tucson railyard.

Wyatt and Holliday were charged with the murder, but Wyatt refused to submit to arrest and left Tombstone for Pete Spence's wood camp, accompanied by his brother Warren and Doc Holliday, where Spence surrendered to Sheriff Behan. The next day, still at Spence's camp, the Earp party killed Florentino Cruz, who was also suspected of involvement in Morgan's death. It was also reported, though never proven, that Wyatt killed "Curly Bill" Brocius in the Dragoon Mountains.

🖝 *Grave marker in Boot Hill Cemetery, Tombstone.*

Wyatt Earp left Arizona for good, dabbling in various ventures, including mining and real estate. However, apart from refereeing the Bob Fitzsimmons vs. Tom Sharkey boxing match in 1896, he did nothing very significant for the rest of his life. Wyatt finally died in January 1929.

Thanks to the legendary gunfight at the O.K. Corral, Wyatt Earp has since been transformed into the most famous lawman of the frontier West, immortalized in books and movies, and all this despite only ever having been deputy sheriff or assistant marshal.

ROMANCING *THE* DESPERADO

Armed guards defend a stagecoach in Wyoming.

WES HARDIN
"LITTLE ARKANSAS"

ALTHOUGH NEVER AS FAMOUS

AS, FOR EXAMPLE, WILD BILL HICKOK, JOHN WESLEY (WES) HARDIN WAS PROBABLY ONE OF THE MOST PROLIFIC MAN-KILLERS OF THEM ALL. THE SON OF JAMES GIBSON AND ELIZABETH DIXON, HE WAS born in Bonham, Texas, on May 26, 1853. His father was a Methodist preacher, schoolteacher, and lawyer. The young Hardin's deeply ingrained Southern sympathies and hatred for African Americans motivated his violent career, which is said to have started in 1867 with a schoolyard squabble in which he stabbed and wounded another boy. He was only fifteen when he shot and killed a former slave known as Mage (or Maje) who—Hardin claimed—had threatened to kill him.

WITH THE LAW in Texas looking for him, Hardin fled to his aunt's house, north of Sumpter, Texas, where in the fall of 1868 he is said to have killed three Union soldiers who sought to arrest him for the murder of Mage. The following summer, he and his cousin Simp Dixon, a member of the Ku Klux Klan, ran into a squad of soldiers near Pisgah and in the ensuing shoot-out killed one man each. On Christmas Day, 1869, Hardin killed Jim Bradley, a gambler from Towash, Texas, after a dispute over cards and the following month got into

JOHN WESLEY HARDIN

BORN: May 26, 1853, in Bonham, Texas

DIED: August 19, 1895 (age 42), in El Paso, Texas; shot by police officer John Selman

ALIASES: Little Arkansas (so named by Wild Bill Hickok), J.W. Swain

OCCUPATIONS: Gambler, school teacher, cowboy, cattle rustler, lawyer, outlaw, and gunfighter

SPOUSES: Jane Bowen, Carolyn Jane "Callie" Lewis

CHILDREN: 2 daughters, 1 son

PARENTS: Father—James Gibson Hardin; mother—Mary Elizabeth Dixon another fight, this time with a circus worker, and killed him, too.

More killings followed, including several state police officers. If all the killings attributed to and claimed by Hardin were true, it would mean that by September 1871, the eighteen-year-old Texan had already killed twenty-seven men, "a fair-sized cemetery" as his biographer puts it.

On February 29, 1872, Hardin married fourteen-year-old Jane Bowen. He was very much an absentee husband, but they had three children together. Marriage failed to change Hardin's ways; more trouble and deaths ensued and he was drawn into the Taylor-Sutton feud in 1873–74. As well as gambling and racing horses, Hardin was now also dealing widely in stolen cattle. After a gunfight in which Deputy Sheriff Charles Webb was killed, Hardin was forced on the run. With a price of $4,000 on his head—dead or alive—he took his wife and children to Florida and Alabama, adding more victims along the way. Hardin was caught and sentenced to twenty-five years in jail for the murder of Webb. He was released in 1894, after serving seventeen years, during which time he had studied theology and law.

Once out of prison, Hardin went to El Paso where he established a law practice, but despite efforts to lead a decent life, he was soon drinking and gambling again. Jane died and he remarried, but soon abandoned his new wife. He was shot in the back of the head by lawman John Selman Sr. with whom he had had a long feud, on August 19, 1895, at the bar of a saloon in El Paso.

In his autobiography, completed in prison, Hardin depicts himself as a pillar of society, maintaining that he never killed anyone who did not need killing. Some regarded him as a man more sinned against than sinning—he was a violent product of a violent time.

John Wesley Hardin.

BILLY THE KID

THE BRIEF LIFE OF BILLY THE

KID WAS LITTLE MORE TO HISTORY THAN A CANDLE IN THE WIND, YET DESPITE THE FACT THAT MOST OF WHAT IS KNOWN ABOUT HIM TOOK PLACE DURING THE LAST THREE YEARS OF HIS LIFE, MILLIONS OF words have been written about him. The date and place of his birth, his father's identity, and where he lived as a child all remain shrouded in mystery. He is thought to have lived with his mother, Catherine McCarty, in Kansas, in the early 1870s. Catherine married a mining prospector named William Antrim in 1873 prior to moving with Billy to New Mexico, where she died eighteen months later. He may have achieved notoriety as "Billy the Kid," but it is thought that his real name was Henry McCarty and he was also known as Henry Antrim.

AFTER HIS MOTHER'S death, Billy became delinquent and was jailed for theft. He escaped and turned horse thief in Arizona, later killing a bullying blacksmith named Frank Cahill in a drinking den on the fringes of Fort Grant. In 1877 he drifted over the border into New Mexico's Lincoln County and became a cowboy for rancher John Tunstall. Now known as William H. Bonney, over the next six months, he transformed from a drifting nobody into a prominent member of the Tunstall-McSween faction and a member of the Regulators (see page 43), participating in the assassination of Sheriff William Brady and one of his deputies, a gunfight at Blazer's Mill near Lincoln in which two men died, and the famous "Five Day Battle" in Lincoln, in 1878.

Pat Garrett.

In spite of his shameless rustling activities and several further killings, Billy seems to have kept hoping for an amnesty, but Governor Lew Wallace withdrew his promise of a pardon. In November 1880, cattle rancher John Chisum and J. C. Lea backed the election of Pat Garrett as sheriff of Lincoln County. Garrett made it his principal mission to arrest or kill Billy the Kid and finally captured Billy just before Christmas, 1880. He was held in jail in Santa Fe for several months and then taken to Mesilla for trial. Found guilty of the murder of Brady, he was sentenced to be hanged at Lincoln, but

BILLY THE KID

BORN: William Henry McCarty Jr.; possibly November 23, 1859
DIED: July 14, 1881 (age 21), at Fort Sumner, New Mexico; shot by Sheriff Pat Garrett
ALIASES: William H. Bonney, William McCarty, Henry McCarty, Henry Antrim, Kid Antrim
OCCUPATIONS: Horse rustler, cowboy, outlaw, murderer
PARENTS: Father—unknown, possibly Henry McCarty or William Bonney; stepfather—William Antrim; mother—Catherine McCarty

fifteen days before the date set for his execution, he escaped, killing the two deputies guarding him.

Sheriff Pat Garrett waited until word came that instead of fleeing south of the border into Old Mexico, where no American law could touch him, Billy was hiding out near Fort Sumner, northeast of Lincoln. Taking along two trusted deputies, he sneaked into the old Fort, relying for help on rancher Peter Maxwell, whose sister Paulita was Billy's sweetheart—a relationship Maxwell wanted terminated. At around midnight on July 14, 1881, Pat Garrett killed Billy in Maxwell's bedroom, marking the end of a brief life that was to become an enduring legend.

William Bonney, aka Billy the Kid.

BLACK BART

ON JULY 26, 1875, IN A LONELY SPOT ON THE ROUTE BETWEEN COPPEROPOLIS AND MILTON IN CENTRAL CALIFORNIA, A STAGECOACH WAS STOPPED BY A MAN WITH A SHOTGUN. WEARING A LONG LINEN COAT, HIS HEAD COVERED with a flour sack with eyeholes cut out, beneath a bowler hat, the bandit politely requested the driver, John Shine, to throw down the strongbox, shouting, "If he dares to shoot, give him a solid volley!" Looking around, Shine saw what appeared to be rifle barrels pointing out from the surrounding bushes. Taking no chances, he tossed down the strongbox; when a frightened woman threw out her purse the bandit refused it, saying he only wanted the Wells Fargo shipment. Told to drive on a short distance, Shine waited until the robber vanished into the woods, then went back to get the plundered express box. He found the "rifle barrels" were no more than sticks poking out of the bushes.

Black Bart.

THIS ROBBERY, which only netted $160, was the first of at least twenty-eight holdups carried out at intervals over the next eight years by the same softly spoken, courteous man. At the scene of one robbery near Fort Ross, Sonoma County, in August 1877, he left a poem signed "Black Bart the P o 8," the name by which the humorous and very untypical Western highwayman became known. He always committed his robberies on foot and never fired a single shot.

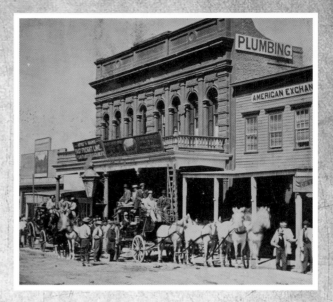

A stagecoach prepares to leave Wells Fargo's Express Office in Virginia City.

A year passed before he reappeared, intercepting the Quincy–Oroville stagecoach on July 25, 1878. He took $379 from the Wells Fargo box and left a scrawled poem ending:

> Let come what may I'll try it on
> My condition cant be worse
> and if there's money in that Box
> 'Tis munny in my purse.

Black Bart always chose stagecoaches with no armed guards, stopping them at the top of a steep rise where the horses had to slow to a walk. There was no pattern to his strikes, which ranged from Yreka near the Oregon border to the mining area south of Sacramento.

BLACK BART

BORN: Charles Earl Bowles (Boles); *c.* 1829 in Norfolk, England

DIED: Unknown, but after February 28, 1888, possibly in New York of natural causes in 1917

ALIASES: Charles E. Bolton, Black Bart the Poet

OCCUPATIONS: Gold prospector, soldier, highwayman

SPOUSE: Mary Johnson

CHILDREN: 3 daughters, 1 son

PARENTS: John and Maria Bowles

In November 1883, when he stopped the Copperopolis stagecoach at the same spot as his first robbery, Black Bart was wounded by one of the passengers and fled. When Sheriff Ben Thorn arrived at the scene, he found a handkerchief with the distinctive laundry mark "FX07." Wells Fargo detective Harry Morse had long believed the bandit was from the San Francisco area, and a systematic search of the city's laundries led to the owner, one Charles Bolton, a mining man who had rooms on Second Street. Just two hours later, while Morse was still at the laundry, Bolton came in, wearing "a natty little derby hat, a diamond pin, a large diamond ring on his finger, and a heavy gold watch and chain."

Morse tricked Bolton into accompanying him to the Wells Fargo office, where he and fellow detective

James Hume questioned him before taking him to his rooms, where letters were found in a hand that matched the poems. Bolton finally admitted his guilt, cut a deal with the detectives, and led them into the mountains where he had concealed around $4,000. On November 17, 1883, Bolton pleaded guilty in a San Andreas court and was sentenced to a very lenient six years in San Quentin prison.

Bolton's real name was Charles E. Bowles (or Boles), born in Norfolk, England, around 1829. The family had emigrated to the United States a year after Charles's birth and settled in Jefferson County, New York State. Charles and his brothers David and James joined the gold rush, returning east after two years. In 1854 Bowles married Mary Johnson and settled in Decatur, Illinois. He served in the

The heavily guarded Wells Fargo Express Co. Treasure Wagon with $250,000 gold bullion from the Great Homestake Mine, Deadwood, 1890.

Union Army between 1862 and 1865 and moved his family to Oregon, Illinois, but in 1865 Bowles left to join the Montana gold rush and never went back. What he did in the decade between leaving home and his debut as a bandit remains a mystery, as does what happened to him after he left prison in January 1888. The unlikely story persists that Wells Fargo offered him the sum of $200 a month to leave their vehicles alone. Whatever the truth, Bolton disappeared forever, and in one of history's ironies, he became something of a legend in California, whereas lawman Harry Morse, who rid the state of so many of its bad men, has largely been forgotten.

GLOSSARY

Affidavit A written statement, signed by a person to say it is true.

Amnesty An official decision to pardon someone convicted of a crime.

Boarding house A private house where people pay to stay and have meals.

Boom and bust An increase in productivity/wealth, followed by a sharp decline in the same.

Confederate Supporter of the southern Confederate States of America 1860–65.

Delinquent Tending to commit crimes or do immoral things.

Gandy dancer A laborer on a railway.

Hand (e.g. hired/ranch hand) A person who works as a manual laborer or on general tasks.

Homestead A house and farmland; an area of land that could be acquired to farm and live on, granted by the U.S. Congress in the Homestead Acts.

Marshal A federal (government) law-enforcement officer.

Posse A body of men assembled by a sheriff to enforce the law.

Railhead A place where rail traffic starts or terminates.

Reconstruction era The period (1865–77) following the American Civil War.

Rustle/rustler To steal/someone who steals animals from a farm or ranch.

Saloon In the western United States, a place where alcoholic drinks are served.

Sheriff An elected official who enforces the law in a U.S. county or town.

Speculator A person who invests money for profit, but risks loss.

Stagecoach A large carriage pulled by horses.

Stockman A person who raises cattle or sheep.

Stockyard An enclosed area where farm animals are kept.

Teamster In the West, a person who drove a carriage transporting goods or freight.

Union The northern states of North America, opposed to the Confederate states in the American Civil War.

Vigilantes A self-appointed group of people who punish someone without legal authority.

Ward A person under the protection/control of another person or organization.

Warrant A legal document authorizing the police or an appointed person to make an arrest or carry out some other action.

FURTHER INFORMATION

Brennan, Stephen Vincent. *The Greatest Cowboy Stories Ever Told*. Guildford, CT: Lyons Press, 2006.

Charles River Editors. *The Icons of the Wild West*. Boston, MA: CreateSpace Independent Publishing Platform, 2013.

Charles River Editors. *Legends of the West: The Life and Legacy of Wild Bill Hickok*. Boston, MA: CreateSpace Independent Publishing Platform, 2013.

Hatfield, Dr. Coleman C. & Davis, F. Keith. *The Feuding Hatfields & McCoys*. Chapmanville, WV: Woodland Press, LLC, 2011.

Laughead Jr., George. *Dodge City (Images of America)*. Mount Pleasant, SC: Arcadia Publishing, 2012.

Masterson, W.B. (Bat). *Famous Gunfighters of the Western Frontier*. Mineola, NY: Dover Publications, 2009.

McLachlan, Sean. *Tombstone – Wyatt Earp, the O.K. Corral, and the Vendetta Ride 1881-82 (Raid.)* Oxford, UK: Osprey Publishing, 2013.

McLeod Raine, William. *Famous Sheriffs and Western Outlaws: Incredible True Stories of Wild West Showdowns and Frontier Justice*. New York, NY: Skyhorse Publishing, 2012.

Murdoch, David S. *Cowboy (DK Eyewitness Books)*. London, UK: DK Publishing, 2000.

Murray, Stuart. *Wild West (DK Eyewitness Books)*. London, UK: DK Publishing, 2005.

True West Editors. *True Tales and Amazing Legends of the Old West*. New York, NY. Clarkson Potter, 2005.

Wallis, Michael. *The Wild West: 365 Days*. New York, NY: Abrams, 2011.

Wexler, Bruce. *The Hatfields and the McCoys*. New York, NY: Skyhorse Publishing, 2013.

Web sites

Billy the Kid: www.aboutbillythekid.com www.billythekidmuseumfortsumner.com

Cow towns: www.kshs.org http://plainshumanities.unl.edu/encyclopedia/doc/egp.ct.011

John Wesley Hardin: http://www.frontiertimes.com/outlaws/hardin.html

Lincoln County War: http://www.spartacus.schoolnet.co.uk/WWlincolnwar.htm http://www.aboutbillythekid.com/Lincoln_County_War.htm

Railroad history: http://www.ushistory.org/us/25b.asp www.up.com/aboutup/history/chronology/index.htm

Wyatt Earp: www.wyattearpmuseum.com

INDEX

Picture credits

Library of Congress: 4, 7, 9, 11, 12, 14 (top and bottom), 15, 17, 29, 30, 33, 34, 35, 38, 39, 41, 44, 47 (top), 52, 53, 59, 60
Shutterstock: 13, 20 (top and bottom), 23, 24, 27, 42, 45, 48, 49, 51
Texas State Library and Archives Commission: 31
U.S. National Archives and Records Administration: 10, 21, 22
To the best of our knowledge all other images are in the public domain and are copyright free. This applies to U.S. works where the copyright has expired, often because its first publication occurred prior to January 1, 1923. See http://copyright.cornell.edu/resources/ publicdomain.cfm for further explanation.